Heaven Help Us

A Modern-day Ghost Story, Inspired by a True Event

Third Edition

Jo Macleod

Tellwell Talent
www.tellwell.ca

ISBN
978-1-77302-813-2 (Paperback)
978-1-77302-812-5 (eBook)

This book is dedicated to the
Spirit of young Rosie Murphy and her
Godmother Rosemary Sullivan-McGinty.

To young Rosie
"When you've been denied justice... you are incomplete.
It feels that God has abandoned you in a stark place...
Mary Debenham to Hercule Poirot-screenplay by Agatha Christie

To Rosemary Sullivan-McGinty
Thank you for your guidance.
I know you are now complete with your son in Heaven.
You have helped rescue millions of lost souls in Ireland
and right a wrong that was done.

Rest in Peace

Contents

Preface

*D*espite the fictional storyline, this book was inspired by a real life spiritual experience that began in July 2004. Thanks to the spirit of Rosemary Sullivan-McGinty, who reached from beyond the grave to guide this unworldly process step by step, and rescue the many lost souls of this historical era. It was through the power of your love for your son, and your need to put things right for Rosie that this book became possible. Thank you Rosie for being brave enough to come forward. I know you are all together now, safe and happy on the other side, and through telling this heartfelt tale of life after death, we can be assured that love has no boundaries.

Introduction

Ireland, 1840-1940

*I*t was a time of great hardship in Ireland. Staying alive was a struggle for everyone. All over the country, farms were raided of crops, livestock and provisions by young Queen Victoria's English armies for her soldiers at war in India and around the world. It was a time of English invasion both in Ireland and Scotland.

The Great Potato Famine of 1840 followed the invasion of the Irish farmlands. Ireland witnessed the starvation of its nation. Only the English aristocracy and landlords had food. Nearly 1.5 million people died in the streets and fields of Ireland while the English looked the other way. The lucky ones, who could, abandoned their homes and left for America and Canada by way of the great liners of the time. Over one million men, women, and children emigrated to America and Canada in the hope of staying alive. They took the chance of a lifetime to survive the notorious journey of death and disease.

The "death ships" or "coffin ships" were nicknamed with good reason. Conditions for steerage passengers were appalling, but the lower deck was all that working class people could afford. Crowded decks made for food shortages and poor hygiene; these were the poor and the tired, the huddled masses who would soon wash over the ports of New York and Boston. People slept wherever they could find a space on deck floors. Men, women, and children died from typhoid, pneumonia, cholera, dysentery, and other diseases caused by the conditions and the putrid diseased air. Most of the survivors arrived at their destination either sick or failing. History writes of the ships that beached on the mud banks of Quebec to drop off the ill and dying. Only the most determined made it. By 1940 more than half of Ireland's population had emigrated to America and Canada. The hatred between the Irish and the English aristocracy remains today and still divides the country into two parts: those loyal to the English Crown, and those who seek Irish independence.

Rosie Murphy was born in 1895 when Ireland was still recovering from starvation and dreadful poverty.

1

Sophie, British Columbia, Canada, 2005

S ophie had been teaching meditation for years. In fact, a significant number of people attended her classes. Occasionally her friends Marishka and Chloe joined her group, and she returned the favour for special occasions. The two groups worked independently on opposite sides of the city.

Sophie's highly developed intuition guided her daily, and being *touchy-feely*, she had learned to listen to her instincts and not brush them aside. Her intuitive sensitivity connected her to everyone and everything around her. Her antenna was always right.

Sophie absorbed energy like a sponge absorbs water, without limitation, taking in the feelings of the world around her. Being an empath--a person who feels energy, she knew people now, more than ever, had to learn to switch off and relax. She could feel their anxiety in her classes. She felt it from the people she encountered in her everyday life, when she was on the bus, at work, or, in the shops. Cashiers who were once so friendly, were now under time constraints to rush customers through the checkout and out the door as quickly as possible, with "goodbye, have a nice day" spouting automatically, as they moved the next person forward. Everybody seemed in a great hurry.

The doorbell rang and disturbed her thoughts. She opened the door to see her friend standing.

"Come in," she said. "I've just made a pot of tea."

Helen entered the apartment, took off her coat, hung it on the hallstand and followed Sophie into the kitchen. The two ladies, now in their fifties, had been friends for over ten years and Helen knew her way around Sophie's home. She reached into the cupboard for a mug and Sophie poured her tea.

"So, what's going on, Sophie?"

"Nothing much," she replied. "I've got a class tonight and I'm just getting ready for that."

"When are you going to teach me to meditate, Sophie?"

"I've told you, Helen, come to the class like everybody else."

"But what will it do to me? You know I'm scared of that hocus-pocus stuff that you do."

Sophie smiled at her friend. "There's nothing hocus-pocus about it. Come over here, bring your tea and sit down," Sophie said pulling out a chair. Helen moved over to the kitchen table.

"Now," Sophie said with a sigh, "I know you find my views strange and some odd things have happened to me, but listen and perhaps you'll learn something new. You might even begin to understand."

The two friends sat at the table facing each other and sipping tea. For once Helen was serious and listened.

"This is how I see it, Helen," Sophie began. "Today's world is too busy for most of us to manage."

"Yes, I agree," said Helen interrupting.

Sophie continued. "Stress is endless and unyielding, especially at work. Bosses seem to want more from their staff in every area, demanding higher commitment with less time for family." Helen nodded in agreement as her friend carried on.

"Home life often becomes inconvenient and difficult, resulting in divorce, single parent families, and insecure children."

Helen interrupted again. "It's pretty sad that life has deteriorated to this level, isn't it, Sophie? But I agree with you; we live in the fast lane today. It's all about the dollar, so where does meditation come in?"

"Well," Sophie said sighing. "In today's world, leisure time has become a pill, an alcoholic drink, or drugs that give instant relief-- you know, the switched-off feeling that most people are looking for."

"I know, Sophie," said Helen, "I know exactly what you're talking about. I see it in some of my friends who drink too much. Every weekend they look forward to their binge just to unwind. I know others who use drugs or smoke 'wacky-backy' to get high. So, yes, I do understand, but how do you stop that, Sophie? The drugs and the drink, it's all part of today's social scene."

"I don't know that we can," said Sophie, finishing her tea. "Our society has created a complete disconnection with the soul." Helen nodded sadly in agreement and Sophie continued on.

"The old ways were not so long ago, when families supported families, propping each other up. They lived in the same area and helped each other out."

"Yes," said Helen again. "My mother's sisters all lived within walking distance of each other and my grandmother lived just around the corner from us. They saw each other regularly--a chat, or a favour: picking up the kids from school, shopping, things like that," said Helen.

"Today that's all changed," said Sophie. "Families are divided by jobs and distance. The modern state of our evolving society separates us." Sophie stood up from her chair and walked over to the teapot. "More tea, Helen?" she asked and continued talking. "Most of us aren't consciously aware of stress levels. We react mechanically, without compassion or consciousness of our feelings."

"Yes, please," replied Helen raising her mug towards Sophie. "You mean we're like robots, just getting on with life."

"Yes, Helen, just like robots. Someone has to help bring people to a safe place, where they're able to relax, and learn to listen to their body, without the use of drugs or alcohol," said Sophie returning to the table.

"I can remember my aunties coming over to our house on a Friday evening after work," said Helen. Mum would have made a pie or something for everyone and they would all have supper together and talk about their week. There was never any alcohol and it only lasted for the mealtime, then they would go home to their own family. I suppose that was their stress-relieving time?"

"Yes, it probably was," Sophie agreed. "I mean, we all want the perfect job and a better lifestyle, and we deserve to have it, but the price today is so high that eventually something has to give. We're not meant to run on high alert all the time. You know what I mean?" Sophie asked her friend.

"I know, Sophie, sometimes I want to get off the treadmill myself, but how? What can we do to stop our roller-coaster society from evolving at top speed?

"Well, I don't think we can stop it completely," said Sophie, "but we can become aware of what's happening around us, and we can use meditation to help us slow down and reconnect."

"Reconnect with what?" asked Helen.

"With our intuition Helen, our inner being, our soul, or spiritual self. Like I said, the old ways have been lost, the very reason to work forgotten. It's not just about more money--when does more money become enough?" Sophie asked.

"I know what you mean, some people just want more and more," agreed Helen.

"People don't listen to their intuition anymore, let alone rely on it. If only they knew how easy it is, and I would like to teach them. It's that simple," Sophie said.

"Does it really work?" Helen asked. "What will it do to me? Can I learn something that I can use in everyday life?" she questioned.

"Of course you can, Helen. It's simple really. It's learning to listen to your body, being aware of your feelings, and taking charge of your reactions. Awareness is the first step. You know, not letting your body dictate what it wants, but you telling your body what you want and need."

"You mean like me wanting chocolate when I know it's bad for me?" The girls laughed together and Sophie jumped up and opened her treats cupboard.

"Yes, Helen, something like that...I just remembered I bought these chocolate biscuits," Sophie said as she placed them on the table.

"Thanks, Sophie, you know me too well," she said as she opened the packet and took one.

"Most people join my classes for health reasons or to control anxiety, or simply to recognise their stress and learn how to stop it from building. They learn to relax. It's that simple," Sophie said. "Come to the class, Helen. Attend every week for the course, do the exercises at home and once you lose your fear of the unknown and relax, it won't disappoint you. You might even learn to control your need for chocolate," the girls laughed again.

"Oh, I don't know that I want to do that! But Sophie, you make it sound so simple and intriguing."

"It actually becomes pleasantly addictive, Helen. You'll find that you want more and more time alone--no TV, radio or computer games. Just yourself and silence, it's a rare sensation, I know you'd enjoy it."

"It sounds very peaceful, Sophie, still a bit far out for me, but I trust you and I could do with some peace."

"Let's go into the lounge, Helen." The girls set their mugs on the counter and Helen followed Sophie into the lounge.

"I love this room," Helen said. "I love this big window overlooking the street." The two girls walked over to the bay window and stood looking down at the people below.

"I can sit here for hours watching people. It's always busy and entertaining," said Sophie.

"I can imagine," agreed Helen looking down into the bustling street below.

"I'm glad you're taking the plunge, Helen. I believe everyone should learn to meditate, from young school children all the way up to adults. It's a healthy thing to do. It's non-invasive, not religious and doesn't interfere with anyone's form of thinking. It helps children be less fretful and more relaxed and gives them something to concentrate on when they're anxious, especially at school."

"Could it really help school children?" asked Helen.

"Oh, yes," replied Sophie. "Visualization is a wonderful tool. It fills you with tranquility and helps you become aware of your feelings. It really does help," said Sophie seriously. She turned her gaze from the window and looked directly at Helen's face.

"Meditation is a very personal experience, Helen. It's different for everyone," she paused and sighed. The girls looked at each other and Sophie explained further. "With practise, there could be a spiritual connection. Only you can hear the whisper of your neglected soul. I've had more than one extraordinary experience through meditation. But, in the beginning it's about learning to relax, and it really works, Helen, it really does," she said in earnest.

"Sounds beautiful--still mysterious though," said Helen hesitating.

"No mystery--it's just relaxing, that's all it is, but in a different way to what today's society does. There's no noise, none, just silence," Sophie paused and then continued. "It's a unique experience as I said--it's different for everyone and every time a different experience. No two people feel the same while meditating. It develops with practise, and slowly you become the master," Sophie explained. "It's like growing the perfect rose and producing a beautiful bloom--it takes time."

"Ah..." Helen said finally with a smile.

"With patience and nurturing, in time the buds will open fully and display their unique beauty. The perfume is intoxicating, permeating your entire being and absorbing all negative energy within and around you. Its peace is dreamlike and magical, quite indescribable," Sophie said with a sigh. "Did you know that roses absorb negative energy? That's why it's always peaceful in a rose garden," she said.

"Okay, now I'm interested. You make it sound very alluring, and mentioned extraordinary experiences before. I want to hear more about that too, so when do we start?" Helen asked.

"Come to class like everyone else, it's only once a week. In the beginning, you'll learn to empty your head of unwanted thoughts and clutter, and just relax. Soon you'll connect with your intuitive side. With practice, you'll learn to control your life more effectively. Start this week, Helen, learn to relax--that's all."

Sophie loved to people watch, and as the weeks passed she observed the dynamics of her group changing. In the beginning, most newcomers were anxious and agitated, their energy static with nervousness and insecurity. She taught them how to listen to the quiet calling of their body. How to take control and help themselves get well by breathing and imagining beautiful settings. By the end of the first session, the energy had changed to a calm and tranquil confidence that everyone enjoyed. They were at ease, relaxed, and looking forward to the next session in a week.

The girls left the window and made themselves comfortable in the easy chairs. "Would you like the fire on, Helen?" Sophie asked.

"No, I'm fine thanks," she replied. Sophie continued to explain more hoping to ease Helen into the idea of joining the class.

"Visualization is key to relaxing in the beginning, and it gives you something to concentrate on while learning to breathe and empty your mind. It sounds odd but it does work."

"What kind of visualization do you mean, Sophie?"

"Just focusing on a beautiful scene in your mind can change the energy vibration in your body. Changing your pulse, changes the way your body is feeling and results in an energy shift. You can go from being anxious and nervous to being peaceful and relaxed."

"Really," said Helen surprised, "just by looking at a pretty picture?"

"Absolutely--it's like a breath of warm summer air has softly caressed your face, soothing you completely."

"Oh, Sophie, you're so impassioned about this. I've never heard you talk this way before. I'll start this week I promise, but I do want to hear about these extraordinary experiences you've had."

"Good, you'll be surprised how much you learn from it, and you really will enjoy it, I promise you," Sophie said and carried on talking.

"When I was young I was ill a lot. Always feeling aches and pains all over my body, a bit like rheumatism. Every winter I got pleurisy or bronchitis or something of that nature. By the time I was in my early twenties I had realised that it wasn't just the city smog and dampness that made me ill. It was people too--their bad energy affected me. If I was around ill-tempered or aggressive people, I seemed to absorb their dark energy and in a short time I got sick," she told her friend.

"Really?" said Helen listening closely?" Sophie realised she had finally caught her friend's interest.

"My first strange experience happened after my hip dislocated during the birth of my daughter. I was in the hospital for months, drugged all the time because of the pain. The doctors didn't know what to do with me. Finally, they sent me home wearing a steel-boned corset. I spent the next two years doped out of my head on pain medication and tranquilizers. I was high for two whole years of my life--it was a terrible experience," she confided.

"I had no idea, Sophie, you never said anything."

"It's a long time ago now," she said reminiscing.

"What happened to you, Sophie?" Helen asked. "I mean, how did you manage to get back to normal?"

"Well, one night a friend took me to a healing service being held in a church out-of-town. I went reluctantly as a non-believer. She made go me because of the pain I was in. I think she was fed-up listening to me moaning? What happened to me that night changed me, and after that I started to learn about meditation," she told Helen.

"This sounds interesting, go on, Sophie, what happened?"

"I went forward for the hands-on-healing from a male volunteer. I knew nothing about the man; he was a stranger to me. He laid one hand on my left knee and the other hand on the back of my left hip. I felt the most tremendous heat from him, so much so I was sweating profusely. Then he stopped and stood back from me.

'You've got some powerful friends *over there*,' he said and smiled at me as he walked away."

"Creepy stuff, Sophie," her friend said. "Go on, tell me more."

"I walked out of that church upright with absolutely no pain. On the way out, I went to the back of the hall where volunteers were raising funds for the church. I saw a book with a picture of a man on the front cover and picked it up. It was the same man who had just given me the healing, and I bought the book. I told the lady at the counter. 'This is the same man who gave me my healing tonight,' I said as I handed her the money. She laughed and smiled while handing the book back to me. 'No, it couldn't have been him,' she replied, 'he's been dead some fifteen years or more.' What she said shocked me, and as it turned out, he was a famous spiritual healer. I had never heard of him and knew nothing about spiritual healing, but it was the same man, I swear, who had given me hands-on-healing that night."

"Oh my goodness, Sophie, what happened next?" Helen asked eagerly.

"I looked back and he was gone. The altar was empty and there was no one around. I asked my friend if she saw anyone and she said 'no.' I gave myself a shake, wondering if I had imagined it all, but everything else around me was real. I checked, my pain--gone for the first time in years. I could stand with ease, and walk without limping. The experience changed my life and compelled me to learn more about it."

"Oh, Sophie, this sounds really weird. I've never had anything like that happen to me."

"I know it's weird. I don't normally tell people about it. I've always known I was different and all my life I've had people tell me I'm nuts, a weirdo, laugh at me, humiliate me, mock me for things that have happened to me. Finally, I learned to keep quiet and not talk about it to anyone," Sophie confided. "Most people scoff when the word 'medium' or 'psychic' is used to describe a gifted person. I've found that they are the very people who are genuinely afraid. I can feel it from their energy, and so I don't disturb their thinking. It doesn't matter any longer that these people don't believe me, and no amount of proof will ever convince them, so I just let it go. I know now that they're on a different part of the same journey we're all on, and they'll come to the point I'm at in their own time," she said reassuring her friend.

"Oh, Sophie, how lonely for you."

"It is, and the saddest thing is to hear your friends talking about you from a distance. You can't say anything about it or let them know you heard them. In some cases, I hear people's thoughts and that's awful if it's about me."

"How sad for you," her friend said with true compassion in her voice.

Sophie was a clairsentient medium, known today as an empath. Occasionally she used her gift to help friends, but she had never set herself up as a psychic who charged for sitting. She believed her gift was given to help others and herself. People came to her as if by magic. She was always willing to listen and help them if she could. She had come a long way since then, and now it was time to come out from the shadow. It was her time. The world was awakening to their own consciousness, realising that they had a share in creating the world around them.

"Now, it doesn't seem important to convince people there's another energy more advanced than we are," Sophie continued. "It seems pointless to try to persuade a non-believer when that person's not advanced enough in their own evolution to understand. It's like trying to teach a seven-year-old child advanced math, when they're still struggling with their times tables, you know what I mean?" she asked.

Helen nodded her head in agreement. "Yes, Sophie, unfortunately I do."

Sophie continued. "Those who don't believe are simply not ready, not interested, or, are even afraid of the idea that we're not alone in this vast universe," she said with a sigh. "Did I ever tall you about Eagle Feather Helen?

"No, you haven't, and I'm all ears now," she replied.

"He's my *Spirit Guide*. He came to help me with something I had to do. It was my first rescue and the first time he showed himself to me. It became my quest--a test of faith. I would never have been able to complete it myself," Sophie said staring into space, as if remembering. There was a silence but Helen remained quiet, eager to hear the rest of Sophie's story, then her friend continued.

"I still get flashes of scenes in my head and I have to pinch myself. The whole event was so surreal and unbelievable. At times I think it was all a dream. Then I'm thankful that Eagle Feather sent me a keepsake in the form of a little metal figurine--a token from him to me. A reminder that something unworldly had happened, not of this dimension or timeframe."

"Can I see the figurine Sophie," Helen asked.

"Of course," she said, wanting to prove his existence. "He's in my bedroom. I'll get him for you." Sophie left the room to fetch the small cast iron figure and returned quickly handing it to Helen.

"Oh my, he's so detailed, I can actually see the characteristics on his face, it's amazing," said Helen.

"Yes, isn't he. Quite amazing, and I still talk to him, and at times I can feel him close to me, but he hasn't appeared physically since the rescue," Sophie said a little disappointed.

"How did he come to you, I mean how did you find him?" Helen asked.

"A lady at work bought him when she was on a cruise. She knew he wasn't for her but felt compelled to buy it. When she returned to work and heard the story she came to my desk and gave him to me. It shocked me because it looked exactly like him."

So, now you know my story, Helen, well some of it anyway."

Helen pursed her lips reassuringly and Sophie smiled back expecting judgment of some kind.

"That's quite a story. It's not easy being different when people don't understand you or think you're a bit eh--*off your head*. I feel for you Sophie," she said. "I trust you. I know you're a good person who wouldn't intentionally hurt anyone. That's what's important to me in our friendship," Helen said.

"Thank you, Helen. It means a lot to hear you say that. Over the years I've become hardened to people who have no compassion or understanding of extra sensitivity. I try to avoid their negative energy at all costs and stay clear of them. But I can feel your compassion and I know you believe me, so thank you for that," she told her friend.

"So Sophie, tell all, I want to hear the whole story from beginning to end. Don't think you're getting off that lightly. You have my total and undivided attention and I want to hear everything," Helen said adamantly.

"I'll do my best Helen, but it's a long and rather fantastic story, you know? It began with a visitor, a spiritual visitor," Sophie said.

Over the years, Sophie's sensitivity had grown acute. It was normal for her to feel another presence--energy from the other side--a *visitor* she would call them. However, her recent visitor was different and wouldn't leave her alone or go away. The presence lingered with her for weeks, following her around in her home, wanting her attention and yet staying in the shadow unidentified. Sophie didn't know that the spirit needed her help.

Finally, she decided it was time to find out who this unearthly being was and what they wanted. She spoke out loud to her ghostly companion in a soft and gentle voice.

"I can't see you, but I can feel your presence and I know you can hear me. I want to know who you are and why you've come to me?" she said aloud. "I feel you're in great need of help because of some disturbing, traumatic event. I know you're suffering. I can feel your anxiety and your fear, and I promise I will help you if I can," she offered.

Sophie made her way into her bedroom and sat in her chair in front of her dressing table. She lit a beeswax candle in front of the mirror as she always did for her prayer. "This is my sacred place to meditate," she said quietly. "If you can, and you wish to, you have my permission to show yourself to me in the mirror." Sophie was confident that her visitor would show herself because she could feel her desperation and knew she had come for help of some kind.

She made herself comfortable, closed her eyes and began breathing deeply while focusing on the brilliant Divine life light. She could feel her visitor close to her as if standing right by her side.

Almost instantly, Sophie fell into a deep trance-like dream, and found herself in the countryside--a farmyard, she thought. She could see fields all around her, and smelled a stench that could only be farm animals, mixed with the smell of wet grass after a light rain. She couldn't see anyone else around but felt that she wasn't alone either. She stood on the grass in front of what looked like an old rundown farmhouse, or a cottage from an age gone by. A soft breeze caressed her face and felt so real she wondered if she could be in two places at the same time? Sophie knew this was her meditation and without fear released herself to the Divine Universe to reveal its mystery to her.

Then the work began as her spirit visitor channelled her memories. She shared her whole life, her happiness and her sadness, the birth of her children and the grief of losing a child. She shared her fears, her regrets, her guilt and her suspicions. In turn, Sophie felt her visitor's deep pain, her anguish and regret for not doing more to help her Goddaughter.

As the channelling continued, Sophie shared every detail of the visitor's life. The more time they sat bonded in meditation, the stronger their connection became. Information filtered through steadily. The spirit wanted Sophie's help and for that reason she allowed her to share her innermost secrets, every thought and desire. For Sophie, it was like watching a movie and feeling all the emotions attached to the events as they unfolded. Finally, the spirit shared her shocking discovery. When she died, to her horror, she saw two child souls, still grounded in the old farmhouse--trapped in time as ghosts. That dimension was now behind her, since she too had passed over. The spirit knew she couldn't do anything to help them by herself. She knew she couldn't bridge two worlds on her own, and became frantic with fear and a desperate need to help them. The spirit's heartache was heavy; her torment without end, and her only release would come when the two child souls were safe with her on the other side. She had to find a way to somehow rescue them and bring them over with her.

Sophie now understood the events of the past leading to the present, and the need for their spiritual connection. She realised what the spirit was asking, as she slowly opened her eyes and gazed into the mirror in front of her. There, in the shadow of the candle-light, stood a tall, slender young woman in her mid to late thirties. She was painfully sad and full of grief, as she stood wringing her hands nervously. She needed help to bridge the two worlds and make the rescue happen. This was why she had come. Sophie humbly accepted the honour bestowed on her, and believing that the Divine Universe would guide her, she resolved to do her best to help them all. She thought she saw a faint smile of relief on her visitor's lips, as a single tear spilled over and slowly rolled down her cheek. The spirit thanked her new friend, and Sophie felt the ache in her heavy heart lift, and her soul lighten. Then, as the candlelight flickered, the spirit faded into the shadow and disappeared from the mirror.

This is their story.

2

Italy to Ireland - Marcello to Marcel, 1894

Marcello Gonnella was a handsome fifteen-year-old Italian. He was short and stocky, with broad shoulders and well-developed biceps. He looked strong as an ox, and he was. His soft dark eyes were large, round, deep-set, and brooding. He had long, thick black eyelashes that any young lass would envy, and heavy dark eyebrows. He had an unusually small, almost flat nose for an Italian. Not like that of a Roman nose, but straight, short, and broad. His face was roundish, with cherub-like chubby cheeks, and a heart-shaped mouth with full lips. His curly dark hair gave him a boyish look, which he hated. Marcello was masculine in every way and had a serious need to let everyone see that he was stronger than anyone else.

Marcello's father died while serving his country in the army. As the only child he had grown up alone with his mama. Rosa loved her son deeply, but their close relationship stifled him in his youth. He was over protected and smothered by her attention. She would not allow him to play sports for fear of injury, and refused to let him join in the usual rough and tumble at school. As a result, the other boys picked on him from an early age. His mother regularly arrived at the school to find him in yet another fist-fight. She blamed the other boys for picking on her bambino, but as others knew, it was often Marcello who did the provoking. He enjoyed proving that he was stronger, and a better fighter. He was often verbally insulting, and became a bully with cruel tendencies.

As a short, skinny boy, Marcello determined to make himself muscular and strong. He started training at home when he was seven years old. He found a book on boxing and exercised daily following the advice and guidelines. By the age of twelve, Marcello was developing biceps of a young man above his age. When he was fourteen, most people at school stayed away from him, knowing him to stir up a fight to prove his strength. He relished the power and enjoyed watching the defeated boy limp away humiliated. Marcello seemed to grow in height as he witnessed his opponents' suffering, releasing some of his own pain at the same time.

At fifteen, Marcello had no friends. He was a loner. He spent his time working out doing his exercises, and preparing for the call of duty to serve his country. It was only one year away, and he looked forward to it. He would show the world his courage and pride in serving. He was afraid of nothing and nobody. He didn't react to pain like other people. He showed steely control and determination and bowed to nothing. He was mannerly and polite, but somewhat stiff and stern in his outlook for a young person.

It was springtime in 1894 when Rosa decided it was time to put her plan into action.

"Marcello, I want to talk to you," his Mama announced casually. "I've decided that we should take a trip to the Vatican City in Rome. I want to show you all the splendour of our religion and our culture. You're fifteen now, and old enough to understand the ways of life. What do you think of that idea?" his mother asked.

"Why Mama, what a great idea. When do we leave?" he asked.

"We must go to the city first and catch a train to Trieste, we can travel from there," she replied. "Are you excited?"

"Oh yes, I'd love to get away from here and see the world."

"We leave in a few days. I just wanted to know how you felt about leaving home. However, I see that it doesn't seem to bother you?" she said flatly.

"No, it doesn't Mama, not in the least," he replied honestly.

She always knew she would protect him and had a plan in her mind. At sixteen, all boys entered the regular army to serve their four-year term of duty for their country. Rosa was adamant that her son would never serve in any army, not for any country, not even Italy. She saved her money all of her life for this, and now the time had come. Unknown to Rosa, neither she nor her son would ever return to Italy.

Rosa was thirty-six years of age and had been a widow since Marcello was just a one-year-old. She was a good-looking woman, delightfully plump in all the right places. She had full, round bosoms and shapely hips with a decent incline for a waist. Several men had come courting after her husband died, but Rosa loved her man and knew in her heart that no one would ever take his place.

"I'm sorry, signor," she would say. "I am not available. My heart will always belong to my dead husband " and she would close the door immediately on the gentleman. In time, the suitors stopped calling, and she was left alone to look after her son. She made it known that she would never marry again.

Marcello's eyes were like his mothers. It was obvious seeing them together that they were mother and son. Even their stature was similar, albeit Marcello was a sturdy, maturing teenage boy. His mother was a petite and curvaceous young woman. Rosa had talked for years about visiting the Holy City of Rome and taking a tour of the Vatican and all its history. She planned it this way and made her family aware of her upcoming trip.

"I want Marcello to know about his religion and his country, its background and history. What better way to educate him than to travel and experience it?" she told them.

"It's a wonderful idea," her parents agreed.

"Good, I'm glad you agree with me. Here, take my house keys--we're leaving next week. Marcello's very excited."

Rosa was planning a trip further than Rome. She planned to sail on the big ocean liner to the United Kingdom and on to Ireland. She was in search of a small village out-of-the-way, where Marcello could settle down and work--a place remote enough that the Italian army would never find him. When it was safe again to return to Italy, Rosa would send for him. Until then, she would know that he was alive and well.

It was early March. The weather was warming up which made for lighter packing and gave Rosa more room for her young son's clothes. Marcello had never travelled before--excited to leave his hometown. Once in the city they caught a train to the dockside where they boarded one of the sailing ships on a route through the Mediterranean and northbound to the United Kingdom. There were many ports where they could disembark and connect with a sailing to Dublin, Ireland.

"Where are we, Mama? Not Italy, that's certain?"

"No, we are in England and will board another ship to Ireland. I know you'll love it there," she told him.

It was a soft language and he listened carefully, as he did know English. He would stand on the deck staring into the ocean for what seemed hours. The sea was hypnotic and relaxing to him, deep and dark, with a mysterious energy and silent power that somehow calmed him. Finally, they arrived in Dublin, Ireland, where Marcello's new life was about to begin. Here the people spoke with another new and even softer accent.

"I can understand these people better. I could listen to their talk all day," he remarked to his mama. Unlike the harsh brogue of the English dockside workers, the Dubliners accent seemed soft and warm to him, with a lilt that he enjoyed.

"I'm glad to hear that Marcello, you'll pick it up more quickly," she replied.

They had reservations in a medium-sized family boarding house on the edge of Dublin city, with easy access to the city amenities and its historical interests. To her relief, it was a convenient location.

"I booked a twin room with a bathroom for our privacy. I hope you appreciate the expense, enjoy it while you can?"

"I do, I do, Mama. Thank you." It was an expensive luxury she chose to pay for, rather than sharing the main lobby bathroom with the other guests.

She had not yet explained her plan to him.

"Why have we come so far from Italy, Mama?" he asked. "Are we going to visit the Vatican City on the way back home?"

"We'll talk after dinner tonight," she replied dismissing his question.

Rosa knew she had to tell him everything soon.

The boarding house was fresh, clean, and inviting, not palatial in any way, but it had a friendly atmosphere and it catered to family groups. The dining room had ten tables, and they were able to reserve a small round table at the window overlooking the river.

"Supper is served between five and seven o'clock," the receptionist advised offering a schedule. They were both used to eating later in the evening but adapted quickly. It was a simple meal. Steak pie, mashed potatoes with carrots and peas, followed by pudding, homemade custard, and apple pie. They didn't serve coffee at all, and tea followed every meal with sweet biscuits.

"That was different, Mama, but very nice."

"That's good. You won't miss the pasta then?" They both laughed and finished drinking their tea.

"I thought we'd take a stroll down by the water later--there are some things I want to explain to you."

"Yes, I've been waiting to hear why we're not in Rome. I expect we were never going there at all. Am I right?" he asked.

"Yes, Bambino, you are," she replied.

"Don't call me that. Especially in a public place," he said annoyed. "It's embarrassing. I'm a man, not a baby," he said showing his anger.

"Of course not," she agreed trying to calm him. "You're my son and I forget how quickly you are growing. I won't do it again. I'm sorry," she said apologising.

It was six-thirty in the evening and still light as they left the boarding house for their walk.

"What do you think of the people?" Rosa asked.

"I like them, they seem friendly and I love the way they talk." They walked on a little, up the embankment of the river and came to a bench overlooking the water.

"Let's sit here," she said. "I have something to tell you." Marcello looked at his mother inquisitively as he sat beside her on the bench. He knew she had a plan--she always did, and he was eager to listen.

"Marcello," she said earnestly. "I have something to tell you. I don't want you to speak until I have finished. Please don't interrupt; there will be time later for questions. I want you to listen and think about what I say before you make your response. Do you understand me?" she asked.

"Yes, Mama, I do." His mood was more serious as he waited for his mother to start. Rosa composed herself in a dignified and confident manner as she prepared to tell her story.

"I was heartbroken when they told me your papa was dead. I didn't know what to do or what would become of us. I was a young woman, and I knew I'd never marry again. Your papa was my only love--I had no interest in other men. With a young child, I was afraid for both of us. But we struggled and we managed. I saved all the money I could because it gave me comfort and security for you now," she told him and continued. "I was often afraid for your well-being, that something would happen to take you away from me," she said slightly embarrassed. "I'm sorry if I was over protective when you were at school, but you are my only bambino, my child," she looked at him adoringly. "Are you listening to me, Marcello?" she asked sharply. He was sitting straight on the bench his head down--bored, and she could not see his face or gauge his mood.

"Of course I am," he replied slightly annoyed and wishing she would get to the point.

"I knew the day would come when I would have to say goodbye to you if I wanted you safe and alive. So I prepared for this day, and now you are ready. Marcello," she said with a sigh. "We are not going to Rome."

"I guessed as much," he replied slightly confused, "but where are we going? I'm sure you have a plan?"

"Yes, I do," she continued. "You will stay here in Ireland safe and away from the Italian Army. They will never think to look here for you," she said pleased with herself.

"What?" he interrupted now shocked. "I'm not going home to Italy at all?" he asked irritated.

"I don't want you to go into the army like your papa did. If we stay home in Italy, they will call you up to do your service in a few months time. That is why we left for this vacation while you are still fifteen years of age," she told him.

"But ... " he interrupted again.

"Don't talk now," she said in a raised voice. "You promised not to interrupt me," she continued. "You are not be going back to Italy with me. In five years, your conscription will be over, and if it's safe for you to return home, I will contact you to come." She finished speaking and remained quiet for a few moments, waiting for his response.

Marcello sat quietly absorbing what his mama had said and trying hard to control his temper. He was not afraid of being left alone. But he was angry at her manipulating schemes and always arranging his life.

"I want to serve my country like Papa. Did you ever think of that?" he snapped at her and took a deep breath through his nose to suppress his anger.

Rosa continued. "I have enough money for you to pay your way while we arrange for a place to live and find you work. We will change your name to Murphy--a common Irish name. Also, you should get used to being called Marcel instead of Marcello. No one here will ever know," she assured him and continued.

"You can say that your papa was Irish, that we came on vacation from Italy to see the land of his birth, when a terrible accident happened, and only you survived. In time, your accent will change, and you will learn to speak their language. You'll survive and have a happy life." Rosa paused for a moment and glanced slowly at her son for his reaction.

He was furious--his mouth closed tight and controlled. She continued more quickly now seeing how angry he was and fearful that he might turn on her.

"I'll tell people you fell in love with a girl in Rome and you ran off together. I'll say that I stayed as long as I could but that the police could find no trace of you, and the time came when I had to leave without you. I'll be able to grieve openly for my lost son. I will miss you--you must know that. But as a mother who loves her child, I'll have some comfort in knowing that your papa's blood and mine will continue through you. You will live, marry and have children, and we will see each other again one day, I promise you that," she insisted and continued quickly again.

"You shouldn't have to die for a country that doesn't know you exist. They gave me a little money when your papa died, but I was young and alone with a baby. They didn't care that I was afraid. So, it is my decision that they will not get you as well." Rosa finished and sat quietly.

There was silence as she waited. His face reddened, and she could see his rage. He was about to burst out in anger when she turned to him.

"Say nothing now, we'll talk more tomorrow."

She rose from the bench and began walking along the embankment at the water's edge, leaving Marcello to deal with his anger. When she glanced back, she saw him pounding the bench with his bare fists and bawling in frustration at what she had done. Rosa quickened her step. She wanted to put some distance between them. She must have walked a mile along the embankment when she realised it was getting dark and time to make her way back to the boarding house. She turned and headed back towards Marcello. She could just make out his figure sitting on the bench and braced herself as she approached.

His head bent low, his hands covering the front of his face, she suspected he was crying--his cheeks were wet and stained. He didn't speak but stood up following slightly behind her. They entered the boarding house silently and went upstairs to their room.

Rosa was already planning for tomorrow. They had to find suitable lodgings and a job for him. She didn't give his grief a second thought, or think for a moment that he wanted to join the army or was looking forward to serving his country. She didn't consider his feelings at all.

Rosa prepared herself in the bathroom and went to bed without a word to her son. Marcello followed after her. There was a hostile silence between them that she ignored. Although Marcello's anger had subsided slightly, he lay awake staring up at the ceiling imagining ways that he could get even with her for manipulating his life.

It was dark and quiet and he could hear his mother breathing as she slept on the other side of the room. His thoughts drifted through a variety of things he might enjoy doing to her. He wanted revenge for what she had done. He could suffocate her in her sleep. She would be out of his life forever. He could stab her to death with a knife, and enjoy seeing her suffer. He had come to realise how much he disliked her, and once again, she had managed to cheat him, manoeuvring his life to suit her needs. He vowed this would be the last time. He promised himself that.

He began to think differently about his situation. He never had friends like other boys, and blamed his dominating mother and her overprotectiveness. At last, he thought, this was his way out. Finally, he would be his own man, free from her smothering motherly indulgence, never bending to her again. All through his life, every time he had an opportunity to show his masculinity, she stepped in and stole his moment of glory, making him look silly and soft in front of his peers. At school, they jeered him and called him "Mama's Bambino," and even now, she took away his chance to become a soldier. He hated her, and would be glad to be free. He just hoped she left him enough money to live on. With that last thought of hatred for his mother, Marcello rolled over and fell asleep.

Early the next morning, Rosa used the washroom first and dressed quickly. Marcello followed, and silently, they went downstairs. They had the usual Irish breakfast and finished with tea. There was no conversation. Marcello wondered what his mother had arranged for the day. He knew she had plans as she always did.

First on her list was a visit to the Registry Office to change his name to Marcel Murphy.

"We need his original baptism certificate te change his name in this country," advised the registrar plainly in his soft Irish voice.

"But we are from Italy, and I don't have it with me," she replied.

"Then there's nothing te change," the Registrar told her in a somewhat aloof manner.

"Sir, excuse me, is there any documentation required for him to work?"

"What kind of work?"

"Oh, labouring or something manual, he's young but very strong, you see?" she said as she gestured towards her son.

"I understand more than ye t'ink misses," he replied. "The best place te find casual labour is in the pub if ye dare go there, misses, but the youngster can go himself, he's old enough."

With that, the registrar dismissed them, waving his hand towards the door. They left without further discussion relieved that there was no paper trail and he could to pick up casual work without legal documentation.

"From now on your name is Marcel Murphy, even to me," she said. "I will probably forget from time to time, and you must correct me when I do," she said.

"Yes, Mama," he replied in a flat tone.

They spent the rest of the day looking for lodgings and work. They found a lodging house where the family had beds to let. Not rooms, as expected, but single beds in a room of many. Rosa didn't like this idea, but when she heard the cost of renting a bed, she thought better of the situation.

"Marcel, you're going to have to get a good job before you can afford a whole room for yourself alone."

"Yes, Mama, I understand."

The house they visited had two large rooms for lodgers--six beds in one and four beds in the other. All the lodgers were young men. There was an outhouse toilet and separate washroom with a sink and a tub for bathing. It was freezing in the outhouse. At home Rosa had a tub inside the house for bathing her son. She would boil pots of water for her bambino and personally washed him down until, at the age of fourteen, he told his mama, "I can manage." She didn't argue with him and left him alone to bathe for the first time.

The lodging room with the six beds had one vacancy. Rosa accepted it immediately before someone else did. There was no place for personal storage.

"Keep your packing case under your bed locked. Never leave your keys around for someone to steal." She spoke to him in Italian so that the others wouldn't understand her.

"*Si, Si, Mama,*" he replied quietly.

Rosa turned to the landlord and his wife and explained.

"I'm returning to Italy on business, but my son will be staying until I send for him."

"Yes misses, we've come across this arrangement before. He'll be fine here wit' us while yer away, we've our own boys the same age."

They knew that Rosa was deliberately avoiding the government's conscription into the army. They had read about such things in their newspaper, but it was not their business. They had no such thing in Ireland. Most young boys were eager to join the military where they had food, a bed with a roof over their head and got paid. So the idea of running away from the army didn't make any sense to them.

Rosa paid them the first month's rent plus one month in advance. After that, Marcel would pay them directly.

"When you want to leave you'll have to give notice a month ahead and your last month will already be paid for. Do you understand how it works, Marcel?"

"Yes, Mama, I understand " he sighed controlling his impatience. She shook hands with the landlord and his wife and they left. Marcel Murphy would move in on the first of the month--a few days away. Next on her list was the International Bank where Rosa exchanged her money for Irish pounds.

"Now, Marcello--sorry, Marcel," she interrupted herself, "it's important that you understand this: never, never, under any circumstances, let anyone see that you have cash about you. You must keep this secret from everyone. If they find out you have money, they'll steal it away from you, and you'll have nothing. Keep it in this pouch and hide it inside your boot, it's the place your papa used for his money pouch," she told him. "He said he could always feel it there and knew it was safe," she ordered. "Never leave it in your room or under your pillow or anywhere you think is safe. It isn't. Someone will find it. Promise me you'll always carry it with you everywhere, even when you are sleeping. Tuck it inside your sock and never let anyone see it. Do you understand how important this is, *Marcello--scusi--Marcel?*" she said again.

"Yes I do, Mama," he sighed impatiently.

Rosa handed him a leather drawstring pouch. Inside was one hundred Irish pounds, enough money to live comfortably for many years. She kept just enough for herself to get home to Italy, and gave everything she could to her son.

"If you find work pay your rent from your wages and keep the pouch money intact. Only use it when you must, and it will be there for you in an emergency. If you need to buy boots, use your wages. Not the pouch money. Do you understand?" she said with anxiety in her voice.

"Yes I do, Mama," this time he replied seriously.

Marcel understood--the pouch money was his safety net, but otherwise he had to earn his living and pay his way. He had a lot of pride for his young years. He would keep the leather pouch tucked inside his sock and held in place by his boot. He would get used to the uncomfortable feeling in no time, knowing what was at stake.

They spent the rest of the day looking for work and heard about the open market where work was often available. They also heard that every month there was an auction on the outskirts of the city where the local farmers brought their livestock for sale. There was always extra work preparing stalls for the animals.

They made their way around the city, learning the tramcar routes and fares. Most people walked to their destination as trams and pony traps were expensive and used mostly by the gentry. There was one tramline that went up and down the main street, in a straight line. Workers used that to jump on and off at will without paying, and you could hear the *'clippie'* shouting at folk who skipped their fare as they jumped off the tram.

Rosa thought the locals were friendly, but that didn't fool Marcel. He knew city people were quick to act, shrewd, and dishonest. From now on, he would trust no one, or risk, losing his money pouch. He wasn't afraid. But, he was a little paranoid. He didn't believe people were warm and friendly without an ulterior motive. He was suspicious, and wouldn't trust anyone enough to get close to him or call them 'friend.' However, he was so wrong about the Irish. He knew nothing of their history and their struggle to survive.

That evening, on their way back and after much argument, Rosa eventually gave in and let Marcel go to the pub alone.

"Don't forget to tell them your name is Marcel Murphy."

"Yes, Mama, I know," he drawled.

The Irish people were a law unto themselves and loyal to the grave. To betray a trust was the worst sin of all. A traitor would face death by shooting, no matter how young they were. In extreme cases, the locals would take control, and publicly tar and feather the guilty to guarantee a slow death. The police wouldn't dare intervene in these situations knowing the local heavies would avenge any interference. The Irish were proud, strong, stubborn, and hard-working. They were a bit rough around the edges but prepared for anything life could throw at them. They were quick to learn and ready to earn their place in society.

Most Irish people had a profound, unshakable belief in God. Indeed, it seemed to Marcel that they constantly prayed the Lord's name out loud all day. "Be Jesus Himself," or "Lord God give me strength," or "by God's Holy name," and it went on all day. They seemed to ask God for help one way or another. They had a duty to survive hardship. This, Marcel would learn although he would never understand their unending sense of fun and laughter. Marcel's personality was much more sombre--life was a serious business, not taken lightly. The Irish could make a joke out of any situation and turn it into something funny when it was actually sad, unfortunate, or even tragic. It was their way of coping with the most horrible of life's hard knocks. They laughed and joked with each other, and about themselves too. They could drink beer until dawn, and get up and go to work all day with a hangover from Hell itself.

Marcel would learn about manhood in ways he had never dreamed of. These Irish lads, boys his age, survived working anywhere, doing anything that earned them a living and put a roof over them in the cold winter. They did the hard manual labour wherever the work was, digging, carrying, and building anything. That was the Irish way.

"I'll wait in the dining room for you," she said, "don't be long, we can eat together and get an early night."

Marcel had different plans, but that would keep for after supper when they were alone in their room. He would have his say before bedtime that night. He left his mother and went 'scouting' to the pub alone.

Marcel didn't realise that he was handsome, or that his energy exuded a wave of interest wherever he went. People around him could feel it, but not his loving mama. To her, he was just her beautiful boy and like other mothers, she wanted her son safe and to live a happy and fulfilled life. He spent half an hour in the pub watching and listening to all he could. Then he left for the boarding house and supper with his mother.

They ate silently with no conversation, then went upstairs for the evening.

Rosa used the bathroom first to wash and change. She returned ready for bed, and as she crossed the floor, announced excitedly, "We have another busy day ahead of us tomorrow. I'm looking forward to more adventure, are you, Marcel?" she asked.

"No, Mama, there's no need for you here any longer. Tomorrow you will go home." His voice was cold and adamant. Rosa turned quickly.

"What do you mean?" she said in surprise. Marcel interrupted her in a louder, more commanding voice. "Tomorrow you will go home. I don't need you. Do you understand?" he said coldly. His anger was beginning to get the better of him as he struggled to hold his temper.

Rosa spoke in her mama's voice to him, softly, gently, pleading. "But Marcello, bambino, we were having such a good time. I thought tomorrow we could visit some other places." Marcel had controlled his impatience with her all day and finally let go. A flush of anger rushed up his neck and into his face. He began shaking with rage as he turned on his mother and yelled.

"I am NOT your BAMBINO or your MARCELLO--I am a MAN." He continued in a more controlled and quieter voice. "Tomorrow you will go home and I will be free of you forever."

"Bambino," she protested; and he couldn't stop himself. Rage took over, and he lunged across the room and thrust his hands around her neck. In his anger, his hands tightened as he squeezed hard to strangle her. Shocked and startled, Rosa's legs weakened and she staggered backwards, falling on the bed with him on top of her. Her leg came up automatically as she went back and landed him a swift and hard knee in his groin. Marcel released his grip on her throat, and rolled over on the floor. Bent on his knees, his hands covering his groin, he reeled back and forth moaning in pain. She had without intention averted her own death, for, in his blind rage, he would surely have strangled her. She didn't move at first but lay quietly in fear, trying to understand what had just happened.

"God forgive me," she whispered. "How could he do this? How could anyone do this thing? Please God, forgive me, whatever I have done to make this happen." She pleaded as she prayed into her pillow. At that moment, she lifted up her quilts and bedding and went into the bathroom and locked the door from the inside. She would sleep there in safety that night and come out in the morning.

Rosa stood still in the middle of the bathroom floor breathing deeply and still in shock. She arranged the pillows and bedding on the floor in a daze, and made herself as comfortable as she could. Bewildered and confused, she didn't know this person--he was not the son she had raised, not the boy she loved, not her bambino. Where did this monster come from? Who was he? She felt ashamed and baffled. *What happened to provoke such hatred from him,* she asked herself? *How could he do that to me, his mama? He attacked me. My son had his hands around my neck.* Thoughts raced through her mind, and it was hard for her to admit that Marcello, her beautiful son, had tried to kill her.

"God help me," she cried to herself. *Only the saints above can understand this, for I cannot. He has always been a good bambino, but now I do not know him.* Rosa cried softly in fear that he might hear her and try to break into the bathroom. She felt mortified, humiliated and confused. Her belief shattered, and she did not recognise her son, that she loved so much. The boy she knew did not have a dangerous temper.

"Please God, help him, forgive him," she prayed quietly. "He needs help, I need help. Forgive me for having such a son." Rosa had never witnessed Marcel's rage and was deeply ashamed. She recalled him and the many fights at school and now realised who the bully was. In her embarrassment, she wanted to hide away from the world and so wrapped the blankets around her tightly, her head under in the darkness. She prayed as she cried, pleading to God for forgiveness for raising a monster, a son who she now realised she did not know at all. Finally, she fell asleep.

The next morning before breakfast, Rosa packed her suitcase ready for the long journey back to Italy. She sat in silence at the table by the window, her stomach anxiously churning while waiting for Marcel to awake. They would have their last breakfast together, and she would settle their final bill at the desk. Rosa was going home to Italy. Broken and sad, she had lost her only son and was silently devastated. Her world had collapsed.

When Marcel awoke, he gathered his things together and went into the bathroom. No one spoke. The room was quiet. She knew now that her son would be alright--he could take care of himself. She was still in shock but accepted that he didn't need or want her around. She felt empty inside, like the pain that comes with the death of a loved one. Rosa tried hard not to think about the night before, but the shock, fear, and panic were already inside her and wouldn't go away. She couldn't look at him and kept her head lowered and turned away. They ate breakfast together for the last time in silence. Rosa picked at her food, but she was unable to eat anything and managed only to sip her tea.

Marcel Murphy accompanied his mama to the ferryboat in Dublin, where she would sail to the mainland. He would be rid of her smothering love forever and at last he would be able to live life on his own terms. He waited beside her in silence until she handed her ticket to the ticket master. He then kissed her on the cheek showing no emotion and said goodbye as if nothing had happened between them. He handed her baggage to her and then turned and walked away. She had no words, only pain and said nothing. Marcel did not look back, not even once.

Rosa's heart broke. She stood rigid holding on to the handrail. She was trembling all over and afraid to move for fear that her legs would give way beneath her. She was helpless to stop him and watched as he walked away in final abandonment of her. *God forgive him, how could he be so cruel and heartless to me, his Mama? When did he become this cold and unkind person? He is not my Marcello, not the boy I know.* She felt emptiness and the deepest limits of despair, exhausted at the thoughts going round in her head. Lonely and shattered, Rosa boarded the ship and found herself a bench in a quiet corner of the far deck towards the bow. She sat down and began to sob quietly. *What can I do? Marcello my boy, my beautiful bambino has gone, and this new Marcel has rejected me. He does not need me or want me in his life--he hates me.* She felt alone and drained, isolated with no hope.

Rosa reached the pit of her endurance. After a moment, she stood up and walked towards the bow of the ship. Without hesitation, she pulled herself up over the railing and threw herself into the cold darkness of the Irish Sea. Rosa hit the water with a force and descended into the deep, icy blackness. She felt the sting of the freezing water in her lungs and gasped a breath as she descended into the abyss. She didn't struggle as she took in breath after breath of icy cold water, sinking down until it became black, and there was no light above her. She prayed all the while to God for his forgiveness that she couldn't live in this world without the love of her son. It took Rosa three minutes to drown.

3

Doune, Ireland - 1890-1900

Rosemary Sullivan was a local girl. She was born and grew up in the village of Doune in County Kilane, about forty miles south of Dublin. She lived at home with her mammy and daddy and her two older brothers. They were a close-knit family, hard working with a good sense of fun, and like everyone else in the area they farmed their land to survive. She was in the vegetable garden digging up spuds for her mammy when she heard her daddy calling from the kitchen door at the back of the house.

"Rosemary, me girl. I need ye te ride wit' me up te McGinty's farm. Finish up what yer doin' and come wit' me. Are ye clean enough te be seen? I see not. Get a quick wash an' make yerself respectable. We might just drop inte the local on the way home, ye know?"

"Right ye are Daddy, I'll be right wit' ye."

It was thirteen miles between McGinty's farm and where Rosemary lived on the outskirts of the village. It was not a journey she had often taken, but she had been there as a child on the pony and cart with her daddy and knew the route. As she remembered, they owned a lot of land and there was much farming to do.

She had known Sean McGinty Junior for most of her life but not closely, just as the son of a neighbouring farmer. He was a few years older than she was and known locally as a hard worker that his daddy relied on heavily. Sean was a solid and clear-headed young man. He took life seriously and didn't indulge in frivolities, but he did have a sense of humour and could laugh and joke too. He knew his place and his duty and willingly took over the hard work that his daddy could no longer perform. Unknown to Sean, Mr. McGinty Senior was quietly looking for a suitable young lady that might make a good wife for his son. She was strong and able to think for herself--no prissy little girl would survive the work on his farm.

It was springtime in 1893. Rosemary was seventeen years of age, old enough to go into the ladies' lounge at the local pub and have a glass of lemonade. Mr. Sullivan had just returned from the monthly market. As usual he wanted to drop into the pub to show off his profits. However, he had a duty to perform first--he had to settle some business with his neighbour Sean McGinty. It being the monthly market day, Mr. McGinty Senior would be expecting him.

Rosemary finished up in the garden and threw off her boots at the back door. She slipped her feet into her only shoes and hurried inside to wash up. Then she changed into her cotton dress and white cardigan, which she kept for special occasions. She tidied her hair piled high on her head and rushed outside to climb up on the trap beside her daddy. She was a dutiful daughter, always willing to help when she could. She had grown into a dependable young lady, respectable and well thought of locally. She could hold her own but was not afraid to get her hands dirty either. She loved her daddy's company and enjoyed going with him. *She might even meet up with some of her friends in the village,* she thought?

"Thank ye, Rosemary, that was quicker than yer mammy takes. Now let's be off." He eagerly pulled on the reins, and the horse trotted down the driveway on the rough turreted path that led towards McGinty's farm.

Sean McGinty Senior had lived on the farm all of his life, passed down from his father and his father before him, as was the custom. He and his family had survived the famine years and held on to their land despite the struggle. Most of his brood, now married, had their own farms, and a couple had left Ireland to settle in America. However, his youngest son, Sean Junior, would remain home and inherit the farm and the way of life that went with it. Mr. McGinty Senior, highly respected in the area, was known to lend a hand financially in difficult times--the reason for Sullivan's trip today was to finalise another short-term loan. They pulled up outside the farmhouse, and Mr. Sullivan jumped down from the trap and went inside.

"Come along inside, Sullivan me man, I've been expecting ye."

"How're ye doin' today, Mr. McGinty?

"I'm well thank ye, Mr. Sullivan," he replied.

"I'm here te make final payment te a debt well received an' appreciated, Mr. McGinty," he said. "I'm going inte the village for a celebration pint, will ye kindly join me, sir?" he said as he handed over a small package to Mr. McGinty.

"How very generous of ye and thank ye for the invitation, but not tonight. It being market day I'm expectin' some other visitors, ye know? No need te count this though," he said as he accepted the package and placed it on the table in front of him. The two men talked casually about the day's events at the market. Mr. McGinty liked to hear of the goings on, as he was older now and not often able to make the long journey. After some conversation, Mr. Sullivan made his leave, thanking McGinty for his kindness.

"Good day te ye, sir, and thank ye," he extended his hand towards Mr. McGinty.

"A pleasure indeed," said McGinty and the two men shook hands.

When they arrived in the village, Mr. Sullivan helped Rosemary down from the trap and walked her into the ladies' lounge, which was empty.

"I'll send ye in a glass of lemonade."

"Thank ye, Daddy, and take yer time, enjoy yerself. I'll be just fine right here on me own, somebody's bound te come in te talk wit' me," she said.

The publican Jimmy was behind the bar working on his own. Jimmy's wife had been sick for some time, and the barman complained to Mr. Sullivan.

"I can't keep up these long hours much more ye know, it's doin' me in slowly," he sighed.

Mr. Sullivan was not a heavy drinker but, like everyone else, he did enjoy the odd pint of beer at the local pub where he could exchange pleasantries and hear the gossip. The pub also served as a local meeting place, where bartering and haggling were common, and business of all sorts took place. If anyone wanted to know what was going on locally, then best go to the village pub. A good publican could tell of the latest news from the furthest parts. Mr. Sullivan was not slow to act, and jumped at the opportunity of a job for his daughter, Rosemary.

"Why, Jimmy, me daughter's the very lass te help ye run the place. Ye know her well and she's honest as the day's long. Ye'd be able te go aboot yer other business, and she'd help oot wit' Mary too. She's a real good lass, as ye know. What d'ye t'ink?" Mr. Sullivan asked.

Rosemary was the youngest of Mr. Sullivan's three children. She took to her brothers' ways and copied them in almost everything they did. She would never let anyone down if she had given her word on something. People liked her and knew her as a good Catholic girl who would never do anything that was wrong. Rosemary was not a stunning beauty. She had a heavy-set jaw line and square chin that gave her a slightly masculine look. She was tall with big farm hands used to doing heavy work. She had long legs that could stride once to most people's two steps, and she had large feet for a young woman. Her dark hair she wore up off her face and her small, deep-set eyes, which she kept down most of the time. She was a quiet girl and shy of most people unless she knew them well. She didn't speak unless spoken to first, and when she did speak, her head bent down to avoid eye contact, although her reply was firm and confident.

Rosemary lived all her life on the family farm where she helped her mammy and daddy with whatever they asked of her. She was a willing worker, anxious to please her parents with any request. She never gave it a moment's thought that it was not fitting for a young lady to do some of the work she helped with. She was just glad that her daddy relied on her, and felt proud that he did. She loved her daddy and her mammy dearly, and everyone said she had a heart of gold.

At seventeen, Rosemary stood tall and straight--her large, rough-working-hands clasped in front of her confidently. She was quietly proud of her ability but appeared somewhat ungainly in comparison to the usual petite young girls of the day. However, Rosemary was not ugly, either. She had a fresh look about her face, lovely soft, pink cheeks, and high cheekbones. People remarked on her unblemished, clear white skin, her ruby lips, and her beautiful broad smile. However, that softness didn't fool anyone for she could certainly handle herself with the men. Being taller than most of them and having two brothers was a blessing at times. She spoke up for herself when she had to but didn't force her opinions in any way unless asked to.

Jimmy thought a while--seemed to mull the idea over--suddenly turned to Mr. Sullivan and announced loudly.

"Yes, send her in te see me."

"Alright then, Jimmy, I'll go fetch her now. She's in the ladies' lounge."

"Indeed, man, go bring her in, and we can talk a bit," Jimmy replied with interest. Mr. Sullivan knew the pay would be low if only a couple of coppers a week, but he was also thinking ahead.

His daughter Rosemary was not a social type of girl and had never shown any interest in the romantic side of life. She was a practical girl, serious and hard working, but still had a good sense of humour and enjoyed a joke or two. It didn't matter to her that she wasn't petite. In fact, she was glad people knew she could handle things on her own. It made her feel more independent, like she had a purpose. She worked as hard as any man around and didn't need anyone to look after her. She could see to herself.

Her daddy was no fool, either. He knew that the few coppers she earned, she would save. This would be a welcome dowry to any young man seeking a wife in these parts. Working behind the bar would put Rosemary up front in public view for all to see how hard working and able-bodied she was. She was everything desired for life as a farmer's wife. She was strong enough to fetch and carry for herself, and healthy enough to bear a large brood of children, which most farmers wanted. "Yes," Mr. Sullivan thought, his daughter had a better chance of finding a husband working behind this bar, and he needn't fret about his fields--he knew his sons would manage. Mr. Sullivan made his way into the lounge to fetch his daughter.

"I believe I've found ye a job working for Jimmy here in the bar. Mary's sick again, and he can't cope himself any longer. It's too much for him. Would ye like that, girl, te work here I mean?"

"Why, Daddy, d'ye t'ink I could do it? I mean it's a man's place in the bar, not like in the ladies' lounge, ye know?"

"Of course ye can. Once ye get settled into the work, and people see yer able, ye'll earn their respect and ye'll get te know everybody in the land. Wouldn't that be grand?"

"Oh, Daddy, how exciting, meeting all those people and having a job of me own that I get paid for doin'," she was thinking aloud. "I'd love it, and save every penny I could. I'd be able te give you and Mammy somet'ing te help out wit' t'ings at home," Rosemary said excitedly.

Mr. Sullivan took her hand and guided her to the men's bar to meet Jimmy. She knew that it was usually a man's place of work, but Rosemary was not offended in the least. She could handle any of them, and she knew most of the locals who frequented the pub. She knew it was hard work, low pay, and some other local might be more able than she. Her main quality that Jimmy would appreciate, and she was known for, was her honesty and trustworthy. He knew she would never steal from him. Rosemary was quietly confident she would get the job, and she did.

The pub was in the village, about five miles from her home. She would have to walk there and back every day, and was suddenly grateful that she had a good pair of heavy walking boots. She would need them now more than ever. She could pick up some speed walking, and not be afraid of spraining her ankles. She could do the five miles in just over an hour at a quick walk.

Rosemary felt a new sensation come to her. She wasn't sure if it was a sense of freedom or independence? Rosemary, she would work here for the next 7 years of her life. She would spend long days and often hard labour, lifting barrels and changing kegs. She got to know all the local drinking men and even the non-drinking men among them. Rosemary intervened in a few brawls in her time too, and occasionally had to throw some fighting beggars out into the street when they had exceeded their capacity. Yes, she certainly proved to the locals that she was every bit as capable and more able than most men. She earned their respect over the years doing the hard work and the bidding of a publican.

It was in her second year working at the pub that she made it known to her customers that she was looking to buy a bicycle. It was getting near market day, and most of the local men would be going to the city to buy or sell livestock. Rosemary thought if she made it known now that someone might keep an eye open for such an item, ands tell her about it when they returned from the market.

Only then, on a sure thing, would Rosemary arrange to go to the city on her day off to view, and perhaps buy the bicycle she desired so very much.

"I'm looking for a lady's bicycle, in good condition," she announced to everyone one night. "It has te be sturdy enough for the rough roads in these parts, not paved like they are in the city, ye know?" she pointed out. "I can't afford a brand new one. But I'm looking for a good quality, second-hand one. Maybe one that belonged to a wealthy city lady now tired of the fashionable park riding," she declared. "If ye keep a lookout for me and let me know, I can stand ye a pint of beer for yer trouble if it works out, ye know," she announced to everyone.

Sean McGinty Junior was standing at the bar enjoying his monthly half pint of Guinness when he looked over to Rosemary.

"I'd be glad te keep a look out for ye, Rosemary--it'd certainly save ye all that walking."

"Oh, thank ye Sean, that'd be grand."

"T'ink not'ing of it, we'll see if I get me half pint free next month?" and they both laughed. Sean finished up his drink.

"Goodnight now," he said as he made his leave.

"Don't forget te keep an eye out for me bicycle now," she called after him.

"I will, I will," he said turning to look at her. "Goodnight now," he replied. The twinkle in his eye caught her off-guard and she blushed slightly. Goodnight Sean," she said quietly as a tingle ran through her.

She had been walking the journey between her home and the village pub since she started and had saved every penny she earned. She did give her mammy and daddy a little for her keep and food. They were grateful for her financial contribution. None of her brothers earned an income and still worked the fields every day for their daddy. Rosemary's parents were proud of their daughter, for her independence and her frugal ways with money. They both knew that she would be a good catch for a man with a practical mind. It would be just a matter of time for the right man to come forward and claim her as his wife.

4

Rosemary Sullivan is 19 Years of Age, 1895

R osemary was proud of her job, and her ability to deal with the men as she did. She needed everyone to see that she could cope, to win their respect. After a time the locals thought highly of her for toughing it through the hard times. Now, two years on, she held her own firmly, stood her ground and won. Rosemary enjoyed the social side of the work. People understood that even though she might not take part in the conversation, she was certainly listening.

"Ask Rosemary, she knows everyt'ing that's goin' on in these parts," people would say, and she did. Customers wanted her opinion and would openly ask her.

"What d'ye t'ink, Rosemary?"

She enjoyed the interaction on equal terms, and knew she was though of as wise, for a lady. They suspected that she would save her money, and of course, she did. She was a rare commodity in these parts. Each man viewed her differently from then onwards. Not that Rosemary noticed, of course. She thought they were polite, well-mannered and friendly, and she liked that, but kept them all at a safe distance.

It was a quiet day when Sean McGinty and his son Sean Junior came into the pub. They were on their way home from the city, having been at the market. Old Mr. McGinty was in fine fettle, happy that he was able to make the trip and watch his son do his bidding. Sean Junior had made a good price on his cattle, and feeling generous, Mr. McGinty Senior offered to celebrate with his son's profit.

"The drinks're on me, boys," he announced loudly at the bar. Of course, they all knew each other, being neighbours for many years, and so a pleasant afternoon covering the events of market day followed. Now old Mr. McGinty was at the bar paying for his drinks when he offered, "A drink for yerself Rosemary?"

"Oh, I don't drink, Mr. McGinty, but thank ye anyway."

"Of course ye don't, a young lady like yerself, but do take for a lemonade and enjoy it in yer own time."

"Why thank ye Mr. McGinty, that's very kind of ye, I will." Rosemary took Mr. McGinty's money and included the lemonade for herself in the total.

"Thanks again, Mr. McGinty," she said as she handed him back his change.

"Not at all, Rosemary, yer welcome. I see ye can count too, not only a lady, but educated as well. Ye'll make some lucky man a fine wife. Are ye walking out wit' anyone?"

Rosemary looked down, embarrassed and replied hesitantly in a low voice that others could not hear.

"No, no one, sir. I spend me days here working, and it's late when I get home, but I am looking for a bicycle, te get me home earlier."

"Sure it's a man ye need, he'd keep ye home alright--not a bicycle to get ye home." The crowd laughed aloud as old Mr. McGinty continued.

"Here I have a young man--about yer age too, right here wit' me." He placed his arm on Sean Junior's shoulder, "And he's no wife either, what d'ye t'ink 'bout that?"

Both Rosemary and Sean Junior glanced quickly at each other and blushed. Rosemary lowered her head and busily started drying beer mugs. Sean Junior interrupted his father.

"I t'ink ye've had enough te drink now, Father, let's get ye home before ye spend all our profits."

"Aye, yer probably right, Sean, let's be off. Goodnight, and thank ye, Rosemary. I hope I didn't embarrass ye too much."

"Goodnight, Mr. McGinty, no offense taken." Rosemary's eyes darted over to Sean Junior and quickly away again. She busied herself picking up their empty jugs, and wiped down the countertop where the two had stood. The men made their way towards the door and out of the pub.

A slow evening followed, and Rosemary's thoughts drifted to having a family of her own, one-day. She had never contemplated the idea before, not being much of a day-dreamer. However, while drying jugs and mindlessly cleaning the counter, the thought somehow slipped into her mind. The idea floated around for a few minutes, long enough for her to imagine herself with an infant baby of her own. For that instant, Rosemary felt full of love for the child, a feeling she had never experienced before, and just as suddenly she snapped back to reality when she heard her boss Jimmy shout out.

"Help me, Rosemary, go fetch Doctor Connelly for me, I t'ink Mary's dying!"

Rosemary quickly threw on her shawl.

"I'll be quick on me feet--back soon." With only two men left in the bar, Jimmy was not worried about Rosemary leaving. He stood around for a few minutes, thinking about all the years he and his Mary had worked there--*long, hard hours in the pub for what? She's so weak and sick all the time, what was it all for? I should have sold this place years ago, but who would buy it? No one around here has any money. No matter, someone might have turned up, and we could have gone to America wit' our boys,* he thought quietly to himself.

Rosemary's long legs took great strides as she ran down the road to the doctor's house. It could only have taken her five minutes at most to get there. She frantically banged on the door with her large fists, loud as she could, in case they were at the back of the house, as most would normally be.

The door opened, and there in front of her stood the doctor.

"What the dickens is all the noise about?"

"Quickly, Doctor, Jimmy Hughes says Mary's dying. Ye've got to come now, Doctor, please?"

"I'll get my bag and coat." The doctor spun around and grabbed his coat and bag from behind him. Together they ran up the road to the pub. When they arrived, the two men were still sitting at their table, talking quietly and sipping beer. Jimmy was not there.

"He'll be upstairs wit' Mary. Over here, Doctor." Rosemary ushered him up through the back stairs behind the bar to the house above. Jimmy heard them coming and came out of the bedroom to meet the doctor at the top of the stairs.

"In here, Doctor, I t'ink she's still breathing."

Doctor Connelly knew the room well. He had helped deliver all six of Mary Hughes' children and confirmed three of them dead at birth. It was not unusual in those days to lose a child at birth. Often the mother would lose too much blood during the delivery, or there might be other complications during the birth. Mary Hughes had never been a strong woman. The fact that she gave birth to three sons who lived was a miracle in itself.

Mary was a frail, small-boned little lady. She was quiet as a mouse and always getting sick with colds, pneumonia, and other ladies problems never spoken of in those days. Many times she would have to leave Jimmy alone in the bar to go to bed and rest. He never objected and would urge her to go and lie down. He had always loved her very much in his own quiet way. Now he was wondering what it was all for? All this hard work and saving every penny for their growing boys to give them a start in life; just like the start that Jimmy and Mary had received from Jimmy's father, when they first got married. They had both wanted the same for their boys and were happy to do with less for themselves to that end.

Old Mr. Hughes had turned up a big surprise for everyone when he offered a substantial amount as a deposit for the young couple to help buy the pub. He knew it would give them a living, independence, and a roof over their heads. He wouldn't have to worry about them all the time, but he had no idea how much work there would be. Neither did Jimmy or Mary realise what a toll it would take on them.

There was a lot of cooking. Mary had to prepare food every day for people coming in for lunch. She had a pot of soup or stew on the go at all times, along with fresh, homemade bread every day, her own jam, butter and cheese. There was a lot of work involved, and on top of looking after her own three boys, their weekly washing, ironing and keeping her house clean, it was a lot. Mary had a busy life and never a minute spare to relax on her own. Now, with all three boys gone to America, Jimmy thought they would have some time for themselves. Then Mary got sick, and looking back he wondered if her heart broke when her boys left. That would explain a lot, he thought to himself. He wished now that they had sold up back then and gone to America with their boys. It would have been a new life for them all, and maybe, just maybe, Mary wouldn't be dying now if they had.

Mary never complained or mentioned her boys after they left. She knew America would be good for them, and she was glad they all went together. She did receive a short letter from her youngest boy, Seamus, with news of their landing and where they were living. They were doing well, with good jobs earning good money. They had decent digs with an Irish landlady who included washing and ironing for an extra one dollar a week. Mary was happy to know they settled alright, but she did miss them terribly. Their leaving left a great void, and only her boys could fill that emptiness and make her happy again. However, she said nothing to anyone and now Jimmy wondered about her sickness, which seemed to turn far worse after her boys left. *Could it be that Mary was dying from a broken heart?* Then as quickly, he turned his mind back to the present.

"In here, Doctor" Mary lay on the bed, her eyes struggling to open and her breathing shallow--almost silent. Doctor Connelly listened to her heart and then whispered something to Jimmy. He went on to check her lungs, and shook his head in despair. Mary had a high fever and was delirious, as she lay in the bed unaware of how ill she was.

"How long has she been sick like this, Jimmy?"

"About a week now, Doctor, I t'ink. She took badly last weekend. She's had not'ing to eat, won't even have soup or a cup-a-tea." Mary remained lifeless in the bed, not aware that Doctor Connolly was there at all. He was seriously afraid that he was too late to stop this illness. He took Jimmy outside of the bedroom and spoke quietly to him.

"Jimmy, Mary's very sick, very sick indeed. She has pneumonia. Her lungs are full wit' fluid, and she's very weak. They're testing a new drug in London at present, but it hasn't been released for use as yet."

"Is there anyt'ing ye can do for her, Doctor?"

"Jimmy, ye have te be very brave now. Mary's dying, Jimmy," he said softly. "She doesn't have much time left and cannot be alone--she needs ye wit' her. If ye need me at all, day or night, come get me or send Rosemary and I'll come." Doctor Connolly made his leave and left Jimmy alone with his wife. He sat on the edge of the bed beside Mary, beloved wife of forty years.

"What'll I do without ye?" he spoke quietly. "I've had ye wit' me since ye were a girl, just seventeen years old. My little lady, petite and so frail--I was always proud of ye being my wife. Birthing all those babies and our three boys that survived." Jimmy paused for a moment remembering the hard times Mary had delivering her children.

"I know that was hard on ye, but ye did it for me. I'm sorry, Mary, that our life was so hard. I thought it would be more fun than work, and it was for me, for a while at least. I see now it wasn't for ye, all that cooking, cleaning, and taking care of our boys and our home, it was just too much. Ye never complained though, not a word of regret from ye in all these years--a labour of love it was."

Gently, Jimmy lifted her small hand in his. Her hands dry and rough with hard skin on the palms from being in and out of water so much, was now limp to touch, and he began to cry. Tears welled up in his eyes and slowly spilled over and rolled down his cheeks. He didn't sob or make a sound--just sat there holding her hand. She was like a little child in the bed, so small and delicate, he thought, as he gazed lovingly at her. "What will I do wit'out ye?" he whispered. Then he let the tears come, silently and slowly down his face.

Mary died that night in her sleep. Jimmy was sleeping in a chair at the side of the bed, and when he woke in the morning, she was already gone. He dressed quickly and went straight for Doctor Connelly. It was Wednesday at six o'clock. The doctor came to minister over her body and write-up the paperwork. Mary would be buried on Saturday--three days after she died.

Rosemary continued to go to work every day, even though the pub didn't open. She helped Jimmy with preparations, cleaning, and such. He just wanted company, and he couldn't think straight so Rosemary would help him. He had come to rely on her for almost everything. It would be a dry village that following week as the pub closed for grieving. A week after the funeral, Jimmy opened again.

Rosemary had been a blessing over the years, but now Jimmy had other things to consider and big decisions to make. Having her around was a great comfort to him. She busied herself making sandwiches and tea for the people coming to pay their respects. Jimmy was not up to his usual social self, but under the circumstances he put on a brave face and did his best, and Rosemary, of course, helped him get through things.

"Rosemary, would ye consider staying overnight here for a short time, just until we get through all this? I'd like ye te ask yer parents if that'd be okay wit' them, would ye do that for me?"

"Of course, I will, Jimmy, and I'll let ye know tomorrow morning, alright."

The funeral day arrived. Most of the village attended at the chapel, as almost everyone in the area was Catholic. Mary had a lot of well-wishers and good friends, albeit she had been a quiet and gentle little lady. Everyone had liked her, and she was known never to have a bad word against anyone. There was a solemn sadness for her loss throughout the villagers. Many of them had known Mary's kindness and quiet ways through personal experience in one way or another. She was one of the first people you could ask for help in the village, and she never spoke to anyone about it. Mary was known for her integrity as well as her hard work and good deeds--those who knew her, would miss her.

Mary was laid to rest in the cemetery behind the chapel next to her mother and father. For Jimmy, it was all so final, and he was now alone in the village. After the funeral, people returned to the pub for tea and sandwiches. They made small talk for a short time and left quietly, giving Jimmy a pat on the back and telling him to keep a "stiff upper lip, time's a great healer." It didn't take his pain away. That dull, stabbing emptiness in the pit of his stomach, would that ever go, he wondered?

Is this the feeling that you get when a loved one dies? He wondered. *A pain to remind you that there was someone there, and now they're gone, you're alone in the world and they're dead?* He asked himself the same questions over and over in his mind--*why, what's it all for?* Jimmy closed up for the evening after everyone had left and poured himself a brandy. He didn't usually drink, but felt he could do with something to help him sleep.

"Would ye like a drink, Rosemary?"

"Thank ye, but no thank ye. You go ahead, Jimmy. It'll help ye settle for the night."

He sat at the bar drinking his brandy without speaking then turned to Rosemary.

"Ye can go upstairs to bed if ye like, lass, I'll be fine?"

Rosemary continued to clear up. "Will ye be alright on yer own?"

"I'll be fine. I just want te t'ink some t'ings through, ye go on up. I have a letter to write to the boys, telling them about their mother. I was going to send a telegram but had second thoughts about that. What d'ye t'ink I should do?"

"You should write to them, Jimmy, a telegram would be cold and official, and she's their mammy, ye know. It would be better in a letter and more personal from their daddy."

"Aye, I t'ink yer right, goodnight Rosemary. Ye've been a great help te me these last days, and I want ye te know that no one else could have done for me what ye've been able te do. I thank ye from the bottom of me heart, and I know Mary would want te thank ye, too. I'm so lucky te have ye. Thank ye lass and goodnight." With that, Rosemary went up the stairs to her room and left Jimmy with his brandy and his thoughts.

In the days to follow, life at the pub slowly got back to normal. The usual customers came in for lunch, and Rosemary was kept busy cooking and cleaning and serving at the bar. Jimmy was not around--he seemed to have other personal things to attend to. He had sent his letter off to America by first-class mail, and he was now seeing a solicitor to complete some other legal details.

Rosemary never asked questions--she just got on with the work at hand. She was behind the bar when she heard a couple of old fella's talking about the new people who moved into the village. Not just one family; it seemed several had arrived but not related in any way. It was just coincidence that they came to the village around the same time. One of the new people was a young man--an Italian it seemed, with a strange name for an Italian.

"Oh, and what would that be?"

"They call him Murphy, Marcel Murphy, and that's not an Italian name by any means--but it seems his father was a Murphy? He's working as a farm hand up at McGinty's place. Their boys have gone now, and there's only young Sean and the old fella left te do the work. No doubt he'll drop in here for his supper at the end of the day. Ye'll see him then."

"Aye, aye," replied the other. "Then there's a couple of new families moved in down the bottom of the village--a lot of girls in one of them, no boys at all. The father died recently, and the widow had to move out of her farmhouse for new tenants. I t'ink there's four or five girls in all, young teenagers by the look."

"Not too many young men in these parts te go around, so many young girls. They'll have their competition cut out for them if they're looking for suitors," the other man interjected.

"Of course, of course," and they continued between them.

Rosemary listened on casually, taking note that there was new blood in the village as she carried on working. A few days later, a girl came into the bar asking if there was any work available. Rosemary knew she could do with the help since Jimmy was never around. She was alone most of the day with kitchen work and the bar. She thought she would just ask Jimmy if he might be willing to take on another girl? Maybe he would consider even just a few hours a day over the lunch and supper times for the cooking? Rosemary never complained about too much work, or it being too busy for her alone. So, when she broached Jimmy, he was quite surprised at the request.

"Well, I have a few t'ings going on at the moment and I have an idea coming up in the near future. We might take someone on for a few hours here and there te help ye. Yes, Rosemary, tell her she can start on Monday, whatever hours ye t'ink ye'll need her, base rate, of course. Oh, and Rosemary, while we're on the subject, I've decided te give ye a pay rise for all yer hard work here. We'll talk more about that later." Rosemary stood silent for a few minutes, surprised at the rise, and glad to get the extra help. "Thank ye, Jimmy, thank ye very much," and she continued on with her work.

The new girl was Philomena Logan, Flo for short. She was fifteen years of age and said she was a hard worker, which was what Rosemary expected. No slouching allowed in her bar. There was much work to do, and quickly too. She showed her new friend the ropes and Flo learned quickly, although she was not much help when it came to changing the barrels. Flo was a small-framed girl and not strong like Rosemary. This could have been a drawback for Rosemary. However, she ignored that because Flo could cook extremely well. She worked quickly and learned fast. She was a quick mover where Rosemary moved slow and deliberate. Flo showed her talent in the kitchen, cooking up a storm for her unsuspecting customers.

"Me mammy taught me everyt'ing. She's a great cook, and I love te do it," she told Rosemary. The aroma from Flo's kitchen drifted outside and down the street. It gave the villagers something to talk about. Her Irish stew and her broth became a favourite of the locals. She made her own butter, cheese, creams, and jams, too. She also made her own bread, scones, biscuits, sweet breads and cakes, including puddings, which the men loved. People started coming to the pub more often after she started, and life became quite busy.

Flo wasn't afraid to get her hands dirty, and could certainly show a nippy tongue with the men if they got out of control. Rosemary knew Flo would be able to handle herself, and that was necessary for a young girl behind a bar full of workingmen. Indeed, Rosemary now tired of making simple, quick meals, was happy.

"The men love puddings and sweet t'ings, just wait and see," Flo said.

Rosemary was very pleased with her, and they worked well together, laughing their way through the long hours and hard work. As a young girl, Rosemary had spent her time competing with her two brothers, and was not in the kitchen with her mammy, as other young women were. As a result, her cooking was basic. Having Flo around was much more fun and made the day pass more quickly. It was just a month after Flo started work when Rosemary approached Jimmy again.

"Jimmy, I was wondering if I could offer Flo full-time work in the kitchen? She's bringing in more customers every day wit' her excellent cooking. People in the village are talking about her and coming in te try her food," she explained. "Also, it gives me more time in the bar and tending to paperwork and other t'ings that take a lot of me time. I do need the help, Jimmy," she finished.

Indeed, Jimmy had noticed a difference in the food being served and made many complimentary comments about Flo's cooking himself.

"That's up te you Rosemary. If ye feel there's a need for Flo then go ahead and hire her. So long as ye keep a record of the wages an' all, the books--ye know." Jimmy saw that the two girls were working well together, and it settled him somehow.

"Rosemary, will ye come upstairs when it gets quiet. I'd like a word wit' ye." "Certainly," she replied and some fifteen minutes later turned to Flo and asked, "would ye watch over the bar please? Jimmy wants te talk te me." "Of course," said Flo. "If it gets too busy, just call me," she said as she went upstairs to Jimmy. He was waiting for her in the parlour of all places, which surprised her. It was Mary's best room, which she kept for special company. Jimmy motioned Rosemary to come in and make herself comfortable on the sofa. She sat down a little awkwardly and unsure of what was happening.

"Would ye like a drink?"

"No thank ye, Jimmy, but don't let me stop ye, you go ahead and have one."

Jimmy poured himself a brandy as he did when he needed some Dutch courage. He downed it quickly and poured another.

"Rosemary, I have somet'ing I want to tell ye and somet'ing I want to ask ye," he said pouring his second drink. "I don't want ye to answer me tonight on this. I want ye to go home and talk it over wit' yer folks first. Come back to me wit' an answer in a couple of days." With this Jimmy took a deep breath then made his announcement.

"Rosemary, I'm going te America--I've decided. Since Mary died, there's no reason for me te be here. Me boys are in America, and they're all doing just fine for themselves in the police force in New York. I've no family left here and me nearest relative lives in the North of Ireland. I'm not even sure he's still alive. I don't want te grow old here on me own, and so I've decided te sell up and go." Jimmy paced the floor away from Rosemary, his hands clasped behind his back and his head down, then turned pacing back towards Rosemary again.

"As ye know, I saw me solicitor and have all me papers in order. I have the pub on the market and am just waiting for a buyer. I know that can take time, and I don't have the time te wait around. So, I'm going now while I still have some years left in me, and before I'm too old te make the trip." Jimmy reached the dresser again and lifted his glass. He took another drink and set the glass down again and continued.

"Rosemary, I want ye te run the pub when I go." He stopped speaking for a short moment and paced across the floor again, his head down as he pondered.

"Should ye decide te do this, I will, of course, pay ye a stipend of twenty pounds a year, for yer honesty and hard work, until the place sells. I want ye te live here as if it was yer own home. Yer food and boarding will be part of yer weekly wage although I will continue te pay ye as I do presently, including yer new rise in pay. Just keep the place clean as ye always do, and continue te run the pub, cook, and of course, record the takings and bills out," he said.

Rosemary remained quiet as Jimmy began again.

"Continue te do what ye've been doing these past three years wit' the addition of now overseeing Flo's work and pay. I'll give ye me solicitor's personal details as he'll be our only contact while I'm away and until the pub sells. He'll advise ye on anyt'ing that ye cannot determine yourself. He's a decent man and I trust him." Jimmy paced the floor his hands still clasped behind his back, and continued talking as if thinking aloud.

"I know I can rely on ye te make yer own decisions. Ye've a good head for money, and ye know the business well enough. The house upstairs will sell as is, furniture included, apart from anyt'ing that ye might want for yerself--a keepsake from Mary and me. So ye would have te inform the solicitor what ye would like te keep for yourself and he will put that in the inventory, which comes te me when the place sells. I'm leaving everyt'ing--I want te travel light. I know Mary would want ye te have her good t'ings, ye know, her dishes, silverware, and the like." He lifted his glass and took another large gulp of brandy.

"This is a great honour, Jimmy, and I'm glad ye feel ye can trust me wit' yer business. I'll do me best not te let ye down," Rosemary said seriously.

Rosemary lass, ye could make yourself a good income by doing this for me."

"I'm so grateful for the opportunity, Jimmy, thank you," she said still trying to take it all in.

"Ye could have a nice dowry, but I want ye te talk it over wit' yer family first. I know it's a lot te ask ye te live here alone and not see them as often. This would be yer home for whatever length of time the sale would take.

"Yes, Jimmy, I'll discuss it wit' me Daddy and Mammy tonight. It's a generous proposal," Rosemary replied.

"I hope ye'll give this yer serious consideration, it's a lot te take on. Ye can give me yer answer on Friday this week. Today being

Monday, ye'll have the week te visit and talk t'ings through wit' yer folks. I've not mentioned this te anyone else, only me solicitor knows about it. I suggest we keep it that way just between us, ye know what the gossip around here is like?" Jimmy finished his brandy and motioned Rosemary up from the sofa to go back downstairs to her work.

"We'll talk on Friday evening." Jimmy again motioned her out of the parlour and went back to his brandy, glad to be over with his proposal. Although he knew it was a good offer, he hated leaving a young girl like her in such a responsible position. But there was no one else he could trust, and no other way that he could leave to go to America. He hoped her parents would see the dowry as a motivation.

"Thank ye, Jimmy, I won't let ye down." Rosemary went downstairs, slowly taking in Jimmy's plan--excited at the idea of earning so much money, and stunned at the offer of running the place without him around. He was certainly showing more confidence in her than she had in herself. She gave herself a brush down, straightened her piny, and went back behind the bar to work. She said nothing of her conversation to Flo, and Flo would never ask or pry into another person's business.

The mood was light-hearted in the bar that night. Rosemary was happy and noticed that there were quite a few new people in for supper and drinks, so they were busy all night. Flo commented on the handsome young man up at the back of the room. She'd never seen him before.

"D'ye know who he is, Rosemary?" she asked.

"No, he's new around here, I t'ink?" Rosemary replied looking up at the new face.

"He's gorgeous," Flo said dreamily. "Look at those big dark eyes and ruby lips, just teasing for a kiss." Flo let the words spill out of her mouth before she could check herself. She looked startled towards Rosemary, and they both burst into laughter.

The newcomer was eating his supper and enjoying the local Guinness. He decided on Flo's stew and mashed potatoes.

"That was delicious, thank you," he said softly in a strange accent that Flo had not heard before. Flo smiled at him softly, unable to find words as her heart fluttered and skipped a beat.

"Look at him now, Rosemary, isn't he handsome?" Rosemary looked up and saw him, then, she winked at Flo and the two girls laughed. They worked on through the evening, making comments and joking about the handsome new face in the bar and the strange accent he had.

"I wonder where he comes from? Maybe he's the new hand up at McGinty's farm. I heard some talk about him earlier last week," said Rosemary.

"I don't know, but I've never heard such an accent before. He's probably French or somet'ing like that wit' those dark eyes and dark hair."

"How old d'ye t'ink he is, Rosemary?"

"Oh, I don't know, I haven't seen him close up like you, but he looks like around seventeen or eighteen, I t'ink?"

"Hmm, maybe," Flo shook her head in agreement but couldn't take her eyes off the handsome new face and giggled excitedly while dashing in and out of the kitchen as she spoke to Rosemary. Business was certainly picking up and Rosemary was about to become the local residential publican in charge of the village public house.

5

Marcel Murphy is on his Own

After leaving Rosa at the ship, Marcel made his way back to the city. He checked himself of all the things that he should keep in mind. Of most importance, and first on his list, was never to let anyone know that he had money. He kept the pouch in his sock inside his boot as Rosa instructed. It was annoying, but he was conscious of it being there all the time. At night, he slept with his socks on, and the pouch still inside. He only removed it when he was alone and it was safe.

First--find a job, he thought. Tonight he would go to the pub and listen and watch--no alcohol, just a lemonade. He was not a drinker, as he would find out soon enough.

The pub was exciting for him, noisy, busy, and full of action. It seemed that people from all walks of life gathered there; a few gentlemen having a quiet drink, reading their newspaper--as well as workers out for a night on the tiles, and other groups. Then there were the ladies....

"I see a new face here, some beer for the boy, bartender," one woman called over as she wrapped her arms around Marcel's neck and kissed him on the cheek.

"No, no, not for me, I have lemonade. I came looking for work," he jested.

"Why that's what I'm looking for too--let me show ye? I can change the boy in ye and make ye a man for just a shilling," and she continued to wrap herself around his body. The crowd laughed, and Marcel angrily pushed her off.

"I'm not a boy, and have no need for tutoring tonight. Now get your hands off me and go away," he scowled at her coldly.

"Huh, too tight, I see," and she skulked away. He was standing at the bar drinking his lemonade and scanning the room. He heard talk about the young woman who threw herself off the ship in Dublin and drowned in the sea. No one seemed to know who she was. Marcel knew it was Rosa, but he didn't show any interest or knowledge of her. He had no remorse, no guilt, no love, no loss, no emotion whatsoever towards his mother. He was just relieved that she was no longer in his life, and at last he was his own master.

He found it easy to ask around for work, people were friendly and helpful towards him. Of course, Marcel was handsome and had a boyish charm about him--something innocent; made them want to help him. He heard a group talk about work on the railroad. They travelled every day and returned to their digs every night.

"Might there be work for me, too?" he interrupted. Marcel was strong and flexed his muscles to show off.

"Let's have a feel at them. I t'ink ye've got something stuffed inside te puff them up like that?"

"No, no it's real muscle. I've been working on them for years."

"Look here," said another, "I've been digging an' haulin' for years, bet ye can't beat these rocks?" There followed a comparison as each young man rolled up his sleeves to show off his physique. They all laughed, but the oldest one, Sean agreed.

"Okay, looks like ye've worked at it, I'll give ye that much, but what about yer stamina, can ye keep up the pace all day, I wonder?"

"Just give me a chance and I'll prove to you that I can and more," Marcel coaxed.

"Well, wit' braggin' like that I'm tempted to take ye on, just to see for meself what yer worth. I'll have te try ye out first," said Sean, who was in charge.

"Be ready te come wit' us in the morning. I'll give ye a try--see what yer made of, and then I'll decide if yer good enough te be one of me crew or not."

"I'll be ready," replied Marcel seriously.

The crew had come together through necessity. They were all orphans turned out at the age of fifteen, according to workhouse rules. Sean knew he needed a crew to bid for work and had taken to watching for the best workers wherever he was. Finally, when he had selected the best for his own crew, he got them together and made his bid as their boss. He was the most sensible of them--his decision was final. Sean found their first work at the auction halls, Sean found their digs, and it was Sean who made sure they were at work every day without fail. He would bid for work, ensuring that they were never without a job. He negotiated hours, rates, and terms for the crew. Business came by word of mouth. He had his head on straight and kept his crew in line. They had earned a good reputation and were known always to turn up.

Sean was the oldest being twenty years of age. Frankie was next at nineteen, then Brendan also nineteen, and his younger brother Damian, eighteen. Then came Ciaran at seventeen. They seemed a good bunch and Marcel could learn a lot from them if Sean was willing to try him. He determined to impress them all.

"As long as ye can keep up wit' the work, yer in," Sean told him. So, Marcel got his first job as a labourer on the railroad. He enjoyed the hard work--flexing his muscles. The money was fair, it paid his way and that was important to him. He stayed with his new crew until the job finished, and they were all paid off at the end of the summer. The lads moved around the country wherever the work was found. Marcel enjoyed their company and learning the ropes. He managed to save some money, too, as he didn't spend any of it on beer like the others. His time for drinking was coming, but he didn't know that yet. Sean landed them a job at the auction rooms in Dublin. He was always one step ahead when it came to the work.

"That's why I'm the boss. Ye need te be ahead te keep up," he told Marcel. "There's a big livestock auction coming up, the owners need new stalls. We need te turn the soil, drain and clean, and then build new stalls. We're heading into winter; the diggin' gets hard. Are ye in?"

"I am," Marcel replied.

"Ye'd need te move into our digs, if yer te travel wit' us. We move in one unit, ye know?"

"I'd be glad to."

It was a done deal, within a few days he'd moved in with his new crew; he was one of them now. All six lads shared one room together. The landlady was great. She did their washing for extra money. She cooked for them and prepared a packed lunch every day. For the first time in his life, he had friends and began to enjoy being part of the group. He had never known such good times. He learned the Irish patter, the blarney, the local jargon, and the crew had a laugh teaching him some new words. Marcel saved quite a bit of money although no one ever knew where he put it.

"Yer mammy will soon be rich wit' ye sending all yer money home te her?" they teased.

"I hope she is." He was content to let them think that and didn't argue the fact. They never got to see his pouch. That was his secret.

Marcel was turning sixteen years old the next week.

"Time for ye to learn te hold yer beer like a man, Marcel me lad."

It was January in 1895, and still bitterly cold. They were all working the next day, but tonight they were out on the town celebrating Marcel's sixteenth birthday.

"Guinness all round please, barman, a young man here is coming of age tonight," announced Damien. Each took a turn and bought a round of drinks, but not Marcel. It was his birthday, and his drinks were free for the night. By the time they had reached the fourth pub on route to their lodgings, Marcel--drunk as a lord was laughing at everything he saw. They took turns holding him upright while heading for the last pub nearest their lodgings. Here they had something to eat with their last drink of the night. It was the Irish whiskey that finished Marcel off. The rest of the evening went blank for him when he collapsed on the floor in a drunken stupor. The lads laughed it off and carried him home to bed. As Sean was taking Marcel's boots off, he saw the bump in his sock. He knew immediately that this was Marcel's stash. He didn't touch it and left his socks on his feet.

The next morning they were up as normal, except Marcel who was still in a drunken sleep. Frankie got a metal pot and spoon and banged on it into Marcel's ear to waken him. They got him out of bed, dressed him, and dragged him to work. It was Marcel's first ever hangover. His head was pounding, he was dizzy, and found that his mouth didn't work properly. He was slurring his speech uncontrollably and didn't understand what was wrong with him.

"This is the evil that comes with the pleasure of beer," Sean told him. "Ye have te learn to hold yer liquor and still function the next day or become as a loser."

"I c-c-can work's well's any 'f yis-ss can," Marcel stammered. He tried to stand but lost his balance stumbling time after time. He couldn't hold his beer like the others, and that bothered him. Through his double vision, it looked that they were working as normal. He would show them that he could do it--just like them. He tried to keep up with them to prove his worth when all he really wanted was to sleep. The crew just laughed.

As the day wore on Marcel began to sober up, and realising how drunk he had been he remembered Rosa's warning about his secret pouch. He prayed it was still there. In his drunken state he was unsure what had happened He couldn't take the chance to look now. He waited for the right moment to check his sock, and when the time came, he was so relieved that his pouch was in place and realised how lucky he had been. "How did I get home?" he asked, concerned.

"Sure we carried ye back te the digs, took yer breaches and yer boots off and left ye te sleep on top of the bed wit' the quilt over ye," Sean told him.

"Who took my boots off?"

"Why, I did, Marcel, and I never touched your socks or that lump either. Yer secret's safe wit' me," Sean replied. The boys looked each other in the eyes. They both knew what was on Marcel's mind.

"We all have our stash somewhere," Sean said. "The sock isn't a bad place te hide it, but there are other places too," he said. "No one else saw yours, only me and I didn't touch it. I know it's for yer mammy and she probably needs it more than we do. Anyway, yer one of us now, and we take care of each other. Yer secret's safe wit' any of us, like I said, we take care of each other. Right?" Sean slapped Marcel on the back.

"Right." Marcel nodded, unconvinced.

"Where do you keep your stash?" he asked Sean.

"Now that would be tellin', wouldn't it? I used te keep it in a pouch on a string around me waist. I tucked the pouch inside me breaches, but that got awkward, ye know, danglin' there and hittin' me *boys* all the time. So I had te change me secret place."

They both laughed out loud--it lightened the atmosphere, but Marcel was still unsure. Could they be so friendly and honest, he wondered? He just wasn't prepared to take the risk and vowed he would never get drunk again. From then on Marcel would buy his round, but he would only ever have one or two pints of an evening.

"I'm in training you know, not like you hardened drinkers," he bantered.

"Aye, yer a wise man--small steps, that's the way."

Marcel continued to keep his pouch in his sock for the time being. He would be leaving the group soon and had decided that if another opportunity turned up, he was ready to move on. He had enjoyed the learning experience but he couldn't make any permanent attachments, and it was time to go. He wanted to get out of the city and felt the urge for somewhere new. They were at the auction halls when he began talking with young Sean McGinty and his father Sean McGinty senior.

"That's some nice cattle you have there, sir. I take it you farm in these parts?"

"Aye, about forty miles south of Dublin give or take, inland away from the city and a long journey te get here."

"I'm looking for work inland never seen much of the country since I've been here--don't suppose you're in need of workers?" Sean Junior knew only too well that they were always in need of workers, but he wasn't sure if his father would agree.

"What d'ye t'ink, Father? This young man's in need of work, perhaps we could make him an offer?"

"Aye, we're always looking for good labourers," said old McGinty, "but what would take ye out of the city, surely there's more work here than in the countryside?"

"I want to see the countryside, and the work is seasonal so that I could move on when I wanted to?"

"Of course, it's a good way te get around working as ye go, so te speak. The pay is average, but ye can use our barn te sleep until ye get a more permanent place. Me daughter usually provides us wit' daily breakfast, not that she's the best cook, but it's filling when yer hungry," he said.

"Yes, that would tide me over until I found a place," replied Marcel.

"Most young labourers don't stay around for long; farming is hard work, long hours and more a way of life by necessity. But if ye t'ink ye can muster the work, we'd be willing te try ye out."

"I'll be finished here at the end of the month. I'd be able to make my way to your farm after that. How long do you think it would take me to get there, walking, catching a lift here and there?"

"Ye might make it for spring planting. We always need help then and it would be perfect timing for us."

"Indeed, I'll see you in the spring then," Marcel said as they shook hands.

The deal made--Marcel had a new plan in mind. He got the address of the farm and kept it in his secret pouch. He had no intention of telling the others. He just wanted to disappear quietly, and when the time came, that's what he did. They were all in the pub enjoying a pint after work.

"I'm not feeling good; I'm going back to the digs for an early night. I'll feel better after a good sleep." Marcel stood to leave. "Enjoy yourselves," he said, "I'll see you in the morning," and he left. When the rest of the crew returned, Marcel was gone, baggage and all. The landlord told them he paid up in full and left.

Marcel would enjoy walking this journey, seeing the country-side, and luckily had good walking boots. He made his way to the outskirts of town where he booked himself overnight into a small hotel near the train station. He knew it was expensive but he wanted a good meal, a bath, and a comfortable bed for the night. He paid upfront at the counter.

The receptionist showed him to his room, which had an adjoining bathroom with tub. He paid the extra for hot water in advance and couldn't wait to get into the tub. He handed in his laundry. It would be ready the next morning, washed, dried and pressed. Oh, such luxury as he lowered himself into the hot water. He sank down remembering the delight and sheer ecstasy of a bath. When it began to cool, he reluctantly got out, quickly dressed in his best clean clothes, and went downstairs to eat. He could smell the aroma coming from the dining room, and it was making his mouth water.

All he had lived on for months was sandwiches and bacon and eggs. He was ready for a real supper.

He had never tasted Hearty Irish Stew or dough balls, and ordered that. It was delicious, and he savoured the tender meat, the tasty firm vegetables, using the dough balls to mop up the gravy. It was delicious. Feeling indulgent he asked for the homemade rice pudding with fresh fruit and cream. It really satisfied his sweet. He finished with a cup of tea, and a homemade scone, fresh butter, and jam. He liked the hotel--the food and the service was just what he needed, and he went upstairs for a good night's sleep in a clean, comfortable bed. The next morning after breakfast, Marcel booked himself out of the hotel but first asked the receptionist. "Which way to Doune?"

"That way," she pointed. " About forty or fifty miles in that direction," she smiled.

"It's a long walk, how long do you think it will take me?" Marcel enquired.

She smiled again and offered some advice. "I t'ink it'd take ye about a week, maybe more in bad weather. Ye'll need te rest overnight, and there's nowhere between here and there for shelter, just open country," she told him. It was the end of January and still cold, especially at night he thought.

"There's a shop further back towards the village where ye can get yerself some camping equipment. Make yer journey more comfortable, ye know?" she suggested.

"Thank you, I think I'll take your advice," he replied, and set off towards the shop. He bought himself a one-man sleeping tent with a waterproof covering on the outside for when it rained. It went up quickly with just four pegs and was perfect for overnight. It also had a waterproof groundsheet sewn in that he was grateful for. He bought a sleeping bag, water container, a Tilley lamp with paraffin, and some new thick woollen socks. He already had a tin box to keep food in. He made his way to the grocery shop where he bought some fresh fruit, cheese, cooked meat, and bread and filled up his water container. Now he was a more prepared as he set out on his walk towards his new life.

The road, roughed out and burrowed over time, looked well used. He walked for as long as he could during the daylight, and slept by the roadside at night. The sky was clear and cold, but he was well wrapped as he lay there looking up at the night stars. Finally, he slept with his head inside the sleeping bag for warmth--glad of the camping gear. He awoke to the freshness of the countryside, the breathtaking views and the lush shades of green all around him. In Italy the fields were mostly burnt brown. The space here seemed never-ending--fresh air freeing him of his past, now he was eager to start life on his own terms.

Many hours later he arrived at a little farmhouse set back off the road. He made his way up the path, knocked on the door and waited. In time an older woman with greying hair opened the door.

"I'm on my way to Doune for work. I was wondering if you could spare me some hot water for tea?"

"Of course, just wait here," she replied. Marcel sat down on the ground and waited. When she returned she beckoned him inside.

"Come in, it's ready," she said. "Just sit here," as she pulled out a chair. Marcel sat at the table. She poured out the tea and offered him some freshly baked bread and homemade butter. Why don't ye wait outside for me man, he's looking for help himself and might make ye an offer?" she said.

When he arrived, Marcel told him of his plan to walk to Doune for work.

They struck a deal, and invited him inside to eat with the family. He slept in the hayloft inside the barn. It was warm and cosy and better than the roadside. The next morning the farmer called him in for breakfast--bacon, eggs, toasted bread, and butter. *What could be better*, Marcel thought surprised that he missed his bacon and eggs.

"Thank you for the hot breakfast--much appreciated," he nodded to the wife. He ate quickly and readied himself to go with the farmer for the day's work. They would return for supper at dusk. It was a long day, hard, heavy work with only a sandwich and a drink of water the entire day. When they returned at night, they directed him to the outhouse to wash before supper. He changed into clean clothes as he always did before sitting at the table--surprised to see the farmer still in his working clothes but made no comment.

The farmer was a neighbour of McGintys, for generations back. They were Brendan and Kitty Garrity and knew the McGinty family well. Marcel impressed him, especially changing for supper. Brendan Garrity knew a good thing when he saw one. Marcel was robust, strong, and a hard worker.

"McGinty did well to take ye on," the old man said. "Will ye give me another day? I could do wit' yer help. I'm on me own here ye know?" Marcel agreed. Mr. Garrity promised he would drive him in his pony and trap towards Doune. That would save Marcel a few cold nights on the roadside. He slept under cover of the warm hayloft and ate a hot breakfast before setting out with Mr. Garrity in the morning. He enjoyed the freedom of the space in the open fields, and he liked the physical work.

They returned to the farmhouse at dusk, cleaned, and readied for supper. Two days later, Mr. Garrity, true to his promise, readied the cart and pony, and drove Marcel on the country road towards Doune. They covered many miles, and talked casually to fill time.

"Well, this is where I let ye off lad. Just keep in this direction and ye can't miss McGinty's place. It's on a bit of a hill, ye know, so ye'll see it before ye get te it. Good luck and thank ye for all yer hard work."

"Thank you, sir, and Mrs. Garrity, too, for your kindness and hospitality, much appreciated."

Mrs. Garrity had made up a food package for him, something different from his bread and cheese, and homemade--always tastier.

His walk was easier now and he had a spring in his step. Mrs. Garrity's homemade scones and egg pie, was so tasty, he loved it. Marcel enjoyed the Irish food. However, there were times when he'd just love to have a plate of homemade, hot pasta with olive oil and Parmesan cheese. One day, he thought to himself, one day, perhaps. His mind drifted back to his home in Italy. He remembered his mama making homemade spaghetti with Parmesan cheese and tomato sauce. The aroma filled the house, and he could almost taste it when a wave of nostalgia suddenly came over him. How friendly these people are, he thought. They have nothing much but still willing to share what they have with a stranger. In Italy, they would have shooed him away, and the door closed in his face. He had a good feeling about his future as he walked.

It was nine o'clock at night when he arrived at Ballydoune Farm in Doune. There was still a light on inside as he made his way up the pathway towards the front door of the farmhouse. He knocked on the door and young Sean McGinty answered.

"My goodness, ye've arrived, come on in, come inside," Sean said warmly.

Marcel entered the tiny room to see old Mr. McGinty sitting close to the fireside in a comfortable, well-worn chair.

"Come on in and sit yerself down," said old Mr. McGinty. "It's been a long walk ye've had, are ye hungry?"

"Thank you, sir," he replied.

They made Marcel feel welcome as he sat down on a chair beside a wooden table away from the fireside.

"Kate, Kate," shouted old Mr. McGinty. "Our new farmhand has arrived and he's cold and hungry. Will ye get him some food?" Kate McGinty appeared from behind a doorway beside the fireplace. There was another room, Marcel hadn't noticed. Perhaps it's a bigger house than he first thought. Kate smiled down at Marcel.

"Hello," she said in a soft whisper of a voice. She was a small-framed girl in her early teens, with fair hair and blue eyes. She seemed shy as she busied herself at the fireplace getting food for Marcel. There was a large pot on top of the big black iron cooking stove that also supplied heat to the room from a small opening at the front of the unit.

"That's a fine cooking unit you have there, sir," remarked Marcel.

Old Mr. McGinty nodded and smiled over at Marcel. "Yes, it's been a great convenience te us all since me wife passed away. Saves a lot of work and keeps the place toasty warm."

Kate took down a plate from above the stove and scooped up a ladle of soup from the pot. She handed it over to Marcel at the table.

"Here ye go, heat ye up. Would ye like a bit-a-bread wit' it?" Marcel had to listen hard to understand what she was saying, her voice was so soft and quiet, but he understood.

"Yes, some bread, thank you," he replied. Kate passed some bread for him and went to fetch water to make fresh tea for them all. They made small talk while Marcel warmed himself with the soup. The bread, made that morning, was still reasonably soft, good enough for soup he thought to himself as he wolfed it down quickly. Mr. McGinty Senior spoke next.

"Excuse me for asking will ye, but what was it that brought a fine young man like yourself to the shores of Ireland at this time in yer life?" Marcel was ready and replied immediately without hesitation.

"Well, sir, I was on vacation with my mama and my papa, touring Europe. My papa was Irish, we were visiting the city and while crossing the street, we were hit by four horses drawing a carriage. The carriage came round the corner so fast it couldn't stop in time. My parents were both killed, but I survived because Papa threw himself on top of me to save me from the horses. I went to the orphanage and then on to the workhouse, and when I was fifteen, they turned me out to work and find my own way--as they do."

Old Mr. McGinty nodded, satisfied with Marcel's reply.

"Aye, life is cruel, but we all just have te get on wit' it, don't we? Where did all this happen te ye?" he asked.

"It was a city called Belfast." Marcel quickly remembered hearing about a large city called Belfast in the pub. His mind was quick and he made his explanation without fault. Mr. McGinty again satisfied with his answer, settled himself in his chair again and puffed on his pipe.

"Hmm Belfast--a big city, it is that, alright. Ye look te be a fine strong young man, and ye'll be needed about here in the next while getting the fields ready for the spring planting. Are ye up te that young man?"

"Yes sir. Indeed I am," replied Marcel confidently.

"Good," said Mr. McGinty as he motioned to his son.

"Now Sean, take Mr. Murphy here, show him the barn where he can sleep until he finds a place te settle."

"Right ye'are, Daddy. Will ye come wit' me?" he said to Marcel as he motioned in his direction. Marcel stood up from the table.

"Thank you for your hospitality, sir," he said and nodded to Kate as he followed Sean out the door to the barn.

"I have a lamp," Marcel said, "is it alright to light it in here?"

"Well," Sean said, "the barn's full of hay? If yer lamp falls over and sets the hay on fire, we'll all be after yer guts." Marcel nodded in understanding. "Just be very careful wit' it an' it'll be okay," Sean said. "Use the beam hooks," he said pointing to the beams above him, "not the floor where it could fall over and start a fire."

Marcel smiled back at him. "Thanks, I'll be careful." He lit the lamp and hooked it to the beam above his head. It cast a good light around him, and he could see that it was a large barn stacked full to the rafters--made the place feel warmer inside than it was outside. He had his choice of where to settle for the night, no matter where he decided to settle, he would be warm and out of the cold night air. He got his things out and readied himself to sleep in his bag, taking care to put out his lamp first. Marcel slept like a baby all night long.

The next morning he awoke early to the sound of a cockerel. It was around five o'clock. Farm life began early, and he was aware that the others in the house were already up and ready. Sean saw Marcel at the barn doors and shouted over to him. "Come up to the house for something to eat before we start work." Marcel went straight over. Kate was in the kitchen.

"Come in and sit yerself down at the table."

"Thank you," he said and sat down. She served up hot oats followed by toasted bread with fried eggs, bacon, and tomatoes and a nice hot cup of tea to wash it all down.

"It's always yesterday's bread at breakfast, that's why it's toasted," she said.

"It's great," he replied. "Thank you." He could see that Kate had a lot of work on her hands cooking for the men. Life was hard for her he thought--no modern kitchen fixings to help her. She had a well outside where she would fetch her water. Like everyone else in the area, she made everything from scratch, every single day, which meant bread most of all. Milk came from their own cows, and she made butter and cheese from that, skimming the top skin for the dog. Nothing went to waste on the farm, especially food. There was washing to do--water to boil on the big stove that they were so proud of, and her only luxury. It baked the bread, cooked the stew, boiled the water, and heated the house all at the same time. Some farmhouses had one if they could afford it, but not all. They were expensive to buy, but in the long run they were a blessing to the working farmer's wife and worth every penny.

Kate was Sean Senior's youngest daughter and had run the house since her mother passed away the year before. She was just a girl herself, only eighteen years of age and already regarded as a spinster; she had no suitors and only a few young men were available. Young Sean was just twenty-three years of age and Sean Senior, his father, was without question looking for a wife for him. Sean Senior knew the ways of life in this quiet countryside and he knew if he didn't find Sean Junior a wife and produce children soon, his son would have nothing to work for as he grew older. The men sat together and ate breakfast in earnest. Mealtime was a serious business.

"When yer finished here, we'll go up together and ye can show our young man here the ropes te get him started, Sean."

"Yes, Father, I can do that," Sean said. Kate had prepared some hot tea and bread to take with them. They wouldn't be coming back to the farmhouse until evening.

"Here's yer lunch box for the day," she said handing the package to Marcel to carry. "It's for all of ye's," Kate said.

"Oh, thank you," Marcel replied as he took the box. The two men stood up from the table to leave and start the day's work; Marcel followed behind carrying the box. The air was fresh with a slight mist settled over the fields as they walked, and it was cold, icy cold.

"We're up in the north field today," Sean said. "We need to turn the soil ready for planting next month so it is well broken and loose te let the air through it." Sean's breath was visible in the cold air as he spoke.

Mr. McGinty Senior remained silent and let his son take the lead. Marcel looked around amazed at the panorama before him. "Is all this land yours?" he asked. "Aye," replied Sean, "an' it all needs digging before spring comes."

It was hard work--the soil was rock-solid and difficult to dig, but this pleased Marcel and gave him an opportunity to prove his strength to the McGintys. He knew they would be watching him, and he was about to prove his worth.

Marcel could do more than his size would at first suggest. Sean realised quickly that it would be wise to keep this fellow around for as long as possible. He could do the work of at least two men. He was no slacker and seemed to enjoy the race.

Old Mr. McGinty impressed too, although not one to praise the efforts of a paid farmhand. The morning fog cleared as the sun broke through and exposed the span of the farm. It seemed to

Marcel that the McGintys had a lot of land but he didn't stop to ask questions and carried on working. He knew that would impress them more than his talking.

They stopped for lunch half way through their day. They worked about six or seven hours, Marcel thought, when Sean called time. Lunch was cold but welcome. Then they went straight back to digging and turning with earnest, breaking up the hard soil to let it breath. Their day was shorter now--just a few hours left to work. Marcel knew the McGinty's wanted as much of that field turned by dusk or even finished if possible. He got stuck in at the work again as if he was just starting fresh as a daisy. The other two men watched in amazement at his enthusiasm, and then continued on with their own patch. It was beginning to get dark when old Mr. McGinty finally announced quitting time. Marcel thought about another six or seven hours had passed since lunch. He loved the lack of restriction, openness, and freshness and knew he would enjoy this life. His working days would be dawn till dusk. The space gave him freedom and he felt happiness from it. He was glad to arrive at Doune.

"Come te the house for supper later on," old man McGinty offered.

"Thank you, Mr. McGinty, I appreciate the offer," Marcel replied.

They started to pack up their working tools and headed back to the farmhouse.

"Don't forget the box, Marcel, we'll be needin' it for tomorrow's lunch," said Sean.

When they returned to the farmhouse, Marcel fetched a bucket of fresh, cold water, took it back to the barn with him, washed down and changed into clean clothes. Then he went up to the farmhouse for supper. Mr. McGinty Senior took note but said nothing. Marcel noticed that they had washed up but hadn't changed their clothes--surprised that they would sit at the table wearing the sweaty working clothes of the day. He said nothing about it--vowed never to sink to that level. He had always been clean about his person.

He took pride in his appearance and personal cleanliness, as his mama had taught him. He didn't know that the only other set of clothes either of the McGinty men possessed was for weddings and funerals only. They each owned one set of working clothes. There was nothing spare, no extras. Everyone had the basic necessities only.

The next evening, to Marcel's great surprise, both Mr. McGinty Senior and Sean Junior had washed and changed into their better clothes for supper. This would be the way of things in the future. McGinty Senior would not be shown up by any young foreigner--not at his table, in his house, or his country!

The days passed quickly and in no time his first week was behind him. Marcel had found the family friendly but a little private in their ways. It seemed to him that no one questioned old Mr. McGinty on anything. His word was the last and final word, without argument. Everyone seemed to have a place in order of seniority. The days went by like clockwork--even the cockerel awoke every day at the same time. Sean and Marcel were getting along just fine, Sean giving direction, and Marcel following as asked. Sean was very impressed with Marcel's physical attributes.

"How did ye ever get muscles the likes of that?" Sean asked him. Marcel told him the story of living in a large town and being picked on at school. Sean--amazed that he even went to school--optional in Doune, listened on.

"One day I found a book, like a catalogue, in the street. Someone probably dropped it because it looked expensive with its shiny cover on the front. When I picked it up and looked inside, it was about how to build muscles to create the perfect biceps and other bodybuilding exercises. I took it home and every day after school I did the exercises. I read it from cover to cover many times over and kept it hidden for years. It was my secret. In time, I saw a difference in my body and kept up with the exercises. It wasn't long before the boys at school kept their distance from me, I can tell you." They both laughed and worked on.

"Saturdays are a different routine," said Sean. "We go into Doune and go te the pub for dinner on the way home. It's more of a social afternoon than anything--ye get te meet up wit' the neighbours and hear what's going on in the last week or so. Would ye like te come wit' us?"

"Oh, I'd like that very much," Marcel replied. That gave him something new to look forward to. The pub was about five or six miles from the farm and the only way there was either walking or by pony and trap.

Mr. McGinty Senior would be going, and so they would take the pony and trap, as he was not able to walk the distance any longer. There would be room for Marcel on the back of the trap. Kate sometimes came with them to do a little shopping in the village, or just to see some friends and find out what was going on. There was a lady's cubicle in the pub--she could meet up with her friends and talk the afternoon away over a glass of lemonade. Women were not seen in the public bar--it was only men who drank and ate there. It was not against the law, but frowned on. Only occasionally, or at funerals and weddings and the like, would you see any women in the public bar. The villagers held to their old ways and were slow to move with the modern times.

Marcel was looking forward to going and made sure he had clean clothes for the event. He wanted to make a good first impression and he did, especially with young Flo. She was the most impor- tant person of all--the cook, and Marcel loved his food. After that first visit, he started going to the pub every evening to eat. He had breakfast with the family and Kate in the farmhouse, but he looked forward to Flo's cooking in the evening, and he relished the idea of something new and different every night. She never disappointed him, her food was fabulous, and he complimented her on every meal. They laughed together and got to know each other quickly. Flo, intrigued by his accent finally asked him:

"What part of the world was it that gave you such a beautiful soft voice?" Marcel was secretly delighted that she liked his accent.

"I come from Italy, but I will never go back there. I have no family left, just me." Flo, sensing his secretive side didn't want to intrude further, and so she didn't ask any other questions.

"Oh, I'm sorry for yer loss, and yer most welcome te share me beautiful country wit' me anytime." Marcel smiled and didn't take offence at Flo--he liked this young lady who cooked so well and seemed so friendly towards him.

"May I ask you a question?" he replied earnestly. "Where did you learn to cook so well?"

"Why me mammy taught me everything I know, and then I like to experiment a wee bit too, ye know, just te try somet'ing new like," she chirped happily. He seemed lonely to her, and she thought he might be missing his home country as she gazed at his big dark eyes, so soft and innocent. Flo could have dropped into his lap there and then if he had asked, but instead she just smiled down at him silently.

"Well, she did you a great service--your food is excellent."

"Why thank ye very much, I hope ye come back for more."

"Indeed I will, I certainly will." Flo made her way back to the kitchen. Before Marcel left that day, he went up to the bar and spoke to Rosemary. "Would it be possible to speak with the young lady who does the cooking?" Rosemary looked around the room--it wasn't busy at the bar.

"Certainly, wait a minute, I'll get her for ye." Flo appeared from the kitchen wondering who wanted to speak to the cook. When she saw it was Marcel, she just smiled, blushed slightly and walked over to him.

"How can I help ye?"

"Well, I wondered if perhaps we could both help each other a little. When do you finish work?"

"Around eight o'clock."

"Well then, I'll come here for eight o'clock and we can sit at one of the tables and discuss my offer."

"Offer," said Flo intrigued. "Okay, I'll see ye here when I get off work." She nodded her head in agreement and smiled at him again as he left.

"Rosemary, what d'ye t'ink o' that? He wants te sit wit' me and talk." Rosemary smiled at Flo in a knowingly way.

"I think he has a soft spot for ye. Just as well ye'll be sitting here an doin' yer talkin'." Flo's eyes widened at the thought, and the girls laughed together. She blushed a little in excitement wondering if he liked her, because she surely liked him. She began singing as she worked, wondering all the while what he wanted.

"My, my, what it takes te get a song these days," said Rosemary in jest. Again the girls laughed and continued on with their chores. When eight o'clock arrived, Marcel showed up as promised. He walked around the village getting to know the area--and chilled through when he returned to the bar. Together he and Flo took a seat at the back of the room away from the bar. He seemed to favour that space more than any other in the room.

"Why d'ye always sit up here at the back of the room?" she asked him.

"Well, I can see everything in front of me from here," he said rubbing his hands together for warmth. "I see the people coming and going, it helps me get to know the faces."

Flo smiled at him. "Well, what's this offer ye have on yer mind?" she asked.

"I was wondering, since you are such an excellent cook, if you knew how to make pasta?" he asked.

Flo looked at him a bit perplexed. "Pasta, no I'm sorry, I don't know what pasta is. Is it a food?" Marcel laughed out loud, and

Rosemary looked up at them--enjoying themselves, she busied herself at the bar.

"Yes, oh yes," he replied in all seriousness. "Pasta is a food. Italians eat it almost every day. If I find out how to make it, would you try to make it for me? I'd buy all the ingredients. I miss my pasta a lot," he said. Flo, surprised and elated at the same time, wanted to help him.

"D'ye really t'ink I'm good enough te do that?" she asked.

"Absolutely, you are a great cook--I will find a recipe and we will try together in your kitchen--yes?" he suggested.

"Oh, I'd have te ask Rosemary about that. She's the boss around here. She's in charge of everything, but if we were te do it on me time off then I don't think she would be offended. I'll ask her first and let ye know what she says."

"That would be wonderful," he said eagerly. "I really appreciate your work and your time, and I would pay you for that, so thank you very much. I'm sure other people who come here to eat would also enjoy it."

"Well," replied Flo, "we'll see what Rosemary t'inks of the idea, she's the boss as I said. Then if she agrees, we'll see how it turns out and what it tastes like, too. Rosemary might decide to let her customers taste it, but I don't know," Flo said hesitating.

"I do thank you for asking permission on my behalf."

"Yer most welcome," Flo replied.

"Now our business is over, may I walk you to where you are going? It's getting dark outside."

"How nice of ye te ask, but ye don't really need te. I live just down the street at the bottom of the village."

"Then I will walk you down the street to the end of the village," and he smiled at her with his soft dark eyes. Flo's heart melted and she had no intention of saying no--she just couldn't. They made their way towards the door and passed Rosemary at the bar.

"Goodnight, Rosemary, see ye in the morning," said Flo beaming.

"*Buona notte, signora,*" and doffed his cap in respect as he passed Rosemary. She looked at Flo, who seemed lit up with happiness, her eyes flashing and sparkling like little diamonds.

"Yes, darlin', see ye in the mornin', goodnight now," she replied as she winked an eye at Flo and smiled at them both. Rosemary continued cleaning up. It was nine o'clock in the evening and getting dark outside and although the pub didn't officially close until ten o'clock every night, she settled herself for the last hour behind the bar in her comfortable high chair. She was able to lean over the bar resting her head in her hands, taking a few minutes shut-eye before closing. It was seldom that anyone came in after nine o'clock. But it did happen on occasion, and it was the law to stay open until ten o'clock. Only on holidays and bereavements could the pub be closed, by penalty of losing the liquor license. So Rosemary slept in her high chair at the bar for the last hour on most evenings.

Just then Jimmy appeared coming downstairs from the house above.

"I thought I'd catch ye before ye closed up for the night. I knew ye'd be alone and wanted to tell ye about me plans te leave for America." Rosemary shook herself awake to listen to Jimmy.

"I'll be seeing me solicitor next week and he should have the paperwork ready. I'll bring a copy for ye te sign our agreement."

"That's grand Jimmy," she replied.

"If and when the pub gets bought over, ye'll receive another stipend and be given yer choice of any furniture ye want te keep. At that time, our business will be over, and ye can move home wit yer family," he explained.

"I understand " Rosemary replied.

"The only next opportunity would be if the new owner wanted te keep ye on for working the bar or Flo for the cooking. But that would be up te the new owner," he finished.

"Well, Jimmy, it's a grand offer and I'm keen te please ye, as ye know," she said. "I won't let ye down," she promised.

"I know ye won't, I'm relying on ye te do yer bit. Ye've not let me down yet and I'm not expecting ye te now. So do yer stuff and make it work for us both," he said. "We'll both profit out of this yet. I know I can trust ye. Now after next week, ye'll be on yer own and the rest will be up te you. Can we shake on it?" he asked her, extending his hand. Rosemary was serious as ever, but still digesting the new situation and getting used to the idea of being the boss.

"Of course, we can shake on it, Jimmy," as she extended her hand.

Jimmy returned upstairs for the night. Rosemary began to close up and prepare to make her way home, all five miles of it. At least it was dry, she thought to herself. What a night, so much has happened in one evening. *Perhaps I won't need to buy a bicycle at all now?* She left the pub as usual and started her walk home. Marcel approached returning from his walk with Flo.

"Good evening again, Rosemary." He sounded happy and confident. "Is this you finally getting home?"

"Yes it is, and what a beautiful clear night. The stars are out te keep me company on me walk."

Quickly thinking, Marcel replied. "Do you want me to walk with you a little of the way, to the end of the village, at least?"

"Oh, ye don't need te do that. I come this way every night on me own." Rosemary saw the disappointment on Marcel's face and instantly changed her mind.

"But of course ye can walk wit' me. We can enjoy the stars together. It'll be a change for me. Thank ye for the offer." Marcel smiled back at Rosemary--she could see he wanted to walk with her. He continued talking as they walked. *Quite the chatterbox* she thought, and now she understood what Flo meant about his accent.

"People are so friendly here, I find, don't you?" he remarked somehow eager to please her.

"Of course, but I was born here and so ye tend te take these things for granted after a while. It's good te hear a stranger say something nice about the place. I notice ye come in every night for yer supper. Where are ye working?" she asked.

"At McGinty's farm. I just arrived last week and they're letting me sleep in the barn until I find lodgings. Do you know of any lodging places locally?" he asked.

"Not off the top of me head. But let me t'ink about it and ask around for ye," she offered.

"That would be good of you, very decent, indeed. I don't know the people like you do, and you would be a better judge of the distances for me to travel back and forward to McGinty's farm," he said. They continued talking as they walked together along the dark roadway and finally reached the end of the village.

"Well, ye should start heading back if ye want te get some sleep before the mornin' comes, ye've a good seven miles ahead of ye now. Thank ye for yer company, it was a pleasure walkin' wit' ye. Goodnight now," Rosemary said and Marcel doffed his cap at her once again.

"Yes, I should start back. Thank you, too, for your company and your kind offer of help with lodgings. I'll see you tomorrow at supper time." Marcel turned and headed back towards the pub and home to McGinty's barn for a sleep. Rosemary watched him walk away. *He's short, but sturdy,* she thought. *He looks very strong wit' those big thick arms of his. He must keep himself in shape working the way he does, but he seems nice enough. I can see why Flo is so smitten wit' those big dark eyes of his,* she thought to herself. Rosemary continued on her way home enjoying her thoughts on what had turned out be a very eventful evening.

It was frosty and clear in the cold night air and the darkness of the black sky made the stars twinkle all the brighter. Marcel didn't feel the cold in his happiness and his newfound friends lifted his spirits somewhat, so he put a spring in his step and quickly made his way back to the farm. His thoughts drifted back over the evening's events and how lovely Flo was. He realized he was smitten and wanted to impress her. *Can I really be this lucky to have met such nice people in this small place* he asked himself? But where to find a recipe for pasta, he wondered, when he remembered his friend Michael from the Dublin Hotel. He would help. It'll be fun, being with Flo, and making his favourite pasta. He relished the thought for a moment remembering the taste from his childhood and smiled to himself as he suddenly felt how cold it had become. In no time he reached the farm and headed straight for the barn. It was reaching midnight and young Sean McGinty came out of the house just as Marcel was entering the barn doors.

"My, yer late the night," he called out.

"Yes indeed, just getting acquainted with some new friends," Marcel replied.

"The people 'round these parts 're not used to foreigners. Ye'll find them a bit nosey but they're harmless enough, just inquisitive, ye know?" said Sean.

"Oh, I find them very friendly and pleasant, I was just walking the lady from the pub down the village and mentioned that I was looking for digs, and she offered to ask around for me. Isn't that good of her?"

"Ye mean Rosemary?" Sean asked surprised.

"Yes," he hesitated, "Rosemary." Marcel noted a look of surprise and perhaps even a pinch of envy in Sean's eyes.

"Rosemary's well thought of in these parts, everyone knows and respects her. I'd be careful not te step out of line wit' her if I were you," he warned Marcel.

"Oh, nothing like that, she was friendly because I'm new here, and I eat in the pub every night." Sean backed down a little, enough for Marcel to notice a change in his mood.

"Well then, just be polite and mannerly wit' her, that's all I'm saying. Goodnight now," he said and went inside.

"Goodnight," replied Marcel as he entered the barn to settle for the night. He fell asleep smiling as he recalled Rosa's word--*a small village in the middle of nowhere*. She would be happy for him, just the kind of place she meant for him. He didn't think any more of Rosa. He knew she was dead.

Marcel was up with the cockerel when everything to came to life. A new day and he could see Sean waiting for him in the courtyard. Together the men made their way to the pony and cart--they were working in the further field that day. Kate had sent out some freshly made tea, bread, and a couple of boiled eggs for each of them.

"Such good people," he thought. "Good morning, Sean," he said in a happy chirp.

"Good mornin'," Sean replied dryly. "Come get yer tea and bread before we start, and here's a couple of eggs. Ye need the protein te keep those muscles of yours in shape." The two men sat together on the cart drinking their hot tea and chewing at the almost-stale bread.

"Dip yer bread in the tea--it goes down easier, no chewing needed. Ye know it's yesterday's bread, and God only knows what she puts in it te do what she does te it." They both laughed and Marcel had a go at dipping his bread in his tea. It worked just like Sean said. It definitely slid down easier.

Life here seemed to have a natural flow to it. Everyone involved in the hard work, doing his or her own bit and somehow they all seemed to interact with each other. Marcel felt he was on the verge of becoming part of something he'd never experienced before. Back home in his own country, his aunts and uncles left Rosa and him alone to fend for themselves. They wouldn't get involved. Rosa's was a single family without a man at the helm. Here, in this little country, everything was different. Old Mr. McGinty Senior was the head of the family with his son Sean obeying his father's wishes at every request, no questions asked. The people in the village looked up to the McGinty family, knowing them as long-standing farmers of their land. Other people looked to them for advice and often went to them for help in some way or another. It seemed to Marcel that the family must have earned that respect somehow, and he wondered what they did to get such an esteemed position in a small place like this.

Marcel knew nothing about Ireland or its history; how the English armies had raided the farms, taking their crops and animals, leaving only those farms that belonged to the English aristocracy untouched. He didn't know how many died on the side of the roads and in the fields, from malnutrition and starvation. This, followed by the potato famine, left the ordinary people with nothing and Ireland's farmers famished, or heading to the "coffin ships" going to America. If they survived the journey at all, they had a slim chance of a future.

The McGinty family held fast during all those years, determined to farm the land again and stay independent of the English land-owners. They did what they had to do, to rid the land of its sickness and grew nothing for years. They spread manure, fed the soil, and turned it without planting to regain its natural healthy state. They learned to survive on morsels of food. They heard weekly about their neighbours dying, and continued steadfast in their prayers that God would protect them and not let them starve to death. Marcel knew nothing of any of this.

6

January-February 1895

*I*t was the end of February, cold, wet, and the days were short and dark. The farm took on a new routine with Marcel joining the workforce. Kate was unusually diligent about making sure the men were well fed before they started work in the mornings. Although she was a timid young lady and cooking was not her strength, she did make an effort to lure Marcel into her kitchen. After all, he was the only new male blood in the area for years, and they were about the same age. She made sure there was hot food to eat first thing, usually hot oats followed by eggs and toast with tea, or sometimes with bacon. She made an effort to make bread daily, as was not her normal routine. Her father noticed that she was trying to impress the young man.

"Ah, Kate, me girl, it's good that yer turning the young man's head wit' yer cookin," he sighed. "Ye know I appreciate the hot breakfasts, but I don't want ye te be disappointed either." There was a warning in his voice as he reached towards his daughter and cradled his arm around her thin bony shoulders. "Ye see there's a bit of competition in the village. So don't be settin' yer sights too high, that way it's not so far te fall if his feelings take him elsewhere--ye know?" He winked at her in jest and smiled knowingly. Kate blushed at his directness and she turned on him in her own defence.

"How could ye say such a t'ing, Daddy and humiliate me like this? I was just trying te do me bit." She ran into the bedroom to hide her embarrassment and sat down on her cot, disappointed that Marcel had eyes for someone else already. *Now what--she thought--perhaps going to New York might be my only chance of a life.* She could take the big ship and go to her aunt who settled there. Her father had already given his blessing, and had mentioned it to her many times. She would find a husband there--so many young people alone and lost in a new country searching for a partner, or so she heard. The problem was that she was afraid to travel so far without a companion. She knew that she might have to give in to her fear if she wanted a life of her own. *Aye,* she sighed, *America might be the best place for me.* She pulled herself together and went back into the kitchen. Her father stole a glance at her obvious disappointment, but he was glad that she knew why, if Marcel didn't return her favours.

"There's always America, ye know."

"I know, Daddy, I know," she said in defeat.

Each night Marcel washed and changed into clean clothes before making his way into the village for supper. He looked forward to something different every night and was never disappointed. The walk home was about five miles, but it got easier after the first few times. In the beginning, he carried a flashlight, but he didn't need that now--he was familiar with the dirt track back to the farm. He returned most nights around ten o'clock and went straight to bed in the hayloft. It was warm, and dry. He always slept well, and woke with the cockerel in the early morning.

Marcel realised that Kate was making an extra effort on his behalf. He had earned their respect and they all knew that he was worth his weight in gold. He was a real hard worker, and always thankful and mannerly towards Kate, but he didn't want to give her any false hope and remained a little distant. He liked her enough, but his heart, already set on someone else who, unlike Kate, loved to cook. Marcel had thoughts of staying in the area for a time, maybe get to know people better and even settle down if things turned out as he hoped. He still had his mama's pouch money intact, and had savings of his own since his only expense was his food each night at the pub.

It was at the beginning of the month when Jimmy told Rosemary that he had bought his ticket for the ship to America. She would take over as landlady according to their "Agreement" immediately. Rosemary's parents helped to move her into the house above the pub, adding a few personal items from her own bedroom to make her feel more at home in Jimmy's house.

With all the events happening in her own life, Rosemary had completely forgotten her promise to ask around for lodgings for Marcel. One night on his way out after his supper, he approached the bar to speak with her.

"I was just wondering if you had heard of any lodgings around?" he asked.

"Oh my goodness, please forgive me, Marcel. There's been so much going on around here lately it totally left me mind that I had said I would ask around. I'll look into it right away, and get back te ye as soon as I hear anything," she told him, somewhat embarrassed to have forgotten her promise.

"Thank you, Rosemary, I know you've been busy," he replied. Rosemary didn't waste any time and began asking around if anyone knew of digs for Marcel--surprised at the response.

"Even if I knew of lodgings I don't t'ink they'd entertain taking in a foreigner, ye know?" said one of her locals. What was she thinking--Rosemary hadn't thought of that at all. She just saw Marcel as another casual farm labourer passing through. There were lots of them around, roaming the countryside looking for work of any kind that paid or just fed them and offered a roof for a while. She never thought of him as a foreigner, even though it was obvious that he was. Now, she felt even more responsible, and vowed to help Marcel find a place to live. She thought about her parents' place, but they were far out of the village and so she decided it wasn't any better than where he already was. Anyway, he would have twice the distance to walk, to and from the pub, and to and from McGinty's farm. It wasn't a good idea. She worked on as she thought about it and then turned to Flo to ask about the night before.

"Well now, are ye going te tell me what it was all about or not? Ye know I met him on the way back from yer house, and he walked me te the end of the village as well. He seems a very well-mannered young man, so what was the big confab all about?" Rosemary asked.

"Cooking, and food. What else?" Flo replied in a flat tone. The girls looked at each other and burst into laughter.

"He misses his home country and t'inks me cookin' is grand, and t'inks I would be able te make him Italian pasta," she said rolling her eyes at Rosemary. "I told him I'd never heard of it and didn't know what it was or how te cook it. He said he would get a recipe for me and help me wit' it, and I've a favour te ask of ye Rosemary," Flo said.

"What's that Flo?" she replied.

"Well," Flo continued "if he does get the proper ingredients and a recipe an' all, will ye let me cook it in yer kitchen on me day off? He said he would buy all the right ingredients next time they make a trip te Dublin and look for a gadget that makes the right shape of pasta. It was all about food," Flo sighed.

"Well now, you know of course that the way to a man's heart, is through his stomach," said Rosemary hopefully.

"Never was a truer word spoken," replied Flo.

"So, Flo, what is pasta?" asked Rosemary. "I've never heard of it meself," she said.

"I've no idea, I was just happy that he was asking me te cook for him," she replied. "Rosemary," she said more seriously, "would it be okay for us te use yer kitchen te cook it? It would all be proper and above-board ye know, and he said he would pay for everything if only he could taste some pasta again. I'd love te be able te do it for him. Just te see the look on his face when he tasted it proper--ye know?" Flo looked at her friend, pleading. "What d'ye think, Rosemary? Please, please, let me try, I promise wit' all me heart, it's just cooking," she implored seriously.

Rosemary turned to look at Flo and they stared at each other for a few moments. She could see her friend was begging her. She paused long enough to give it some serious thought.

"Okay Flo, you can give it a go when he gets the proper ingredients," Rosemary agreed. "It'll have te be when the pub is closed, on a Sunday afternoon, after Mass. That's the only day and time yer not working, he's not working, and I'm still here te oversee what's going on. That way it'll keep those idle tongues from wagging," she said. "We wouldn't want te give them ones around here somet'ing te gossip about, not coming from this respectable public house--would we?" Flo squealed out loud in excitement and threw her arms around Rosemary.

"Thank ye, thank ye, thank ye, Rosemary, I won't disappointed ye, and we won't give anyone reason te talk about us either. I'm just dying te try this pasta stuff, I've never heard of it before now. I don't know what it tastes like, but Marcel says it's delicious and we'll like it. It's so exciting. He'll be delighted, thank ye, Rosemary, thank ye so much my friend," she said gratefully and relieved that she had given her this time with Marcel.

The monthly visit to Dublin was due soon. Marcel had become friends with Michael when they met at the auction halls some months ago. He was the head chef at the Dublin Hotel, only the most high-class place in the city. He would be able to supply the ingredients and instructions to make the pasta, and find one of the kitchen gadgets to make the long spaghetti-string shape and the sauce to go with the pasta. Michael was the right man to help. Marcel would make him an offer he couldn't refuse.

His intuition was right. Michael was open to dealing, barter or otherwise, to make a few extra pounds. His conscience was clear--he didn't break any laws either. He just used his position and stretched his authority a bit, to pave his way and get what he wanted. He was Irish, Catholic, and a married man with six children. Any extra money he could make was always welcome. He didn't ask questions and he didn't expect any in return.

They arranged to meet at the back entrance to the kitchens the following month on market day. Michael would have all the ingredients required. He would write up a step-by-step recipe for the spaghetti and for the sauce for Marcel's young lady friend to follow. Michael would order a small-sized spaghetti grinder with a handle for her to make homemade spaghetti.

"I want five pounds for the lot. I have te order the grinder for the spaghetti, and there's enough ingredients te make pasta for months," Michael said.

"That's a lot of money, I didn't realise it was a bulk order. Wow--and what about the instructions?" Marcel asked.

"It's in the package here. She just needs te follow the step-by-step guide and once she gets the hang of it, ye'll be eatin' pasta for years," he laughed.

The month went by quickly but not fast enough for Marcel. He couldn't wait for the day to come when he and Flo would be alone in the kitchen, cooking pasta together. They had come to know each other well in that month just talking about their plan, and Flo laughed when Marcel tried to explain what pasta looked like and how it tasted.

Her smile softened him and loved to hear her laugh. She had such a girly giggle that it made him laugh too when he heard her. They were just right for each other and it was obvious that something more was in the air between them--they each lit up like a bright star when the other entered the same room. Their cheerfulness affected people around them. It seemed everyone wanted to catch some of that happy dust and soak it up.

It wasn't long before people were asking Rosemary when the wedding was due to happen. Rosemary of course, being the friend she was, feigned all surprise when confronted with the question.

"Why, they're just two young people who like each other's company," she said in their defense.

"Aye, aye, just you wait an' see, I'll prove ye wrong." The gossip had started already--it being such a small village, any change in events was bound to cause talk. Marcel was walking her home one night after work when she confessed something to him that embarrassed her.

"Ye know, Marcel, I've something I need te tell ye."

"What is it, *mio amore?*"

"Don't laugh at me when I tell ye," she whispered quietly.

"What in the world could make me laugh at you, *mio amore?* Of course, I won't laugh. What is it?" he asked her.

"I can't read Marcel," she confessed timidly. "Ye understand? I can't read the instructions that Michael has written out for me te make yer pasta," she told him, apologising

"Oh, *mio amore*, no need to worry about that, I can help you. I can read even in English so I can read the instructions and you can follow me," he told her reassuring.

"I should've known ye'd come up wit' something, clever man ye are. Ye've an answer for everyt'ing, Marcel Murphy. That's me man alright--an answer for everyt'ing," she said relieved.

He felt good and sighed in satisfaction that he was able to calm her fear. Just being with her made him feel good. He was now involved with her, rather than just being a supplier and recipient. Now she needed him, and needed his help, and he would lead her through the whole procedure, step-by-step. Everything was falling into place just as he knew it would.

Market day finally came for the McGinty family. Marcel's plan went smoothly. Michael and he met at the rear entrance to the kitchen behind the hotel as arranged. Michael delivered the package and accepted the cash--very pleased with the money.

"Nice doin' business wit' ye, Marcel. If yer ever in need, I'm yer man. I can get ye anything yer lookin' for, I've contacts for everyt'ing, ye know?" Michael told him.

"Thank you, I'll keep that in mind." They shook hands and parted on good terms. Marcel had brought a packing box on wheels for his supplies. He knew he wouldn't be able to carry them around with him in Dublin. When he finally met up with the McGintys for the journey home, Sean helped him lift the box onto the cart.

"My word this is heavy, what in God's name's in it?" Sean asked.

"Yes indeed, it's heavy, and thanks for your help," he replied. The two men lifted it onto the cart, but Marcel didn't offer any information as to the contents.

Sunday finally arrived and Rosemary had agreed to allow Marcel and Flo to use the kitchen for their cooking experiment. All three of them gathered in the kitchen after early morning Mass. Rosemary's interested was to see the contents of the case, as was Flo's.

Marcel opened the case and began to empty some of the items onto the table. Everything was in bulk, so for tomato paste there were twenty-four little jars, as would be supplied to the hotel. There were twenty-four jars of black olives, twenty-four small bottles of olive oil, and twenty-four small bottles of garlic oil. There was a huge sack of special durum flour that they had never heard of. It was all there, twenty-four of everything, dried herbs and spices, all of which the girls knew nothing about, and there was the hand grinder to make the spaghetti. The girls examined it carefully and decided they wouldn't know what to do with it.

"Never seen anything like it before."

"Me neither," said Flo examining it inquisitively.

Marcel couldn't hide his excitement and happily readied the ingredients that they would need for the cook-in of the year.

"This will be the best pasta ever," he announced loudly.

"Oh, I don't know about that now." Flo seemed a little unsure as if she had taken on more than she could handle. Marcel was so eager he dismissed her hesitation, smiled and kissed her suddenly on the cheek.

"Don't worry so *mio amore*, I'll be here to help you, and you're an excellent cook, the best in the land."

She blushed at the kiss, which was so unexpected. She tried not to show her embarrassment but was secretly pleased that he had kissed her cheek so naturally, without a second thought. She wondered to herself what "amore" meant. She had heard him use that word with her before, but she didn't know its meaning.

"I'll let ye get on wit' it," Rosemary announced, and left the kitchen to them. She headed back to the bar to make some preparations for the next day. As always, she had lots of paperwork to catch up on. Marcel and Flo started reading through the instructions and preparing the ingredients as directed. All was very quiet and serious between them as they worked together following recipe that Michael had carefully written out for them, step-by-step.

"The spaghetti part is easy, just that the flour is different and felt strange," Flo said working the dough. Marcel was curious about the little machine, but when he finally put it all together as directed, there was a handle to turn and an obvious place to insert the dough.

"Well, that part was easy," he said. The sauce was another story and he read the instructions aloud. "Place two tablespoons of flour in a saucepan and slowly add the olive oil. Mix to consistency of a sauce. Open one jar of tomato paste and add to sauce slowly, all the while stirring. If the sauce gets too thick, add some cold water slowly and continue stirring to the right consistency. Add one teaspoon of basil, one teaspoon of rosemary, one teaspoon of oregano, and garlic to taste, salt and pepper as required."

"It's just like making a gravy," Flo said.

"This recipe is for a large amount to feed an army in a hotel. How much do you think we should use, Flo?" he asked.

"I'm not sure what it should taste like. I've never used these herbs before, so I think we should start wit' just a pinch of everything and then taste it. Ye'll have te taste it, 'cause I don't know what it should taste like."

"Good idea," he said. "Can I leave you to do that since you know how to make gravy?"

"Of course, I'll do a little bit at a time and add slowly," Flo said.

"Let me know when you think it's ready for me to taste it and we can decide from there," he said.

Marcel took over the dough that Flo had made. It was time to try the machine and see if he could handle it properly. He inserted the dough and turned the handle and delightfully, out came the long tube-like shapes of spaghetti at the other end. Flo thought that this was it ready to eat and Marcel laughed out loud.

"No, no, now we have to cook it in boiling water and oil."

"Oh, thank goodness for that, I didn't really like the idea of the dough." They continued diligently working away at their creation.

"Oh, my, this is starting te taste quite good, Marcel, what d'ye t'ink?" She turned to him with a spoonful of sauce for his opinion. Marcel tasted it carefully, slowly savouring the herbs.

"Just a little more garlic and oregano I think, but not too much, we don't want to spoil it at this stage. We're almost there, *mio amore*." Flo started to get quite excited seeing that he was seriously happy so far. She carefully made the second additions of the ingredients, slowly adding a pinch as he had suggested and tasted it again. It was different from anything she had ever tasted before but pleasant and she liked it. Then Marcel tasted it and low and behold.

"Just like Italia--back home--*perfecto, perfecto*," he exclaimed in excitement. He lifted Flo up high in the air and down again as if she was a little girl. She let out a cry of delight as he dropped her down on the floor. They both laughed out loud and at that moment he wanted to kiss her on the mouth but hesitated. Flo noticed his withdrawal and sensing a discomfort quickly put her attention back on the sauce and removed it from the heat.

"We don't want this precious sauce te burn now do we, now that it's been perfected for such a fine Italian gentleman's dinner."

"Indeed." Marcel's head was looking down, slightly embarrassed that he had held back.

"Now, what do we do wit' the spaghetti?" she asked, changing the subject.

"Why, we cook it of course, in a pot of boiling water and oil. When cooked we drain it and that's it--all ready to eat with the sauce on top and some sprinkled Parmesan cheese."

"Well then--let's do it. I'm dying te taste it, and I'm sure Rosemary will be too, after the unusual aroma coming from this kitchen." The cheese did smell strange, but she didn't say anything to him for fear of upsetting him further. Marcel took a pot and filled it with water from the tap.

"Looks like you have a problem here--your water is backed up?"

"Oh, it does that from time te time. It gets blocked outside at the drain wit' leaves and foliage, and we have te go out and free it up," she told him.

"It's quite something to have running water inside these days," he remarked.

"Yes, it was one of the t'ings that I was glad of when I came for the job. Most places still have a well outside, but Jimmy had this place modernised for Mary years back. He liked te make things easier for her--you know?"

They stood closely together, their bodies almost touching while they waited for the water to boil. Flo just wanted to swoon into his arms and embrace him but instead she stood still. Finally, the water began to bubble. Marcel slowly added the spaghetti and as it softened he added more, just a little at a time until he thought there was enough for them all for a meal each.

"It says to add salt to the water, perhaps just a pinch to give it taste," and she added some salt as she would to gravy.

"I'm getting very excited at this. I couldn't tell you the last time I had spaghetti," he said. It was ready. Flo lifted the pot to pour out the water before it overcooked. Then she poured the spaghetti into a dish and Marcel, still reading the instructions, poured a little of the olive oil over the top and forked it through.

"Why is that done?"

"Well, it says to stop the pasta from sticking together. It looks perfect, Flo, thank you for doing this."

"Yer welcome, Marcel."

"We should give Rosemary a call, let her know it's ready to serve. We can all sit together in here and enjoy this Italian creation," he said. Marcel called for Rosemary who joined them immediately.

"I'm ready for this, I'm really hungry," she said. She sat down at the table with them and Flo announced.

"Will I be Mother?"

"But of course, *mio amore*, as the cook you must serve the dish." "Do you know how to lift the pasta and put it on the plate?" he asked.

"Oh, I hadn't thought of that. Could ye show us how it's done, please?" she asked him.

Marcel picked up a fork and a large soup spoon. He twisted the fork around a string of spaghetti and placed the spoon underneath the fork so that the pasta wouldn't fall off. Then he lifted the fork and dropped the pasta on Rosemary's plate. He did the same for Flo and the same again for himself.

"We can have another helping when we finish this one, this is the tasting test," he said in fun. He picked up the other dish and spooned the sauce out over the pasta. Then he lifted the hand grater and grated the Parmesan cheese on top of the sauce.

"It looks grand, " said Flo.

"Hmm--smells delicious," said Rosemary.

"That's it, now we can eat." They quickly bowed heads in thanks to God for bringing them together and helping them to make this spaghetti.

"Thank you, Amen," they all said in unison.

Both girls tried to copy Marcel in the way he lifted the pasta. They tried again and again to keep it on the fork long enough to get it into their mouth. It was a challenge to them both, and time and again it fell off the fork onto the plate. They laughed as Marcel showed them over and over, how to do it. Rosemary eventually gave up and used her spoon instead.

"I'll never get te taste it like this, and I'm too hungry te wait." She heaped the spoon full and quickly into her mouth, her eyebrows raised in surprise.

"Well, this is different, but I t'ink I like it. It's tasty," she said savouring the new flavour in her mouth. "Indeed, this is delicious," she said piling more on her spoon.

Flo continued to try to pick up the pasta with her fork. Adamantly, she wouldn't admit defeat, but every time she thought she had it safely on the fork and opened her mouth it fell off again. They laughed together, and finally Flo used her spoon like Rosemary had done--surprised at the taste.

"Hmm--it's good, really tasty, not too bad for a first try," she said.

Marcel had already finished and picked up the bowl to have a second helping.

"This is simply *magnifico*, Flo. What can I do for you to show my appreciation and gratitude for this superb meal?" he asked her.

"Yer thanks is enough," Flo replied delighted that he was enjoying it and appreciated her efforts. "No more thanks required," she repeated.

The three friends sat around the table talking and eating as if they'd known each other for years. They were comfortable with each other, and their conversation flowed easily. Finally, they all finished eating and thanking each other for allowing them to use the kitchen and make it all possible.

"That was delicious, simply delicious," Marcel said. The two girls agreed.

"Yes, it was worth the attempt and thank ye for yer help, Marcel. It turned out grand indeed," Flo said.

"Well, it was a joint effort, and I couldn't have done it without you, Flo, or your kitchen, Rosemary," he said.

"Yer welcome, Marcel," Rosemary replied, "I'm glad te be able te offer ye a little taste of yer homeland."

"Thank you," he replied gratefully. "To show some appreciation I'll go free up the blocked drain outside," he said as he stood up from the table.

"You might have te dig a little, sometimes it gets choked wit' leaves and twigs and t'ings. Oh, and there's a compost heap 'round the back of the old coach house. We use that for the rubbish and scum from the drain," Rosemary told him.

"That's no trouble--I'll find it," he said. He went outside to find the drain, carrying a bucket and shovel. Marcel worked at the blockage until he finally heard the sink begin to drain freely. He called out to Flo. "Turn on the water tap to see if it's free-flowing."

"Right ye are," she replied. It was, and he went in search of the compost heap with the scum. When he saw the old coach house lying empty and disused, his curiosity got the better of him, and he went inside for a look.

Surprised to see the size of what had once been the coach house, he imagined it in full use in its time. *It must have been a busy place with four separate stalls for horses. It would have serviced all the farmers in the area and riders passing through the village from around the country,* he thought to himself. He wondered why it wasn't in use now. The local farmers still used pony and cart for most of their travel and indeed horses were still used for work in the fields by most farmers.

The top opened up into one large area where there was a built-in fireplace on the exterior wall with a flat plate and a large hook above for hanging something heavy. *Perhaps this is where they shod the horses and made their shoes,* he thought. At one side next to the fireplace stood an old table and a couple of old chairs. On the other side there was empty open floor space and several large hooks lined up on the wall. There were some remnants of old hay bundles lying around on the floor, a few tools, forks, nets and spades from the garden. The ceiling was high, and the beams open with chain links and hooks for hanging a lamp in a few places. Marcel's mind began to race ahead and he actively took note of all the details. There were no windows at all. *Why would there be in a stable,* he thought? *The place is dry, no leaks in the roof, it's solid and spacious. I could turn this into a very comfortable place to live. It only needs a few things done to it, and I could do all the work myself. What a great space. It's close to the pub for meals and only a short walk to work. I'll talk to Rosemary and ask her if it's possible to rent the place. I could turn it into a home for myself easily,* he thought excitedly.

He came out of the stables and went round to the back of the building. The compost heap was just where he expected it. Then he saw the vegetable garden already prepared with onions, carrots, potatoes, peas, cabbage, green beans, turnips, and other vegetables. *Well, I wonder who takes care of all this? I don't think Rosemary has any other help around the place--why, the girls must do this themselves,* he thought. He knew Rosemary got her meat and milk delivered by various farmers from around the area. Flo says she makes her own bread, butter, and cheese just like Kate does. *Who tends the vegetable garden* he wondered again?

Marcel would talk to Rosemary about their mutual needs. He couldn't let this opportunity pass him by. The pub was a lot of work. He thought she might be interested in some help in the garden on a permanent basis, and perhaps maintenance around the property? It could make her day less stressful. The vegetable garden was certainly time-consuming. He would talk with her today. He was sure they could come to a mutually beneficial arrangement.

7

Marcel's New Digs, February–March 1895

After freeing up the drain, Marcel returned to the pub where the girls were clearing up dishes. He replaced the shovel and buckets where he had found them on his way back.

"Well, that's fixed now," he said. "Rosemary if you have a spare moment there's something I'd like to discuss with you."

"Why, of course, Marcel, we can sit here at the table. What is it?" she asked. Flo busied herself with the dishes, but she did overhear some of the discussion between Rosemary and Marcel.

"Rosemary, when I was cleaning the drain, I saw the coach house and went inside out of curiosity--you know?" he said trying to excuse himself. "It's a good building, warm, dry, and has a fireplace for heat in the winter. I was wondering if I could live there in exchange for labour in the garden and around the property? That way no money would be exchanged, and you would always have me on hand to help out with anything you needed."

"It's a bit unusual te be living in the stables," she replied.

"I could turn it into a nice comfortable place to live without much bother," he told her. Rosemary thought for a moment quietly.

"Ye know, Marcel, I t'ink it's a grand idea and it would be good te have someone like yerself close by for t'ings that turn up--ye know? I'll go upstairs right now and talk te Jimmy. He's still here until the mornin', and I'd like his opinion. Just wait here," she said and went upstairs.

"What a grand idea Rosemary," said Jimmy. "If he's willin' te work the vegetable garden, and take care of any other little t'ings ye might need around the property. What a grand trade-off, don't ye t'ink? As ye know, I'm going in the mornin', and it'd ease me mind te know you girls had a man around the place that ye could turn te if ye need help. Ye have me permission te settle any deal ye want wit' this young man."

"Thank ye, Jimmy, I t'ink it's a grand idea meself," she said as she returned to the bar.

"Jimmy agrees wit' me. It's a grand idea, Marcel. Ye can move in when ye want. Ye take care of the vegetable garden and any other small jobs around the place and ye have the stables as living quarters in return for yer labour," Rosemary said.

"Deal," said Marcel, and they shook hands on it.

"That's grand what a good idea, I'm delighted for ye," Flo agreed.

Marcel, happy with the new arrangement, and although grateful for the barn at Sean McGinty's place, preferred not to share his bed with the smaller creatures of the country. He would make the old coach house a proper home. He told Sean the good news about his new digs. Sean too, was happy to know there would be a man on the premises after Jimmy left.

"But what then?" he asked Marcel. "Sounds like ye mean te stay around for a while, maybe settle down." he jested.

"We'll come to that when it happens, the pub could take years to sell," Marcel replied, ignoring the last question. He was not in the least concerned. He knew somehow that the pub wouldn't sell quickly and by the time it did, he would have fixed the coach house up into a good living place. If the new owners wanted rent, Marcel might pay if it worked out for him. Meanwhile, it was rent free in return for his labour on the property and the work on the vegetable garden. He was very pleased with the arrangement and wasted no time getting started on the work. Every night after supper Marcel left the bar and went directly to the stable where he worked until it was time for bed.

It wasn't long before he had the place ready to move in. He cleaned it up and made ready the fireplace so that he could have it warm in the evening when he came home from work. He had running water in the yard right outside his door. He found an old trough used for the horses, which he took inside and fixed up to use as a basin to wash in. In time, he would have this place the way he wanted, and it would be warm and comfortable for him through the winter months next year. Marcel was keen to work on it every evening after supper behind closed doors.

The girls were curious but didn't interfere.

"What d'ye t'ink he's doin' in there?" Rosemary asked Flo.

"I don't really know. He hasn't mentioned te me, but he's out of here sharp when he finishes his meal," she offered Flo in response. Marcel seemed busy with whatever he was doing. He had made himself a front door, much like any other front door you would see in a typical home. He simply made a new entry in the old existing stable doors, so that he didn't have to open up the complete stable door every time he wanted in or out. Inside the house, there was a table, two chairs, and a bench, all of which he cleaned up and renovated to look good as new. Presently he was working on making himself a bed from solid wood. He wanted one that could hold a proper mattress, a new modern one made from horsehair, wool, and silk. He had seen them in Dublin, and they were expensive. Not only were they comfortable and warm in the winter, but also cool in the summer--and would last a long time. He would pay a handsome price for this luxury, knowing it would give him the comfort he wanted. He had decided he was staying in the area and had plans to settle down.

"Why, yer spending a lot of money on this place of yours," Sean said.

"Well, after many years of living rough, and I want a little comfort and luxury now that I have a place to call home."

"Sounds like ye intend staying around here for a long time then?" he teased again.

"I like it here and I've made some friends, such as yourself and your family. You've all been kind to me, and it's a long time since I had any friends or family," he said.

"Well, as ye know, we're more than happy te have ye workin' for us. I'm glad te hear yer stayin' around, and we can rely on yer big muscles for a long time te come." They both laughed.

Every month on their trip to Dublin, Marcel bought something for his new home. He had new bedding, the horsehair mattress, two new horsehair pillows, extra material for upholstery, some dishes, cooking pots, cutlery, and spare wood. Everything had come via Michael at a discounted price arranged between them. Sean and Mr. McGinty Senior--both impressed, commented on how much work he was setting himself up for. People in the village had heard of Marcel's spending spree in Dublin, and all were eager to see how his place was shaping up after all his work.

"Not many people in these parts can spend money like that on such home comforts. What d'ye t'ink about it" was the local gossip? "Where did he get all that money he's spending?" they asked. Rosemary was behind the bar working but offered her verbal support and interrupted.

"Most people would have family te help get a new home started, some giving this and that te set the person up. He's no family here and has te do it all himself, make his own t'ings. He's a hard worker and obviously very frugal wit' his money. He's been livin' rough and savin' hard for years by the looks. I t'ink he's doin' grand by himself." Reluctantly the tongues stopped waggin' and found another subject to gossip about.

In no time, the coach house was looking great from the outside. It had a new and complete facelift, freshly painted and cleaned. Marcel had his privacy and a home at last. As for the inside, he had worked hard to make it look good and comfortable. His homemade bed was a grand feature of the one stall placed next to where the fireplace was so that it was warm and cosy. Finally, Marcel had the bed he missed from his childhood; comfortable, warm, and luxurious with his new emerald green satin quilt, filled with duck down.

The kitchen was taking shape, too, and albeit one large space, he had areas sectioned off with furniture. At the fireplace was the stove-top-hot-plate, his basin for washing, and a cupboard for dishes and pots on one side of the fire. On the other side of the fireplace, he had a table, two chairs, and a bench--now finished. He was making another bench with a solid back support, a comfortable enough sofa to lean back on and rest his head. He would upholster it with the material he bought in Dublin. He imagined himself and Flo sitting comfortably by the fireplace talking, in the dark winter evenings. The sofa reminded him of his long-lost home in Italy. His new home was looking very comfortable and warm. Marcel had a natural flair for making things and he enjoyed his accomplishments. He was in the process of making a side table for his bedside, when the girls' curiosity got the better of them.

It was a Sunday morning and the girls were returning from Mass, when they decided to go around to the stables to see what Marcel was up to. They knocked on his front door surprising Marcel, and waited for an invitation inside.

"Well, are ye not goin' te ask us in?" Rosemary asked. Flo stood in the background smiling bashfully but curious to see what he'd been doing these last few weeks. Marcel stood back, opening the door wide and offering a clear pathway for them to enter.

"I'm not quite finished what I'm working on, but since you can't wait for the surprise, you can come in for a few minutes," he said reluctantly. "You can't tell anyone what you see. I'm going to invite some people around for a house party--a tradition we have in Italy, to celebrate a new home. So, you must promise me," he pleaded with them.

"Of course we won't tell anyone," offered Rosemary.

The girls entered Marcel's home. Flo's jaw dropped when she saw inside. To their amazement the place was lovely. He had painted everything white, the walls, ceiling, and beams. It gave the place a cottage feel and made the room brighter. He hung two large oil lamps from the central beam in the roof, lighting up the entire space. They were easy to reach as each one hung from the beam by a long chain with a hook on the end for the lamp. They gave the place a warm, inviting glow. As the girls walked in, on either side of the space, they saw an empty stall, clean with a new wood floor, but no furniture. Further on, the next stall on the left was his new bedroom. The lamp from the central beam threw a shadow into the room allowing enough light for them to see it clearly. He had installed new wood flooring in all the main areas and was working his way forward. Only the two front stalls awaited furniture.

His bedroom consisted of a beautifully carved wooden bed, independently positioned in the middle of the room against the back wall. The carved headboard and footboard had big square posts on each end that made the bed look strong and sturdy. There were two side tables with a shelf, made from the same wood, on each side of the bed. It was the latest in fashion that he had seen in Dublin. No cot beds in this house, too old-fashioned for Marcel. The bed was a simple oblong shape, and the mattress rested inside of it. He was still working on the footboard, but the headboard now finished, looked great pushed flat against the wall.

"Where did ye get this quilt from, Marcel?" asked Rosemary.

"It's just beautiful," said Flo.

"It's the latest fashion in bedding from Dublin. I have a friend there who has contacts for everything. I just told him I was looking for a quilt made from silk, filled with duck down feathers, with an emerald-green satin cover. They're warm in winter and cool in summer."

"It's beautiful, Marcel, so luxurious compared te what we have at home. I love the satin fabric unlike our homespun, and the emerald-green is so rich," she sighed. "It's grand against the white sheets," said Flo.

The girls examined the new horsehair mattress under the white cotton sheets and stroked the new pillows in their white cotton case covers with great envy. There was nothing else in the room. They sat on the edge of the bed and sighed in approval. This was more than either of them had expected, much more. Marcel was feeling quite pleased with himself and proud of his work.

"This is my kitchen area over here, and this is my dining area over here, almost finished," Marcel said pointing. "When I have my sofa finished, this will be my area in front of the fireplace to sit quietly and read or just watch the fire," he told them with pride. Marcel had cooked and eaten his breakfast already, but had not washed up his dishes, which were in the basin waiting for water.

"Look here, ye have a proper basin and unit for yer dishes and yer washin'. It's grand Marcel--ye've done yerself proud, so ye have," Flo said.

"Ye certainly have," agreed Rosemary.

The fire was lit, and the place was warm. A pile of logs sat at the side of the fireplace for convenience. The girls remarked on the hot plate.

"Ah, yes," he said, "this would have been where they melted the iron for horseshoes and then poured it into the mould. All I had to do was fix the hot plate over the top of the open fire, and use it to cook on, just like a black iron. I lengthened a chain above the open fire for a pot of water. I keep the water warm constantly for the convenience, and made a ladle to spoon the water from the pot. It works well." Flo smiled, obviously impressed, and that made him feel good.

"Yes, ye really have thought of everything haven't ye, Marcel?" Flo said. Then the girls saw the old table, the two chairs, and the bench that he was working on.

"What're ye doing wit' these?" asked Flo.

"I'm refinishing them to make them smooth and clean."

"What a difference it makes. The furniture looks new in the places ye've re-finished," Flo said. He had made a couple of shelves above the basin for soap and kitchen utensils, and had also just finished a box cupboard with a door. He lined the cupboard completely with tin to keep his food cool.

"I don't want the local critters helping themselves to my food. So, I made this one for perishables and hung it on the wall away from the fireplace where it's cooler."

Marcel, pleased that the girls were obviously impressed by his handiwork, was still working on his sofa-bench for beside the fireplace. He showed the girls his upholstery material.

"My uncles in Italy had an upholstery business. I always watched them as a boy, and I still remember some of the things they showed me. I'll try it and see how it turns out. I know exactly what I want, and it should feel very comfortable." The girls, amazed at his attitude, encouraged him. He would make another two chairs for the table--there would be enough for everyone to sit around it. He still had some work to do, and he didn't want anyone to see it incomplete.

"Don't worry, we'll keep yer secret for ye," Rosemary said.

"Promise me, not a word to anyone?" he pleaded.

"Indeed, not a word. It'll be our secret," assured Flo. Finally satisfied that they had seen everything, they made their way out and left Marcel to get on with his work. The girls chatted while crossing the courtyard towards the back door of the pub and went inside. Marcel stood watching as they walked away, content in the feeling that they were all good friends.

Finally, Marcel's renovations finished, he wanted to celebrate.

"Flo, I want to have a party--'Italian style' for my new home and my friends. Would you make the pasta again for me?"

"Of course, I will, ye only need ask me and I'd be glad te help." She was truly impressed at what he had accomplished in the old coach house and wanted him to settle down and be happy in her small village. She also realised that a feeling of tenderness was forming between them. They both felt it, and each one was aware of a growing desire. However, Marcel was not quite ready to commit. Flo would give as much time as he needed--she knew that they would be together soon. They were falling in love, and she wanted it to happen in its own time.

As the March trip to Dublin was due, Marcel thought he would plan his party to coincide with that. He could buy his supplies without everyone knowing and surprise them all. He wanted to say thank you to his friends for helping him settle in the village. He spent more money on good wine suggested by his friend Michael, who gave him a discount as always. Michael had become a dependable source for goods of any kind, at a good price.

Marcel didn't scrimp; he paid for quality and told Michael to get him the best of cheese and veal to make scallops with cheese and ham to go with the spaghetti. He knew his friends had never tasted veal before. He had it all arranged in his mind and just had to ask Flo to do the cooking. The scallops he could cook himself on his hot plate, as he knew what he wanted and how to prepare the breadcrumbs with extra herbs mixed in.

He was quick to learn anything new and not afraid to try for himself. Although he never actually cooked before now, he took advice from Michael and followed his instructions to the letter. Flo need only cook the spaghetti and Marcel was confident she would do that perfectly.

Everything was ready. His table was laid out with his new cutlery and dishes, water glasses and wine glasses. He had place mats and table napkins held together with sparkling silver rings. He had bought an oblong-shaped silver plate as a centrepiece for his table into which he arranged wildflowers and roses for an extra touch. He had a crisp, starched white cotton tablecloth on the table. The chairs, now beautifully finished with the same shade of emerald-green velvet that Flo liked. Marcel had missed nothing.

He invited Sean McGinty, Mr. McGinty Senior, and young Kate, and of course, Rosemary, Flo, and himself. That made six people for dinner. He wanted a warm, casual evening, with good food and good friends. Most of all he wanted to impress Flo. He even paid Rosemary for a couple of jugs of beer for the men. She was glad to do the favour and bring the beer with her. He knew the men would appreciate that more than the wine after their meal.

"Of course, what a grand idea," Rosemary agreed.

They arranged the celebration for the first Sunday in March--it was the only day everyone could attend. The pub closed Sundays, and the McGintys could arrange the feeding to give them the afternoon off. Mass was normally over by noon, and everyone would be ready to eat after that. Marcel left nothing to chance and was ready to meet his guests when they arrived for dinner. The McGintys arrived in the cart as expected. Sean took the horse and cart around to the back of the pub, unhooked the cart, and tied the horse up. He placed a heavy blanket on the horse's back, left a trough of water, and filled the horse net with hay. He knew they were going to spend the afternoon and wanted the horse settled and comfortable. Rosemary and Flo arrived shortly after the McGintys, carrying the jugs of beer, which they placed on the side table, away from the fire where it would keep cool.

"How beautiful everything is, Marcel," said Kate. "Did ye really do it all?" she questioned as she stroked the new upholstery.

"Ye've done a grand job of everything, and the furniture's grand," agreed Mr. McGinty Senior.

"Something smells good," said Rosemary. Everything was ready as Marcel showed them to their places and began to wait on his guests. He positioned Rosemary opposite Sean and himself opposite Flo. First, he poured cool water into each glass, indicating that the second glass was for white wine to have with the meal. He had the wine cooling in a bucket of ice water. He then fetched down a large dinner plate, which held the cooked scalloped veal with ham and cheese. He placed it in the centre of the table. The second hot plate contained the spaghetti, and finally, he had a separate small pouring jug filled with the sauce.

"Would you like me to serve?" he asked.

"I t'ink it's better if ye do it," Flo replied smiling. "Yer the only man here who knows how te pick up the spaghetti and serve it. It's all new te me, and the rest of us," said Flo.

Marcel lifted Mr. McGinty Senior's plate first and with the silver tongs picked up a large scallop. Then he replaced the lid as not to let the heat out of the dish. Next he spooned some mushrooms and asparagus on the side. He then wrapped the spaghetti around a large fork and lifted it on to Mr. McGinty's plate and finally poured some sauce on the top and sprinkled some Parma cheese as the finishing touch. Mr. McGinty was speechless, especially having been served first, acknowledging his seniority.

Marcel methodically and quickly served the rest of his party in the same fashion. Each impressed by their plate, he finally sat at his place and announced grace. They each bowed heads and Marcel lead the prayer.

"Thank you, Father, for the food we eat here today. Thank you for guiding me to this village and for bringing these good people into my life." Together they said, "Amen."

"Please, my friends, eat and enjoy."

Marcel opened the first bottle of chilled sparkling white wine.

"This is the very best champagne from France for my dearest friends," he announced. Everyone cheered, and the girls giggled with delight as the bubbles went up their nose. There was no shyness between them, and the wine helped to put everyone at ease. They ate and drank in comfort, each enjoying the new and different tastes they were experiencing. They were all having fun learning how to keep the spaghetti on the fork, placing the spoon beneath to hold it in place. Marcel demonstrated many times. He made it look so easy as each tried and their food fell back onto the plate.

"It's easy," said Sean, "just watch me," as his spaghetti fell to the plate again. Rosemary laughed out loud and gave it another try but again the spaghetti fell from her fork. "Look," said Sean again, "put the spoon under the fork and lift it, like this," but once again his spaghetti fell from the fork. They all laughed out loud. Finally Sean declared aloud. "I've got this under control. This is easy," he said as he started using the spoon alone. Again everyone laughed and Rosemary smiled as she joined him using her spoon too.

"I'm glad ye gave in Sean, now I can eat wit' me spoon too," she laughed placing the fork on the table.

He's got a good sense of humour, she thought to herself. *Not the sombre man he seems all the time.*

"Where did a boy yer age learn te do all the t'ings ye can do?" asked Kate. Being about the same age, she wanted to know how he had gained all this knowledge and experience. Her remarks made Marcel feel vulnerable and inadequate, but he defended his upbringing proudly.

"I used to watch my uncles working in their workshops. Their expertise always amazed me. Also, I was the only child in the family and Mama would include me in everything she did, even the cooking. It was lucky that I enjoyed learning these things. I watched and learned," he replied defiantly.

"Although I was young, I still remember clearly how my uncles worked. I thought I would try to do it myself, and although my work is not perfect, it is good enough for me and I am happy with the outcome. My furniture is comfortable, and the food tastes good, too." He smiled over at Kate, satisfied with his response.

"Everyt'ing looks grand " Flo said. She realised that Kate had offended Marcel by calling him "just a boy."

"Why, only a mature young man could do as well as ye've done, Marcel. Yer obviously a quick learner and good wit' yer hands." Marcel recovered his manliness and composure quickly enough.

"Thank you, Flo, I'm glad you think so."

"It's grand indeed, well done young man. Yer a man of great strength and hidden talents, too, and here's te ye," said Mr. McGinty Senior as he raised his glass in a toast to their host.

"Cheers," they cried out together. The atmosphere was more to Marcel's liking now. His guests accepted him as a mature man with strength and ability, and that meant everything to him. They continued to eat and talk as he filled the girl's wine glasses while the men enjoyed a glass of beer. He wanted everyone relaxed and knew that wine at the beginning of the meal would do the trick, but not to overdo it. He didn't want anyone drunk or feeling ill. They finished their first course and sat around the table, joking and talking casually--complimented Marcel on the house and the dinner. Mr. McGinty Senior enjoyed the meal so much he began to jest.

"Now we know ye could take over Kate's job too anytime, but I don't t'ink she'd be able te fill yer shoes as well." They all laughed out loud as Mr. McGinty continued to describe in detail how Kate would do in Marcel's work. Even Kate herself thought it was funny and joined in the joke without resentment.

The room was pleasantly warm and Marcel knew the white wine did the trick. Relieved that everyone was at ease, he announced that he had yet another surprise for his best friends.

"Yesterday in Dublin I arranged with my friend at the hotel, to buy some fresh-made Italian ice cream. He put the ice cream in a special container to keep it for a day or two without spoiling. I have it today for our dessert." Marcel went outside to fetch the box. It looked quite large for the amount of ice cream it contained, but he explained that the shell contained the ice that kept the contents frozen overnight.

"Ice cream!" said the girls in excitement. Marcel quickly opened the box to expose the still-frozen ice cream.

"Michael prepared it especially for us, and he managed to get strawberries to go with it. The hardest part was keeping it frozen but now we can open it and dish it out," he announced.

"My goodness, Marcel, it's a long time since any of us have had ice cream, let alone strawberries at this time of year," said Mr. McGinty Senior.

"Indeed, Father, I can't remember the last time I had ice cream at all," said Sean. "What a grand treat and strawberries too. I'm think we're payin' ye too much!" and they all laughed again.

"Then the more we will enjoy it. Now let's eat." Marcel passed the small dishes out to everyone at the table and then poured out the last of the white wine. "Here's to good friends," he said raising his glass to toast.

"To good friends," they cheered in unison. They continued to talk about everything from Flo learning to make spaghetti to laying the fields in preparation for the spring planting. Suddenly and unannounced Mr. McGinty Senior broke into song. Young Sean McGinty smiled at Rosemary and nodded his head, knowing his father was pleasantly drunk.

"It must have been the strawberries that did it," said Sean jokingly. "Now we have te listen te his singing too," and again Rosemary laughed. They didn't spoil it for the old man who was enjoying himself and immediately joined in the song with him. Rosemary sang along and Sean and Kate did also. Marcel didn't know the song, but tapped along with his foot. Flo smiled and sang with the group, enjoying the fun. At the end when Mr. McGinty had finished, Marcel sang his own song in Italian. It was quite a beautiful song, even though no one knew what he was singing about.

"It's a love song wit' such a lament?" said Mr. McGinty.

"I believe yer right, Father," said Sean. "A beautiful ballad like that--hmm singing about his true love." Rosemary nodded to Sean in agreement.

"I don't know what's come over me," said Marcel smiling at Flo. "I don't usually sing in company--it's the wine," he sighed. "I feel so relaxed, and it is a beautiful love song," he said whimsically.

"Yes, indeed it is," said Flo. They talked on for some time enjoying the last of the beer and the wine when young Sean McGinty realised that it was after four o'clock.

"I hate te be the one te break up the party," said Sean, but we'd better be leaving to get back in time to feed the animals before nightfall."

"Might I offer you a glass of beer for the journey?" said Marcel.

"Not for me," said Sean, but Mr. McGinty Senior was more than happy to oblige knowing that he could rely on his son to see the animals fed and watered when they got home. Young Sean McGinty knew he shouldn't risk drinking more, and so his quiet refusal accepted with understanding, Marcel was not offended. Rosemary, Kate, and Flo sat around the table still talking to each other while the two men enjoyed their glass of beer.

"I'll stand you a beer, Sean, on another occasion."

"I'll remind ye of that later, Marcel," and they laughed.

"It's been a grand afternoon altogether. Thank ye for a lovely meal and good company too," Sean said to Marcel as he glanced at Rosemary and smiled.

"Thank ye for such a lovely afternoon and yer hospitality. I'm proud te know ye and te be yer employer, and I want ye te know ye can stay wit' us for as long as ye want," said old Mr. McGinty with a smile.

"Thank you, Mr. McGinty, I too am glad I'm working for you."

"Enough of this now, we have te get back te the farm. We'll see ye in the morning, Marcel. Thank ye for everyt'ing, it was very nice of ye. Goodnight te ye all," said Sean glancing again towards Rosemary.

Marcel walked them to the door while Rosemary and Flo began to clear up, both laughing, and singing--slightly tipsy themselves. Sean McGinty went around the back of the house to fetch the horse and trap and walked them to the front for Mr. McGinty was first up on the trap. Kate always sat behind her daddy and as usual Sean was in the driving seat--made their farewells again as Sean pulled on the reins.

"See ye in the mornin'," he said pulling away.

Marcel went inside to find the girls clearing away the dishes.

"Enough of that," he said. "It's time for us to have a song and a dance." He began to sing a dancing song and stood up beside Flo to show her how to make the moves to the song as he danced. Flo tried to follow his lead, and soon Rosemary was doing the same and they were all dancing around the floor together as Marcel sang the song. In the end, they laughed and fell to their seats to recover. Then without warning another song started and it went on like that for some time.

The three friends sang the afternoon away, the two girls singing together at times and then Marcel singing alone as if to try to better their last song. They enjoyed the competition and laughed and danced together with great ease and amusement. Finally, Rosemary fell to her seat exhausted.

"Time for me te go, I have some t'ings te ready for tomorrow," she said.

"Awe, no Rosemary, don't leave yet, it's still early enough," begged Flo.

"No," replied Rosemary, "I must go now. Ye can stay and have fun for a while yet. I'll see ye in the mornin' as usual." Rosemary readied herself to leave, and Marcel walked her to the door. He closed the door firmly behind Rosemary and headed directly towards Flo standing at the table. His strut was confident and full of intention, and she wondered what he was thinking? He walked straight to her, put his arms around her tiny waist, and pulled her close to him.

"Flo, I am so happy today," he confessed. "Because of you, and Rosemary, and the McGintys, I feel I have a family again. I work with people I like, and now I have a real home of my own. Do I have you, Flo?" He took her tiny hands in his and gazed into her eyes as he spoke.

"I know you like me, don't you?" His voice was soft and unsure at first, but when Flo melted into his arms, and he caught her, he knew his answer.

"Ye know yer me man, Marcel--no one else will ever take yer place." Marcel's self-confidence soared as he kissed her softly on the lips. Her heart was bursting to please him as she responded eagerly with love.

8

Love is in the Air, March 1895

Flo knew she was in love with him even before that afternoon. Having waited for so long she knew she would hold nothing back. Her body yearned for him now and she freely surrendered to his touch. She felt only love for him and knew he loved her every bit as much. She would deny him nothing. Not now. He had made his intentions clear to her and she would give her all, her whole self, even her soul if he asked her.

"I was afraid to do that before, but now I feel sure we are right for each other," Marcel assured her.

"Yes, I feel it, too," she whispered. He put one arm under her legs to lift her and cradled her like a baby in his arms. She gazed into his eyes with love and tenderness as he slowly carried her into the bedroom and laid her on the beautiful quilted bed. It felt so welcoming to her, like lying on a bed of soft cotton wool. She knew she couldn't resist him and didn't want to. Her heart was exploding with desire. He sat down beside her and kissed her, first on the neck and then again on her mouth. They embraced each other willingly. She knew they were going to make love. She could feel the excitement rise in her stomach, her heart beating louder, as she felt it thud against her chest.

"Gently," she said to him in a soft voice. "Yer me man, Marcel, take me gently." Marcel kissed her softly on her lips and stroked her face with his finger, feeling her smooth, young skin. He could feel her body relax to his touch as she kissed him back--relieved to feel the approval of her lips. His mouth found her neck, and he continued to smother her with kisses as he undressed her slowly. Her blouse buttons slipped open with ease, as did her under-vest, exposing her small round breasts. His touch was soft and warm, and she wanted him more and more. Her mouth kissed him back, and his tongue and hers collided in an embrace neither had felt before. He continued to loosen her clothing, and she found herself undoing the buttons on his shirt then the buttons on his breeches. His body was ready for her as she could feel his manhood strong and ready to make love, pressing hard against her body.

"*Amore*," he said in a soft whisper. "Are you sure you want this?"

"More than anything in the world--I know I want ye," she replied softly. At that, Marcel raised himself from the bed and quickly threw his clothing to the floor. Flo hastily did the same, and there she stood in front of him completely naked. He slowly raised his head and looked at her small, shapely body, his hands stroking her white skin and gently touching her smooth, firm breasts. Flo gasped in excitement at his touch. Marcel reached over and pulled down the quilt to expose the white virgin sheets. She lay on the bed--he beside her. He kissed her eager month while gently moving on top of her and slipped inside her body with ease.

They fit perfectly, like a pair of snug leather gloves--moving together in rhythm. He was gentle with every move. She kissed his cheeks and his ears and ran her fingers through his thick, curly hair as she surrendered to him. Their movement was as one, first gently and slowly, and then faster, and deeper. Her heartbeat quickened, and she became aware of feelings deep in her body that she had never known existed. She wanted more--didn't want him to stop. His thrust quickened and touched her someplace inside that almost made her cry out with delight, but she did not. She didn't want to alarm him.

She felt the sweat from his brow on her face and kissed him again and again on his cheeks as she continued to sway to his rhythm. She gave out a shrill sigh of delight as they continued to move together, both breathing heavily and holding each other passionately. He kissed her breasts, and she smothered his head with kisses in return. Their body heat was unbearable under the new quilt, and Marcel kicked it to the bottom of the bed to give them some air. Finally, they could go no longer, and he relaxed and let go. She felt the body rush exploding from deep within as she relaxed, and they climaxed at the same time.

His body slumped on top of her, and he kissed her mouth as he rolled to her side. They lay together quietly, limp, for a moment as she turned to see that he too was as exhausted. They said nothing to one another but lay side-by-side in silence feeling their satisfaction and contentment. She saw the sweat on his forehead and reached up with one hand to her brow to find that she too was wet with heavy perspiration. Finally, Marcel turned to face her and with one finger stroked her cheek.

"*Amore, mio amore*," he said to her softly, repeating these words again and again.

"What does it mean?" she asked him, whispering.

"It means, 'my love,' you are my love," he replied as he leaned over to kiss her gently on her lips.

Flo couldn't have been happier--she felt full, complete and free after these long months waiting for him to come to her. She knew they would be together forever, now that they had sealed their love. Everything in her world was right.

"Promise me one thing," Marcel said to her softly.

"Anything," she replied warmly. He looked into her eyes like a little boy pleading, and she could see that he was serious, as he spoke almost in a whisper.

"Just love me, never leave me, that's all I ask of you," he said. She felt a deep loneliness from him.

"Yer me man, Marcel, now and forever. I'll never leave ye," she replied and kissed him fully on the lips.

They lay together for a few moments in silence, just enjoying each other in their satisfaction.

"Well now," he continued talking. "That was more than I ever expected. It was something marvellous, wonderful, fulfilling, exciting, and exhausting all at the same time and only you could give me all of that. We should do that again soon," he said, and they laughed together.

"It seems we've christened yer nice new bed and lovely linen," she said.

"Just like a woman to worry about the linen. I have no regrets," he said looking into her eyes. "Do you?" he asked in earnest.

"Now, yer teasing me, ye know I don't. Yer me man, Marcel, and there'll never be anyone else but you."

"I bought all this for you Flo. I did all of this work for you, to impress you. I love you, and I knew we were falling in love." Marcel lowered his eyes and looked down as he spoke. "I've never felt like this for anyone in my whole life. I've always been able to walk away with no regrets and never look back," he admitted. "Then, I met you and everything's different. I want you with me, always, wherever I go I want you with me. Flo, *amore, mio amore*, I love you. I will never love another, only you *mio amore*. Will you marry me, please, Flo, be my wife, marry me?" Flo lay beside him in the warm, cosy bed feeling wonderful, yet humbled.

"Ye did this all for me?" she repeated in bewilderment. At that moment, she knew she would always be able to count on Marcel. If ever she needed anything in the world, Marcel would be the one person she could rely on. Overjoyed and deeply touched by his need to make her feel so special, a tear spilled over her eyes and gently rolled down her face. She was weeping with love for him, and he felt it, too.

"Of course I'll marry ye, there's no one else in the world I want te spend me life wit' but you. I love ye." He rolled over towards her, and they kissed passionately on the lips. Marcel spoke again, but this time he was looking for an immediate reply.

"Promise me that you'll never leave me, promise me now, we'll be together for always and you'll never leave me alone." His question sounded anxious, and she knew he needed her reassurance.

"I promise ye, I promise I'll never leave ye, I promise," she said, imploring that he would believe her. Somehow she understood his need to hear her say those words over and over, and feeling full of love for him, she kissed his cheek and held him close to her breast like a frightened child. They lay together for what seemed the rest of the afternoon, talking, laughing, and planning their life together. They made love again, gently and playfully taking the time to explore the others body and feel their passion freely. Marcel admitted to her that he had always wanted a special friend of his own. He had never had a close friend before now, not once in his lifetime. Now, he had someone to share with, who, understood him and accepted him as he was.

"I'll never change ye. Yer me man, perfect exactly as ye are. I'll talk te me mammy first, but ye know I'll be sixteen in two weeks, and old enough te make me own decisions then. Legally she couldn't stop me even if she wanted, after I'm sixteen. Ye'll have te come home wit' me te meet her."

"Flo, tell me what happened to your daddy?"

Flo paused. "He got pneumonia and died last year. That was why we had te move out of our farm and live in a small cottage in the village. Mammy couldn't run a farm alone, but we needed a place big enough for all us girls," she explained and continued. "I think she'll be glad in a way that I'm leaving. It'll give the others a little more space. I'll talk te her today when I get home, and perhaps ye can come te me house tomorrow evening after work."

"That's fine with me," he replied as he continued to run his fingers over her smooth white skin.

"What kind of wedding do you want, large or small?" he asked her, smiling.

"Well, I'll be the first of our girls te wed, so me mammy will want te be there, and me sisters too. I'd rather have just a wee group, say Rosemary and perhaps Sean McGinty as the witnesses, and then come back te the pub for a real celebration wit' all our friends and family."

"That's a good idea," he agreed. They lay together for a while longer, just holding each other gently, and in their contentment they drifted off to sleep.

Marcel awoke first and sensed that it was late. He opened the door to take a look outside.

"Oh no, it's dark outside. We must have slept the afternoon away, and now I have no idea what time it is."

"Neither do I." Flo jumped out of the bed and began to dress herself. Marcel returned to the bedroom and quickly threw on his clothes.

"We should go over te Rosemary and find out what time it is."

"Yes, and we can tell her our news and ask her te be one of our witnesses." He agreed and together they readied themselves to leave. Flo was happy in the knowledge that she would be coming to live in this home that Marcel had made for them. She wondered about having a window somewhere on these walls. Otherwise, she might never know if it was day or night. Marcel was thinking the same thing.

"We need a window, at least one if not two," he thought out loud. "I'd like you to think about that and where you might want your windows."

"Yer amazing Marcel--I was just t'inkin' that meself when ye said it. Ye can do anything, can't ye, even make a window where there isn't one. How will ye do that?"

"With wood and glass and clay," he said and they both laughed.

"I just have to work out how much it will cost and give it a go." Together they walked around the back of the pub to the rear entrance and knocked on the door for Rosemary. She arrived soon enough and opened the door to them.

"Come in, come in," Rosemary said. "Is this the two of ye just now after yer party, Marcel?" she asked surprised. "It was a grand dinner and a grand party wit' us all there. I loved every minute of it, but now look at the time, and ye've been in there alone all this time?" she smiled, knowingly? "What on earth were ye up te, or should I not be askin'?" Rosemary said with a smile.

Marcel spoke first, and wearing a quirky grin on his face as if very pleased with himself, he continued.

"First of all, would you tell us what time it is? I don't have a clock in my house yet but can see that I'll definitely need one now."

"It's eight o'clock in the evening. Now what have you two been up te that ye lost track of the day?" There was a silence between them, and both Flo and Rosemary looked at each other and began to laugh. Marcel joined in as well.

"Should I put the kettle on?" said Rosemary and then continued talking as if to herself. "Silly question, I'll put the kettle on, sure there's a story to listen to, alright."

They followed Rosemary into the kitchen where she put on a kettle of water for the tea. They all sat down at the kitchen table in silence. No one wanted to speak first. Finally, the kettle boiled for the tea and Rosemary poured it into the pot with a couple of spoons of loose tea leaves.

"I t'ink we need a strong cuppa," she said. Marcel looked at Flo and winked at her beneath his long, dark eyelashes. She just melted and knew everything would be fine. It would be grand--her man was in charge of the situation. Rosemary brought out the teacups and saucers and filled three with tea.

"Would anyone like sugar or milk?" In unison, Flo and Marcel both replied, "No thank you."

Rosemary sat down at the table and looked at Flo first.

"Do ye have something te tell me, or something te ask me?" Flo looked over to Marcel, who promptly took the lead and replied to Rosemary.

"Both," he said. "First, I've asked Flo to marry me. Second she has accepted, and third, would you like to come to our wedding and be a witness for us along with Sean McGinty, if he accepts?" Rosemary's mouth dropped open in shock. A couple of seconds passed when she suddenly realized they were waiting for her reply.

"Well, this is news, indeed," she said excitedly as she stood up from her chair. "Congratulations te both of ye's. Congratulations," she said as she leaned over to kiss Flo on the cheek, and then turned to shake Marcel by the hand. "I'm so happy for ye both, but Flo, I hate te cast a shadow now. Are ye sure yer mammy will let ye marry so young? Yer not yet sixteen years old?" Rosemary said more realistically.

"I'll be sixteen years old in two weeks. Mammy can't object after that. Legally I'll be old enough te marry, and anyway I t'ink she'll be happy for me. She knows we're walking out together, and when I tell her how much I love him, she'll be happy for me, I know she will," Flo replied confidently.

Marcel sat quietly, saying nothing but watching Rosemary's response to the news. He could tell she was not entirely supportive.

"Why Rosemary, do you think we shouldn't marry yet? Too young or what do you think? We love each other, so why should we wait when we both know in our hearts that we want to marry now."

"Oh, Marcel, ye make it sound so simple, and yer so confident about taking care of Flo. I don't see how any mammy could disagree wit' ye when ye speak," Rosemary replied.

Marcel replied quickly. "I will speak to Flo's mammy tonight in fact, and not tomorrow. I'll ask for her blessing on us this very night."

"In that case, I think ye'll find a little nip of whisky will help wit' yer question. I suggest ye take a small quart wit' ye. After ye've had yer discussion, ye'll offer her a nip in her tea. That's the way it's done around here, so if yer a man she'd expect that of ye," Rosemary said.

"I might offer ye both a little nip in yer tea now, by way of me congratulations as is our custom here. Jimmy always said it was good for the soul when settling or celebrating something unexpected." Rosemary reached into the cupboard behind her to retrieve a bottle of house whisky and quickly tipped a nip into each cup of tea.

"Now," she said raising her cup. "Congratulations to the both of ye, I wish ye every happiness in yer life ahead." Flo was smiling so hard that she almost burst into tears as she jumped up from the table and threw her arms around her friend.

"Thank ye, Rosemary, ye've been so good te us, thank ye," said Flo. Rosemary laughed back.

"Now is there anything else ye want te tell me?" she asked with a wink in her eye. Flo suddenly blushed and smiled again at her friend.

"Not'ing, not today anyway," she replied, laughing. Marcel also smiled at the two friends. He knew how close they were.

"A secret shared by three of us," he said and they all laughed.

"Then ye'd better get yerselves down that road before yer mammy goes te her bed."

"Yes, although I think she'll be sitting up waiting for me te get home," said Flo.

Rosemary handed Marcel a quarter-bottle of whisky for his pocket. "It's on the house," she said. "Jimmy would want ye te have it." Marcel accepted the whisky gratefully and slipped it into his jacket pocket.

The young couple made their way to the back door and headed 'round onto the street and down the village. Rosemary stood watching, and wishing them all the luck in the world. Her thoughts drifted towards Sean McGinty. He impressed her at the dinner party--not the gloomy stern type she thought him at all. *He was actually surprisingly funny,* she thought to herself. It wasn't often anyone got to witness such love in these parts. It was mostly just hard work, sad news, and making ends meet. *That's probably why the Irish are so good at making fun out of anything and everything,* she thought. *It's their way of entertaining themselves and making others laugh while breaking the harshness of the daily routine at the slightest chance of a smile,* she thought.

"Ye've got te laugh," Rosemary said aloud to herself, "misery just kills ye if ye let it," another of Jimmy's sayings.

Rosemary was beginning to understand what life was all about. Everyone in Ireland was going through the same hardship. She knew she had been very lucky what with Jimmy and the pub work, and now taking over for him completely in his absence. She wondered how he was getting on and if he liked his new country? She was very grateful to him for setting her up this way. One day she would have a substantial amount of savings, and that was unheard of for a young lady of her class.

She knew that a cash dowry would make her a desirable wife, and her thoughts slipped back to Sean McGinty. She was secretly hoping that he might be interested since she decided that she liked him. Sean always seemed a little shy and awkward with the ladies, she thought, but that wasn't a bad thing either. He was a hard worker, kind, and good to his animals. He had a good sense of fun in him, she saw that today, and he knew the bad times of Ireland. His family had somehow managed to survive and stick together. She also knew that some of his relatives had left on the ships to America, and were still living there.

The McGintys were survivors, Catholic, and stubborn to the bone, just like she was herself. She felt that she and Sean McGinty could make a good match, and all Rosemary wanted in return was to have children, lots of them. She had no delusions about herself. She knew she was taller than most girls, larger boned and not as feminine as the likes of Flo. However, she wasn't ugly. She had beautiful soft rose-coloured skin that everyone commented on. She was a hard worker and could match any man around--that was important. She was strong for childbearing and could endure the hardship of the Irish ways without complaint. She knew farm work and crop sowing and the long days alone. She could hold her own as a farmer's wife. Her only wish was to have a large happy family. She imagined lots of children sitting around her table on a Sunday after Mass, eating breakfast, laughing and joking. She longed for that day to come, especially now that Flo was going to marry first.

Rosemary smiled to herself and went back inside the pub to her reality. She cleared away the cups and saucers and washed them up for Flo to have a clear kitchen in the morning. Then she did her final check of the evening, and it being Sunday, went upstairs to have an early night's sleep. She just couldn't get Flo out of her head. She knew that they had been "intimate" that afternoon, after everyone left and they were alone. She imagined them in that brand new bed, with the luxury of the new bedding--the clean white cotton sheets, and puffed up pillows, filled with that expensive horsehair and silk. Everything was so new and clean; it must have been wonderful--she chuckled to herself, looking forward to hearing Flo's story. They had become true friends, and she wanted everything good and happy for Flo. Rosemary had a good heart, and it was now obvious to her that Marcel had his own plan in mind. Indeed, pleased for them, she wished them a life of happiness, and hoped things would go smoothly with Flo's mammy that very evening.

The couple reached the front door of Flo's mammy's house. They lived in a stone cottage on Main Street in Doune Village. It was a typical terraced cottage in a row of five. They had a front room and back kitchen downstairs and upstairs two bedrooms. Marcel knew that Flo had four sisters and couldn't imagine how so many would fit into one bedroom. He didn't know that Flo slept with her mammy in her big bed so that there were only two to a bed in the next room. Flo opened the door and shouted in before she entered the main room where she knew her mammy would be sitting by the fireside knitting. As she entered the room, her mammy looked up.

"Ah, at last, yer late. Did ye have a good time wit' yer friends?" Then she saw someone enter the room behind Flo and stopped knitting, waiting to see who was with her.

"Mammy, this is Marcel, I wanted ye te meet him tonight because... At that moment, Marcel cut in and stepped forward in front of Flo. "How do you do, Mrs. Logan," he said, holding out his hand towards her.

Mrs. Logan stood up and offered Marcel a seat opposite her own. Flo danced on the spot in anticipation.

"Go and put the kettle on for a cup of tea please Flo," her mother said. Marcel sat down, and squeezing his cap in his hands asked Mrs. Logan if she had a good day. They began to exchange small talk. Mrs. Logan knew all along what was going on. She didn't make it difficult for him but decided to play along.

Flo returned with a tray of cups, saucers, and the full teapot. She placed it on the side table beside her mammy and began to pour the tea. She handed her mammy a cup first, then Marcel, and then she sat down on the chair next to Marcel with her own cup of tea.

"Now then, what's all this about, visiting at this time of night?" She was not annoyed but wanted Marcel to get to his point, as it was already late. Marcel cleared his throat.

"Mrs. Logan, I have come here tonight with Flo to ask you for your blessing and permission to marry your daughter."

He managed to get it all out in one sentence, and couldn't believe his luck that he did. Flo, amazed at his courage, just smiled over to her mammy. Mrs. Logan looked at Marcel, who was now slightly nervous and then turned to Flo whose eyes were sparkling like diamonds. She had never seen her daughter so lit up and happy. She looked again at Marcel more studiously this time, and saw a nervous young man who was obviously committed to her daughter. Marcel began again.

"Mrs. Logan, I want you to know that although Flo and I met just a couple of months ago, I knew immediately that I loved her and want her with me for the rest of my life. I have a home for us to live in and I am working hard to make our furniture. Flo loves what I have done to the house, and can see from today that I am very capable of looking after her. Mrs. Logan, I want you to know that I love your daughter, and she has told me that she loves me, too, and agreed to marry me with your blessing. Mrs. Logan, please say yes, I beg of you, or my heart will break with disappointment. Mrs. Logan..." Marcel began to plead with her again, but this time Mrs. Logan interrupted.

"And where is this house?"

"It was the old coach house behind the pub. I've converted it into a real home for us to live in. I just need to put a couple of windows in it because it's dark inside with no daylight, and we lost track of today because we couldn't see outside."

Mrs. Logan looked over at her daughter, who, now perched on the edge of her chair, was smiling nervously. Her eyes danced back and forth between her mammy and Marcel.

"Mrs. Logan, please don't break my heart. I love Flo and will take good care of her forever more, I promise."

He continued rambling, "Mrs. Logan--" he began again, and Mrs. Logan interrupted.

"I can see how happy ye are, Flo, and ye seem te me te be a nice young man. I'll give ye my blessing on one condition, that ye be married as Catholics here in the local chapel. I don't want any talk or gossip starting because yer both so young." Flo screamed and jumped up to kiss her mammy in excitement. Then she quickly turned to Marcel and threw her arms around his neck and kissed him on the mouth. Mrs. Logan blushed slightly but seeing how happy her daughter and Marcel were, became quickly at ease with the situation and her decision to let them marry. The door opened slowly, and Mrs. Logan motioned them into the room.

"Come on in ye girls, we have news here for ye all te hear." The sisters entered the room dressed in thick flannel nightgowns shy in front of a stranger in their home. They heard the noise upstairs and knew something was happening and just had to come down to hear what it was all about.

"Girls, this is Marcel." Flo proudly waved her hand in his direction. "He has asked me te marry him, and I've agreed. Mammy's given her permission tonight, so we'll be posting the banns at chapel this weekend for a wedding in four weeks' time." Flo babbled out the news excitedly.

Marcel suddenly remembered the whisky and produced the small bottle from his pocket.

"Mrs. Logan, I believe it is your custom, so can I offer you a nip in your tea to cement our agreement?"

"I'm surprised ye know of such t'ings. Of course, I'll take a nip," she said as she extended her arm, holding her teacup and saucer towards him. Marcel poured the whisky into her cup. The girls were so excited at the news, jumping up and down in joy for their sister, wishing her happiness and lots of children.

"What kind of wedding will it be Flo, a big white wedding or a quiet vestibule wedding?" asked her younger sister Marie.

"I don't know yet--we haven't decided, but I'm sure we'll all be busy sewing these next few weeks te make somet'ing nice te wear."

Mrs. Logan began to discuss what material she had for a white gown for Flo. They were all drawn into the conversation, excited about the event. Marcel was quite overwhelmed by all the females surrounding him.

"I think I should head home now and leave you all to your preparations. It's been a pleasure meeting you, Mrs. Logan, and thank you very much for your blessing." Mrs. Logan shook Marcel by the hand once again and wished him congratulations and together with Flo they walked Marcel to the front door. Once there, Mrs. Logan wished him goodnight and left Flo with him as she returned to the front parlour where her daughters were planning what they were going to wear to this very special occasion.

Flo and Marcel stood together in the dark of the street with their arms around each other in an embrace.

"Well now, Mrs. Murphy, to be, this has been a very successful day and an even more successful evening." Marcel's hands coupled her face, and he stared deep into her eyes as he continued to speak.

"Flo, I love you. I'm so happy I could burst with joy," Marcel whispered to her.

Flo whispered back to him, her eyes still sparkling excitedly. "Marcel, I'm so happy too, and I love ye so much. This's been the best day of me life, and I'm so looking forward te being yer wife."

They kissed passionately, enjoying the feeling of holding each other once again. They stood in silence not wanting to part until finally Marcel said he must get home and sleep for work tomorrow. They kissed again, and he turned quickly and walked away from her, unable to look back until there was a distance between them. Flo watched him walk down the street and out of sight in the darkness and finally turned and went inside. Her mammy was waiting for her--the whiskey had obviously taken its effect as her face was somewhat flushed red, and she seemed very happy.

"He seems a nice lad. I hope ye'll both be very happy, but now it's time for sleep. We all have work tomorrow, let's te bed," she ordered.

"I love him so much Mammy, I know we'll be happy." Flo and her mammy climbed the stairs together to go to bed, both feeling jubilant, and both a little flushed for different reasons.

That night, neither Flo nor her mammy could sleep for thinking and planning the wedding. Mrs. Logan was a little concerned what the neighbours might say about her young daughter getting married. She knew most people would think that Flo was already pregnant. She would have great delight in telling everyone that Flo was in love with a charming young man who also loves her. As was her duty, Mrs. Logan would talk to the priest on Sunday after Mass and make the necessary arrangements for a chapel wedding. That would stop the gossip dead in its tracks. Flo was not pregnant, and Marcel was also Catholic. If Flo had been pregnant, a quiet vestibule wedding would be normal. Since she was not there was no need to hide anything, and a chapel wedding would look good for Mrs. Logan.

She would look out what fabric she had in her hamper to see if anything was suitable to make a beautiful gown for Flo. There may even be enough for a dress each for the girls. She had her work cut out for her over the next month--five dresses to sew, and she relished the challenge. Luckily she had her treadle sewing machine that her husband had bought for her when they first came on the market. They were well off that year with extra crops and good sales at the market. The bonus was the unexpected birth of a second bull calf, which Mr. Logan sold at the market for a handsome sum. All the girls received something special from their daddy and Mrs. Logan got her sewing machine. What a wonderful year that was. They were all so content on their farm then. She remembered the happy days when her husband was alive, before he got sick with pneumonia and died. Mrs. Logan lowered her head to pray for Flo and Marcel. She spoke quietly to her husband telling him what a nice young man Flo had brought home.

"Well, Francey, our first daughter's found herself a husband and her just turning sixteen in a few weeks. He's a nice young man and it's a good match for Flo, she loves him. He's Catholic of Italian background and orphaned here in Ireland. He loves her, Francey. It's plain te see on his face when he looks at her, and that's what matters. Remember, we were so young ourselves when we got wed. Just twenty years old. It feels so long ago now Francey, and yet I remember it like it was yesterday. So, Francey, we're preparing for a wedding, and everyone's so excited about it. We're settling into village life as well, and it's not so bad after all. I still miss ye, but I know yer watching over me, and the girls and everyt'ing will be just fine. Goodnight now, Francey, and thank ye, Father, Amen."

With that thought and the help of the whiskey, Mrs. Logan fell into a deep sleep. Flo, on the other hand lay beside her mammy in the bed, and no matter what she thought of, she just couldn't sleep. She was so excited about everything and pleased that her mammy liked Marcel and had no objections to her marrying him, even though they were both so very young. She would ask Marcel if he could go to Dublin and buy some silk for her wedding gown, and her mammy would sew a beautiful gown, the nicest gown ever seen in these parts. She must talk to Marcel tomorrow about the wedding. Since her mammy wanted a Catholic wedding, she was hoping he would choose a chapel wedding at the main altar, which was bigger than a small gathering in the Vestibule at the side of the chapel.

Flo understood her mammy's concerned about the neighbours. The locals would never actually say anything directly to her. However, they would gossip about the possibility among themselves. She was also concerned that they could be right, but not a breath of that to anyone. She put that thought out of her mind immediately, concentrating on her beautiful gown and how it would look--white silk, with lace trimming, and she fell asleep dreaming about the smallest details of her wedding gown.

9

A Secret Shared

The next morning Flo was so tired she could barely pull herself out of bed to go to work. She had bread to make and cheese to churn, and still tired, it was only six o'clock in the morning.

"Come on," her mammy called. "Get up and get te work before ye lose yer job, and then there'll be trouble wit' you getting married an' all."

Flo pulled herself out of bed and scrambled to get ready for work. By the time she dressed and was ready to go, she was awake, and ready for the day's work.

"I'll be straight home tonight after work, Mammy. I want te get te bed early for a decent sleep, I'm exhausted."

"Good girl ye are, dreamin' all night long and now I see yer tired. I hope for yer sake yer day is quieter than usual. See ye tonight, my lovely," her mammy said cheerfully.

Flo hurried up the village street almost sprinting towards the pub. She knew Rosemary would be waiting to hear all the news about yesterday. She also knew that she couldn't tell about certain intimacies that Rosemary was especially interested in hearing. She knew that Rosemary wouldn't let her off, not wanting to miss out on anything that happened after she left.

Flo cringed a little in embarrassment at what she knew she had to tell her friend, but she also knew she would have to make

Rosemary swear to an everlasting secret. If word ever got out and her mammy heard about it, there would be blue murder in these parts! Finally, she arrived at the pub door. Rosemary was waiting inside and opened the door to her as she arrived.

"I saw ye comin' down the street, so I knew ye'd be there when I opened the door."

"Aye, aye," said Flo as she entered the pub and headed straight for the kitchen. Rosemary followed directly behind her. Flo took her hat and coat off and hung them up as usual. She turned to pick up her piny and wrapped it around her laughing out loud as she looked over towards her friend.

"What 're ye laughing at? Ye know I'm dying to hear what happened yesterday after I left the coach house. Tell all, tell all and nothing missed out," Rosemary demanded.

"Ye must promise never te repeat what I'm about to tell ye," Flo warned her friend. "If word ever got back te me mammy and family, I'd be an outcast forever and me mammy would never forgive me. Now d'ye promise in God's holy name never te repeat what I'm about to tell ye?"

"Aye, aye," said Rosemary. "I promise in God's holy name, never to repeat anything that yer about te tell me. In the name of the Father, and of the Son, and of the Holy Ghost, Amen." Rosemary crossed herself in the Catholic way to seal the promise. "Now tell all, and don't miss a t'ing out," she ordered.

"I'll put the kettle on," said Flo. "I can talk while we work or we'll have not'ing for the suppers tonight."

"A good idea," said Rosemary.

Flo was still excited, her eyes twinkling like the stars, and she was as bubbly as she was the day before. She took out the dough prepared the day before and began to knead and roll it one last time to ready it for the oven. She went over to the churn bucket and handed it over to Rosemary.

"Here, ye can churn while I knead the bread. At least that way we'll have bread and cheese, and the cooking will get done." Rosemary didn't argue. She took the churn bucket and started working it to make the cheese. The kettle was ready, and soon the teapot was full. Flo poured out the tea and still kneading, she began her story.

"Well, after ye left yesterday, I thought that I should go home meself and not be seen spending time alone in the house wit' Marcel. So, I was about to leave when he came back from showing ye out. What happened next was a miracle, Rosemary," said Flo. "He walked straight towards me, put his arms around me waist, and told me that this had been the best day of his life. He said he was so happy he could burst wit' joy. He had friends that he never thought he would have in his life and that he had met me," she said modestly. Flo's sincerity touched Rosemary's heart and she smiled tenderly at her friend.

Flo continued with her story. "He said he had always been able to walk away from people and not look back, but I was different. He said he wanted te be wit' me, for always. He told me he loved me and asked me te marry him." Flo sighed looking into space and smiled again. Rosemary's eyes grew wider, and her mouth dropped opened in great surprise. She had expected something but not a full-blown proposal.

"Go on, go on now," she said anxiously, and Flo continued.

"I just melted; I fell into his arms and we kissed for the longest time. I've never felt that way for anyone in me life and it was wonderful," she whimpered. "He told me that he had known from the very first time we met and spoke te each other that he was going te marry me. He said he loved me from that moment on and that everyt'ing he had done from then on was for me," she told her friend timidly.

"The old coach house he converted for a home was for me. The furniture he was making was for me. The luxurious t'ings he was spending his savings on was all for me." Flo took a deep sigh as great tears spilled over in her eyes and rolled down her cheeks. She didn't bother to wipe them away but kept on working the dough, and then continued her story.

Rosemary churned furiously but couldn't take her eyes off Flo.

"He wants our home te be beautiful and loving and inviting wit' nice things in it, for me. It was all for me all along." Flo beamed with pride as she sniffed more tears of joy and could hardly see what she was doing as she kept kneading the dough, turning it and throwing it on the table as she spoke.

Rosemary was speechless and continued churning mechanically, her eyes glued on Flo.

"Then, he asked me te marry him again. He said he wanted te speak te me mammy before the day was over te ask for her blessing and consent, and he did last night," she sniffed. "What's more, me mammy likes him, too, and gave her permission for us te wed. Oh, Rosemary, I'm so happy, I love him so much." Flo was bursting with joy, her face beaming brightly. Love sparkled in her eyes as she finally finished her story.

Rosemary's eyes gaped open as she stared back at her friend, waiting for the conclusion. "What happened next? I want te know the next bit," Rosemary said seriously.

"Well," said Flo, "I said yes, I would marry him and told him that I loved him too. Then, he picked me up in his arms and carried me through te the bedroom. He laid me on the bed and started kissing my neck, and I kissed him back." Rosemary's eyes grew even bigger, and she was intent on listening to every word Flo said as she pounded harder and faster, turning the handle on the cheese bucket.

"Then it happened," Flo said.

"What happened? What happened? Tell me what happened next?" interrupted Rosemary, almost shouting. Flo replied in a whisper. "We made love--passionately, lovingly, all afternoon long, until we finally fell asleep, and woke up not knowing what time it was."

"Oh my goodness, ye's never did, did ye?" Rosemary exclaimed in excitement. "I want to know all the details," she said as she continued to churn the cheese, which was getting more and more solid.

"Rosemary, I t'ink the cheese's ready for setting now and me dough's ready for the oven."

"Okay," said Rosemary, "but don't t'ink yer getting off this lightly. I want the details. I want te know what it was like, you know, how it felt an' all." Flo laughed out loud and then giggled sheepishly.

"Rosemary, it was grand I've never felt anyt'ing like it in me life. It was warm, gentle, passionate, and loving. I swear I could feel him touch the pit of me stomach inside me, tickling me like, someplace really deep inside me. We just seemed te fit perfectly," and Flo sighed again.

"Well now, was there any pain?" Rosemary asked.

"Absolutely not, not even a might of pain. Like I said, it was all so natural and perfect, nothing to fear at all," she said matter of fact and with confidence. "It was the most beautiful and wonderful feeling I've ever felt, and then finally after a while, there was what felt like an explosion inside me. Oh, my goodness, it was ecstasy, the most pleasurable feeling ever, and I know I want more," she giggled.

"What happened next?" Rosemary asked, impatient to hear more.

"Then, we just lay there in each other's arms declaring our love and talking about getting married right away. We made love a second time, and then we both fell asleep," Flo said somewhat flushed but with a shy little smirk on her face.

Rosemary, enthralled and speechless at the same time, but had about a million questions to ask.

"No more talking now, we've got work te get through for tonight and I need te recover from what I just told ye. I can't believe I'm tellin' ye all this, it's like a confession." Flo looked up at her friend without raising her head and smiled teasingly.

The girls worked together as quickly as they could, preparing the evening meals. Rosemary continued to ask questions now and then, some of which Flo would never have thought of. However, she answered her friend as best she could. She could see that Rosemary was digesting every word as she filtered everything Flo said slowly, and repeated her words quietly to herself until she got a complete picture in her mind. Rosemary gazed over at her friend and saw she was lost in her dream working and smiling at the same time. It was clear to her that Flo was in love.

Rosemary secretly began to think about her own life and wondered what would happen to her. Would Sean McGinty ever declare his undying passion and love for her? She couldn't see him doing that and thought not. He was not that kind of man. He was a kind man alright, but also practical. He dealt with life just as he would a business proposition. In fact, it wouldn't surprise her if he made a proposal as a bargaining point for marriage. She laughed to herself because she would do the same thing too, and she understood the ways of someone like Sean McGinty. Perhaps he would suit her after all, even without the romance.

"It'll a busy month now wit' a weddin' to prepare for. How exciting," Rosemary declared!

It was Monday, and Flo's mammy was in a flap about material for a wedding dress. Flo had told her that Marcel goes to Dublin every month with the McGinty's and she decided to visit his house to ask if he could buy some nice material for her to make Flo's dress.

"Well now, I'm glad you asked about that. You see I've already bought something--something very special for Flo." Mrs. Logan looked at him puzzled.

"What d'ye mean?" she asked.

"The last time we went to the market I ordered a dress for Flo. I have a contact you know, and he can get anything I ask for through his business," Marcel said confidently and continued. "I knew before I asked Flo that she'd say yes, and I took the chance to get her something special made up. I've already paid for it myself. I've also bought a gold wedding band and have it ready for her finger. It's a solid gold band Mrs. Logan, the finest gold," he told her excitedly. "I think you should come in to see the dress for yourself, Mrs. Logan, I have it all boxed up and hidden away." He opened the door to let her pass inside. Mrs. Logan stood looking at him in amazement.

"How did ye know what size te get for her?" she asked him rather sternly.

"Oh, Kate helped me out with that a while back. The dress is a size eighteen waist and the ring is a size five, small. Kate and Flo are about the same size and build," he said. "I'm pretty sure everything will fit her, but I would like your opinion on that," he said. Again Mrs. Logan stood staring at Marcel, her eyes in disbelief at his self-confidence with her daughter.

"And how did ye know she'd accept yer proposal?" she asked him defiantly.

"Mrs. Logan, I love Flo with all my heart and I know she loves me, too. I just knew that if I asked her she would say yes, and she did."

"I hope that's all ye've been asking her for, and I'm sure ye know what I'm talking about now," Mrs. Logan replied quizzically with a stern look on her face. Marcel blushed at the thought and immediately lowered his head in embarrassment.

"As I said before, Mrs. Logan, I love Flo and would never do anything to hurt her in any way. I can promise you now this very day to take good care of her in every way for the rest of our lives together." Mrs. Logan glared at him coldly.

"Well, there'd better be no babies for at least nine months from the marriage date. I can't have people around here talking and pointing fingers--bringing shame on the rest of me girls. That wouldn't do at all and make it all the harder for them te find a respectable husband. D'ye understand me, Marcel? I would have te disown me own daughter te protect the others."

"Yes, Mrs. Logan, I understand. Will you come through now to see the dress?" he asked.

"Of course, I'll be happy te do that, but not immediately. I'll come down tonight. Flo's coming straight home from work te have an early night. Will ye be alone?"

"Yes, I'll expect you after supper time."

At eight o'clock Mrs. Logan turned into the courtyard to Marcel's house behind the pub. Flo was just leaving through the front door of the pub for home. She had already said goodnight to Marcel and told him earlier that she wanted an early night. She didn't know that her mammy was going to see him. She just wanted to get to her bed. Mrs. Logan entered the house--impressed at how new and clean everything looked. She hadn't noticed earlier when her mind was on another matter. She complimented him on his work as he ushered her towards his kitchen where his new table and chairs beckoned.

"Please sit down, Mrs. Logan," he said pulling out a chair for her at the table.

"I'll get the box." Marcel left the room and went into the bedroom where the dress was hidden in his newly finished wardrobe. He returned to the kitchen holding a large white box. He placed the box on the table and began to open it carefully. Mrs. Logan looked eager to see the contents, and as Marcel slowly undid the crisp white tissue paper, her eyes grew larger and larger in anticipation. She was speechless, her eyes now wide as could be, and her mouth gaped open. She paused silently in awe.

"It's absolutely beautiful," she said in a whisper. "Oh my, what a grand dress, our Flo will love it, and she'll look beautiful in it. Can I lift it out?" she asked, almost afraid to touch it.

"Of course, Mrs. Logan, you'll have to look closely to make sure it'll fit her. I know I'm not allowed to see the bride in her gown before the wedding, so I'm counting on you to help make it fit. I have some extra material if you should need it."

"Well, ye thought of everything. It's satin and lace, isn't it?" she asked.

"Yes," he said with pride, "the finest satin and Italian lace, encrusted with small pearls around the neck and the sleeves."

"Well, I could never have made anything as luxurious as this. It must have cost a fortune?"

"Only the best for my Flo. I told you I would take good care of her, Mrs. Logan, and I will. I promise you." Mrs. Logan examined the dress carefully for size. She looked closely at the waist and the top part of the dress to make sure it was not too small. Then she held it at her waist to see if it might be too long. It was not.

"It'll fit fine. It's perfect, and I don't t'ink I'll have te make any adjustments at all."

"I also have this as a headpiece," said Marcel, unwrapping a second box to expose a short white veil made from the very same Italian lace attached to a pearl comb to hold the veil in place.

"It's simply grand and I know she'll love it. When will ye give it te her?" asked Flo's mammy.

"In a day or two. I want her to have it to try on at your home, but I'd like to show it to her myself. I'd like to see her reaction," said Marcel smiling. Mrs. Logan, impressed at how romantic this young man seemed, began to feel easier towards him. She realised that he had been on his own for a long time and finally found a young lady that he loved and wanted to spend his life with.

Philomena Logan was a petite girl, small boned and light as a feather. Although she was a hard worker, she had spent a long time ill with female troubles when she first became a woman the year before. Mrs. Logan worried about her daughter in that regard. She was well aware of the pains and difficulties some women had to contend with every month. Her daughter was one of those unfortunate young women who suffered painfully at that time of the month. Now she knew that Flo would be alright with a husband who loved her as much as Marcel seemed to. He would take care of her daughter and let her rest when those times came. Mrs. Logan, although somewhat envious of the young couple, felt sure there was no need for her to worry about Flo.

The wedding would be set for the first Saturday after Flo's sixteenth birthday. Mrs. Logan, Marcel, and Flo went together to make the arrangements. When they returned from the chapel, Mrs. Logan put on the kettle for tea and Marcel announced that he wanted Flo to come back to his house.

"I have a gift I want you to have but I couldn't bring it here with me. When you see what it is, you'll understand. Then we can come back here and have tea with your mama," he said. Of course, Mrs. Logan knew what it was. "You should go wit' him," she said as a tear welled in her eye. "We'll have tea when ye get back, go now," as she ushered them through the front door. A little envy creeped into her heart--her husband was dead and she still ached for him--but she pushed it away wishing she could be there to enjoy watching Flo get her dress from the man she was about to marry.

Finally, the young couple arrived at the coach house and went inside. Flo was anxious to see what the gift was, and Marcel was anxious to see her reaction. He hoped that she wouldn't be disappointed. When he came back into the kitchen with a large white box, Flo had no idea what it could be. Marcel laid the box on the table and stood back.

"Open the box, *mio amore*."

"What is it?" she asked.

"Open it and see." She took the top off the box and saw the white tissue paper inside. Now she was even more curious, her stomach turning over in excitement.

"What is it, Marcel?" she asked curiously. She opened the tissue slowly and carefully, and there laying gracefully set in the box, was the most beautiful dress she had ever seen. Her eyes opened wide in delight as she gazed in bewilderment at the gorgeous wedding gown that lay before her. She carefully lifted it out of the box, and her eyes became even more dazzled as she held it up against herself.

The dress was stunning. It was cream coloured Italian satin covered with the finest Italian lace. It had a scooped halter shaped neckline, encrusted with pearls from one shoulder to the other. The short sleeves, slightly gathered at the shoulder, came down to the elbow, edged with lace frills and encrusted with pearls and a little satin bow. The skirt was long and A-shaped at the front with a small train at the back. It had a thick satin pleated waist belt at the front, which tied into a huge bow at the back. It was a very modern, posh, Victorian wedding dress, and Marcel had paid handsomely for it. He also bought himself the perfect outfit to offset Flo's dress. He didn't want anything to spoil their day. He did have to use some of the money from the pouch his mama had given him. However, he assured himself that Rosa would have wanted the best for her bambino and his future wife. He was right, she would have.

"Oh, Marcel, how exquisite and strikingly gorgeous. It must have been expensive?"

"You mean after the emerald satin quilt on the bed," he replied. They both laughed and she danced around the room holding the dress up in front of her.

"I'm so glad you like it."

"Oh, it's simply beautiful," she replied, holding the gown close to her.

"Not nearly as beautiful as you are, Flo, *mio amore*." They kissed and held each other for a few moments, enjoying their happiness. Finally, Marcel said it was time for them to get her home with her new dress.

"Your family will be waiting to see what the gift is."

"Yes," she agreed and began to fold the dress carefully so as not to crease it in any way. She carefully followed the lines already set in the gown and placed it gently inside the box, covered it with the tissue paper and replaced the box lid.

"I'm the happiest woman in the world."

"I'm happy for you, and me, too," he replied.

"We're going te have a wonderful life together, I just know it. Great t'ings will come te us. Everyone will be happy for us, I can feel it Marcel," she said joyously. Flo was on cloud nine, hypnotised by love.

"Let's get going, *mio amore*, your mammy will be waiting for us with more tea." He kissed her on the mouth and took her by the hand. They both laughed out loud and left the coach house. Flo took his arm with great pride and Marcel carried the box as they walked together down the village street to Mrs. Logan's house. Indeed, her sisters were waiting patiently to see what the gift was. Again, Mrs. Logan put on the kettle for tea as Marcel had predicted. Then came the opening of the box and Flo gently lifted out the most beautiful gown the girls had ever seen. Great excitement filled the room as Flo's sisters "oohed" and "aahed" at the wedding dress and the short veil with the pearl comb.

Marcel finished his tea and was able to make his leave to get back home. It had been a long day and a lot of walking. He would be glad to get home and have an early night in bed. Flo walked out to the front door with her fiancé, taking his arm in hers as if she was taking ownership of him. The display of public affection pleased him. No one in his life had ever wanted to own him before--apart from his mama. It gave him a sense of power that he had not felt for a long time. They kissed in the shadow of the closed-door and the darkness of the street.

"Goodnight, *mio amore*." He began his walk back home again. They would see each other again tomorrow in the pub when Marcel came in for his evening supper. Flo watched him disappear as he walked up the village street and became so small he was out of sight. Then she sighed to herself and went inside to deal with her younger sisters and her mammy's questions. It had been a grand day, one she would never forget.

The next morning Flo was up bright and sharp and full of life. She arrived at work early to get started cooking. When she arrived however, Rosemary was waiting to hear how everything had worked out the night before.

"Don't miss anyt'ing out now. I want te know everyt'ing from the beginning te the end of yer day," she said.

"Okay," said Flo, who was tending to the daily chores of the kitchen almost in a remote motion. She recited the events of the day before as if it was all a dream. Rosemary listened to every word.

The wedding gown was the biggest surprise, and Flo described every pearl, frill, and bow in detail. Then she described the head-dress, veil, and, the pearl comb for her hair. It seemed to Rosemary that her friend was still dreaming as she listened to her fantasy.

"Rosemary, I t'ink I have the most romantic man in the world. I'm so in love wit' him, and he has the most wonderful taste in clothes and furniture. He seems te know all the latest fashions in everyt'ing. I'm so lucky, Rosemary."

"Indeed, ye are," her friend agreed. They continued to work on while Rosemary listened to Flo going over and over the same details again and again. She didn't get annoyed--she was enjoying listening to Flo as much as Flo enjoyed repeating herself.

They posted the wedding for Saturday morning at ten o'clock in the chapel. The next few days, were hurried and exciting, bustling with preparations of all kinds. Mrs. Logan was at her best making arrangements and kept busy sewing the girls' dresses for the wedding.

Sean McGinty loaned the pony and trap to the couple for the day and Marcel wasted no time in preparing it for the wedding. He covered the carriage with white sheets, and placed white satin cushions on the seats and tied red and white ribbons, bows, and fresh wild flowers all over. He transferred it into a spectacular bridal carriage. When it turned up at Mrs. Logan's house, they were all speechless. "What a romantic I'm marrying," Flo said to her mammy and sisters smiling.

When the bridal carriage pulled up at the chapel what a surprise to see so many people. The entire village and surrounding neighbours, as well as strangers from other villages had come to see the much talked about wedding dress that Marcel bought in Dublin. Everyone had heard about the young couple's love story and wanted to see the gown that the gossips said "definitely wasn't homespun and must have cost him his life savings." It had been a long time since the village had hosted such luxury.

Flo deliberately walked slowly into the chapel. She wanted people see her gown and hear their comments. The wedding party was already seated in front of the altar, waiting for the bride. The priest gave the signal when he saw Flo enter the chapel and the organist began to play "The Wedding March." Everyone stood up and turned towards the aisle to watch her pass. She was stunningly radiant and beautiful. Marcel was very proud when he saw her and sneaked a quick wink as she took her place beside him. The priest began the ceremony and it seemed no time to Flo when her new husband placed the wedding band on her finger. Everything went according to plan with family a few friends and invited guests in attendance, a small but good-sized group for a village wedding. A few villagers had quietly slipped in at the back of the chapel to see the young couple in their finery. They threw rice and wildflowers over the newly weds to wish them good luck as they left the chapel. Both Flo and Marcel were in their element and soaking up the loving energy from the enthusiastic gathering outside.

"May ye be happy and love each other all yer married life!" people shouted at them.

"Good wishes te ye both and lots of healthy children!" the crowd called out.

"Blessings and good wishes for a happy life together!" People called out dreams of happiness and love and that pleased Flo and Marcel very much. The wedding party returned to the pub where Rosemary and Mrs. Logan had previously prepared the food. Mrs. Logan had insisted on doing the cooking and bringing it down to the pub so as not to have Flo cooking for her own wedding. She also baked the wedding cake, which looked professionally baked and tasted delicious.

"I've taken a few days off work, which means we can go to Dublin for a short trip. I can show you the shops, and we can eat at the Dublin Hotel where Michael is Head Chef."

"Oh, Marcel, ye t'ink of everything. How wonderful," Flo exclaimed with pride. It was such a blissful day. Arrangements went according to plan with no glitches whatsoever. Sean let Marcel borrow the pony and trap for the trip to Dublin. After the young couple had eaten, cut the cake, and changed clothes for their journey, they were ready to set off for Dublin and the beginning of their exciting new life together. Flo had never been to the city. Marcel was in his element showing her around. He climbed up on the front seat of the trap and leaned forward to help pull Flo up on the other side. The crowd was happy and excited for the young couple and waved them off with shouts of joy and laughter.

Many hours later, somewhat exhausted and dishevelled, they arrived at their little hotel, went straight to bed and fell asleep immediately. It had been a long trip to Dublin. They both laughed about it the next morning over breakfast.

"You must promise never to tell anyone about our first night together?" Marcel pleaded.

"I would never embarrass ye like that, especially in light of how ye made it up te me when we woke up in the morning."

It was in the morning, when Flo awoke to find herself lying in bed with a sleeping Marcel that she became full of love for him. She wanted to pinch herself to know that she wasn't dreaming.

She woke him gently, first with a kiss on the cheek, then on his forehead. He opened his eyes and smiled softly back at her. Then he moved closer and kissed her on the mouth. They began to make love without hesitation, and once again Flo's movements were in perfect unison with her new husband. For the second time in her life, Flo felt complete abandonment, joy, and a deep pleasure that was both emotional and physical.

Marcel was careful and gentle, as he didn't want to hurt Flo in any way. The couple united in enjoying the motion and the pleasure of surrender as they moved passionately together. Flo felt that same surge of deep penetration followed by the overwhelming explosion from deep within, as Marcel relaxed, released, and let the body rush come. Once again, they reached climax together. They lay quietly in each other's arms just loving one another and realising that they were now married.

"That was to make up for last night, *mio amore.*"

"Yes, I know it was," said Flo and they laughed together.

They had two wonderful days in Dublin, sightseeing everywhere that Marcel could remember. They ate at the Dublin Hotel. Marcel introduced Flo to Michael and he them give a short tour of the hotel. They walked hand in hand along the riverbank, he pointing out the big ships on their way to America and the islands on the other side of the world. Finally, after their two days, they had to pack up and head back home to start work and married life.

"This trip will always be our most treasured, loving memory, *mio amore,*" Marcel said.

"Indeed, it will, a dream honeymoon wit' the love of me life," she agreed and kissed his cheek.

10

After the Honeymoon

Flo returned to the pub, preparing food for the regulars. Marcel was back on the farm working in the fields with Sean McGinty. Everything was in its place--people doing their daily duty as normal. It was hard for the young couple, having to return to everyday reality; it seemed to Flo that she was living in a dream and missed Marcel every moment they were apart.

Rosemary had never-ending questions of every kind, wanting to know details of all that had happened on the honeymoon. The pub was busy and full of life again, people talking, laughing, and plenty of questions for Flo. She tried to keep to the kitchen away from folks, and busy herself with her cooking and so forth. It was hard to avoid the most awkward question from everyone.

"When are the babies coming?" everyone was asking her. Flo was most embarrassed at such questions into her private life. She had never even considered a baby, and this made her think about when her last cycle had been. In the rush of all the excitement she had forgotten, but now thinking about it, it must have been in February. Anxiously, she began to wonder if it was possible that she was already pregnant? *I hope not*, she thought. *It would be better te have some time wit' Marcel before we start a family. I won't bother him wit' such an idea just yet, best te be sure first.* She put that thought to the back of her mind and tried to forget about it.

It was the end of April already, spring was in the air, and crops were showing signs of sprouting. Spring was always a busy time in the world of farming. Some would say farming was always a busy time and Marcel would agree. He loved his days out in the fields. It gave him a sense of power, to use his great strength working with the soil. He appreciated the space around him when he worked, and felt such freedom. He could look up from wherever he was and see the nature of things all around him. Marcel understood that everything came in its own time when nature decided it was ready. He was happy for the first time in his young life. He couldn't remember ever feeling this way before, not about anyone, or about anything. Flo made him feel alive, complete and fulfilled in every way. To her, he was her man, strong and muscular. To him she was his little lady, small and petite in all the right places, confident and able in the kitchen.

Marcel loved Flo's cooking and had shown her many Italian dishes, which she was able to adapt for customers at the pub. Instead of the usual vegetable soup, she might add some tomatoes and pepper to spice it up and perhaps a little pasta in there too. People noticed her new recipes and commented with enthusiasm. She loved to experiment with new tastes and add the herbs that Marcel had introduced her to. She would try a dash of garlic in her stews or some basil and rosemary in her salads with lemon and olive oil. No one was ever disappointed in Flo's cooking.

Rosemary, of course, was just glad to have Flo around to do it all. She used to have to do the cooking as well as running the pub, changing the barrels, and the other "men's work." It was a busy place, and they both worked hard, but between the two of them they coped. Marcel attended to the vegetable patch. He added a small row for herbs--easy to grow, and he made sure they were never short of anything. He kept the kitchen drain clear and any other work that Rosemary asked him to do. He was more than glad to help and began to feel a sense of belonging in this small village--as if he'd found his place in the world.

Rosemary had not heard from the solicitor since Jimmy left for America and wondered if she would ever hear anything from him? She continued to keep the books up to date, bank the weekly takings, and send him copies of everything that she had done. She did, of course, continue to pay herself and Flo, every week as arranged. She kept an adequate amount of cash available for repairs and paying the local farmers who delivered her milk, eggs, and meat supplies. She kept that money separate from the cash takings, in a little tin box with a lock on the front. She kept the key to the box in the till where only she and Flo could find it.

Market day was coming due.

"Do either of you ladies need anything from the market?" asked Marcel. He was happy to do a bit of shopping--it gave him a reason to look around while Sean was talking business with the other farmers. Rosemary remembered that she had asked Sean McGinty about buying her a bicycle some time back. She had forgotten to ask him if he'd seen anything suitable, or even had a rough cost for a decent second-hand one. Then, of course, everything changed, and she didn't really need the bicycle as she was living in the village. She asked Marcel. "It would be a great favour te me if ye could find out how much a second-hand bicycle would cost?" She still had a secret fancy of owning a bicycle and riding around the countryside on her time off.

"Of course I'll keep a look out. You just want to know how much it might cost, yes?" Marcel nodded.

"Yes, Marcel, I'd like an idea of what a decent second-hand one would cost me."

"No problem, I'd be glad to do the favour."

Flo didn't need anything, except some new recipes for his Italian food.

"I'll look for a proper cookbook, an Italian cookbook, my gift to you for making me happy and cooking my favourite Italian dishes," he said.

When he arrived back home from the market, Marcel gave Flo the new Italian cookbook.

"For being my wife," and he kissed her on the cheek.

"Thank ye, Marcel, ye know I'll enjoy learning the right way te do it for ye. Ye'll just have te read it out for me, like the first time." He smiled over to her remembering.

"Marcel," she said quietly, and more serious now. "I've something I need te talk te ye about." The hair on the back of Marcel's neck bristled as if she had walked over his grave. She sounded worried, and he turned to her, immediately concerned.

"What is it *amore*, why so serious?"

"Oh Marcel, it's almost May, and I haven't had me monthly for April yet. I can't even remember having one in March."

"What monthly?" he said curiously.

"Ye know what I mean," she said, slightly embarrassed. "Me monthly, ye know what, girl's monthly, things that happen every month to girls?"

"Oh, oh, your monthly, oh yes that monthly," he said understanding. "Now I know what you mean."

"You haven't...had...any..." he asked hesitating. "Should we be worried?"

"Yes, I t'ink so. If it's two months now, we would be having a baby in December, and that's too early according te what me mammy's calculations will be. Oh, Marcel, I'm so worried." Marcel walked closer to Flo and put his arm around her shoulder.

"Don't worry, *amore*. If it happens we'll deal with it then, but not until then." He turned Flo to face him and then kissed her softly on her lips. "Don't worry, *amore*, it'll be okay," he reassured her. Flo began to clear the table and wash up their dishes as Marcel went outside to cut wood for their fire. When he had left the room, he took on a different attitude.

Wow! He thought to himself holding his head with his hands and pacing back and forth. *It's too early, not now, not yet. Mrs. Logan would certainly have a fit and as she warned us she would have to protect her other girls first. There was no knowing what she meant by that, and Flo would suffer for it. No, please God, no baby, not yet at least.* He continued chopping and cutting although they had plenty of wood inside. However, it kept him busy and let his head deal with the idea that Flo was probably pregnant. *Poor Flo, she's worried. I should go to her and see how she is, my poor little amore,* he thought to himself. With that, he put down his axe and went inside to Flo.

She had finished clearing away their dishes and was preparing their morning breakfast. Flo liked to feed Marcel a hot-cooked breakfast before he left for work in the fields and always had a well-packed lunch ready for him to take with him. His work was so labour intensive she knew he had to keep up his strength. Marcel was physically strong and muscular, something that Flo admired when they first met. Suddenly Marcel came in to the house and went straight over to where she was preparing his lunchbox. He turned her around to face him and placed his hands on her shoulders.

"Now listen *amore*," he said sternly, "I want you to know that no matter if we're having a baby or not, that I am here to protect you. I'm your husband; your man, remember? I'll be here to deal with your mammy, no matter what. I don't want you to worry about it. Right?" Flo struggled to stop herself, but she had wound herself so tightly that she burst into tears.

"Oh Marcel, I'm so sorry. I didn't mean te do this te us, not now. I hope I'm not having a baby yet, but I'm afraid that I already am. Can ye forgive me?" She leaned her head on his shoulder and continued to wail.

"There's nothing to forgive, it takes two to make a baby, and I'll deal with your mammy if we have to." Flo controlled herself and wiped her face with a cloth.

"Yes, Marcel, yer me man alright, a good husband and I know I can rely on ye te deal wit' me mammy, if we need te that is."

May came and went, and Flo had no monthly. Neither did she have any other side effects and that confused her, but a little bump was starting to show in the pit of her tummy, even Marcel noticed that.

"Will you go to the doctor?"

"Not yet, I'll wait another month or so. I don't want people seeing me at the doctors just yet." Before long it was the end of June and time for Flo to confess that she had started to notice little signs indicating that she was pregnant. Her breasts were fuller, and her body seemed to have blossomed and appeared more round and curvy. Also, she had a strange feeling in the pit of her stomach one day and had to sit down. She suddenly felt her tummy turn upside down, and she felt sick. She knew the term; she had heard her mammy with her friends talk about it once, and it somehow stuck in her head.

They called it the *quickening*--folklore said it was the time when God the Father sent the Holy Spirit into the female's body to install a soul into the foetus. Only then would the baby be connected to God and deemed a living soul. Now, Flo knew she was having a baby and would go to the doctor for confirmation. She told Marcel. She knew that he wasn't happy about their situation, but neither was he annoyed and showed no regret. He didn't feel anything towards the event and would simply deal with it as it arrived. It was more important to him not to upset Flo.

Flo was becoming secretly excited about her condition--except for her mammy of course. Her mammy would be so angry there was no knowing what she would do. Flo would just have to let Marcel deal with her and hope for the best. She didn't tell anyone that she was going to see the doctor. Rosemary heard from one of her regular customers.

"I see young Flo's wit' child?" he said testing Rosemary.

"I don't t'ink so, not yet anyway," replied Rosemary.

"Well I saw her at the doctor's yesterday, what else could it be?"

"I'm sure we'll find out soon enough, not that it's anyone's business," Rosemary said sharply. As it was, Flo was pregnant, about twelve or fourteen weeks along. The doctor had given her a birthing date of December 12th, but even that was too soon to placate her mammy, and Flo knew it. She told Marcel what the doctor told her, and how she needed to take care of herself and get plenty of rest. Flo knew that she had to tell Rosemary immediately, or her friend would be annoyed with her, and she didn't want that to happen. The next day Marcel told Sean that Flo was going to have a baby, and Flo told Rosemary.

"I heard yesterday from old Mr. Docherty when he was in the bar--he said he saw ye at the doctor's. It must have happened right away. What a shame ye's didn't get more time te yerselves first. Oh, well, we'll manage somehow. Just try te enjoy it. Don't worry it's in God's hands now. He'll work it all out ye'll see." Rosemary said.

At first Sean congratulated Marcel and then commiserated with him.

"It would have been better if ye'd been spared a little longer perhaps a year, but nature has its own timing."

"I agree, and I know there will be trouble with Mrs. Logan. As long as Flo doesn't get hurt, that's my main concern," Marcel said to Sean.

That evening Marcel and Flo went down the village to see Flo's mammy and break the news to her. As Flo had thought she was not happy about it, and not happy about the date Flo gave for the baby's arrival.

"Ye must t'ink I'm stupid or somet'ing, d'ye t'ink people around here can't count? What's wrong wit' ye? We'll see when this little one is born. If this baby comes earlier than expected, I'll have te leave this village and take me girls elsewhere, where no one knows us. If I have te do that, it'll be on yer heads, the two of ye's, be warned." There was no way to stop Mrs. Logan and she continued to rant. "Only wrong t'ings come from wrong doings; ye'd better not be lying te me 'cause if ye are, ye'll pay the price yerselves. I told ye before, my girls would be shamed, and people wouldn't want their sons coming near the Logan girls, you mark me words," she warned them, pointing her finger at Marcel. Flo and Marcel understood what Mrs. Logan meant. They knew the ways of these local people, and they knew that everybody would be counting the weeks until this baby was born. The couple just prayed that the baby stayed put until late in December. They left Mrs. Logan's house feeling somewhat depressed and made their way home.

"She didn't congratulate you, Flo, and this is her first grandchild," said Marcel, a little annoyed.

"I know," said Flo quietly. Marcel looked at her, understanding her disappointment. He could feel her pain. He put his arm around her, and they walked up the village street towards their coach house. At least there, they knew a friendly fire waited to warm their hearts again.

Flo continued to work at the pub and took great pleasure in her cooking. More people came daily to eat. Her food had earned a far-reaching reputation for being good and cheap. The days rolled on through summer, and it became obvious that Flo was carrying a child.

"Congratulations, when's the baby due?" customers would ask in a well-meaning way.

"I hope yer goin' te carry on workin' for a while, we'll miss yer cookin' when ye go," was a constant remark.

Rosemary was anxious for her friend and tried to help her out as much as she could, carrying trays of food from the kitchen out to the pub floor. Flo appreciated the help. There was a genuine caring between the two girls.

Flo gave most of her money to Marcel when she got paid. She kept only a small amount for food and housekeeping. She didn't need much, and their supper was always whatever she had made that day at the pub, which she paid Rosemary for, albeit with a large discount.

Marcel was a master at saving money and could be relied on to provide anything they needed. He had replaced all the money he had used from Rosa's pouch for the wedding. Now he had started a box for their own savings, which he kept on the top shelf of the wardrobe in their bedroom. Flo never asked how much it contained. She just knew that whatever she needed, it would be available when she asked for it.

Marcel busied himself in preparation for the baby and was making a cradle, rubbing the wood down with wire wool to make sure it was smooth to the touch. He didn't want Flo or his baby to catch a splinter. He was so thoughtful of every tiny detail. He also made a stand for her to keep the baby's clothes and other belongings. It had a flat surface on the top just the right height for her to lay the baby. He was taking the matter seriously, as he did everything that concerned his little lady. She was very proud of her husband and delighted in telling people of his handy work.

Summer was closing, and it was time for Flo to bring out the soup pot again and think about hot warming stews for the colder days.

"Will ye be able te keep working te help me out? I know I can't cope wit' this business on me own," Rosemary asked.

"Of course, I'll stay as long as I can te help ye out, Rosemary, and I'll be right back te work after the baby's born, too."

"How can ye?" she asked again.

"I can bring the baby in its pram into the kitchen. Sure it sleeps most of the day for the first months anyway. If it's here wit' me I can hear when it wakes up and needs me."

"Why, Flo, if yer sure then I'd be glad te try it and see if it works for ye. I know I can't run this place meself." Both girls knew that there was no extra help in the village. Not anyone that Rosemary could trust in her pub.

The days passed quickly into winter. The pub was busier than ever, and Flo continued to turn out her delicious stews, soups, and puddings. Customers just kept coming and coming from far and wide to taste her delights. Her cooking had become quite a legend in the area, and people would make the trip out to the little village pub just to taste for themselves how good her cooking really was. Rosemary's weekly takings kept going up and up and that would herald good news for a prospective buyer.

It was just December first when Flo awoke in the middle of the night with pains in her lower stomach. She got up out of bed wondering what was happening to her. She could feel pains in places she had never felt before, and immediately when she stood up her waters broke and came gushing forth. Flo screamed in shock and Marcel jumped out of the bed. He saw the wetness pooling beneath her.

"What do you want me to do for you?"

"Get Rosemary te fetch the doctor, quick!" she said anxiously.

Marcel rushed out of the house and across the yard to the back door of the pub, which led into the kitchen. But, he couldn't get in--Rosemary had locked the door. He shouted up to Rosemary in the room where she slept, banging his fists on the door at the same time. Rosemary was a light sleeper and awoke almost immediately. She hurried downstairs and opened the door knowing ahead what it was.

"Rosemary will you go fetch the doctor? The baby's coming and I must stay with Flo. I don't want her alone."

"Of course," said Rosemary reaching for her shoes and quickly throwing on her overcoat and shawl. Her long legs made it down the road quicker than any. In no time she was standing at the front door of the doctor's house, banging loudly on the door. The doctor aroused from his sleep and ran downstairs to the door.

"Rosemary, what can I do for you?"

"It's Flo, her baby's coming, can ye come, now?"

"Of course, let me dress and fetch me bag." In minutes, he returned looking dishevelled and half-dressed, and together they ran up the street to the pub and around the back yard into the old coach house. Marcel opened the door and quickly ushered them to the bedroom where Flo lay writhing on the bed. Marcel had placed as much sheeting as he could find beneath Flo, to help save the new bedding and mattress. Rosemary remembered she had found rubber sheets upstairs in the house when she was going through some boxes after Jimmy had left.

"It must have been what they used when Mary's boys were born, I'll go get them." Quickly she fetched the rubber sheets and returned. The doctor and Marcel lifted Flo and Rosemary placed the sheets under her body. Marcel insisted on having a cotton sheet on top of the rubber for Flo's comfort. She was feeling very hot, and the doctor began to check how far down the baby was in the birth canal.

"Ye must have started earlier today?" he questioned her.

"No Doctor, I had no pain at all today, just a little discomfort a few hours ago now, but I am on me feet all day, ye know, in the pub."

"Your baby is being born now, Flo. I want ye te try te control yer breathing. It'll help ye te relax and not tense up. Now breathe deeply and slowly and when I tell ye te hold your breath, do so until I tell ye te breathe again. Do ye understand Flo?" Doctor Connelly asked.

"Yes, Doctor." Flo was a little soldier when it came to pain, she would suffer silently and say nothing until the pain had gone. Afterwards she would tell how bad it had been, but not at the time. It was as though she needed her concentration to keep the pain at bay. Marcel sat beside her holding her hand and helping her with the slow breathing. Rosemary busied herself boiling water in the big pot for the doctor. They had plenty of clean cloths to use, and Marcel had banked the fire up full to keep the place warm for Flo.

"Let's see now," said the doctor, "it's two o'clock in the morning now, and ye've been up about an hour or so, but when did ye start the contractions?"

"I haven't had any pain until now; I told ye that already, Doctor."

"Oh my, I can see the head coming down now. When I say 'push,' push as hard as you can." He placed his hand on her stomach to feel the contractions.

"Now push, PUSH HARD ... " With that, the baby's head was completely out, and Flo continued pushing when the doctor told her to stop. He took a close look at the neck, made some adjustment, and felt another contraction starting. Again the doctor shouted to Flo.

"PUSH!" She began pushing as hard as she could. Marcel kept holding her hand and suddenly, in one push, to Doctor Connelly's astonishment, the infant shot out like a bullet into his waiting hands.

"I've never seen the likes of such a fast delivery in all me years," he said. "Now let's take a look at her." He lifted the baby up and over to the table that Marcel had brought from the kitchen. Doctor Connelly removed the cord and cleaned out her ears, eyes, and nose. The baby cried, and Flo was almost in tears when Doctor Connelly placed the new-born flat on Flo's stomach.

"She's perfect in every way," the doctor said. "She's a little small, so I would say she's an early birth by a few weeks. I weigh her at five pounds, which is small for a baby. They are usually anything from seven pounds upwards, and seven pounds is average, so she is small," he repeated.

"Now young lady," he said as he turned to Flo. "We have to give you a thorough examination to check everything is out, and you are clean inside." Again he placed his hand on Flo's stomach and this time he pushed down quite hard. A small amount of blood and water came gushing out.

"Ah," he said. "This is what I was looking for. It's important te get it all, and now I know you're clean inside." With that, he turned to Rosemary. "Would ye be good enough te finish here for me? She just needs a good clean with sterile water." he asked.

"Of course, Doctor, I'd be glad te help." Rosemary was grateful she was given a chore. She quickly put the pot on again for more water and readied the things she needed to clean Flo thoroughly.

The doctor spoke to Marcel quietly. "It was the easiest birth I've ever experienced, so quick and so clean in comparison," he said. "Now bring the baby and Flo in te see me in about six days. If ye have any concerns before then come te see me immediately." He made his leave, congratulating Marcel as they walked together towards the door.

"I must say ye've made this into a warm and comfortable home te live in. I'm very impressed wit' yer work," said the doctor.

"Thank you for everything, Doctor." Marcel saw him out and closed the door behind him. Then he returned to the bedroom where Flo was sitting up, trying to pull the rubber sheet out from under her.

"Let me help you, what are you trying to do?" he asked.

"I just want it flattened out; it's all rolled up under me." Rosemary entered the room with the cooled sterile water and boiled wipes to wash Flo. She was meticulous in her cleanliness. She made sure everything boiled and was sterile, to avoid any infection, just like her mammy had taught her.

"Let me help," she said to Marcel, who went 'round to the other side of the bed. Together they yanked the rubber sheet under Flo to make it more comfortable for her.

"Ah, that's better, Rosemary, thank ye for being such a great help. Yer a very good friend indeed, ye are," said Flo. Rosemary accepted the compliment silently and lifted the baby to wrap her in a blanket. She then handed the infant over to her daddy. Marcel's face lit up at first then he panicked a little not knowing what to do with her.

"Just hold her a little while, until I clean Flo and then she can take her from ye." Marcel sat down on the chair holding his new daughter, and looking at her with some pride and much curiosity.

"Such little hands and fingers. Look, Flo," he said, lifting the baby's tiny hand to show the new mammy. Rosemary gave her friend a thorough wash down and changed her gown. Then she removed the soiled sheets and replaced a clean one on top of the rubber sheet. She plumped up her pillows and went over to Marcel to take the baby from him and give her to Flo.

"Little love, how tiny she is," Rosemary said softly.

"Thank ye, Rosemary," Flo said as she cradled her daughter and gently placed the baby's mouth on her breast. She began to suckle immediately, as if she had been doing it for years.

"Look, Marcel, look, she can do it all on her own," Flo exclaimed. "What name will we give her, Marcel?"

"Well now, what about calling her Rosemary, after our good friend here?" he replied.

"Oh that would be lovely, and I'd be honoured."

"Yes, that's grand and we can call her Rosie, for short," Flo agreed.

"How lovely," said Rosemary. Marcel, however, didn't think that was such a great idea. His mother's name was Rosa, and he had disliked her very much. Flo didn't know anything about that part of his life, and he didn't want her to. He said nothing about it and found himself agreeing with the two girls. The baby would be named after Rosemary but known to everyone as Rosie. There was nothing unusual about that in these parts. Often people were given a name like Ann and called Nancy or some other nickname.

Marcel became momentarily reflective and withdrawn, as he remembered his mama. Although he never had any affection for her, he knew she would have loved the baby girl and been proud of her son. His mama would have spoiled Rosie to pieces and relished the pleasure of doing so, but his mama was dead. He showed no emotion and told no one about her. She was out of his life.

Flo saw the change in his mood immediately.

"Is something wrong, Marcel?"

"No, no, it's nothing really. I just had a sudden thought of my mama who is long dead. No matter, let's enjoy our baby girl, our little Rosie." He gave no more thought to it and turned his attention to Flo and their new daughter.

"Well now, is there anything ye'd like me te do before I go home?"

"Yes," replied Flo quickly. "Would ye bath little Rosie and dress her for me? Ye look so natural and confident wit her. Second, would ye do us the honour of being her Godmother, along wit' Sean McGinty, when we ask him that is?"

"Yes, te both questions," Rosemary replied, beaming.

She immediately prepared the bath and readied all the little things she would need to wash and dress little Rosie. It was like second nature to her; she knew what to do and how to do it. Rosemary was in seventh heaven bathing little Rosie, and it was obvious to the young couple that she knew what she was doing.

Marcel brought the new crib through and made it up with the mattress he had made and covered in crisp new cotton. Then he took out the surprise gift he had already bought in Dublin for their new baby.

"What's that box?" said Flo.

"It's a surprise for you," he said as he handed her the box. She opened it in excitement and lifted out a beautiful baby quilt, blue on the one side and pink on the other. Again Marcel had excelled himself. The quilt made of the same silk and horsehair as their own, would keep baby warm, or cool, in her little crib. Flo was so happy she asked him to come closer so that she could kiss him.

"Yer the most wonderful husband a girl could ever have," she whispered, but loud enough for Rosemary to hear. Rosemary looked over at the young couple with tenderness and smiled, hoping that one day she would experience the same beautiful feeling of motherhood.

Rosemary bathed, dressed, and fed little Rosie and it was time to lay her in her crib to sleep. She was so proud and confident and enjoyed caring for the infant without hesitation or nervousness.

Flo noticed how easily Rosemary handled the baby and asked if she could have lessons, please? They all laughed together.

"I must go now, it'll be time te get up and dressed again soon."

"Thank you so much for everything, Rosemary. You've been wonderful and a great friend to my Flo," said Marcel.

"Yes, Rosemary, ye've been wonderful, thank ye so much. I hope yer not too tired today."

"I'll sleep for a little then come over later for the lunchtime people."

"I've some food we can use te tide over the lunches today," Flo said.

"Ye'll do no such t'ing, indeed," said Rosemary in a raised voice. "Today, ye'll stay in bed and recover yer strength, I'll manage meself, and don't ye worry."

"Oh Rosemary, I can't let ye do all that yerself."

"No, no, you can't do it all yourself Rosemary," said Marcel. "I'm going to take today off at the farm, Sean will understand. So I can come to the pub and help out. Flo can tell me where everything is and what I need to do. Rosemary you can cope with the pub as usual, people will understand " he said.

"Oh, that would be grand Marcel. I feel better already. I'll see ye all later," she said.

Rosemary put on her coat and shawl and crossed the yard back to the pub. She had no idea what time it was until she saw the big clock behind the bar. It was five o'clock in the morning. It had been a long night indeed, but she would be able to catch a couple of hours sleep at least before morning arrived.

Flo instructed Marcel on the potato stew she had planned for the day. All the ingredients were ready in the cold press. "Just put them into the pot wit' the beef and let them all cook together," she said. She told him where her secret stock bottle was and how much to use. There was also a pot of vegetables ready to make buttery carrot soup, and she told him what to use, how much, and again what stock to put into it. "Sounds delicious," he said.

Marcel was good at taking instructions, and everything went like clockwork. People congratulated him on becoming a father, albeit their calculations left them wondering about the timing of the birth. Marcel knew that he should go down the village to see Mrs. Logan before someone else told her the news. He arranged with Rosemary after the lunch time was over that he would clean up and head down there quickly and come back again to help out. He took some of the soup and stew over to Flo. He knew she had to keep up her strength now that she was feeding a baby. He told his plan and left the coach house to make his way to see her mammy.

Marcel knocked on Mrs. Logan's door; she answered immediately. "Come in," she said and went to put the kettle on.

"Don't bother with tea for me. I've just come to tell you Flo had the baby in the night. We have a little daughter. Her name will be Rosemary after Flo's friend, but we'll call her Rosie," Marcel continued talking. "The baby is early and underweight, the doctor says. She weighs five pounds, which he said is small for a girl. Both Rosie and Flo are well, and that's what's important." He seemed to ramble on and on without pausing, just to stop Mrs. Logan from saying anything that might upset him. He didn't really care for the woman but had to put on a show to please Flo, until now that is. Finally, she appeared from the kitchen where she had heard every word. The expression on her stern face was enough to tell Marcel that she was angry.

No congratulations, no words of love for his Flo or little Rosie, Marcel thought to himself as he faced her.

"I warned ye both not te lie te me, and now the proof that ye've been lying all along, it is," she snapped. Marcel cut in before she could say anything else.

"Mrs. Logan, the baby is early and underweight, according to the doctor by about three weeks. Flo and little Rosie are going to need help to become strong and healthy." Marcel continued to talk in a loud and commanding voice. "I've told you before that I love Flo and that I will always take care of her no matter what. I don't really care if you think we are lying to you--that's not important now. You can ask the doctor yourself if you don't believe me," he continued in a raised voice.

"I care about Flo, and you haven't even asked after her condition or the baby's; your first grandchild and you've shown no interest in her or Flo at all. You seem to care more about what people might say?" he said with a wave of his hand.

"You can do as you please, frankly I don't care, but don't blame your actions on us," he said firmly. "You have a choice; you can enjoy our little family and your first granddaughter, or stay resentful and spiteful all your days on your own. The choice is yours," he said defiantly. "I'm leaving now and I hope you'll choose to come up to the coach house to see your daughter and your granddaughter. Remember it's your choice and I won't waste time over your decision. Goodbye now." Marcel walked out the front door, slamming it behind him.

Mrs. Logan stood still, furious and frozen to the spot. Marcel's distinct lack of interest in her opinion angered her.

"Well, how absolutely disrespectful," she said out loud to herself. "How dare he speak te me like that in me own house, foreigner that he is, the nerve of him? Not so charming now wit' his pretentious sweetness and hollow kindness?" She sat down sulking quietly. She had not managed to twist things to her favour, and it angered her that Marcel was not afraid of her. She was quiet for a long time in her thinking and finally realised that Flo was a married woman with a husband who would look after her and stand up for her. She no longer had control over her daughter, her husband did, and Flo would turn first to Marcel for anything that she needed, not to her mammy as before.

Things had changed, and Mrs. Logan did not like the feeling of being dethroned for one moment, not in favour of a young, short, Italian boy! Her anger did not subside as the day went on. She relived the incident in her mind a thousand times, and each time she became even more offended by him.

I'll fix them, she thought to herself. *I'll go te Dublin and take the girls wit' me. She'll be alone here wit' only him te keep her. She'll be sorry. One day, when she needs me again, I won't be here for her. She'll be sorry* she thought to herself spitefully.

Mrs. Logan was being cruel and vindictive, but she didn't care about that. She just wanted to hurt Flo and her husband. She was envious of their new family, and seeing them so happy reminded her that her man was dead, and she was alone except for her daughters. She was jealous of her their happiness and couldn't help herself. Flo found love in a young man who would protect her and support her always. Her mammy was bitter and resentful that her husband died and left her to cope alone. Her jealousy took over and she fiendishly wanted revenge for making her look foolish.

The very next day, her mind made up, Mrs. Logan went to visit the moving company to arrange to empty her house of its contents and move everything to Dublin. She would have her belongings placed in storage until she was ready. It would be expensive, but she would use her savings for the move. She wrote to her sister in Dublin.

> *Dear Bridget,*
>
> *Events have made it impossible for me to live with my girls in this village any longer. I am coming to Dublin to live with them and would be grateful if you could offer sleeping accommodation for us until I find a suitable house. Flo is now married, and I am one daughter*

less. I look forward to hearing back from you as soon
as possible.

Your loving sister,

Mrs. Logan didn't go to visit Flo and the baby. She instilled in her own mind that Flo lied to her. Vindictively, she would cut Flo and her family out. She hoped it hurt them as much as her own jealously hurt her. She mailed the letter to her sister and waited for a reply. In the meantime, she told her girls that they were to have nothing to do with Flo and Marcel. They were not to speak to her if they met. If they saw her coming down the street, they were to look down at their feet until she passed them by. They were to have no more to do with Flo ever again.

"Why, Mammy, what did our Flo do?" the girls questioned.

"She lied te me, and yer te have not'ing more te do wit' her again," shouted Mrs. Logan. At that, the girls started crying.

"Go upstairs and don't come down until ye's can control yerselves." Rowena, the youngest wept and didn't understand what was happening. She loved Flo dearly and was so looking forward to seeing the new baby.

"Why do we have te go te Dublin? I want te stay where we are, here in the village, I like it here."

"Don't worry about it all, there's nothing we can do just now. At least we'll be together. Poor Flo's the one who'll be alone, and we haven't even see the baby," said Annemarie the second oldest. Teresa and young Rowena sat on the bed holding each other and crying. They all loved Flo and Marcel, and they didn't really understand what was happening, or why. All the girls wanted, was to see their sister's new baby.

"Mammy won't hear of it," said Annemarie. Whatever had happened, Flo and her new family were now exiled and on their own.

Marcel arrived back at the pub and continued preparing food for the suppertime customers. Flo had told him about her extra stash of bread that she prepared every day. That would tide him over for a couple of days until she got back on her feet. She kept them in separate bread-boxes, three to a box in the cold-store cupboard. She instructed him on her secret way to freshen them up.

"Ye'll have te take the lid off, put a damp cloth over the top and place them back in the slow oven for fifteen minutes," she said.

"What a trick, how clever my little wife is," he smiled at her and kissed her cheek.

Marcel managed the kitchen with ease since most of the preparation had already been done. He just had to follow Flo's instructions, prepare the orders from Rosemary, put the food on the plates and deliver them to the customer. It was easy, he thought. He gave no further thought to Mrs. Logan, knowing that she would use the excuse to hurt Flo and that he had to shield her from her jealous mammy.

It was past eight o'clock in the evening when Marcel cleaned up and went home to Flo. He had prepared two meals to take with him from the pub. When he arrived home, Flo was sitting up in the chair in the bedroom with little Rosie at her breast, feeding.

"What a beautiful sight," he said as he entered the room and kissed Flo on her cheek.

"How have you two little girls been today?" Marcel stooped over his little daughter to study her tiny face. "She's beautiful, Flo, just like you, *amore*." He stroked her little face gently with the back of his finger.

"We've both had a really good sleep today. Rosie slept most of the afternoon, and I did, too. Did ye go te see me mammy?"

"Yes, I did. It was not good. She is very angry with us both, called us liars, and may leave the village as she threatened to do."

"Oh Marcel, can't ye talk some sense to her?"

"I doubt that very much, she's determined to leave the village and blame us for the move. Let her go *amore*, let her go." Marcel sat down beside Flo and put his arm around her.

Flo felt sad for she loved her sisters very much. She would try to get a message to them before they left the village. Marcel gave himself a wash and changed into clean clothes. Then he set the table for their supper, and together they sat down to eat Flo's butter carrot soup followed by Irish potato stew.

"Delicious, even if I cooked it myself?" and they both laughed.

They talked at length about their day. Flo spoke again about her mammy, and Marcel reassured her that he could not change her mind. Mrs. Logan wanted to leave and totally shunned them. That was the truth of the matter, and they would have to live with it.

"We are a family now," insisted Marcel as he took Flo's small hand and stroked it. "We have to stick together and care for each other. I'm sorry about your mammy, but I can't do anything to change her mind. We have to let her go and get on with our life *amore*," he said pleading. Flo knew he was right and agreed with him.

"I'd love te see me sisters before they all leave," she sighed.

"There might be a way," said Marcel. "Leave it to me and I'll see what I can do. Tomorrow I want to go to see someone about a perambulator for Rosie. I got a tip today at the pub about one and I want to check and see if it might do for her."

"Always one step ahead my man is," said Flo congratulating him as she spoke. Marcel cleared up and washed the dishes. Then he helped Flo back to bed returning the crib into the bedroom with them.

"Perhaps I should put some little wheels on the underside of this crib to make it easier to move around?"

"What a grand idea," said Flo.

"Right then, I'll do that," he said as he undressed for bed. They settled down together in the bed and lying closely he turned and kissed her on the cheek.

"Goodnight *mio amore*."

"Goodnight, Marcel." They both slept soundly until six o'clock in the morning when little Rosie woke for her first meal of the day.

The days rolled by, and Marcel took Flo to see the doctor as arranged. Everything was fine, and he was especially surprised at how well she was coping with the new baby.

"Never known any birth te be as easy as ye had it," the doctor said. "Ye were very lucky." Flo agreed and let the doctor check her over as required.

"Baby feeding well?"

"Yes," replied Flo.

"Good, well that's about it, come back te see me in three months wit' the baby."

Flo and little Rosie were doing very well. Marcel was so pleased that there were no problems with either of them. Flo returned to work at the pub, bringing little Rosie in her new perambulator with the bouncy wheels. It was very comfortable for the baby, and Rosie was no problem to anyone. She seldom cried, just when she wanted something.

Rosemary, thrilled with little Rosie, loved to hold her and play with her at every chance. Marcel had arranged for the baptism, and that went well with both Rosemary and Sean McGinty standing for the baby as Godparents. They had a nice day back at the coach house after the baptism. Flo had made a cake for the occasion and Marcel stole the show once again by giving the new Godparents a gift each. For Rosemary, he bought a silver cross on a silver chain.

"Oh, how gorgeous! I love it and I'll always wear it wit' pride. My first piece of jewellery." For Sean, Marcel had bought a timepiece for his pocket, the latest in fashion.

"They call it a pocket watch," he said to Sean. "The most modern of jewellery for men." Sean seemed impressed.

"It's grand," he said, "now I can never be late again," and they all laughed.

The group had become good friends, helping each other out through such ordeals. It was that same day when Marcel asked Sean for a big favour, the most he would ever ask in his life.

"Sean, you know that Mrs. Logan is leaving the village for Dublin."

"Aye, it's sad for Flo that her mammy's leaving this way."

"I wanted to arrange somehow for her girls to have a visit with Flo and little Rosie before they leave. They've never seen the baby and Flo just wants a chance to say goodbye."

"Yes, keep talking, I'm listening."

"Well, I wondered if there was a chance if you would be my accomplice in crime and keep Mrs. Logan busy for an hour or two some day soon? I could smuggle the girls to our house while she was visiting with you and make sure they were back home before their mother returned."

"What kind of plan d'ye have in mind?" Sean asked.

"Well now, Mrs. Logan is a seamstress and I wondered if your Kate might want a dress made for her?" Marcel suggested. "I would pay for the material and the sewing, and you'd have to invite Mrs. Logan to your farm to get Kate's measurements and go over the style of dress she wanted. That would keep her busy for two or three hours, enough time for the girls to come visit with Flo and Rosie."

"What a grand plan, Marcel," said Rosemary.

"Mrs. Logan would surely want the extra money for her new start in Dublin," said Marcel.

"It would take her at least a couple of hours te get te yer farm, Sean, visit wit' Kate for her measurements and return home," explained Marcel.

"How would she get up te the farm, Marcel?" Rosemary asked.

"Well, that's the thing." Marcel replied. "Sean would have to come to her house with pony and trap to pick her up, take her up to the farm, and then bring her home again. That way we would be sure she was with you, and the girls could come up to the coach house when she was gone," Marcel said. "Are you up for it, Sean? Please say yes for us? I can assure you God will be all forgiving, it's for a good cause."

"Well, Marcel, ye've put me in it this time haven't ye? But as ye say it's for a good cause, and God's already forgiven me for the lie. So, I'm up for it. When do ye want it te happen?"

"Next Sunday," Marcel replied.

"Okay, when I leave here today I'll go down the village te her house and ask her if she's interested, and if she is I'll make the arrangements te pick her up next week."

"That would be great, Sean, I owe you for this."

"I know ye do." The two friends shook hands. Sean realized that it was probably the only way that Flo would see her sisters before they left for Dublin and that her sisters would see baby Rosie. They all thought it was a grand plan.

"Such a shame that it has te be done like this but I understand why and agree wit' ye. It's the only way," said Rosemary.

Sean McGinty made the detour after leaving his friends that day, and Mrs. Logan was, as everyone thought, more than happy to earn a few extra shillings. She would expect Sean McGinty as arranged the following Sunday after chapel.

When the time arrived, Sean picked up Mrs. Logan and drove her to his farm to visit with his young sister Kate. Mrs. Logan took Kate's measurements and talked about what kind of dress Kate wanted. She had brought some patterns with her for Kate to look at, just to give the girl an idea. Marcel had managed to relay a message of the plan to Annemarie. She and her sisters would be ready to leave the house as soon as their mammy left the house with Sean. Once the pony and trap was out of sight, the girls hurried to the coach house to see Flo and baby Rosie. Marcel could not be seen in the village with the girls, or near Mrs. Logan's house. It was safer for the girls to make their own way to the coach house.

The plan worked wonderfully. Flo and baby Rosie were waiting and ready. Flo had made a cake and had plenty of milk for the girls to drink, knowing that they were always thirsty. Baby Rosie, dressed in her best pink outfit, looked like a little doll. Flo, delighted they had decided to take the chance and visit against their mammy's express orders thanked them for coming.

Annemarie, Teresa, and Rowena were all young ladies with a mind of their own. They knew that they were in trouble if their mammy found out about the visit, and so each pledged to keep it their secret until death.

The girls cooed and awed over little Rosie, each one taking her turn of holding the baby. They ate cake and drank the milk. They talked about everything that had happened and how their mammy was still angry with Flo and Marcel. They laughed together about some past memories, and then they shed a few tears when it was time to leave and get back home. They also had their chores to finish before their mammy got home; otherwise she might suspect something. They didn't want to draw any attention in that direction. Annemarie promised Flo that she would write, and when they had an address that Flo could reply to, she would send it. The girls hugged and kissed baby Rosie and Flo, and thanked Marcel with a kiss on his cheek for arranging the secret visit.

"We'll never forget ye and we'll be back one day," said Annemarie as she ushered the girls outside and down the village road again towards their house. They waved goodbye as they walked away, not knowing if they would see each other again.

"Hopefully no one'll see us. Just keep quiet, most people will be inside having supper," Annemarie said. "I hope the fire's still lit and I don't have te set a new one. Get straight into yer chores and get them finished before Mammy gets home, and not a word about this te anyone, d'ye hear me?"

"Yes," agreed the other two girls.

"Not a word te anyone. If mammy found out she'd whip the lot of us," Teresa said.

Flo--so thankful that Marcel had arranged the visit, sat quietly thinking and wondering why her mammy would do such a thing? Why was she so angry with her? She didn't really understand. She couldn't comprehend that her mammy was actually jealous of her and Marcel. They were in love--any mammy would be pleased about that surely? The date of the baby's birth wasn't that early to make people suspicious. No one had said anything untoward to Marcel, Rosemary, Sean, or Flo. So why would her mammy think something so bad? Why did she want to pick a fight wit them? She wondered if she would ever see her sisters again. *One day, perhaps, when they are old enough and have enough money to get back to her, perhaps one day*, she thought sadly.

Marcel could feel her sadness and came to her side. He put his arm around her shoulder and gave her a gentle hug. He made everything just that bit easier. At work the next day Marcel thanked Sean.

"It was a good thing that you did for me yesterday, and thank Kate for the secret, from both of us, if you would."

"Ah, it was not'ing. Kate was happy te be getting a new dress, so payment enough for the secret. There's not'ing more important than family and friends, Marcel. I'm surprised at Mrs. Logan not even wantin' te see the baby."

Kate's dress arrived two weeks later, fully finished and tailored to fit her perfectly. However, with the delivery of the dress came the news from Mrs. Logan that she and her family were leaving the following weekend for Dublin. She didn't ask after Flo or Marcel or baby Rosie. Even Kate thought it a bit shocking that Mrs. Logan wouldn't be interested in her first-born granddaughter.

Marcel decided not to tell Flo that they were leaving so soon. She had not mentioned her sisters to him since their visit. He believed she had come to realise there was nothing he could do to help the situation.

The weeks were turning quickly into spring. Rosie was growing fast and looked the picture of innocence. She was beginning to develop her own little features. It was plain to see that she had taken her mammy's fair hair and blue eyes. She did have her daddy's big round eyes and dark eyelashes that made her even prettier.

Flo was kept busy in the pub kitchen. Rosemary was happy that the takings were increasing and knew it was all due to Flo's cooking. Word continued to get around, and new people arrived more and more often.

It was almost March again, and Flo would be seventeen years of age. Marcel thought about giving her a birthday party and talked to Rosemary about the idea.

"Yes, that would be a grand surprise for her and we'd all enjoy the celebration. A break from all this work, ye know, and the long winter."

The monthly trip to Dublin was due in a few days. Marcel would arrange with Michael for a birthday cake. One not made by Flo, and some special party food that he could bring back with him. Rosemary and Marcel decided on some basic food supplies, and other requirements for a party: balloons, streamers, paper pull-crackers with little gifts inside, and of course, the cake.

It was Sunday afternoon after chapel when Flo and Marcel arrived back at the coach house. Marcel was aware that some friends had gathered inside and were waiting for them to return for the surprise party. Marcel opened the door for Flo and Rosie. Suddenly people appeared in front of her cheering. "Surprise! Surprise! Happy Birthday, Flo!" She delighted in the surprise. Marcel told her that it had been his idea to cheer her up after such a long, dark winter.

"Happy Birthday, *amore*." He leaned forward and kissed her on the cheek. Flo was shaking with excitement and dashed into the main room where everyone gathered waiting. She handed Rosie to Rosemary who removed her outdoor clothes. Rosemary loved fussing over Rosie.

As usual, Marcel had a roaring fire on the go and so the house was warm and cosy. The table, spread with all sorts of finger food, pastries, cold meats, cheese, little biscuits, fresh butter, cream, and various fruits and juices was colourful and looked delicious.

Michael did Marcel proud as always. They sang the "Happy Birthday" song to Flo and pulled the paper crackers, which went off with a bang and surprised everyone when a little gift fell out.

It was a lovely day, and everyone was having great fun until Kate spoke to Flo.

"Did ye know yer mammy went away te Dublin a few weeks ago? Did she come te see ye before she left?" Kate asked. Flo's heart dropped like lead, and she became quiet and sullen, as she replied.

"No, no, Kate, I didn't see her." Marcel tried to rescue the situation but it was no good--Kate had spoiled the day for Flo and everyone could see her sadness.

"Oh, I'm sorry Flo, I didn't mean te upset you. I just thought ye'd have seen her before she left. See the pretty dress she made for me, the one Marcel paid her for. This is it." Kate gave a twirl around for everyone to see the dress.

"Okay, enough of that talk, let it be now. Everybody, gather round, it's time to cut the birthday cake," Marcel announced. He brought it over to the table and lit the candles. They sang the birthday song again to Flo. She blew out all the candles while making her wish and everyone clapped and congratulated her. Flo cut the cake and handed them out. The afternoon went well--apart from the dampener Kate made.

"Wait till I get ye home me girl. I've words for the likes of you," Sean scolded Kate.

Sean and Rosemary talked at length about Ireland and the changes in the last few years. He mentioned more than once that his father was getting on in years and probably didn't have long to go.

"Oh my, is he sick?" she asked.

"No, no, he's just old." They laughed and carried on talking. It was the first time he had really spoken to her of his own accord, and it was as if they were old friends, easy, without any embarrassment or hesitation.

"Do ye remember our farm, Rosemary?"

"No, I haven't been up yer way in many years. How many acres have ye these days?"

"Too many. But not really, there's probably about two hundred acres in all, so it keeps us busy. Why don't I bring ye up te our place and give ye a bit of a tour?" Sean suggested.

"Why Sean McGinty, what would ye be wanting te do that for?"

"It would be a day out, we could have a picnic in the upper fields."

"Me only day off's a Sunday," said Rosemary casually as if it was nothing special.

"Fine then, I'll come pick ye up next Sunday after chapel and we'll take a ride together in the pony and trap. How's that? Ye can bring the picnic, and I'll do the tourin'," he replied quickly.

"That's grand," she said, in her usual controlled manner, but secretly thrilled at the idea. After all, it would be a day out, just the two of them, she thought, pleased with herself.

The party came to an end around four o'clock and people started to make their exit and return to their own homes. Flo enjoyed the surprise afternoon with the only depressing news coming from Kate, which Flo took as a genuine enquiry.

The young couple thanked their guests for coming as they saw the last person leave. They went back inside, cleared up the dishes, and made a cup of tea. They sat down by the fireside together and talked for a short while about their day, how lucky they were to have such good friends. It had been a lovely day they agreed, as they sat drinking their tea and feeling grateful for their lot.

The next day at work Flo asked Rosemary, "What was going on wit' ye and Sean yesterday?"

"What do ye mean?"

"Ye know. Ye were both talking for such a long time together. What were ye talking about for that long?"

"Not'ing in particular, just talking."

"I know there's something yer not telling me, Rosemary Sullivan. Come on now I've had te tell ye all me secrets."

"Well, that's because ye had them te tell and I didn't."

"But now ye have a secret, Rosemary Sullivan, and I want te know what it is."

The two girls laughed and Rosemary finally gave in.

"Sean's asked me out on a picnic next Sunday," she said. "He's going te pick me up in the pony and trap and take me for a tour of his fields. I'm te bring some picnic foods, and we can stop for a bite somewhere nice," Rosemary said smiling. Flo's mouth fell open wide in surprise.

"Finally, finally. He's asked ye out on a date!" exclaimed Flo. Again the girls laughed as Flo jumped up and down in excitement for her friend.

"Not really," said Rosemary a little coy. "He just offered me a look round his farm. It's years since I've been up there, and te make it a nice day out, I suggested a picnic," she smiled and winked at Flo.

Rosemary was quietly excited about the trip although no one would ever have guessed it. She wasn't a fussy type of female. Although, on this occasion she would look out some warm clothing, *something a little more pleasing to the eye for springtime*, she thought.

It was the end of March and still quite fresh outside although not cold this year. There would be wildflowers and daffodils and baby lambs in some of those fields. Even if Sean didn't have any of his own lambs on the farm, the idea of seeing them excited her. She loved nature, and this was one of the best times of the year to see it when everything was springing to life.

Sunday arrived, and Rosemary was ready waiting as arranged. Sean--dressed in his best Sunday suit, as he was coming from the chapel, looked very smart. Rosemary was too, and wore a lovely blue and white dress with a white cardigan and her shawl to keep her warm. Sean helped Rosemary up into the trap and climbed up himself. He took the reigns, and off they set.

"We'll begin our tour up at the top, that way we'll be coming down towards home again when evening falls. We can stop somewhere of yer choosing for a bite on the way down. There's a few nice spots wit' a grand view overlooking the farm."

Flo filled a hamper basket for the two of them. She made sweet biscuits, and there was a bit of cheese to have with them--delicious together. She made boiled eggs mashed with butter and salt, and some sliced ham and tomatoes, fresh bread, soft, chewy, and delicious. There was a flask of hot tea and freshly made scones wrapped in a tea towel, with a little butter and jam, and two red apples. That would keep them going on their trip.

Sean took her up to the high fields first. The view down over the farm was a panorama of delight and beauty. Rosemary impressed by the views breathed a sigh of contentment. The area seemed to span forever throwing up many different shades of green like a patchwork quilt. The air was fresh and clean and a sweet smell of wildflowers billowed around them in the gentle breeze. She took another deep breath as if enjoying the freshness. "It's absolutely grand," she said. "Do ye come up here often?" she asked.

"Yes, I like te come here from time te time. I enjoy the silence," he replied. "It's God's kingdom up here. This is what's it's all about," he said, holding out his arms to display the land below. "Behold the Garden of Eden and we are its caretakers," he sighed. In that moment Rosemary knew this was the man she wanted to marry. They gazed in silence enjoying the beautiful panorama. The occasional distant sound of animals broke their silence and reminded them of the farm below. He pointed out the areas they kept for grazing cattle, and what fields were for planting.

"No matter what the weather's doing, there's always work te be done on the land or to the land or for the land. Somet'ing te do every day of the year," he told her and continued talking. "Life's not easy on a farm, ye know? Ye don't get te choose what days ye want te work. If ye don't keep up wit' the work, the family pays the price in the winter months."

"Yes, I can see there's plenty te be done, but how beautiful it is, Sean," she said. It was a huge area, and Rosemary fully realised the amount of outdoor work involved. "It certainly seems te be ongoing wit' no holidays and no weekends off, like ordinary workin' folk get," she said.

"Aye, that's it, alright. Then there's the money side of t'ings te consider. Always having te keep the bulk for feed or crops or repairs or new equipment. So ye can't go spending yer profits until the year after when ye make more at the market, ye know?" he said. "Not like Marcel spends, no such luxuries when ye have a farm," said Sean.

"I know what ye mean, but I t'ink Marcel is very frugal in his ways, too. He only spends now and then and makes do wit' homemade."

"Aye, he's good that way wit' his hands, I agree."

"He is, indeed," Rosemary said.

Sean McGinty was known as tight with his cash. Old Mr. McGinty was the one who liked to spend it at times, having lived through the hard times. But Sean kept his cash safe, saving it for a rainy day. Rosemary was aware of what they said about Sean, but she was much the same way herself and understood his point of view.

The two young people had a lovely afternoon trekking around the countryside surrounded by the lush hues of green, provoking peace and a soothing tranquility. They relaxed and there was an easy flow of conversation between them. After about two hours, they finally stopped in a little dip in the field, to shelter from the wind. It was time to see what Flo packed for them to eat. Sean pulled up under the only tree for miles around, and Rosemary jumped down from the trap not realizing how high up she was. Sean lifted the hamper down on the grass, and Rosemary spread out the blanket that Flo had set aside for the trip.

Everything was perfect--the blanket was nice and thick so as not to let the dampness seep through. Rosemary opened the hamper knowing what was inside and began unwrapping the carefully packed lunch. She spread the tablecloth and placed everything on top of it and told Sean what they had.

They started with the eggs, ham, and tomatoes.

"Just like breakfast," Sean said. Then they had the biscuits and cheese with some hot tea followed by the scones with butter and jam.

"That was grand, worth the trip just for the food alone," he laughed.

She laughed along with him knowing Kate's handicap in the kitchen, but then she grew serious. "So Sean, tell me the truth now, what's this trip really about? I know ye te be a busy man wit' a lot of work te do. So, on a day when ye could be working, why would ye take the time te show me around yer place like this? What's it really about?" she asked.

Sean looked at Rosemary sombrely, took a deep breath and sighed.

"I cannot lie te ye, Rosemary, and so I'll be straight and give ye me honest answer. I like ye, Rosemary, and I'd like te get te know ye better," he said plainly. "We've known each other as friends for many years, but we don't really know each other, do we? I mean--I know yer honest and hard-working, yer Catholic like meself, and yer a good person. We might make a good match for a team. Like husband and wife one day?" he suggested dryly looking her straight in the eye. Rosemary remained composed and didn't flinch. She was always in control but this time her heart fluttered and she smiled inwardly as Sean continued.

"I t'ink it's only fair te give ye an opportunity te see the kind of lifestyle I have te offer ye. It's a hard life for a woman, and ye need te get te know me a little better than ye do. Ye never know. We might not like one another at all," he laughed, and she smiled along with him.

"Are ye asking that we get betrothed to each other?" she said.

"Oh no, not'ing official like that, not yet anyway," he sighed and took another deep breath.

"I'd just like it if ye would agree te go out wit' me now and then. We could go walking, or perhaps a trip te Dublin te see the shops. Just time together, te get te know each other better. That's all, at the moment anyway," Sean said. Rosemary was quiet for a few moments thinking. She had prayed that this day would come, and God had sent her an answer. Secretly, she was more than interested in Sean McGinty and did indeed view him as a prospective husband, one that would suit her very well. Rosemary's mind raced forward. She imagined herself living on the farm as Sean's wife. She pictured several children, laughing and playing in the yard in front of the farmhouse. Finally, she smiled at Sean.

"Sean McGinty," she replied confidently, "I'd be glad te accompany ye on any walks or visit Dublin on a day trip wit' ye. All wit' a purpose of getting to know ye better; indeed I would be glad to get te know ye." Sean's relief was obvious, and so the two of them shook hands on the deal and laughed together about it.

"We'll keep this our business for the moment," Sean said.

"Of course, but I'll have to tell Flo something. She's good wit' a secret though--I'll trust her wit' this one."

"Yes, I expected as much. You two girls seem te know everyt'ing about each other." Sean smiled knowingly and she smiled back at him and nodded in agreement.

They spent the next while talking about the farm and the way of life for a woman. It wasn't an easy life by any means. The days could often be long and lonely, while the men were out in the fields working. Usually, the wife had a few smaller chores to do apart from the cooking and cleaning, which would take up most of her day.

The wife would generally take care of the chickens, feed them morning and night, keep their hutch clean and safe so other animals couldn't get into it. If there were a sick animal, a calf perhaps, she would be expected to care for it as best she could to keep it alive.

It was interesting for Rosemary to hear since she was not brought up on a farm. Her daddy had a small holding, only enough to grow their own vegetables, and some to sell at the market, perhaps an acre or so. Nothing this big and so it was a completely different life altogether.

She liked Sean McGinty; he seemed a caring person, hardworking, and careful with his money. She thought he would make a good father and provider for their children. Her only hesitation was Mr. McGinty Senior. He was nice enough but a bit harsh with his words; not caring who he embarrassed.

Rosemary was more sensitive than she appeared, and she could see the two of them clashing in time. However, she thought, if it ever happened, it was years away. Sean didn't make decisions quickly, and there would be that "getting to know you better" timeline. So she was quite happy with the arrangement thus far.

"I wonder," she said. "When we go te Dublin on our day trip, would ye show me where the bicycles are for sale?"

"Are you still after a bicycle?" he said. "I thought ye had decided not te bother wit' that since ye moved into the pub?"

"No, I'd still like te have one," she replied.

"My, my, when would ye ever have the time te enjoy it? Sure yer working most days as it is? Never let it be said I didn't try. I'll find out about it on our next trip te the city, prices and all and let ye know," he said firmly. Rosemary took a deep breath of satisfaction.

"Right ye are, and I'll be looking forward te hearing about that."

It was getting late in the day, and they decided to pack up and head back toward the pub. By the time they got there, it would be dark, and Sean still had to feed the animals. They made haste and started back down the hill. They had both enjoyed their time alone, and Rosemary felt a sense of contentment as they drove home.

The next day, of course, Flo was waiting.

"Well now, what was it all about? Tell all or I shall go on and on about it all day," she continued. Rosemary gave a deep sigh and smiled. First of all she made Flo swear to secrecy and promise, never to repeat what she was about to tell her to anyone. Flo promised. Rosemary began to tell her story of the day before with Sean McGinty and his pony and trap trip around the farmlands. Flo excited and delighted for her friend waited to hear everything.

"At last, he's come out of his shell, Rosemary. Sean McGinty finally came forward wit' a proposition for ye, my friend. What grand news, Rosemary."

This union could take years, Flo thought. *At least he's had the courage te ask Rosemary officially. That's a first step. Perhaps we can find a way te speed events up? Some men in these parts don't marry until they're in their forties. So far, this has been a very eventful month. I wonder what could happen next?* she mused. She would talk with Marcel and see if he could find a way to bring these two young people together more quickly. She knew that if Rosemary had to wait for Sean, the courtship could take years, and Flo wasn't waiting that long.

11

Rosemary Sullivan is 24 Years Old, 1900

It was on New Year's Eve in 1899 when Rosemary's life changed forever. Sean came in to celebrate the night with the villagers. After a couple of drinks, along with the celebration mood rising and some Dutch courage, he couldn't wait any longer.

"Rosemary, I can't hold back any longer, or we'll both be old. Will ye agree te marry me now and not wait any longer?"

"Oh, my, Sean. What's come over ye? Of course I will," she replied. Her face was beaming with love and delight as Sean announced the news to everyone.

"Rosemary's just agreed te marry me. We'll wed this coming spring. Drinks for everyone." There were cheers all 'round. The pub filled with excitement for Rosemary. However, had it not been for the cajoling and Marcel clapping and coaxing, she might never have had that first kiss from Sean McGinty. Indeed, it took the crowd clapping and shouting in unison.

"Kiss, kiss, kiss, kiss." Finally, Sean leaned over the bar and kissed her on the cheek.

"Boo!" they shouted and called out for more. They weren't satisfied with that and continued shouting and booing at him when Marcel called out to Sean.

"Give her a proper kiss on the mouth, you know? That was terrible for an engagement kiss."

"Aye, we want te see ye kissing her proper. That was a terrible excuse for a kiss," the crowd mocked.

They all started clapping again and shouting out loud for their proper kiss.

"Lips, lips, lips, lips."

"You can't win this one, Sean," Marcel said.

"No, I think yer right, Marcel," and like the gentleman he was, Sean bravely walked around the bar and pulled Rosemary into his arms and kissed her passionately on the mouth for the longest time.

"Oh, my, Sean McGinty. What's come over ye?" she said again. Rosemary embarrassed at first, blushed. It was her first kiss from him, or indeed any man. She was quietly enthralled being in the limelight but controlled her emotions. The crowds were ecstatic with joy for Rosemary, and she was happy being kissed in full view for everyone to witness. What a grand night it was, and a night full of fun and joviality followed. When the clock struck midnight everyone gave out a loud cry of delight. Sean leaned over the bar and kissed her again, but this time it was more intimate between them.

"Happy New Year, Rosemary. I hope we have lots of children and a long and happy life together."

"Happy New Year, Sean, and I wish for the same."

The New Year celebration continued in the pub until the last person went home at one o'clock in the morning. It was a long night for Rosemary and Flo but a very enjoyable one. Rosemary's heart was full of gladness and joy. She was ready as she would ever be to marry and become the wife and mother she dreamed of being. Little Rosie would be five years of age and Rosemary's flower girl at the wedding.

"Oh, such excitement, Rosemary. I can make Rosie a lovely little white dress and the wedding party will look grand. What'll ye do for a gown for yerself?" asked Flo.

"I'm not sure yet. Me mammy's wedding gown is beautiful and I'm sure it would fit me, and I could do something, te make it special for me own day."

"I might suggest something that could make life easier for us after we're married," said Sean.

"Oh," said Rosemary. "What's that?"

"Well," said Sean. "Why not teach Kate the pub trade? She can move into the house wit' ye before the weddin'? That way she'll be able te work wit' Flo when we go on our honeymoon, and she can live there after the weddin'. We can have the bedroom at the farm te ourselves, except for Daddy, and Kate can stay on at the pub house."

"What a grand idea, Sean, how would Kate take te it?" Rosemary asked.

"Why, she'd love the idea of getting away from the farm and having her own room, of course she would. I can come down here te eat at night after the works finished and bring Daddy wit' me. I could buy some bread te take home te see us over for the morning," Sean said. "What d'ye t'ink?" he finished and waited for her response.

"It's a grand idea, Sean," said Rosemary. "When can she start?"

"Tomorrow. I'll bring her down first t'ing and she can get settled into the routine."

So, Kate moved into the pub with Rosemary before the wedding. As Sean predicted, she loved having her own room and learning the work. She worked well with Rosemary and learned quickly. Rosemary had the time she needed to make changes to her mammy's wedding gown and make it special for her big day.

"I'm glad ye came, Kate. Otherwise, I wouldn't be having this nice gown or the time te make the changes it needs," Rosemary told her thankfully. "Me mammy wore this on her weddin' day, and she's so proud that I wanted to wear it, too. I mean it te look good on me, just wait and see the changes I make te it," she said excitedly.

"I love the new arrangement away from the farm and that life," Kate admitted. "I'm not the world's best cook and I don't care if I never saw another pot or stove again," they laughed together. Rosemary understood Kate's need for freedom and they got on well together. Kate was learning as much as she could in the short time available. She wanted to impress enough to keep her place at the pub after the wedding was over, and everyone was back to their normal work duties.

The wedding plans made, and everything arranged, when an inexplicable event shocked everyone. Mr. McGinty Senior suddenly took ill and died the evening before the wedding. Kate and Sean were both devastated, but Sean was adamant that the marriage should continue.

"I'm not putting the wedding off. We'll just have te work around it," he told everyone.

They took Mr. McGinty's body to the undertakers behind the chapel, and the funeral set for five days after the wedding, not the usual three days. Sean knew that there would be a large crowd attending his father's funeral. Mr. McGinty was well liked and respected all around the area.

"What a shocking t'ing te happen, and how unlucky for Sean and Rosemary," people said.

"Sean's right te go on wit' the wedding, though. His daddy would want it." Most people agreed and gave their support to Sean and Rosemary.

"Ye know, Flo, I'm secretly relieved that it happened this way. I didn't much like the idea of sharing his house wit' him, and I liked it even less that he would share the only bedroom wit' us," she confessed to her friend.

"I understand completely," Flo said. "Marcel and I were so lucky te have our little place at the coach house. We've been really spoiled, and I'm grateful for our privacy." For Rosemary, it was a blessing that God heard her fears and her prayers. Sean was thinking along the same lines, it certainly was a blessing is disguise for them.

Rosemary managed to finish her gown and make the changes she wanted. It was a lovely dress; plain white satin with long slim sleeves and four round pearl buttons at the wrist. The dress fitted perfectly and showed off her long, slender figure. It had a simple round neck edged with pearls that encrusted the front of the bodice in a starburst design. There was a narrow belt at the waist made from pearls and the buckle itself covered in pearls. Flo had suggested the belt to match the bodice and Rosemary made it. She was a good seamstress. The skirt was straight and fitted over the hips, flaring slightly at the bottom and edged with three rows of pearls. Everyone agreed, although very simple in design, it was a beautiful gown and she looked stunning in it. Rosemary wore her hair up as she usually did and covered it with a shoulder length veil, which she pinned in place with pearl hairgrips.

The congregation had shown up in large numbers. Rosemary and Sean were both known far and wide, and everyone wanted to witness their marriage. Rosemary's family were all inside the chapel waiting for her to arrive. People crowded the chapel grounds and all around waiting to see the couple.

She looked lovely as she walked down the aisle towards Sean, dressed in his new suit and waiting patiently at the altar. The organ played "The Wedding March" and little Rosie in her pretty white dress followed behind as instructed.

"My, yer looking beautiful, Rosemary," Sean said.

"Thank ye," she replied. "Ye look nice yerself."

It was a lovely wedding, they exchanged vows and Sean proudly placed the gold wedding band on her finger. When the priest announced them man and wife, they kissed tenderly for all to witness. Rosemary was finally satisfied that she married the man she wanted, as she took his arm and proudly walked out of the chapel with Sean.

Of course, the group returned to the pub for celebrations afterwards. Flo had arranged all the food and catering requirements for the couple and their guests. She toiled long and carefully over the wedding cake, a very special undertaking for her. She loved doing it for her friends. The evening's celebration went like a charm and the pub was open to everyone. Finally, the couple had to leave. They were going to Dublin for their honeymoon. Just three days away and then back home for the funeral and a new life. Marcel was left in charge of the running of the farm, but Sean had arranged with a neighbouring farmer to look in and help with whatever he needed. Kate did a grand job, and it seemed to Rosemary that God was listening to her and answering all her prayers. She just couldn't come to understand how a young newly married couple could share a bedroom with the rest of the family. She would be mortified had Mr. McGinty Senior been sleeping in the same room with them listening to their every move. Rosemary prayed.

Heavenly Father,

How embarrassing it might have been, and I thank ye, Father, for listening te me fears. Not that I wanted it te happen te Mr. McGinty but this way, it was sudden and quick, indeed a blessing. Thank ye, Father, for answering me prayers. I'll always be grateful for yer help; however ye see fit te make t'ings happen. Thank ye, thank ye, indeed. Amen.

"We'll be back in time for the funeral. See you all then and thank ye for taking care of everything while we're gone," Sean said.

"Well ye know yer welcome. Marcel and I would do anyt'ing for the two of ye's," Flo said.

"Have a grand time and don't worry about the place. See you when you get back," Marcel assured the couple as everyone waved them off.

It was as well that Rosemary and Sean understood each other the way they did. They were both of the same cut: duty first and always first, pleasure only after everything else. Rosemary, excited and nervous at the prospects of her first night with Sean, as any young virgin would be--hoped he wouldn't be disappointed in her. She would try to please him; it was her duty to do so.

They arrived at their hotel late in the evening, as expected. They were both drained after such a long trip on the pony and trap, which was uncomfortable at best. Sean carried their baggage up the stairs to the room where, waiting for them, was a bottle of sparkling white wine and some sandwiches, compliments of the management. They sat down together, Sean immediately taking his fill of the sandwiches.

"That was decent of them, they must have known we'd be starving," he said.

"Yes, it was very thoughtful of them," she replied. Sean either overlooked the wine or just plain ignored it, but he didn't open it. Rosemary ate quietly as she too was hungry. Sean finished eating and undressed, being careful to hang his best clothes up properly on a hanger and place them inside the wardrobe. He undressed to his long underwear and went to the bathroom to wash. He returned to the bedroom and got straight into the bed. Rosemary sat for a moment still eating her sandwich.

"Come on Rosemary, we got te get some sleep tonight. I'm exhausted, aren't ye?"

"Oh, I'll be right there."

She hurried to the bathroom where she undressed and changed into her new white flannel nightgown with the lace ribbon around the neck and open down the front to her breasts. She returned to the bedroom and silently slipped into the bed beside Sean. They lay side-by-side for a few seconds not speaking when Sean, without warning, briskly turned and moved on top of her. He roughly jerked her nightgown up and forced his hand between her legs to make a space. He pushed himself into her body. Rosemary gasped in shock but remained silent--surprised there had been no warning, no foreplay of any kind, and a little disappointed. His face was at the side of her head, his arms resting on either side of the pillow. He was breathing heavily into her ear, which annoyed her. He pressed himself up and down, penetrating her awkwardly and painfully at first. Then just as the pain began to subside it was all over, and he withdrew from her body and moved back to his place on the bed.

"Thank ye, Rosemary," Sean said. "Goodnight now," and he switched off the sidelight and went to sleep.

"Goodnight, Sean," she replied quietly.

Rosemary lay still for a moment staring at the ceiling, somewhat bewildered.

Was that it? she thought disappointed. *All this time waiting, and it was nothing like Flo described at all. No kissing, and cuddling or touching like she said.* She felt disappointed but didn't complain and fell asleep immediately.

Sean was not a demonstrative person, not prone to show his emotions like Marcel, and Rosemary knew that. She knew the man she married was not like Marcel in any way, not a romantic at all. He was a farmer's son whose job it was to take the bull to the cow and confirm proper insertion to produce a calf the next spring. That was the way of life on a farm, nature's way. That was her man, her farmer's son, and that was what she prayed to God for, and exactly what she got.

She chastised herself--she hadn't asked for romance at any time throughout her prayers. God listened and replied to her request in detail. He didn't include romance because she didn't ask for it. She told herself it was okay, she wasn't really a romantic and vowed never to compare Sean and Marcel again. They were different types of people. Rosemary had married a reliable, straightforward, no-nonsense, hard-working Irish farmer, and she was proud of that. She determined that they would have lots of children, and she would be loved and cuddled by them. How foolish she had been to listen to Flo's romantic fantasies. She understood her man now and was glad to accept his down-to-earth ways. These were the rules of married life for Sean and Rosemary, and they were normal to her. She understood him and knew her duty as a wife--and mother she hoped to become.

The young couple toured Dublin sightseeing--window-shopping was exciting. They ate at different little places of interest and enjoyed the variety of food. They had a wonderful time together and laughed and joked about some of the things they saw.

"I've never been out of the village this far before now. There's so much te see and so much movement going on," said Rosemary.

"I come here every month te the market, as you know, but I never go sightseeing or shopping outside the market. It's quite the eye-opener for me, too. I'm glad we're seeing it together," he smiled at her. "Let's take the tram and sit on top. We can see everywhere around us from up there," Sean suggested.

"A grand idea, there's so many shops and different t'ings te see," she said excitedly.

Sean realised he had a new friend and partner; that's how he viewed his situation. It was a different concept for him; he was now part of a couple. There were two of them and not just him. Until now he had his daddy's companionship. Mr. McGinty Senior was in charge and told him what to do, when to do it, and guided him in most of the work. Now his daddy was gone, and Sean knew it was his time to step up and take the lead to protect his own family.

He was happily content with Rosemary and knew he made a good choice for a wife. She was strong enough to bear children, which he wanted, and independent enough to cope with life at the farm. He admired the way she handled the pub life. She just walked right in there and took over from Jimmy. That was a big challenge for a young girl. He appreciated her courage and the way she earned the respect of the village people, and himself, too. He was not openly affectionate towards Rosemary, but he would protect her under all circumstances, from now until death; she was his wife.

His opinion of Marcel wasn't important in the scheme of things. As long as he could pull his weight with the work, that's what mattered to Sean. So, when he first saw the speed that Marcel worked, he realised how lucky they were to have him and quickly changed his mind. Marcel attacked his work with sheer determination to finish as much as possible. Sean valued his strength and stamina and saw for himself, that Marcel would just keep going, even when Sean could go no longer. He knew he could rely on him around the farm, and had slowly warmed to him over the years. The two had become good friends--but he would always be a foreigner. He knew that his new wife's friendship with Flo was important, and he would respect that for Rosemary's sake.

The second night in bed was exactly the same as the first night. It seemed to Rosemary that Sean viewed sex as another chore, not as a pleasure at all. It was simply another task to complete before he could go to sleep. There was no warm up, no foreplay, and no romance whatsoever. It was strictly the last task of the day. He didn't seem to get any pleasure from it. If he did, she never knew, and it was over and quickly and efficiently.

"Thank ye, Rosemary. Goodnight now," then he settled into his place on the bed and switched off the light.

She lay there afterwards staring up at the ceiling. *Is this enough to get me a baby?* She desperately wanted one. She would endure just about anything to have a baby, and if this was how it was, then that was fine with her. Rosemary put romance out of her head, telling herself again that it wasn't important. That was Flo's fantasy world, and not her own. She felt lucky being married, and knew that soon she would also be a mother. She prayed every night and morning for a baby. Sean completed his conjugal duties every night without fail. It took him a matter of minutes, and it seemed to her that this would be their nightly routine before going to sleep.

The honeymoon was over all too soon. The young couple returned to the village for the funeral of Mr. McGinty Senior. A large crowd gathered at the chapel--he was known throughout the county to many people.

Mr. McGinty was eighty-four years of age when he passed. He lived through the troubled times in Ireland and had managed to survive it all with his family intact. Some said he had been lucky in life. His farm always managed, somehow, to provide food for his family. Others took much longer to recover from the diseased soil that the blight left in its wake.

Old Mr. McGinty had been smart. He was a young man, not long married with a young wife and small baby of his own. He lived with his mammy and daddy on the farm, and all his broth-ers. They all shared the only bedroom in the house, each to their own cot. At least the young couple had been given a far corner of the room away from the boys, with the parents at the other end. There was a small space between cots, but there was little privacy for any of them.

He heard talk of the soldiers coming to raid the farms in their area for their food and livestock. He knew they would take every-thing they had and leave them with nothing to eat. Unknown to his father, Fin, Sean dug the deepest hole in the ground at the back of his barn, not inside the barn, where some might have suspected. It was outside on the other side of the wall up at the back of the barn. No one would ever think to look there for anything. It was on a small hill overlooking the fields and not comfortable to walk on, as the ground was uneven. He removed a plank of timber from the rear wall so that he could stand inside the barn and dig outside on the other side. He dug deep. He spent days and days digging, but no one knew or became suspicious. They couldn't see where he was or what he was doing. Old Mr. McGinty was wise and planned well for his family's survival. He lined the base and the sides with timber and covered it with tin lining to help protect the food from the wet soil. It would rot in the dampness if he didn't line it properly. It was dry to store vegetables. He painstakingly placed each piece of wood in perfect position to ensure that no water could seep through and spoil the produce. He inserted a large box made of timber and again lined it with tin. He attached ropes to each side with a bar across the top to use as a pulley to raise the box up and down. It was strong enough to hold a heavy weight. He could then access the produce and lower the box back down into the hole again. The deeper the hole, the colder it was, and the longer the supplies would stay fresh.

When he finished, he stashed a variety of grains, oats, and vegetables, bagged and boxed separately, into the hole. He made a wooden lid fit into the hole in the ground some three or four inches down. He covered the lid with soil and grass sods to level it with the ground on top. He finished it off with scattered hay over the top. It blended in with the surrounding area. He marked the slat of timber up high so that he would know where the hole was. It looked no different from the other wood, but he knew the mark.

A few days after he had finished and after the first heavy rain, he walked around to see if the soil had sunk, as it should, and scattered more grass sods on the top. When the soldiers came, they took everything from his father's fields. They took all his livestock, even the smallest newborn chicks. They led his prize bull away, but they didn't find his underground cellar, or his food supply.

The soldiers thought they had covered every part of the farm, but his underground cellar was in a place that no one could have thought to look. He had enough to see his family through the coming winter and more if needed. How long they had to last, he didn't know, and he wasn't aware that the famine was ahead of them.

Mr. McGinty's frugal ways saved his family from starvation. When the famine hit and the fields succumbed to disease, he had them cleared completely. Both himself and his father and brothers were out in the fields every day digging, turning the soil, to let the fresh air in, irrigating and planting nothing that year, or the following year, either. Three years later they could re-seed. By that time, his stocks had dwindled to almost nothing, and they were surviving on oats and onion soup. But not one member of his family had died.

There was no meat available anywhere, not even in the city. A scrawny rabbit was occasionally caught and made into a stew that fed the entire family. Thousands died. Others left for America on the death ships. People fell dead in the city streets, towns, and villages, dying from starvation. Bodies were found lying at the side of the roads all through the country. The body carts went around all day picking up corpses and taking them to the communal cemetery--mass graves, mostly without identification.

The famine was widespread through all of Ireland. People from all around the country flocked to the cities looking for food. Most of them ended up in the workhouses surviving on oats and water. In some cases, it was enough to keep them alive, in others, it wasn't. The workhouses were overflowing, and the death rate, high every week.

Sean McGinty Senior was well-respected by all who knew him. The knowledge of his secret underground cellar died with him. His own father never asked him where his hideout was, although he knew his son must have one, he never asked. Sometimes the food came out frozen--the hole was so deep. He would have to hide it until it thawed. Then he would give it to his wife to cook. Not even she knew about the hole in the ground. They were never to speak about the food their father supplied, fearing where it came from. They were all better off not knowing anything.

Time passed and better days finally came; the soil recovered, and crops began to grow again. Old man McGinty forgot about his hideout behind the barn. His secret cellar was forgotten, and the next generation knew nothing about its existence.

Rosemary, Kate, and Flo had prepared for the number of people coming to the pub after the funeral. In the bar was another group of people, new to the area, who just happened in that very day of the funeral.

"What good food yer servin' here. Ye can tell yer cook I said so, and we all enjoyed it," said the lady.

"Is it always this busy in here?" asked the gentleman.

"Not quite this busy, sir," Rosemary replied. "Today's special, we're catering for a local funeral. We do a good trade though--our cook is well-known for her food and she's earned quite a reputation, people come from all around te eat here," she informed them.

"Yes, the food is excellent, I must admit. It's excellent, very good indeed."

The gentleman looked well dressed and from the city, Rosemary thought. There was a lady and three young teenage boys sitting at the table with him. They were all dressed in fashionable clothes, like Rosemary had recently seen in Dublin.

"What brings ye te these parts today?" she asked the lady.

"Oh, just sightseeing. A day away from the city, ye know," she replied pleasantly.

As it was a Saturday, most people had less work to do, which meant they could stay on longer than the usual time attended at a funeral. People engaged in quiet conversation about Mr. McGinty Senior, paying their respects, drinking tea and soft drinks only--no alcohol for those attending the funeral.

The pub looked cheerful and busy, and this impressed the newcomers. When they took their leave, the gentleman made his way to the bar where Rosemary was working.

"Goodbye now, young lady, and thank ye for yer services and grand food. Don't forget to tell the cook I said so."

"Yer most welcome," replied Rosemary. "Come and see us again."

"We will, we certainly will do that," replied the gentleman and the group left.

"Well, what a nice young family--how very polite and well-mannered they were," Rosemary said. She turned back to her work and gave the family no further thought.

It was a few weeks later when she received a letter from Jimmy's solicitor in Dublin to say that a buyer had come forward and made a very decent offer on the pub. He wanted to know when it was convenient to bring them to the village to view the business and its living accommodation. The news couldn't have come at a better time for her. She was planning on being pregnant soon and wanted to spend her time at home, and not here in the pub. Delighted, Rosemary wrote back to the solicitor immediately.

Dear Sir,

You are most welcome to attend next Wednesday.

I will be expecting you and your party and look forward to meeting you all then.

Yours,
Rosemary Sullivan-McGinty.

Kate and Rosemary made several walks around the house to ensure everything was clean and in order for a viewing customer. They didn't want anything to go wrong that would put the sale off. They were keen to get the place sold and get on with their own lives. Jimmy would be delighted to see the end of the place and finalise the sale. She remembered that Jimmy had offered her whatever furniture she wanted to keep and so with this in mind she had suggested several pieces to Sean.

"What d'ye t'ink, Sean?" Rosemary asked him. "Mary had some fine t'ings, and I've been given permission te take everyt'ing if I want."

This was more good news. The farmhouse didn't have a lot of furniture, just cots with dried-grass mattresses and a rod curtain for privacy. The cots were old and worn, and the bed linen had seen better days, too. Now they could have a real bed with a proper mattress and that pleased Rosemary. She had loved her big bed at the pub; it was so comfortable and modern.

Wednesday arrived--the solicitor brought Mr. and Mrs. Duggan to view the living accommodation at the pub.

"My goodness, I remember ye coming just a few weeks ago, it was the day of me father-in-law's funeral," said Rosemary.

"We were so impressed wit' the place, and the food was grand. At the time we were looking for a business and yer place felt good, we liked it," said the lady.

Rosemary showed them the upstairs rooms. There were four bedrooms in all and one proper full bathroom not long converted by Jimmy for his Mary. There was a large living room, a smaller kitchen, and a separate dining room. Rosemary spent most of her time in the kitchen; it was the warmest room in the house. Mary used to do the same thing. The kitchen was well organised and roomy enough to host a small dining table and four chairs, as well as two easy chairs; one on either side of the fireplace.

"I believe you are to inherit all the furniture," the solicitor said.

"Only the items that I would like," she replied.

"Of course, you are right, but if you wanted, you could take everything. Mr. and Mrs. Duggan have furniture," he advised.

Rosemary knew from his attitude that the solicitor wanted to avoid the trouble of shipping and selling the furniture at the auction rooms in Dublin. It would only bring a small amount of money, and hardly worth the trouble to him.

"I'll have te talk te me husband about it first then," said Rosemary.

The viewing complete, Rosemary took the solicitor and his party back down into the public house area.

"It's just the one large room for the main part. There's a smaller glassed area to create a ladies parlour, away from the men in the public bar. Most people usually sit in this central area. The smaller room is seldom used, but it's good te have if a party wants some privacy, ye know?" Then they took a walk around the back yard and coach house area outside.

"This is where our cook and her husband live. He remodelled the place for their comfort and does any work I need around the property in return. He also tends the vegetable garden. That was the arrangement Jimmy made before he left for America."

"Oh, that's somet'ing we'll have te take under consideration. I'm not sure I want a tenant living so close te me own house," said Mr. Duggan. "Yes, somet'ing te t'ink about. I may want that area for meself te store me automobile. I have three lads of me own who are able te keep the vegetable garden as required; it's one of the reasons that we're relocating te the country," said Mr. Duggan.

"Oh, I wasn't aware of that," said Rosemary. They walked back around to the front of the public house and viewed it from the street.

"Yes, I like what I see. I t'ink it would work well for me family. We'll have te consider the coach house and tenant situation, though," he said again.

"Well thank you, Mrs. McGinty you have been very helpful," said the solicitor. "I'll be in touch with you again should an offer come through. It will take some time, though, as I have to contact the owner in America."

"Will we be given time te make our own arrangements after the sale if it goes through?" Rosemary asked.

"Oh, certainly, there will be quite a few months between the beginning and the end of the process. Everyone involved will get ample opportunity to make their plans work in a timely fashion," he advised.

Rosemary knew that Marcel would be annoyed; he had done so much work to the coach house. Rosemary had never seen his anger and didn't really want to. She had a feeling that with his Italian temperament there also came a hot temper. She thought better to tell him right away that they might lose the coach house.

"Ye might have te look for digs elsewhere if they want the coach house back," she said. "He says he has an automobile and needs a place te keep it," she continued.

"I'm sure when he sees what I've done here, he'll be agreeable to let us stay at least until we find something suitable," said Marcel not showing any real concern. "I might even offer to pay a rent to keep the place on. We'll see when the time comes," he said.

The letter finally arrived from the solicitor in June, advising that Jimmy agreed to the sale, and informing Rosemary that she could remove any of the furniture that she might want. Sean and Rosemary discussed the subject before the letter arrived.

"We should take everything, Rosemary. It'll give us a chance te make the house ours wit' new furniture, and who knows how long it'll take us te replace all the old pieces that're falling apart," Sean said. "It would give our home a facelift. Yes," he continued, "I t'ink we should just take it all. I'm sure we'll use it in time, and very grateful te have it, thanks te Jimmy," he said to Rosemary.

"Oh, Sean, I'm so glad ye feel that way. I wanted te take everyt'ing, too, but I thought it might be greedy of me," she replied. "I'm glad ye t'ink the place needs a facelift, and everyt'ing'll be cherished and put te good use. I don't feel so awful now for wanting it all," Rosemary said with a smile.

"Not at all. Mary'll be happy te know we're looking after her t'ings," replied Sean confidently.

Sean arranged to have the furniture moved up to the farmhouse. Rosemary and Kate would have to come and go from the farmhouse to the pub for the last few weeks before the new owners moved in. Rosemary couldn't contain herself, she was so excited when the furniture arrived at the farm and Sean and Marcel started bringing it in.

"Where d'ye want this big bed?" Sean asked her.

"Up at the far end of the room wit' the head against the wall and the feet pointing into the rest of the room," she said.

"Right, let's get te it." The two men assembled the bed together, and finally carried in the heavy mattress. Once on the bed, Rosemary set to making it up with its beautiful covers and quilt.

"Look at the size of this big bed, Sean," she said as she sat on the bed. "Oh, it's so comfortable." She bounced up and down like a child. "Try it," she said giggling and looked over to Sean. "It certainly might make my job easier wit' all that bouncing," replied Sean. Rosemary blushed and got up from the bed modestly. "I'm just joking wit' ye," he said. "It certainly looks very comfortable."

"Ye'll have te move the curtain rod though," she said. "Kate's bed can go over there on the opposite side of the room, far away from us; feet pointing towards us," she laughed aloud.

"Ah, there's reason enough for that laugh," Sean smiled as he reached up to unscrew the hooks. Another two beds were also placed in the big room, and there was plenty of room for them all. Sean repositioned the hooks in the ceiling to accommodate the curtain rods, including their own.

"Well now, Sean, that was a clever idea, wit' the curtain there. It's as if we have a whole room te ourselves. How grand " said Rosemary, excitedly.

"Yes," he replied. "I thought I'd just put them side-by-side like this; it gives us almost half the room te ourselves." He smiled over at her.

Each bed had its own bedding stored in a blanket box at the bottom of the bed. There was a chest of five drawers and a dressing table with a large round mirror. Rosemary wanted that for herself. Sean positioned the dressing table at their end of the room with the back to the wall and the front facing their bed--stool in front of it.

"Will this do here for ye?" he asked her.

"Perfect," she replied. "I love it, me own dresser. I'll be able te sit and brush me hair here." He placed the double wardrobe against the opposite wall facing the side of the bed. That made room for the easy chair in the corner and the big blanket box next to the chair. The box was full to the brim with sheets, coverlets, and that always-needed rubber sheet for birthing babies. The chest of drawers stood in the central part of the room, shared by all--a drawer for each, she thought? Then Sean placed another mirror on a stand on top of the dresser.

"This is nice for the brood." He smiled approvingly, and Rosemary nodded in agreement.

"Where do you want these two little end tables; I think they go with the big bed?" Marcel asked.

"Over here," she replied, "one at each side, please," she said smiling. "Now the room is complete. I'll just make up these other beds later and it's done. Thank ye so much, Marcel. I'm sure it was much easier wit' ye helping Sean."

"My pleasure," he replied.

The main room inherited Mary and Jimmy's dining room table with six well-upholstered chairs, together with the sideboard that matched the set. Mary stored her best dinner service and her china tea set in it. Everything fitted into the room perfectly. There were another two easy chairs. Rosemary placed one on either side of the black iron stove. That provided a cosy place to take their boots off when coming into the house. There was a variety of carpets and side tables, and Rosemary, surprised to find Jimmy had left the family silver along with Mary's best cutlery service, felt honoured, knowing it takes a lifetime to collect such things.

"I don't understand why he didn't take all this stuff wit' him te America for his boys?" she said, rearranging her new dresser.

"Perhaps he didn't see the purpose of carrying such a heavy load all the way to the other side of the world," Sean said as he worked on.

"Or, perhaps he intended Rosemary te have it all, for being so kind te him when Mary died?" Kate said.

"Well, I love it all and I'll take good care of it and use it well over the years te come. It just seems sad that their own boys didn't inherit it," Rosemary said.

"I'm sure the boys don't care for that sort of t'ing anyway. Wit' their new life in America they'll want all the new-style American t'ings," said Sean.

"I t'ink yer right, Sean. I'm so very glad te inherit it all; proper knives, forks, spoons of three sizes, and other accoutrements, which I'm not sure what for," she said.

Rosemary placed carpets in the bedroom, one inside the front door and one under the dining room furniture. Altogether, the farmhouse had taken on a completely new look, which pleased her.

"Now it feels like a new home and a fresh start for us," she said with a smile. Rosemary looked around her new house with pride and satisfaction--just what she was praying for.

"We'd best get back te the pub and do a last check, just te make sure everyt'ing's in order for the morning," she said with a sigh. Their last night at the pub turned into a double celebration.

"Rosemary, I have te tell ye me good news," announced Flo. "I'm expecting again, another baby due in December."

"That's wonderful news, Flo, congratulations," said Rosemary.

"Perhaps this time we'll have a little boy as a brother for Rosie," Marcel said. "The only problem might be if Mr. Duggan decides that he wants us out of the coach house," he continued. "We'll be hard pushed to find a place in the village where we have as much privacy and quietness as we get here. Let's wait and see they might let us stay until after the baby's born," said Marcel.

"Yes, they might do that," agreed Rosemary.

Marcel was also concerned that they would have to start paying rent, something that until now they had not done. He had plenty of money saved. He and Flo were not a spending couple, only occasionally on a few luxuries over the years. He always replaced what he spent, and of course he had his mama's pouch money too; something he rarely touched, and again always replaced. He would start looking immediately for new accommodation. He didn't want Flo worrying about such a little thing. He would take care of it, as he always did.

"It'll be sad te leave this place," said Flo. "I have such wonderful memories here, in the pub. It's where I got me first job cooking; where I met Marcel, and of course, our home here at the coach house," she recalled. "Living and working here's been a grand experience for me, a beautiful memory for sure," Flo said.

"Our next home will be our forever home; room for lots of babies and not just a make-do place like this was," Marcel told her. "I'll find us a really nice place to live. No more working at the pub, you'll be home with the new baby and Rosie. You two ladies will have more time to spend together visiting each other instead of working at the pub," the girls smiled at each other.

Both Rosemary and Flo were eagerly looking forward to their new way of living. A time of change was in the air, and they were ready waiting and excited to see how it would unfold.

Mr. and Mrs. Duggan arrived the following day with the solicitor. Rosemary drove down to the pub in the pony and trap for the first time by herself. She managed to control the horse just as Sean had instructed her. She was quite pleased with herself. They entered the pub and sat down at one of the tables to finalise their business. She welcomed the family to their new home and business and wished them all well as she placed the keys on the table for Mr. Duggan.

"I've taken the liberty of listing some of the suppliers," she said. "Ye might wish te contract yer own, but these are the people Jimmy used, and I continued using them after he left," she advised.

"This is the ledger," she said as she handed it over to Mr. Duggan. "Ye'll be needing that. Everyt'ing's in it, all in order and up te date," she finished. It contained a detailed list of all wages and running expenses, including the income from the bar since Jimmy left. The ledger recorded the amount of cash placed in the safe every night, then taken to the post office for onward transmission to the solicitor and Jimmy. The solicitor handed Rosemary a banker's order for the remaining stipend, previously agreed with Jimmy. It was a handsome sum of money. She knew Sean would be pleased, and they had already agreed to give Flo a share of it for all her hard work and honesty over the years.

The business finished, they all shook hands and Rosemary stood to leave the pub for the last time. Mr. Duggan interrupted to ask her a final question.

"Is there a copy of the recipes Flo used for the food she prepared?"

"No," replied Rosemary, "I never saw Flo use a recipe. It was all just as her mammy taught her. Not'in' was ever measured out like a proper recipe. She just used her own knowledge and experience when it came to her cooking," Rosemary explained.

The solicitor suggested to Mr. Duggan: "You might wish to make an offer to Mrs. Murphy for her recipes. I don't believe it's a requirement to purchase a freehold public house."

"In the event that there was never any recipe to follow, I'll do that," he said.

Rosemary stood back and had a last look around the room.

"What fun there's been in this place over the years. I hope you and yer family enjoy it as much as I have." Rosemary left and closed the door behind her, leaving Mr. and Mrs. Duggan with the solicitor. She immediately went 'round to the back of the pub to the coach house. Flo was waiting with the kettle already boiled for tea.

"It's so good te have a visitor here," Flo said excitedly. "Come on in, Rosemary, and tell me what happened." Rosemary had just entered the house and made herself comfortable at the kitchen table when there came a knock at the door.

"It's them," Rosemary said. Flo looked at her friend in surprise.

"That isn't them already?" she said and went to open the front door. It was Mr. and Mrs. Duggan and the solicitor as Rosemary had predicted.

"Please come in," Flo said as she opened the door wide to let them pass.

"We're just about te have some tea, will ye join us?"

"Thank you," said the solicitor entering the room, followed by Mr. and Mrs. Duggan. "But no tea for us. We'll take just a minute of your time."

"As ye wish," said Flo.

"Please sit down," she motioned towards the table.

The group sat down at the table beside Rosemary. The solicitor spoke.

"Mr. Duggan has decided that he will require the use of the coach house for his automobile. He will be using it as a garage and a place to make repairs. There is no hurry for you and your family to leave, but he would be grateful to have the use of it when his automobile arrives in September. So, you have three months to look for a place to live. He will not charge you any rent for that period and will expect you to continue to care for the vegetable garden during that time. I believe this was your original agreement with Jimmy Logan?" he said.

"It was," replied Flo.

"There is one other point Mr. Duggan would like me to deal with," he continued. "The recipes you used for preparing the food that your customers like so very much. Mr. Duggan would like to make you an offer to buy them from you. He wants to keep the same customers coming here to eat. Is that something you would consider doing, for a fair price, of course?" added the solicitor.

"It's something I'd like te discuss wit' me husband before agreeing anything," Flo replied. "Although I don't t'ink there'd be any problem wit' yer idea," she continued.

"In that case, I'll leave you with that item for discussion with your spouse. You may let Mr. Duggan know your price when you are ready. We won't take up any more of your time, and thank you for your co-operation."

"Me husband Marcel will contact Mr. Duggan when we're ready wit' a reply," said Flo. "Thank ye for coming," she continued and showed them to the front door. Flo returned to the kitchen where her friend was waiting at the table.

"Well, Rosemary, what d'ye t'ink about that? That'll please Marcel if they offer me money for me recipes. I just hope I can get the amounts right. Ye know the way I cook, a pinch o' this and a pinch o' that. I never wrote anything down," she said.

"Flo, I can remember how much the takings went up after ye started. When yer cooking became known te the customers, the takings doubled, ye know. Jimmy did well te let me hire ye. This is yer chance te make a tidy amount for yer trouble," Rosemary confided.

"Hmm," said Flo, agreeing, "I'd hate te be mean te them, they seem a nice family who just want te make their business work."

"Yes, I know what ye mean. They do seem nice people, and of course we'll help if we can. Marcel will decide how much yer recipes are worth, that's for sure," said Rosemary without a doubt.

"Yes, he will, he's good at t'ings like that," agreed Flo.

The girls sat with their tea chatting for a time until Rosemary realised how late it was getting. She had to steer the pony and trap back to the farm herself. She didn't like steering in the dark.

"We'll come down this weekend when Marcel's home. We can talk about yer recipes then, but I'd better get going before it gets dark," she continued.

Rosemary put on her coat and headed out to the pony and trap, followed by Flo and little Rosie.

"Goodbye, Flo," said Rosemary.

"See ye on Saturday," Flo said, and then turned to walk back to the coach house with little Rosie, who was waving her hand. When Marcel got home, Flo was so excited about her news she just couldn't contain herself and started talking as soon as he got inside the house.

"Slow down, *amore*, slow down, let me get inside and get my boots off," Marcel said, smiling at her.

"Oh, that voice o' yours," said Flo in a soft, weak tone, "makes me wilt every time I hear ye speak."

Marcel removed his boots and jumped up to catch his wife around the waist with both hands. He pulled her close to him and kissed her passionately on the lips.

"Do ye see what a mean? I just melt like butter in yer hands. I love ye so much, Marcel, and ye make me so happy," she said.

He felt strong in her presence. She made him feel like no one else could, manly, king of his castle, and proud as her husband and father of their little daughter. Marcel pulled Flo down to sit on his knee like a little girl and said, "Now that you have my full attention, you can continue with your story."

"First," Flo said, "give Rosie a little kiss, too."

"Of course, *amore*, come here Rosie, come to Daddy," and he leaned down to give her a little kiss on her forehead then turned his attention back to Flo, his main interest.

Marcel was not overly interested in his daughter, and in some ways he resented the attention Flo gave to her at times. However, he did like to indulge his wife and so he viewed Rosie as Flo's toy that she could play dress up with, as any little girl would with her dolly. He knew he simply had to make a noise and Flo was there, attentive to his every wish, qualm, or question. She loved him completely, and Rosie was always in second place. Having kissed Rosie, he turned to hear Flo's story.

"Now, I want to hear everything, you may begin."

Flo was so excited she rushed through the events of the day in what seemed like seconds. However, Marcel did get the most important message. Mr. Duggan wanted to purchase the recipes that Flo used in her daily cooking at the pub.

"Perhaps, we might come to some other arrangement with Mr. Duggan? Perhaps he might be willing to let us stay on until after the bambino is born, and we are ready for a move?" Marcel would mull this idea over and discuss it with Mr. Duggan. He knew their friends were going to meet up at the farm on Saturday suppertime. Rosemary would be able to give him more details of how much the pub takings increased after Flo started doing the cooking. It might be better to barter rather than exchange cash, he thought. He suggested as much to Sean and Rosemary when they met. They both agreed. If Marcel and Flo could stay at the coach house until after the baby was born, and rent free, it would give the couple more time to find a good house locally. He would discuss this idea with Mr. Duggan.

"Absolutely," said Mr. Duggan, "a grand idea. Me automobile isn't coming until the spring now, and I have no immediate need for the storage. Mrs. Duggan would like te learn Flo's recipes, and it couldn't be a better exchange," he agreed.

Mr. Duggan was more than happy with the new proposal. Flo would continue to cook at the pub for a short time. She showed Mrs. Duggan the dishes her customers liked--no recipes required.

She instructed her just as her mammy had taught her. This way there would be a continuous flow of the same people coming to eat. There would be no disconnection or difference in the weekly income, which was of utmost importance. Mrs. Duggan took notes as Flo put together the dishes, in her own way. In exchange, the Murphy family remained living at the coach house rent free, until after the baby was born. The vehicle was due to arrive in April, and there was no real hurry. There was no need for Kate McGinty to work at the pub, not with three big sons to help out. Disappointed, Kate went back to life on the farm.

Mr. Duggan would use his pony and trap like everyone else in the village did. It was a grand arrangement. Mr. and Mrs. Duggan were very accommodating and nice friendly people indeed. Their three sons, Seamus Junior, fifteen years of age, Brendan, who was fourteen, and Paul, thirteen years of age, loved the change from city life. They had so much more to do and more free time. They offered to help out any time without hesitation. The oldest boy Seamus even offered to drive Marcel, Flo, and little Rosie up to the farm in the pony and trap, to save Sean McGinty the drive in the dark.

"I t'ink it's a grand idea on your part, Seamus. But yer up early tomorrow and they'll be late home. Why don't ye's just take the pony and trap and drive yerselves up there and back again," Mr. Duggan suggested. "You know how te care for the pony, and ye can settle him down for the night when yer finished wit' him." he continued.

Marcel, surprised at such an offer, jumped at the opportunity. "How very decent of you, Mr. Duggan. I'm grateful, and I accept," he said. "Don't worry about the pony, I'll settle him down for the night after we get back. Thanks again," he said.

The pony stabled in the coach house in the end stall by the doorway. It was far enough away from the living area that it did not inconvenience the family. It was part of the deal made by Mr. Duggan and Marcel, and Flo didn't mind at all. The pony was out in the field all day and stabled at night only. Marcel took care of this chore, every morning after the horse was out in the field, he cleaned the stable out.

Pub life continued as before with the new owners fully installed and accepted by the locals. Flo came in daily to cook and instruct, bringing Rosie with her. It was about this time that Mrs. Duggan told Flo to call her by her first name.

"It's not like the formal city life in Dublin. People here are so friendly," she said. "I'd be glad if ye called me Marie. Seamus Senior prefers that ye call him by his first name, too. We already talked about it, and he agrees wit' me," she said. "We don't want people te t'ink we're stuck up, ye know?" she finished.

The Duggan family quickly settled into village life. Everyone liked the three boys, and they were all so willing to go out of their way to help when needed. Seamus and Marie were also keen to help in any way to anyone who needed it. Rosemary thought of the similarity between Marie Duggan and Mary Hughes, who had also been loved by the community for her kindness. How curious that the Duggan family should replace the previous Hughes family, who also had three boys?

The months passed and finally Flo was getting quite uncomfortable with her new body size. She spoke to Marie about it.

"I have te stop working now. I'm getting so big; it's tiring te stand for any length of time," Flo told her. "I was t'inking that maybe young Kate could help ye if ye needed her? D'ye mind at all?" she asked.

"Of course, I understand. It's time for ye te care for yourself now. I completely agree wit' ye," Marie said.

Flo had some spare time to spend sitting in her garden relaxing among the flowers Marcel had planted for her. She enjoyed the summer months, and they were into September. She wanted this baby born to get her body back to its normal size. It seemed to her that she had grown enormously with this pregnancy. It was awkward for her to move around, and so uncomfortable no matter if she stood up or sat down. It would be over soon enough, she thought to herself. Rosie played in the garden while Flo sat and watched her from the bench. They spent many sunny afternoons in their garden from then on, enjoying their time together as mother and daughter. Little Rosie understood that her mammy was having a baby and that she would be able to help out with it once the infant was born. Rosie was looking forward to having a little baby around.

It was early November when Flo woke during the night with the most awful pains in her lower stomach. She had but a month to go for the birth and couldn't understand what was happening, but it felt to her that this baby was being born. Flo managed to get out of bed and stand up only to fall back down on the bed. Marcel jumped up quickly and around to the side of the bed by Flo.

"What's wrong?" he asked worried. "Do you want me to do anything for you?"

"I have the most awful pains, Marcel; I t'ink somet'ing's wrong, can ye fetch Doctor Connelly?"

Marcel dressed quickly and ran down the village road to the doctor's house. It was after midnight, and he knew the doctor would probably be in his bed. When he arrived at the doctor's house, he banged hard on the front door. Doctor Connelly was sleeping lightly and awoke immediately. He rushed downstairs feeling the urgency, and pulled the door open wide.

"Come inside, Marcel, while I dress. I'll come right away."

"Be quick Doctor, Flo's all alone in the house and in terrible pain." The doctor dressed himself in minutes and was rushing downstairs, grabbing at his coat and bag as Marcel was opening the door to run up the street again.

They arrived at the coach house only to find Marie inside with Flo, and Seamus Senior stalking up and down outside waiting for the doctor and Marcel to return. They had heard Flo crying out in pain and came to help. Marie was a great help, finding the rubber sheet and the other things Flo had told her about and readied the bed for birthing. Somehow she just knew that this baby was coming tonight!

Flo was lying on the bed writhing from side to side and having a hard time concealing her pain when the doctor and Marcel arrived.

"Quickly Doctor, she's in terrible pain," Seamus Senior said as he ushered them both inside.

He followed and closed the door behind him to keep the cold night air out. He went directly to the fire and stoked it up knowing a long night was ahead and trying to make himself useful. Marie filled the bucket to boil the water and in no time it was ready. She prepared the kitchen table with all the things required for use. There were plenty of clean cloths and as much hot water as she could boil. Luckily Rosie was still sleeping, and Marie kept an eye on the little one. She was sound in her bed in her own stall that Marcel had turned into a pretty pink bedroom for her.

Doctor Connelly took a close look at Flo and examined the birthing canal. The baby's head was surely down, but it was a month early for sure. Flo was bleeding heavily, and Doctor Connelly worried how much blood she was losing.

"The nearest hospital is forty miles away," he said aloud for all to hear. Dare he send Marcel for blood now or not? Doctor Connelly ushered Marcel out of the bedroom.

"Flo's going te need blood, she's losing too much even now," he said showing concern.

Seamus looked at Marcel, who was visibly shaken and interrupted.

"I'll go Doctor, just write out the order. Marcel needs te be here wit' his wife. I'll be quick as I can. No need for the trap, I'll just take the horse."

Doctor Connelly handed a piece of paper over to Seamus with the order for eight pints, Flo's type, and Seamus left immediately.

Flo's pain seemed worse and yet the baby's head was not coming down any further. Doctor Connelly felt her lower stomach.

"Flo, remember the last time, I told ye te breathe and then te stop breathing? Well, I want ye te do it again. Marcel, come over beside Flo and hold her hand. When I tell her te breathe deeply, help her," the doctor said. "When I tell her te stop, get her to pant like a dog when it's running."

Flo started to take deep breaths with Marcel's encouragement. He sat with her holding her hand. She was in great pain and lapsed often, and Marcel had to start her again.

Doctor Connelly was taking great care to watch the baby's head appear and measure how far down it was. The night seemed to go on forever. Flo's contractions started and then stopped again repeatedly. Finally, after what seemed hours, there was movement and the baby's head started to come forward but stopped again. Doctor Connelly seemed very concerned and shouted to Flo, "PUSH, wit' all yer might now."

The baby's head started to move forward again, and much to his fear, his intuition right--the umbilical cord wrapped around the baby's neck, and the baby's face already blue. For sure this little one could die being birthed if it wasn't already dead. He shouted to Flo.

"STOP pushing now and breathe fast, keep her panting, Marcel," he instructed.

The doctor tried as he might to unravel the cord from the baby's neck but it was tightly wound, and he couldn't get a space to insert a finger to make a cut to release the cord.

"PUSH," he shouted, "wit' all your might, and keep pushing."

Flo pushed as hard as she possibly could and finally ran out of breath. She took a big deep breath and pushed again as hard as possible. Suddenly the baby ejected and Doctor Connelly luckily caught it, as it did. He rushed the baby to the kitchen table to untangle the cord from its neck. He tried to blow air into its little lungs. He managed to get the cord unwrapped but the baby's face was blue, and he couldn't get any air into it no matter how hard he blew. He cleaned its mouth and nose and again gave it a smack on the bottom to shock it, hoping it would breathe, but nothing. The baby was already dead. Marie looked on as the doctor tried blowing air into its little mouth, again and again. Finally, she stood forward.

"Doctor, it's no use, the baby's gone, stillborn," she said in a flat voice. "It was probably dead before it was born, wit' the cord around its neck like that. That's why it's come so early," she said.

Doctor Connelly shook his head in agreement as he laid the little body on the table and covered it over.

He immediately returned to Flo who was losing a lot of blood, and this had been his first worry. Marcel asked about the baby.

Doctor Connelly whispered to him. "A boy. Stillborn, I'm afraid. I'm so sorry." Flo was conscious enough to hear and immediately cried out.

"Me baby, me baby, what happened te me baby?" she cried as she slumped into unconsciousness.

Doctor Connelly had but one pint of blood of her type with him and no reserves at home. He fixed up the one pint hanging it from a nail on the wall above Flo's head. He inserted the needle into her arm, hoping it would do until Seamus returned. He knew already that she was going to need much more than he had. Marie washed the little boy's body down and wrapped him in a white sheet.

"How very sad," she said. Her sister had birthed a baby in exactly the same manner, and it too was stillborn at birth. Somehow Marie had known something was wrong when Flo started to come so early. Marcel sat in a chair beside Flo; he couldn't get closer to her if he tried. Afraid of losing her, he held her hand gently stroking it as he whispered comforting words to her. He watched the blood slowly drip down the tube and into her arm. He didn't move an inch as he continued softly talking to her in her unconscious state.

"Flo, *amore*, stay with me. Don't let me be here alone without you," he whispered. "Flo, I need you, be with me, please stay with me, I love you. Flo, *amore*, you are all I ever wanted in this life. I can't be here without you. I can't lose you now, please stay with me, don't go," he lamented. "There will be more babies, lots of them if you want, just don't leave me," he muttered. "You promised you would never leave me. Remember, remember you said that to me?" Marcel continued, repeating over and over to Flo.

"Don't leave me, *mio amore*, please stay. I love you. I can't be here without you. You're my life, and I can't go on without you," he sobbed quietly. "You promised to stay with me, Flo, remember? Stay with me now. Don't leave me here alone. I can't do it without you, I can't be alone again," he begged her.

Doctor Connelly leaned over to take Flo's pulse and realised he was losing her. *Her pulse is very weak. If Seamus doesn't get back in the next few minutes, Flo will die,* he thought to himself. Suddenly there was life in Flo. Her eyes opened, and she turned her face to Marcel and spoke in a soft whisper.

"Promise me, ye'll take care of Rosie?"

"Of course, *mio amore*, I promise, but you must stay with me. Don't leave me alone. Don't go, Flo. I love you, stay with me," Marcel cried in a whisper. Flo lapsed into unconsciousness again.

Marie stood at the doorway to the small bedroom and let the tears roll down her face. This scene brought back so many memories of her sister's lost baby. She felt Marcel's pain and the young couple's loss. It was half past five in the morning. Seamus must get here soon, but it was a long ride there and back, in all about eighty miles round trip on horseback. Marie put the kettle on for tea. At least the doctor would have some and she would as well. Doctor Connelly entered the kitchen.

"If he's not here very soon, we'll lose her, too," he said. Marie nodded in acknowledgement and began to pour tea for everyone. Marcel didn't drink; he continued talking to his beloved Flo. Doctor Connelly drank his tea quietly, watching the last of the blood drain from the bag on the wall into Flo's arm. Again he took her pulse and could barely feel it. She was bleeding to death, and there was nothing he could do but watch. Flo silently slipped away from this world and into the next at quarter to six that morning. When Seamus arrived back with the blood at nine o'clock, it was all over. Flo and her baby were dead.

After cleaning and washing up, Doctor Connelly left saying he would go 'round to the chapel and advise the undertaker of the deaths. Marcel would not move from Flo's side. She lay dead in the bed, and he allowed no one near. He held her hand all the while and spoke to her gently; it was a sorry state to see, for sure. Seamus tried to talk to him, but the young man didn't hear. Marie woke little Rosie and took her over to the pub with her, taking some of her clothes with them. Rosie could stay with them for as long as necessary. There was no knowing when that would be or how long it would take.

Seamus sent his oldest boy Seamus Junior up to the farm to let Sean and Rosemary McGinty know what had happened. He had given Seamus Junior a letter to give them, rather than let the young boy tell them the sad news. He said that Rosie was with them and could stay with them for as long as necessary. However, in the event that Rosemary and Sean wanted to take Rosie with them, then that was agreeable too. He advised in his letter that Marcel was a broken young man who would not move from the side of the body. He would not let anyone take her away, not even the undertaker who came and took the baby's body. Seamus asked that if there was any way for Sean to come down from the farm and help Marcel to release Flo's body; at least then they could continue with the funeral arrangements.

Rosemary read the letter out loud to Sean. They were both devastated with the news. Word spread quickly through the neighbourhood. The villagers came out in mourning for the loss of such a young lass and her stillborn infant. People loved Flo, and of course, many had come to know her through her splendid cooking. How very sad it was for Marcel and little Rosie, they said, such a fine young family.

Sean came down from the farm with Rosemary. They both entered the coach house together not knowing how to handle such a sensitive situation. Rosemary was aware that Marcel had a temper, even though she had never seen it. She knew it lingered underneath, somewhere deep down. She just knew it was there.

They both walked into the bedroom where Marcel still sat in the same chair holding Flo's hand. She had been dead almost eight hours, and he had not released her hand or moved once in all that time. He sat there still talking to her, pleading with her not to leave him. Sean turned to Rosemary.

"Go fetch him a large brandy," and she did so immediately.

"No payment necessary," Marie said.

Rosemary took the brandy into the room and handed it over to Sean, then she stood back not knowing what was going to happen. Sean lifted Marcel's hand from Flo and placed the glass in it. He cupped his hands over Marcel's, in case he might drop the glass. Finally, after a few seconds, Marcel looked up at Sean.

"Sean, *mio amore* is dead. She left me, Sean. She's gone, and I'm alone again," Marcel said, bewildered.

Sean ordered him in a firm, authoritative voice. "Drink this," he said. "Put the glass up te yer mouth and take a big drink--down it in one. Do it quickly. Now," he commanded loudly.

Marcel obeyed Sean's order. He lifted the glass to his mouth and drank the brandy in one gulp. He gave his head a shake and looked at Sean. Then he saw Rosemary standing near the doorway her head down in sorrow. For the first time, Marcel moved--he stood up, stepped back from the bed, then walked out of the room. He had never lost his temper in front of Flo. He felt that he was about to explode, and he didn't want Flo to see him in such a state--even if she lay dead.

Marcel left the coach house and went 'round to the garden where the flowers and the vegetable patch was. There he let go of his anger and rage at God. He yelled at the top of his voice, wailing and bawling as if his heart had been ripped from his chest.

"You up there in your Heaven," he yelled, waving his fists and throwing punches into the air as if he was in a fist fight with someone.

"Why? Why did you take her, why not me?" he sobbed out loud. "She was my angel, beautiful, innocent and full of love. I'm the sinner. I'm the one you want, why take her, why?" he yelled. He beat hard on his chest with his clenched fists and fell to the ground on his knees, still muttering words of despair in his native Italian language.

"*Bastardo*," he mumbled, between sobs and deep groans. "*Bastardo*," he repeated more quietly now. "To hell with you. To hell with you." His voice was quieter now, and exhausted but still on his knees, Marcel began beating the ground with his bare fists, as the tears rolled down his face.

"Hiding from me up in your sky." He looked up into the sky and defiantly shouted out to God. "You coward. Come out and face me," he yelled. "You wicked, evil *bastardo*," he said whimpering. "How could you take her--she was innocent, and she was mine. You could have had me. She was my angel. Why do you want her when I need her so much? Why?" he mumbled crying quietly.

His voice was almost a whisper now. Spent, drained, and still on his knees sobbing in despair, he made strange groans that came from some place dark, deep and very lonely. Finally, he cried himself quiet and sat slumped on the damp ground in silence. Rosemary and Sean heard his cries and felt his pain. "We should let him be te get it all out," Sean said to Rosemary as if he understood his friend's agony.

The undertaker came back at Sean's request and took Flo's body. Sean and Rosemary stayed in the house waiting for Marcel to come inside. They would tell him then that Flo's body was gone. They both waited patiently for their friend to control his grief and finally after hours, and utterly exhausted, Marcel returned to the coach house.

"Flo's gone to the chapel. They know what te do, and they'll take care of her there. D'ye want te come up te the farm wit' us?" Sean asked him.

Marcel quietly said, "No."

"D'ye want me te stay wit' ye here?" Sean asked again.

Again Marcel said, "No."

Rosemary had already changed the bed sheets and covers and disposed of the bloodstained sheets so that he wouldn't see them again. There was no sign that anything had happened. She put on the kettle for tea, and they waited around for a few hours more. Marcel sat at the kitchen table, his head bent down staring at his feet. He said nothing. He drank nothing. He didn't move. Sean sat next to him on one side, and Rosemary sat on the other. They sat for almost three hours in complete silence when finally Sean stood up.

"We must get back te the farm now." He spoke aloud, knowing that somewhere inside Marcel's head, he could hear what Sean was saying.

"I'll tell Marie and Seamus te look in on ye later. I won't expect ye tomorrow, and I'll come down te see ye if I can. We'll collect Rosie and take her te the farm wit' us. Other than that, we'll see ye for the funeral the day after that. I'll come te get ye before we go te the chapel, and we'll go together."

Sean knew that Marcel heard him but didn't wait for any acknowledgement. They made their way to the front door and left the coach house for the last time. On their way, they went into the pub to see Seamus and Marie.

"He's in a terrible state, and there's no consoling him," Sean said. "Best te leave him be--he'll come around in his own time,"

Sean said sadly. "Would ye be kind enough te leave some food for him, Marie?" he asked.

"Of course, I'd be glad te."

"We'll take Rosie wit' us now. She'll be fine wit' us until he comes around and decides what he wants te do."

"She's such a lovely little thing. She doesn't understand what happened te her mammy, but she knows it's something bad and cries for her. She'll be needin' a lot of lovin'," Marie said.

"I understand, and she knows us well, so it's probably better for her te be wit' us on the farm," said Rosemary.

"I agree," said Marie.

Sean and Rosemary left the pub with little Rosie. She would live with them on the farm for the rest of her days.

Marcel was so distraught, he never once asked about his daughter. Nor did he ever recover from the loss of Flo. The funeral day came quickly. It was a sad grieving village that gathered at the small chapel. The numbers were overflowing outside into the courtyard. No one was able to contact Flo's mother--she was somewhere in Dublin, was all people knew. Sean and Rosemary came down to the coach house to fetch Marcel, and make sure he dressed appropriately for the funeral. To their great surprise, he was wearing his wedding outfit for the second time in his young life. Marcel was just twenty-one years of age, coming twenty-two in January. He did not speak to them but motioned to go outside to the carriage. They arrived at the chapel to see the crowds had gathered in their numbers.

"So many people te honour Flo's memory and grieving at your loss, Marcel. It's obvious she was well liked by everyone who knew her." Marcel did not respond to Sean's comment.

It was a very sombre Mass. Marcel did not partake in any of it, sitting quietly with his head bowed down the whole time. When finally the priest finished, the crowds went to the graveyard behind the chapel. Many of the villagers left at that time, as it was their custom to give the grieving family some privacy. It was only Sean, Rosemary, Rosie, Kate, Seamus, Marie, and Marcel at the graveside. The priest said the appropriate prayers and the group replied, all that is except Marcel--excused under the circumstances. He fell to his knees crying as the coffin was lowered into the ground

"No, don't go, *mio amore*, please don't leave me." He sobbed loudly for all to witness and hear his pain. He bent over the graveside, reaching down to the coffin below. Sean pulled him back, and he finally stood up straight and excused himself for his weakness. Marcel marched quickly away from the grave and all the way back home to the coach house. Rosemary nudged Sean, but he said to leave him be. The small group made their way back to the pub for tea and a sandwich, as was the custom. Then Sean and Rosemary went home to the farm with little Rosie, leaving Marcel alone in the coach house with his grief.

The next morning Sean and Rosemary were standing outside the house talking, when, to their disbelief, they saw Marcel marching up the pathway towards the barn dressed in his working clothes.

"Sean, d'ye t'ink he's okay te work? I mean, should we bring him into the house and sit him down?"

"I'll go out te the field and talk te him later, but for the moment leave te do what he wants. It's his way of dealing wit' things."

Marcel did not speak to anyone. He collected his tools and went out to the field where he was working before Flo's death. No one saw him leave at the end of the day. It was this way from then on. He would come and go as he always did in the past. He worked without stopping all day and went home at dark. Sean went out to speak with him that first morning.

"Sometimes it's better te work it out of yer system, and I know ye like te put your strength into yer work. This might be the answer for ye just now, and I'm happy te leave ye te it." Marcel did not respond but kept digging and turning the soil.

"When yer ready, don't forget ye have a little daughter who needs ye, Marcel. She's lost her mammy, but she doesn't have te lose her daddy as well. That's up te you. Ye need te come visit wit' her at least. Let her know ye still care for her." Again Marcel did not respond. Sean waited patiently and then grew tired of his selfishness and left him to his misery. Marcel came and went quietly each day, speaking to no one. It seemed to Rosemary that he had *gone completely inside of himself*, and it was going to take a long time for him to come out again. In the meantime he worked well, and they had nothing to complain about. Every week at payday, Sean would go to him out in the field and give him his wages, encouraging some casual conversation.

Marcel accepted saying, "Thank you," but other than that there was no conversation or response. Sean excused his behaviour, understanding his sorrow. Marcel would go to the house when no one was there and leave money on the kitchen table for Rosie's keep. Rosemary knew what the money was for, and accepted it gratefully. She never saw him, and he never made any attempt to see Rosie. Rosemary and the little girl had bonded well--she was the daughter that Rosemary so desperately wanted.

That year passed by without further disruption. Marcel worked through the winter and the following summer without speaking directly to anyone. He did his work and paid his dues for Rosie, but he did not partake in her life at all. Sean and Rosemary had been married one whole year when she realized that she was finally pregnant and due in December. It was exactly one year after Flo was due to have her baby. She worried that there might be some connection and prayed nightly that all would be well with her unborn child.

Finally, the day came when Rosemary went into labour with her own baby. It was the 3rd of December 1901. The baby was earlier than expected, but not too early to cause alarm.

"I'm going for Doctor Connelly," said Sean. "Kate, will ye stay wit' Rosemary and see te her needs? She'll tell ye what te do."

Kate made ready all the things that Rosemary told her to get out. She also placed the rubber sheet under Rosemary as instructed. She had raked out all the extra sheeting Rosemary told her to get. Everything was on the kitchen table waiting for the doctor's instructions when he arrived. The birthing went well, short in duration, just twelve hours in all, and relatively painless, Rosemary thought.

"It's a healthy little boy," called out the doctor, "about seven or eight pounds, I would say. A healthy weight for a newborn."

Sean was waiting outside the bedroom and heard the news.

"Can I come in yet?" he shouted.

"Of course ye can, sure, he's your son too," Rosemary replied.

Sean came into the room and straight over to Rosemary in the bed. He leaned over and kissed her on the cheek. He was so proud to be a daddy.

"Congratulations, love, ye did us both proud, so ye did. We'll call him Finton after me grandfather, if that's alright wit' ye?"

"Of course it is, and what a lovely name. I like it, but I'll be calling him Fin, if that's alright wit' ye?"

"Sure, that's what me grandfather was called, so it's fine wit' me," Sean said.

Rosemary was so very happy--she had a baby son of her own. Sean, delighted that the baby was a boy--later told everyone that he would have been just as happy had it been a girl. Marcel didn't get involved. He couldn't bring himself to congratulate the couple, once his good friends, and continued to keep to himself.

Rosemary watched him arriving one morning and felt so sad for him. He was so very alone after losing Flo, his one and only love. He was still a young man. Young enough to marry again, she thought, but she knew that would never happen. Flo had been his life, and his love. He would never replace her, preferring to live without love to keep her memory intact. If someone new were to come into his life, then he would have to let go of Flo's memory, and he would never let that happen. Many people tried to help him, but he didn't want their help, so finally they stayed away from him.

Unfortunately, Seamus was getting anxious about his automobile. He had put it off for the whole year because he couldn't bring himself to ask Marcel to vacate the coach house. Now he was going to have to find digs somewhere. Seamus decided to leave well alone until after Christmas. That would be time enough, for his automobile would not arrive until the following March. He would let Marcel have his last Christmas in the coach house, alone with his memories. Seamus would talk to him after that.

12

A Pitiful State, 1901

It was New Year's Eve once again and the pub was crowded. People were celebrating and waiting for the first "Bells" of New Year. Marcel was alone in the coach house as was normal these days. He didn't want to celebrate. He just wanted to be alone. Flo had been dead some thirteen months, and he was still in a state of withdrawal. It seemed to him that his life was over. He died when Flo died. His days would continue, and he would work as he always had and pay for Rosie's keep at the farm. However, for him, his life was over. He just had to get through the days until it was his turn to die. Only then could he reunite with Flo, and he wished that day would come soon. He thought about suicide many times. The only thing that stopped him was his promise to Flo to take care of Rosie. He couldn't break his word to Flo--he still loved her with all his heart. Although he didn't care for Rosie on a day-to-day basis, he paid Rosemary to do that for him. Marcel saw that as fulfilling his promise. He had to work and earn money to pay someone else to be her mammy.

He had never been close to his daughter, and a slow resentment began to build towards her. At times, he thought if she wasn't around he could die...or leave. He could go to America and start again if he had the courage to forget Flo, but he knew in his heart he couldn't do that. He would never forget his love, his Flo. He felt imprisoned and yet isolated--he had to stay and work for Rosie's keep. Marcel's mind raced in a million directions. Over and over he remembered every second of the night that Flo died. He couldn't get it out of his head. These same thoughts consumed his every waking minute every day, as he worked on the land, or on his walk to and from the farm, he thought about Flo and his dead son. It just kept going round and round, the same thoughts repeating, again and again. It seemed he would never be free of it. He had lost all sense of normal life and day-to-day living. His only outlet was physical labour in the fields every day.

The events of the village didn't concern him. He didn't light the lamps in the coach house and only lit the fire for heat. He sat most nights in the dark, alone with his memories of that terrible night. He didn't eat at the pub preferring to eat alone in his home. He ate sparingly and lived mostly on meat that he could fry quickly in the pan with a few eggs. He began to lose weight but remained strong and healthy enough to continue working. However, there wasn't an ounce of fat on his bones, just pure muscle.

Christmas and New Year came and went, and it was February when Marie spoke to Seamus about regaining access to the coach house.

"You need te talk te him, we can't put it off any longer and he needs time te look for digs," she said.

"Yes, I'll talk te him this weekend and get him te start looking for somewhere else te live. He's had enough time now. Yer right, he has te find a new place. It's time he moved on," Seamus agreed with her.

Marcel usually finished work around noon on Saturdays. He always stopped at the local butcher shop in the village for his weekly supplies before going home. Sometimes in the afternoon Seamus would see him heading up towards the cemetery to talk to Flo. No one ever questioned him, or interfered. They just left Marcel to his own grief. Seamus was keeping an eye out for him when he saw him rounding the corner at the back of the pub, heading towards the coach house. He came out of the back door into the courtyard to meet him.

"Marcel," he called out. "Hello there, I need a word wit' ye. Do ye have a minute?" Marcel was somewhat surprised but nodded back in acknowledgement as he walked over towards Seamus. The two men stood facing each other in the courtyard--Marcel's was looking down at his feet to avoid eye contact with Seamus. Seamus took a deep breath and began.

"Marcel, I know ye've had a bad time and everyt'ing, but I really need ye te start looking for somewhere else te live. My automobile's coming from the city soon. I've been putting them off te give ye that extra time, ye know? However, as we arranged some time back, I'll need te take over the coach house.

"Certainly, I'll start looking immediately," replied Marcel in a cold, flat voice and with that he turned and walked through his front door into the coach house.

Seamus sighed. He felt bad but something had to change to get Marcel back into the land of the living. Anyway, it had been in their original agreement, and his auto was coming soon. He mulled things over again in his head, and resolved that there was no other way. Marcel had to leave the coach house. Seamus felt sorry for pushing the situation but a whole year had passed and it was time for Marcel to move on.

Two weeks later, Marcel borrowed Sean's pony and buggy. Not the trap but the buggy, used for moving heavy things around. He mentioned to Rosemary that he was taking it to move his furniture out of the coach house and asked if she wanted any of it.

"But Marcel, ye made every piece of furniture yerself. It's good quality, won't ye keep it for yerself for later on?"

"I don't want any of it--I'm moving into furnished lodgings and everything's provided there," he replied.

"Why Marcel, I'd be honoured to take yer furniture. I know what love ye put into every piece, and I'll certainly use it up here. Why don't I just keep it for ye, until ye need it again?" she said.

"That won't happen, and I don't want anything for it, either. You'll probably be having a large brood here, and you'll need it all in time," he said.

He moved it all into the buggy himself until he arrived at the farm. Sean made himself available to help lift things down and into the room.

"I'd forgotten about the cradle--it's perfect for baby Fin and now I can put this drawer back in the wardrobe where it belongs," Rosemary said.

First they brought in Flo's lovely big bed with the soft horsehair mattress, and all of her beautiful bedding that went with it. Now Katie and Rosie could share a big bed together. Then there was the wardrobe. Rosemary positioned in the other half of the room for her future children to use. They put chairs, the bench, and the table into the barn where they would be useful. There were two cupboards that he had made. Marcel thought Seamus could use them, so he left them on the kitchen wall in the coach house. Rosemary opened the wardrobe to see how much room there was inside when she saw the box on the top shelf.

"What's this?" She motioned to Marcel, as she reached up to lift the box down. Marcel stood still saying nothing. He looked at Rosemary then he lowered his head as his eyes filled with tears. He was silent and sullen at the sight of the box.

"It's Flo's wedding dress," he replied quietly as if something caught in his throat. "I've no need for it. Perhaps one day Rosie might use it if she ever marries? If not, perhaps one of your own girls will. I'm sure you'll be having daughters, too," he said.

"Oh, I see, I won't open it and I promise te take good care of it for little Rosie," she said, placing the box back on the top shelf of the wardrobe.

"I found lodgings in the village with Mrs. Ahern, a widow, not far from where Flo's mammy lived. I have a room of my own, with breakfast, packed lunch, and supper included in the price and washing extra," he told Rosemary.

"That's grand, I hope ye can move on now that the coach house is behind ye," she replied.

"We'll see how it goes?" he said.

Old Mrs. Ahern knew of Marcel and his continued grieving and agreed that he could have her ground-floor room that once was her front parlour.

"I don't need that room any longer and I've already furnished it wit' a single bed, a wardrobe, chair and table for yer use. I'll light the fire for ye every night. So, it'll be nice and cosy when ye get in, and there's a basin and jug of water for ye te wash. I'll change that fresh every morning, too," she told him.

Her house was clean and the bed was warm and comfortable. He didn't need any other furniture. Marcel accepted her terms and moved in immediately. This was the last time he saw the coach house.

"Sure, it's a good move for Marcel. Once he's in and settled into a new way, he'll come back te us," Sean said.

"I t'ink yer right, and I hope for his sake it works out wit' Mrs. Ahern. It's time for him te heal and leave the dead behind. He needs te live again and remember he has a daughter," said Rosemary.

Springtime arrived and it was planting season again. There was much hard work waiting to get the fields ready for the new crops. Marcel worked harder than ever. Work was a tonic for him. He did not take the monthly trip to Dublin with Sean since Flo's death. However, now Sean needed his help as he was taking a cow to the market.

"Will ye come this month?" Sean asked. "I need ye te help me wit' the cow. I need te reinforce the buggy te hold her weight. It's a long journey, and she can't walk all that way. Will ye come and help me wit' her?"

"Yes, I'll help you," he replied.

"That's grand Marcel, and thanks," Sean said. "I'll meet ye in the mornin' at the crossroads at five o'clock and we can get started."

He told Mrs. Ahern that he would be leaving earlier than usual in the morning and needed an extra packed lunch and no supper that night, as he would be late getting back from the Dublin market.

It was a fresh morning and the sun was just beginning to rise. They knew it was going to be a lovely day--no rain! At least it would be a dry ride if nothing else.

Sean was not a great talker, and so the feeling between them was comfortable as they drove carefully along the rough roadway. It was easier on the buggy if Sean kept to the deep tracks formed over the years. After about three hours, it was time for a short break. He pulled up and both men jumped down from the buggy. Marcel got his lunch box, as did Sean. They sat at the side of the roadway eating breakfast and drinking lukewarm tea. It was the only drink they would have until they reached Dublin. The trip usually took some five hours to ride by horse and cart. Sometimes it was longer coming back, depending on how much extra weight there was in the buggy. This trip would be longer as they had the extra weight of the cow.

"It's a fine day for it," said Sean.

"Yes," Marcel agreed. Sean sat beside Marcel, and together they ate their sandwiches-like old times.

"I know how hard it's been for ye, Marcel. We all miss her too, but ye've got te get back te living--that's what life's for, it's for living. Yer young enough te marry again and have another family," Sean said.

"That will never happen," replied Marcel.

"It might be hard te t'ink that way just now, but it's possible," said Sean. "Ye don't have te be miserable for the rest of yer life, that's a choice ye make. It's up te you." Sean was quiet for a moment. "I just want ye te know that Rosemary and I are still yer friends and always will be. We're still here for ye if ye need us. We'll keep Rosie, we know ye can't care for her, but ye need te be her daddy. She needs te know that ye still care for her and that she has a daddy of her own. She's seven years old now, and ye didn't even come te see her on her birthday," Sean said.

"Hmm," said Marcel with his head down.

"Rosemary made a cake and we sang the "Happy Birthday" song te her the way Flo used te," Sean told him. "She was looking for you, her daddy, and ye didn't come. She was so disappointed. She's lost her mammy, but she doesn't have te lose her daddy, too," he continued. "Will ye not make an effort for her sake? Flo did ask ye to care for her, Marcel, t'ink on it. She's yer daughter and she needs ye," Sean finished.

Marcel sat beside Sean, listening to what he said. Finally, he took a breath and replied.

"I have to thank you and Rosemary for helping out with Rosie," he replied. "I will make more of an effort with her because I promised Flo I would do that, and I will," he continued. "What you need to know is that I'm a changed man. I'm not the person I was. I can't smile nor do I feel joy or happiness in any way," he said without emotion. "I've lost the only person in the world who made me feel alive--so it's difficult for me. When Flo died she took my life with her. I have no feelings left in me. My insides are empty, gutted, like a fish. I just want to die, then I can be with her again." There was a silence between the two men and then Marcel spoke again.

"I'll try to be a better daddy for Rosie. Bur, you and Rosemary need to know that it might take a long time for me to feel anything again. If I ever do," he said in a cold and flat voice. "Life will never be the way it was for me. Never again will I feel the joy and bliss that I did when Flo was alive, but I will try for Rosie's sake. When she grows, I can die with a clear conscience that I did my duty by Flo," he finished. There was another silence before Marcel spoke again. "Now I've answered you. I hope you and Rosemary can understand. My life is over--it ended when Flo died. I simply must live out the years ahead, until it's time for me to be free and united with Flo again in death. I look forward to that time, I really do." Sean shook his head in despair and patted Marcel on the shoulder. "I understand my friend, I do... give it time--they say it heals."

"We'd better get a move on if we want to make the bidding at noon." They both climbed up on the buggy and set off at a quicker pace than before.

Rosemary just loved little Fin, and so did Rosie. They played together with the baby every day and often Rosie would sing songs to him as she rocked the cradle for Rosemary. She could remember the cradle from her own home.

"Was this the cradle that I used te sleep in when I was a baby?"

"Why yes, it is. Yer daddy made it especially for ye when ye were born."

"Did he?" Rosie exclaimed in surprise with big open eyes. She was quiet for a moment, than spoke. "I don't think my daddy likes me now," she said unsure.

"Oh, now that's not true. Of course, he loves ye. He's just a bit lost since yer mammy died, but he'll come around again and ye'll see how much he loves ye," Rosemary assured the little girl.

She sighed, feeling Rosie's sadness. She had lost her mammy and daddy on the same day and yet she was such a pleasant little girl. She tried so hard to help out and be of use, always showing willingness with a smile. She was a lovely child, and Rosemary hoped that one day her own daughter would be as loving and willing to help as Rosie. Rosemary promised herself that she would be Rosie's friend, as well as her guardian. She realised that the girl had no one to love her and so she tried her best to show her kindness and affection.

Now that she had her own son, she realised that she couldn't feel that same kind of love for Rosie. No matter how hard she tried, it was different. Still love, but somehow not the same. With mother and child came that magical bond--the invisible cord that connects, all-knowing and all protective. Rosie's cord was disconnected from her birth mother--cut-off...missing. Rosemary couldn't offer that connection to her. It simply wasn't there. She would continue to try hard for the little girl's sake. She did love her very much. However, now she understood the difference she would make a special effort to spoil Rosie a little more often.

In the months that followed, Marcel did make the effort to talk to his daughter. At first Rosie was afraid of him. It was a long time ago that her mammy died and went away. They went for walks together on the farm and just talked about Flo.

"I made a promise to your mammy when she was dying, that I would take care of you until you grew up and I will. I know I haven't been to see you much until today, but I have been very sad grieving for your mammy and wanted to be alone."

"Are ye better now, Daddy?"

"I'm getting better and stronger with each day, but the pain of losing your mammy will never leave me. It will always be with me now. It's part of me inside," he explained. "I know you are probably wondering why you live on the farm with Rosemary and Sean?" he asked. "It's better this way for you--I have to go to work every day, and if you were living with me, you would be alone. It's best you stay with them here on the farm and we visit with each other like this. I promise to get better and come to see you more often from now on."

"Thank ye, Daddy, I'd like that, but I like living on the farm wit' Rosemary and Sean and Fin, too. He's a special friend for me, so ye don't have te worry about me. Just come te visit when ye can and we can do some reading like we used te when Mammy was alive. I miss reading the stories from the books," she said. "I remember you reading te Mammy and me and the pictures in the books that I loved," she reminded him.

"I never thought of that. I'll get you some books the next time I'm in Dublin, that'll keep you busy reading."

"I'd love that, Daddy, and thank ye."

It was 1903 and Rosemary was pregnant with her second child. Fin was already two years old and Rosie was eight. The two children were always together. Even when Rosie went to feed the chicks, she would carry little Fin on her hip, the way she saw Rosemary carry him around. The second baby was another little boy, Damian, and he was only about three months old when Rosemary found herself pregnant for a third time. Rosemary prayed in thanks to God:

"Thank ye, Father, for sending me these beauti-ful children.

I'll always be truly thankful te ye for them all and love them every day.

Amen."

Rosemary's prayers were being answered--she wanted children and imagined herself with a large family. Now God was sending them as quickly as he could, one after the other. She smiled to herself as she rubbed her stomach wondering if this one might be a little girl, a little girl of her own.

She had become used to Sean's ways in bed. Every night before sleep, they had a quick three-minute conjugal duty to perform. That was all it took and Sean always said, "Thank ye, Rosemary," and then went to sleep. As soon as Rosemary became pregnant, he would leave her alone. It was as if he had done his duty and there was no need for sex until after the baby was born. Then six weeks after the birth, he would start again. She could time him to the day. She was happy with the routine and loved being pregnant and having her large family. Her dream was coming true. The family grew, and Rosemary continued to work hard on her own little vegetable garden. She would knit in the evening by the Tilley lamp and the light of the fire until Sean returned home, something she learned from her mother and had no time for until now. She did love to knit these warm cosy sweaters for her children to wear on the cold days of winter. She loved to knit socks using the three little needles that went 'round and 'round. They were easy, and she enjoyed making them quickly. Rosemary was always doing something. She liked being busy.

13

Sophie, British Columbia, 2005

"Hello, is that you, Helen?" Sophie asked on the telephone.
"Yes, Sophie, it's me, what's up?" she replied.

"Oh, it's nothing really. I was just wondering if you were free to come over tonight around seven o'clock? That's all." Sophie asked.

"Sure, I'm not busy, what's happening?" Helen said.

"Well do you remember my friends from out-of-town, Marishka and Chloe?" Sophie asked. "They're coming over tonight and I wanted you here too. I have something I want to ask all of you," she told Helen.

"Sounds mysterious," Helen said. "But, yes, I'll be there at seven."

"Great, Helen, look forward to seeing you then. Bye for now," and she hung up the phone.

When Helen arrived at Sophie's apartment, Marishka and Chloe were already there. Sophie led her straight through to meet them. Helen threw her coat on the stand as she passed and went into the room. Sophie made the introductions.

"I know you already know about my special visitor, and I wanted you to consider a group meditation with me tonight. I'm hoping my spirit friend will allow you all to share the vision she is sending me," Sophie asked. The ladies sat quietly, waiting for her to explain.

"There's nothing to do yet, but how do you feel about that?" she asked. "She's been coming to me for some time now--especially when I meditate, and I know she wants me to help her with something very special," she said. "Would you be willing to try it and see what happens? I mean, if she makes her presence known to you and shares her message. That's really what I'm hoping for," Sophie finished.

"Well, I'm willing to give it a go," said Marishka.

"Me too," agreed Chloe.

"We've nothing to lose and if it helps you, Sophie, why not," said Helen.

"Great," said Sophie, "let's get started."

The ladies sat in their usual circle holding hands, and Sophie gently talked them into a mild restful state. She beckoned her spirit visitor forward to join them and to her surprise she came immediately. They channelled her energy as one collective unit and everyone shared in the vision that the spirit visitor was showing them.

At the end of the session, both Marishka and Chloe agreed that the connection was very powerful. Sophie admitted as much, too. "I feel she's preparing me for an event that I might not be up to," she said. "I might need your help when the time comes, and I wanted to find out if she was willing to let you connect with her energy in the event we need to work together. I'm so grateful she is," said Sophie.

The girls discussed the events in detail over tea and agreed to help Sophie if she needed them. Then they made their way to leave.

"When you know what's what, let us know," said Marishka. "We may have to sit together again before the reveal."

"Yes, I thought of that," replied Sophie. "Thanks for coming everybody, I really appreciate it. Goodnight now and safe home," she said seeing them out.

Sophie felt better knowing that her friends were supportive. She promised to let everyone know when her spirit friend disclosed the agenda and hoped it would be soon. Meantime, her visitor continued to channel Sophie and prepare her for the task that lay ahead. She would only get one chance to get this right.

14

A Family Reunion, 1905

*I*t was in the summer of 1905 that Rosemary received a letter from her mammy and daddy. They still lived on the outskirts of the village at the other end. It wasn't really a long way off, but it was an hour and a bit by pony and trap. It was a challenge with the children in the trap, especially when she was pregnant.

> *Dearest Rosemary and Sean,*
>
> *"We're having a family gathering next Wednesday any time you can make it during the day, and we'd love you to come and enjoy some time with the family. Bring all the children if you can and if Sean can't make it, of course we understand. All your brothers will be home and your daddy and me and your auntie Sissy and Uncle John. It's been a long time since we were all together, and we're looking forward to seeing you all then."*
>
> *Affectionately,*
> *Mammy xxx*

Fin, now four years of age, had come down with a bad cold. It was almost eight miles to Rosemary's mammy's house. She lived down past the pub and on through the village and out again on the other side.

"I don't t'ink Fin's well enough te make the trip te me mammy's place. It's a good hour and a bit on the pony and trap. I t'ink he'd be better in his bed," Rosemary said to Rosie. "Would ye mind caring for him while I'm away, Rosie? I know I can trust ye wit' him being sick. He just needs te drink water, and keep him cool. He'll probably sleep most of the afternoon. Would ye mind staying behind wit' him?"

"I t'ink ye should leave him wit' me. Take Damian and Anthony, I'll take care of Fin. Like ye say, he'll probably sleep all day, anyway."

Kate had chores on the farm every day. Sean kept her to a tight work schedule--otherwise she would get lazy and lie around doing nothing all day. Rosie was now ten years old and glad to help Rosemary and she loved little Fin. She stayed in the house with Fin and sang to him while he slept, but making sure he got plenty of water to drink. The little fellow just lay there in the bed. He had a bit of a temperature but not too much, not a high fever. It seemed more of a bad cold that he had, and he was so tired and sleepy.

"Just sit wit' him, Rosie, and keep him drinking water, as much as ye can get him te take. I've left some bread and homemade jam out for ye both, try te make him eat somet'ing when he wakes up. I'll be home around six o'clock--in time te make supper."

"Have a lovely visit wit' yer mammy and daddy," Rosie said as she waved Rosemary goodbye.

Rosemary started out with Damian, two-and-a-half years old strapped in the seat beside her, and baby Anthony in the straw baby basket behind her on the trap--he was just thirteen months. She was already four months pregnant again and was looking forward to seeing her parents and the rest of her family. It had been such a long time since they were all together.

Rosie sat on the bed with Fin, who was sleeping. She placed her tiny hand on his brow and felt that he was still hot. She went into the kitchen and poured a jug of cold water from the bucket. She fetched a cup and brought it all into the bedroom, in case he woke up and wanted a drink. She sat with him all afternoon, singing gently to him, and stroking his brow. He slept soundly. She didn't notice the change in his temperature. The afternoon passed slowly for Rosie, but she didn't mind sitting with Fin. She was very fond of him, and he was fond of her, too. Suddenly she heard what she thought sounded like the pony and trap coming up the path towards the farmhouse. The whole day had passed more quickly than she thought it would. Rosie went outside to meet them arriving. Rosemary pulled up outside the house and stopped.

"How's Fin?" she asked.

"Sleeping," Rosie replied. "He's been sleeping all afternoon; he hasn't woken up at all."

"Oh that's good," said Rosemary. "Probably do him the world of good. Did he drink anyt'ing?"

"No, he's been sleeping all day like I said."

"Alright then," replied Rosemary. "I'll just get the pony into the stable and I'll be right in. Can ye take Damian and Anthony for me, Rosie?"

"Of course," said Rosie as she reached up to lift Damian down from the trap, and then again for the basket with baby Anthony in it. Rosemary drove the pony and trap into the stable and unhitched the trap. She undressed the horse and walked him into his stall. She gave him a quick rub-down and put his rug on his back. She checked that he had plenty of fresh water and oats then she made her way back to the house to see Fin.

When she entered the room, it was as Rosie had said. He was asleep in the bed. She sat down at his side and gave him a gentle shake, but he didn't open his eyes and slept on. Rosemary gave Fin another shake, slightly more vigorous, and again he didn't respond. A little concerned, Rosemary leaned closer and put her ear down to Fin's mouth, but she couldn't hear him breathing. Now frantic, she rolled him on his back and placed her hand on his brow. He was cold, and didn't seem to be breathing.

"Rosie," she yelled. "Fetch me the mirror, the little one from the kitchen."

"Oh my God," she whispered to herself, "this can't be."

Rosie knew exactly what mirror Rosemary was talking about since it was the only small one they had. The big one was on the wardrobe that Marcel made, and there was one on the dressing table. She quickly brought it to Rosemary who placed the mirror in front of Fin's mouth. There was nothing, no mist on the mirror as there should have been--no breath! She screamed out loud.

"Oh my God, no," she shouted. "Get Sean, quickly, get Sean!"

Rosie ran outside as fast as she could. She knew which field he was working in, and ran as fast as her little legs would take her. She didn't know what was wrong, but she knew that Rosemary was very worried. Rosie reached Sean and shouted over to him.

"Come now, come to the house. Rosemary needs ye quick, come now," she called to him. Sean immediately threw down his shovel and started to run towards the farmhouse. Marcel was working not far away in the next field and saw Rosie waving her arms and then Sean running towards the house. He knew something was wrong and thought he'd better head over to see if he could help. When Sean arrived, Rosemary was howling and moaning loudly as if in pain, holding her stomach. Sean thought she was in early labour. Rosemary pointed towards the bedroom and cried out between moans.

"He's dead, our Fin's dead," she wailed loudly. "My God, what happened te him? He only had a cold," she moaned again. "How could this be?"

Sean rushed into the bedroom where little Fin lay still in the bed. He saw the mirror and placed it in front of Fin's mouth. Indeed, there was no breath. He put his ear against Fin's chest. Again there was nothing. No sound of breathing or heart beating, nothing. He placed his dirty hand on Fin's brow and felt the boy was icy cold.

"My God," he said out loud, and turning his head towards the bedroom door he saw Marcel standing there.

"Go fetch the doctor please, Marcel. Fin's dead and I need te be wit' Rosemary; she's in shock." Marcel nodded his head and immediately went to the stable to ready the pony and trap again for the road. Luckily the horse was given a short time to rest up. Rosemary was in shock, shouting and moaning and crying all at the same time. She sat doubled up in her chair rocking back and forth, while still holding her arms around her stomach as if in pain.

"How could this happen?" she cried out.

"Did he wake at all after I left ye?" she asked Rosie.

"No," replied Rosie. "I thought he was sleeping."

"Oh my God," Rosemary shouted. "It's my fault, I should've been here. I should've stayed home wit' him. It might never have happened," she cried out.

"That's not true," replied Sean. "Ye would've thought he was sleeping too. There must've been somet'ing wrong wit' him. He couldn't just die of a wee cold like that. There has te be somet'ing else that we don't know about. It's not yer fault, Rosemary. Ye can't blame yerself for this." Sean put his hand on her shoulder to console her but she continued to cry out.

"Marcel's gone te fetch Doctor Connelly. We'll find out soon what took Fin, but it wasn't a cold, and it wouldn't have made any difference if ye'd been here. He would still be dead," Sean said. He leaned down to reassure her, but she just cried and moaned out loud.

"My God," she wailed. "Why? He was just a baby, why would God do such a t'ing?" she asked. Rosemary rocked herself back and forth, bawling and still holding her stomach. At times she howled like the folklore Banshee--they talk about in whispers. Legend portrays it as the "death spirit" who calls to announce a family death--its eerie moan not of this world.

There was no sense talking to Rosemary--she was beyond coherence and in a world of her own. She continued rocking, wailing and howling all the time. Sean was beside himself with worry for her and their unborn baby. He knew that something bad, like a shock of this nature, could damage the baby inside her womb. He wondered if that was why she kept holding her stomach. Was she trying to protect her unborn child? He spoke softly now to Rosie.

"I want ye te know that none of this was yer fault," he repeated. "This wasn't yer fault, and ye couldn't have known that he wasn't sleeping. Do ye understand me, Rosie? It wasn't yer fault, and ye've done not'ing wrong."

He took little Rosie into his arms and gave her a hug just as he thought her mother or father would do under the circumstances. Rosie loved little Fin and didn't understand what had happened.

"How could he die? I was just sitting wit' him, singing him te sleep. Why did God want him? He's just a wee boy, and he's my friend." she said.

Rosie felt a deep loneliness, like she did when her mammy died--bewildered and lost. She wondered what would happen to her now. Would they send her to live somewhere else? A little scared, she welcomed Sean's hug and words of comfort. Sean McGinty was not an emotional person, but he did feel that some tenderness was due to the wee girl. She did her best, and after all she was only ten years old.

"Where the dickens is Kate in all this?" Sean asked in a stern voice.

"Kate's down at the stream washing clothes," replied Rosie. "She's been gone all day and she doesn't know anyt'ing about this."

"Go and fetch her, Rosie, please, and tell her te bring everyt'ing back up te the house, even if she's not finished."

"Yes, sir," replied little Rosie, and she headed off towards the stream.

"That Kate," said Sean out loud, "give her a job te do, any job, and she'll take the whole day. She should be up here where she's needed not washing clothes all day."

Kate had always been old man McGinty's favourite. Having been born later in his life, she got off scot-free with everything. Sean was the one who did the work. The other sons had long since left the nest. Two of the boys went to America together. His other brother got married and had a farm of his own in the next county.

Kate had never been held responsible for anything on the farm. She would forget to feed the hens or pump water from the well, and had to be told to do every little chore. Sean often encouraged her to go to America. They had an aunt settled in New York who wanted Kate to go and live with her. However, Kate wouldn't go alone. She wasn't confident enough to go on her own. If only there was someone to go with her, but there wasn't--so she stayed home.

Sean thought that Rosemary probably sent her to do the washing to get her out-of-the-way. She trusted Rosie to watch over little Fin but not Kate. She was a nuisance, and he wished she'd leave and go to America. There was nothing on the farm for her and no young men around for her to marry.

Marcel arrived with Doctor Connelly on the pony and trap. He jumped down and rushed into the house, turning straight into the bedroom where he knew Fin would be. He quickly removed his jacket and opened his bag, ready for use. He leaned over Fin and felt for a pulse. There was none. He placed his hand on Fin's forehead. He was cold. He then felt for a pulse at the neck and again there was nothing. He took out his stethoscope and placed it on Fin's heart. There was nothing, not even the faintest sound of a heartbeat. Little Fin was certainly dead...

"Sean," Doctor Connelly said, "ye know he's gone. There's not'ing te be done here. I am so very sorry--I'll make the necessary arrangements. How's Rosemary faring?"

"As ye can see Doctor, she's not reachable at the moment," Sean replied. Doctor Connelly glanced over towards Rosemary.

"Get her some hot sweet tea and put a nip of brandy or whiskey in it," he ordered. "She's in shock. Marcel can drive me back into the village. If ye have no objection, I'll take the body wit' me for examination and cause of death?"

"Of course," Sean replied. "There's no point in leaving him here, and best he goes wit' ye now." Sean, broken-hearted, knew he must care for his wife and their unborn baby. He knew there was a reason for Fin's death and wanted the post-mortem done on his little boy. He had to know why Fin died.

Rosemary was unaware of what was happening, which was just as well as she may not have been able to let the body go. Doctor Connelly wrapped little Fin's body in a sheet and lifted him up on the trap, placing him on the floor behind the seat. He told Sean to keep Rosemary warm and not to forget the hot sweet tea with some brandy or whiskey in it. That would help her come round.

"This is going te be hard on her, so look after her."

"I will," replied Sean.

"Bring her into the surgery office next week after the funeral's over. I need te make sure her unborn baby's alright, what wit' the shock and all," said the doctor.

"I will."

Marcel drove the doctor back to the village and lifted little Fin's body into the doctor's surgery for him.

"Thank ye, Marcel," he said. "How are ye these days?"

"One day at a time, Doctor, one day at a time," he replied.

"Yes, I understand that, and thanks for yer help today. Tell Sean I'll let him know as soon as I find out what it was that caused the death."

"I will, Doctor," said Marcel.

"Will ye go te the chapel on the way back and let them know what's happened? Tell them I have the body here, and te come for him not tomorrow, but early the next morning. I'll need that time."

"Of course, Doctor," said Marcel. He was a little anxious going to the chapel with such news. He was beginning to realise just how temporary life was. *Without any notice whatsoever, a little boy is dead,* he thought. Marcel had made himself distant with Rosemary and her first-born. The timing was bad for him, and here now there was no time left. The boy was dead, and he didn't even get to know him. *What a waste,* he thought. *What kind of God would do such a thing to a tiny child,* he asked himself? *This God is cruel and sadistic, taking this little life. Just like Flo,* he thought. *She was innocent, too, and loving and happy and everything good in a person, and He took her. What a cruel God.*

Marcel arrived outside the chapel and went 'round to the back door where the office was. He knocked on the door, and the undertaker answered.

"Yes, can I help ye?" he asked as he recognised Marcel.

"Fin McGinty has died," said Marcel. "His body is at the doctor's surgery for examination. The doctor says you're to collect the body, not tomorrow morning, but early the next morning." The undertaker's eyes grew large in surprise, and he nodded his head acknowledging the instructions.

Marcel turned and walked away. He didn't linger one minute extra. He drove back to the farm with the pony and settled him down in the stable. No one came out from the house. They probably didn't hear him or perhaps Sean was busy tending to Rosemary. Then he started his walk home.

It was late evening, almost ten o'clock and Mrs.Ahern was wondering what happened to him. When he finally arrived home, she had already gone to bed and left his supper on a plate on top of the black iron to keep it warm. She had lit his fire, but it was almost out. His room was still warm, so he didn't bother to put on more coal. He washed up, ate his supper, and prepared for bed. Tired and emotionally drained he lay in his bed, warm and comfortable--asking some deeper questions. *What's it all for? What is life all about?* He fell asleep thinking about little Fin's short life, just four years old. *Why did God want that little boy? His son, a bambino, not even born alive? Why did God want these babies?*

The funeral was arranged for three days after Fin's death--their custom. The doctor determined that the little boy had a problem with one of the valves in his heart. He fell asleep and drifted into death painlessly. Fin would not have known he was dying. He simply slipped away into a quiet sleep, his heart beating weaker and weaker until finally it stopped and he was dead. This information consoled Sean, but it didn't help Rosemary at all. She blamed herself for his death, believing that if she had not made the trip to visit her siblings, Fin would still be alive. Sean knew this wasn't true. Fin had a heart condition, and it killed him.

The news spread around the village and neighbouring farms quickly. Most families turned up at the funeral in the little chapel. Rosemary was bereft and unable to speak with anyone. Sean held her up throughout the Mass and at the graveside. As soon as it was over he ushered her up on the trap and took her home. She was heavily pregnant and still visibly shaken. She cried continuously and only stopped when she fell asleep with the aid of a sedative that Doctor Connelly left for her. He advised Sean to let her grieving take its natural course and not to give her with any more brandy. Sean worried about her and their unborn baby.

Kate took over the cooking for a few days to let Rosemary recover. Flo had taught her a lot, her how to make a decent pot of soup, and more, and she enjoyed her time in the kitchen. Sean was very surprised that she could actually cook a half-decent meal, although her bread never did improve. It was always dry and difficult to chew. It was the family joke that they had to dip Kate's bread in their tea to get it down.

It took Rosemary a few weeks before she finally pulled herself up out of bed. She cried the whole time--in the morning, during the daytime, and even through her state of half sleep in the night. When she finally got out of bed, she looked gaunt and pale, her eyes red and sunken into the back of her head.

She began to pray again. She prayed for forgiveness because she was out visiting her family the day it happened. She prayed for the lost soul of her little boy Fin. Then she prayed that nothing bad would happen to her other children. She vowed that she would never leave any of them alone ever again. She prayed on her knees, in the morning after breakfast, after lunch, and in the evening before going to bed. She wanted to go to the graveside every Saturday afternoon to spend time with Fin. Sean took her for fear of leaving her alone. She visited Fin again on the Sunday after Mass, and there she would see Marcel at her only friend's grave. Now, she could understand the loneliness of losing a loved one. That disconnection and separation, the huge hole that it left in her heart and the sharpness of the knife in the pit of her stomach. Rosemary prayed.

> *"Forgive me God,*
>
> *I should have been home wit' him. I know that now and I'm sorry. But I need te know somet'ing? First ye took Flo; she was my only friend, and I know I'll never have another like her. Then ye took Fin, my first-born, my wee boy. He was my heart's desire, and I loved him so much. I have another two wee boys now, and I'm due my fourth baby soon, but why did ye take Fin? I don't understand.*
>
> *Is it me ye want te punish? What have I done? I will repent, I will. I promise ye, if only I knew what my sin was? Please, Father, help me te understand and forgive me, whatever I've done te offend ye. I'm very sorry."*

No answer came, but she continued to pray more often, even throughout the daytime. She hoped that one day she would understand. Rosemary grieved for a long time. She would never leave her children again. Two more babies were born. First Patrick, and finally, a little girl, they named Miriam. Both Rosemary and Rosie were overjoyed.

"It's a girl! It's a girl!" they shouted in unison.

Rosemary's happiness was plain for all to see. She loved her children dearly, but a wee girl, now that was special for her. Rosie grew up knowing babies more than anything. She was now twelve years old, and although a little thin and scrawny, she had a tender heart and a warm nature. They all loved Rosie--she had such a delightful happy outlook. It took a lot to get her down, and she was pretty. Not stunning like her mammy was, but she had lovely golden-brown hair and sparkling blue eyes with long dark lashes like her daddy.

15

A Trip to Dublin, 1908

The Dublin trip was coming up, and Kate arranged to go with the men and do some personal shopping.

"Rosemary, would ye let Rosie come wit' me for the day? She could keep me company and she'd enjoy seeing the shops and t'ings. She's never been te Dublin; it would be a nice day out for her, and I've enough money te take her te the Tea Room for a treat?"

"What a nice idea. Of course, she can go wit' ye if there's enough room on the cart. Ye'd better talk wit' Sean. It depends on how much he's bringing back, but he's not taking any animals so there might be enough room," she replied. "Ye might also want te ask Marcel, she is his daughter?" Rosemary reminded her.

"Of course, I hadn't thought of that." Kate ran off to find Sean and Marcel to clear the idea before saying anything to Rosie. She found them both in the top field having their bread and tea break.

"Rosemary sent me te find ye te ask if it's alright for me and Rosie te come wit' ye te Dublin this time?"

"It's a grand idea, what d'ye t'ink Marcel?"

"Yes, I think she'd enjoy the sightseeing and shopping with Kate, and I can give her some money to spend and make the day special for her," said Marcel.

"Thank ye. I haven't told her yet. I thought I should ask yer per-mission first, ye know?" Kate made her way back to the farmhouse to find Rosie and tell her the good news.

"D'ye mean it, Kate? Really? I can go wit' ye te Dublin? I remem-ber me daddy telling me about Dublin a long time ago, when I was little and he wasn't so grumpy." At the time his story had stirred Rosie's imagination. He made it sound like a fairyland.

"Te t'ink now I'm actually going te see it meself. What a t'rill. Oh, thank ye, Kate, for t'inkin of me and askin' if I could go wit' ye. Thank ye so much," Rosie said excitedly.

Finally, market day arrived for Sean and Marcel. In the back seat of the cart sat Rosie and Kate. They had a five o'clock start early in the morning. The girls had prepared well for the long journey, packing a decent food hamper for all four of them and plenty of hot tea to drink.

Rosie sang out loud as they drove through the village and out the other end to the road that would take them to Dublin city. She was so happy, and for the first time in her life she felt excited and free. She realised she was leaving the farm for the first time in her life. It was like her dream had come true. Rosie had always been happy living with Rosemary and Sean, but she knew they were not her real family--even though she pretended that they were. They looked after her because her mammy was Rosemary's best friend, and Rosemary was her Godmother. Rosie knew she was named after Rosemary. She looked around at the countryside beyond the farm that she had never seen before. It was pretty, tranquil, and peaceful, she thought. Dublin, in comparison, was a big city, bustling with people and full of life, Kate said--she was so excited.

They had no livestock to sell, and so the cart was light for the journey. Sean had a list as long as his arm for not only food supplies for the animals, but also from Rosemary. She wanted fruit of any kind, sugar, and flour, so the cart would be much heavier on the journey back with the two girls and the supplies.

Farming was always a struggle financially, and over the years Rosemary had given Sean most of her savings from the pub. It got them through some hard times in the beginning and helped them buy some livestock. She wanted him to invest in a bull calf. However, Sean refused to use her savings for that. They had only milking cows and twenty laying hens and one rooster. That kept them in eggs and the occasional chicken for dinner.

"Sean, we really should invest in a bull calf. Why don't ye keep an eye out, ye never know, there might be a young'un for a good price?" Rosemary said.

"Aye, ye never know. I'll keep me ears open."

Sean was always careful not to spend money he could ill afford. Neither did he like spending her money on livestock for the farm. However, she pleaded with him and so he agreed to have a look.

Finally, after what seemed a whole day to get there, they entered the outskirts of Dublin city and headed straight for the auction rooms. Sean let Rosie and Kate down from the cart. "There ye go, you girls have a good time, but be back here by four o'clock sharp and don't be late," Sean told Kate.

"We have five hours," Kate said. "Let's start at the shops. Down this way te Main Street. I need te pick up some material and thread te sew a new skirt. Stay close, I'd hate te lose ye on yer first trip." As they closed in on the city it became busier and busier, and Rosie had never seen so many people before

"Everyone seems te be in a hurry," Rosie said. "Where d'ye t'ink they're going?" she asked.

"Sure, they're on their way te work. So, they're in a hurry te get there and not be late. Look, there's the shop I'm looking for across the street," she said pointing. "Stay wit' me, Rosie, we need te cross together." Kate pulled Rosie close to her by the arm and together they ran to the other side of the street. "In here," Kate said and she entered the shop, Rosie followed. Her eyes darted all over the place trying to take everything in at once.

"Here, Rosie, ye can look through these patterns while I look at the fabric. What d'ye t'ink of this for a skirt?"

"It's beautiful, Kate. Yer very lucky te be buying material like that."

"I t'ink I'll have this one. Let's pay for it and I'll show ye around the city. Did yer daddy give ye any money te spend?"

"Yes, he gave me enough te buy a book for meself."

"Okay, then I'll take ye te the bookshop on Main Street. It's a great shop--ye'll love it, so many books te choose from." Kate paid for her purchase and the girls made their way back outside into Main Street.

"This way," Kate said. "We have time te look in the shop windows but not enough time te go inside."

"Look at these shoes, Kate. Did ye ever see anyt'ing so lovely in yer life? See the red ones over there?" Rosie said pointing.

"Oh, they're grand right enough. It's almost lunch time, are ye hungry yet, Rosie?"

"Yes, I am."

"Okay, then let's go this way te the Tea Room. It's a lovely place for lunch, and they make special cakes," said Kate. "Ye'll love it, and they make dinners ye've never heard of before. After lunch, we'll go te the bookshop on our way back. We'll have plenty of time for ye te browse."

"That's grand Kate, thank ye." It was Rosie's first time eating in a public place. The Tea Room was a very popular place for ladies to lunch, and it was quite busy when they arrived. A waitress met them at the entrance and ushered them to a table for two. Rosie and Kate looked over the menu with great intent.

"Ye know, Rosie, I've had the beef broth and it's delicious. I've also had the Shepherds Pie, very tasty and very filling," Kate told her. "I want te treat ye te a pudding or a pie, so I t'ink we should only have one course or we'll be full te bursting afterwards," Kate said. The waitress stood at the table waiting patiently for their order.

"We'll have two Shepherds Pie please--no soup today, thank ye. Then we'll have the dessert menu, tea for two, and the cake stand. Thank ye very much," Kate said with confidence.

Just as Kate had warned Rosie, the food was delicious and very filling. The girls hadn't realised how hungry they were and finished the entire meal.

"I'm stuffed," said Rosie.

"Me too, but we must have the dessert menu and the cake stand te pick from. We'll be full, alright, but we can walk it off on our way te the bookshop," Kate told her.

The waitress brought the dessert menu and handed them a copy each. She left the cake stand on the table along with the cups and saucers, sugar and milk jug, and teapot filled with hot tea.

Young Rosie's eyes almost popped out of her head. She never saw anything like it. On the cake stand there was a strawberry tart, a pink meringue cake, a long chocolate éclair, and a long vanilla and fresh cream slice. On the dessert menu, there was a choice of rice pudding with figs, caramel shortcake, peach pie, and custard with a variety of fresh fruit and trifle with fresh cream.

"What'll ye pick?" Kate asked her.

"I don't know, there's so many and they all look delicious. What's the red one?" Rosie asked.

"It's a strawberry tart, ye'd love it."

"What's the pink one?" she asked again.

"It's a meringue cake, I know ye'd love it, too," Kate replied. "Why don't we have one of each and half them between us? Then, ye'll get te try them both?"

"That's a grand idea, Kate, go ahead."

"No dessert then?" asked Kate.

"No, Kate. I couldn't manage both--I'm already full."

Kate poured the tea and split each cake in half. The girls indulged themselves, slowly savouring the delicate sweetness of each delight. Neither spoke but made sounds of approval.

"Mmm," said Kate.

"Mmm," agreed Rosie, "how delicious."

When they went to leave the Tea Room, they were full to bursting.

"I knew ye'd like it."

"Never tasted the likes before now," Rosie told her.

"I know," said Kate. "I was about yer age, Rosie, when I came for me first trip wit' Sean. We should take a walk down te the harbour where the big ships come in. We've got time, and I know ye'd like te see them. Ye know--the ships that go te America?"

"Oh, my, Kate, I'd love te see them."

"Let's go, then. This way," Kate said and they headed for the dockside away from the busy shopping centre. "The walk'll do us good, after all that food. Ye know, Rosie, I have an aunt in New York," Kate told her. "Daddy wanted me te go and live wit' her, but I didn't like te travel all that way meself."

"Oh, I would go in a minute if I were you," said Rosie quickly.

"Would ye?" replied Kate surprised. "Would ye really go te America and leave the farm and your daddy?"

"Me daddy doesn't really like me," Rosie replied. "I know he tries, but I'm quite afraid of him--he's always grunting and grumpy every time I see him. Rosemary says he never got over the death of me mammy, but I've never known him any other way," she said trying to keep pace with Kate.

"Well, we might be able te do somet'ing about that--going te America, I mean. If yer serious that is?"

"Oh, yes. I mean it," she said. "I'd go if I had someone te go wit' and an aunt te go te. If I were you, I'd have gone a long time ago. There's not'ing for ye on the farm and there's not'ing for me, either," Rosie said matter- of-fact like.

"Rosie, can ye keep a secret?"

"Yes, of course, I can," she replied.

"Rosie," Kate said quietly. "There is a way for ye te go te America--ye could go wit' me. Ye'd have te say that ye were an orphan, and I would agree, and say ye were traveling wit' me. That way ye wouldn't have te pay a full fare like I do," Kate said as they rounded the corner into the dockside. "We can watch from that platform over there," she told Rosie pointing the way. "I've got me ticket money already, saved it up years ago. Are ye serious? Or do ye need te t'ink about it?" she asked. "Ye couldn't tell anyone, not even Rosemary or Sean, and if yer daddy found out he'd skin me alive for putting ye up te the idea," Kate said.

"Okay," said Rosie slowly. "I know me daddy would be angry if I didn't tell him, but I'm sure he'd let me go if I did ask him. Don't ye think?" Rosie argued.

"Absolutely not," Kate said boldly. "If he knew, he'd thrash the both of us, and we'd never get te go te Dublin again. It has te be our secret if we do it. Are ye up for it or not?" Kate asked again. Rosie was quiet for a few minutes thinking. A chance to leave the farm forever--the only home she had ever known. To go to a big country like America where there was a future for her; where she might even find a young man and marry and have children?

She turned to Kate and announced confidently. "Let's do it, where do we go to sign up?"

"We can't go today," Kate told her. "We have te put our names on a list for the next available ship leaving from here, and I would have te pay, now, I mean today," she said. "Thank goodness I have me savings wit' me, so we could sign up today if ye were sure," Kate said.

"Let's go and see when the sailings are due. There might be a ship leaving next month that we could sail on and sign for today?" Kate said. They made their way down towards the harbour office and went to the inquiry desk to ask for the list of ships in and out.

"Look here," said Kate. "There's one next month, and it sails at noon. That's the same time as the auction starts, so we'd be here in time, alright. We could sign up for it today and come through next month wit' Sean and yer daddy. They would never know, and by the time they went looking for us, the ship would be gone and we'd be on our way te America," Kate said defiantly.

Rosie had never done anything deceitful before. She had no reason to hide anything, always being honest and open about everything she did. It was a bad thing to do to Rosemary and Sean--she knew that, and was sorry about it. She also knew that her daddy wouldn't let her go with Kate, at least that's what Kate said. She couldn't ask him, if he said no, then he would know their plan. She had to take the chance and sign up today while she was here with Kate. "Okay, where do we go te sign up?"

Kate led the way to the booking office, she had been there many times before and always turned away. Now that she was travelling with Rosie, it didn't seem so frightening. They were going together, and Rosie would love America. Rosie put her name on the list and marked herself as an "Orphan."

Kate signed her name and paid for her ticket. Ten pounds got them sharing a cabin with another four people; Rosie would share Kate's bunk. Kate opened her purse and showed Rosie her savings. Rosie never saw so much money before. "I've enough for the two of us when we get te America." The booking clerk handed them each a boarding ticket.

"If ye don't have this, ye won't be getting on the ship, and there's no return money if ye don't show up, either," he told them.

It was their biggest secret ever. Kate was so eager to go now, and couldn't stop talking to Rosie about it telling her everything her aunt had written about New York.

"When we get back te Sean and yer daddy, ye mustn't mention a single t'ing that might trigger them te think what we're about." The girls agreed not to talk about it again until next month. Not even if they thought they were alone on the farm, not a word until they were back at the harbour.

They booked the noon sailing on September 2, 1908, Dublin to New York. It was a month away. Kate told Rosie that she must look normal for the trip. However, the weather would be cooler, so she might get away with wearing more clothes than usual. Kate couldn't pack a trunk, either. They would have to make do wearing their ordinary clothes.

Meanwhile, they made their way back into town and went to the bookshop. Marcel was expecting Rosie to spend her gift money on a book. She chose something that cost less than she might have spent and kept the change. Then they returned to meet up with Sean and Marcel at four o'clock for their journey home to the farm. Marcel and Sean were still loading the buggy with supplies.

"My, ye've got a lot of stuff," said Rosie.

"Everyt'ing that Rosemary asked for and more," replied Sean. "What did ye girls get up te, have ye had a good time?"

"It was wonderful, Kate took me te see the shops and the fashions. Then we went te a tea shop for lunch, and we had a cake each, and I had Shepherds Pie. It was delicious. Then we went sightseeing down te the harbour, and we went te the bookshop. I bought a book and then we came back here. What a wonderful day it's been. Can I come back again wit' ye next month?" she asked. Everyone laughed out loud at Rosie's obvious excitement.

"We'll see," replied Sean. "Now jump up and get settled down. It's a long ride home, and I'm sure ye'll be tired now wit' all that walking around the city." He helped Rosie up on the rear bench with her new book, and then Kate with her small parcel of material and threads. The cart now loaded with supplies, would make for a slow journey home. Sean was right, though, Rosie was exhausted. All the new food, excitement, and a new secret that weighed heavily in her heart made her tired and sleepy.

They didn't stop to eat this time as the sun was starting to set. Soon it would be evening and then dark. They preferred to keep going and get home a little earlier. Kate unpacked the hamper to see what the men had left them to eat. There was still some bread and a lump of cheese, so she sliced the bread and cheese and handed a piece to the men. Both Rosie and Kate were still feeling full after lunch. They continued their journey. Marcel took the reins while Sean had some food--everyone wanted to get home as soon as possible. It had been a long day, and they were all tired out. Rosie didn't sing this time. Instead, she lay her head against Kate's shoulder and quickly fell asleep. The men talked between themselves about the auction. Sean told Marcel that he had let out word that he was looking for a bull calf. Marcel nodded in understanding.

"Did you hear of any on offer?" he asked.

"Yes, but just born two days ago and not ready for market until next month," he replied. "When we come back in September, the bull calf will be up for auction then. I'll tell Rosemary about it and see if she still wants te buy one. I'm sure she won't have changed her mind. She's quite adamant, ye know," he said. "The problem with buying at this time of year is the winter. The calf seems te need its mother more in the winter. Often ye have te bring it inside te the warmth te keep it alive. Oh, well, I've told her all this before and as long as she knows before she makes up her mind."

Sean rambled on for a while longer, and Marcel nodded and made the occasional response. They were going as fast as the horse could handle at a steady trot. Sean was patient--he knew his horse and its speed, and he never used the whip on him. Finally, they rounded the road that took them through the village, and on up towards the farm. They reached the farmhouse and stopped outside at the door to let the girls off. Kate woke Rosie.

"We're home--time te wake up." Rosie opened her eyes and saw Rosemary standing at the front door smiling.

"Come on in girls, I've made a stew for us all, and it's delicious." Rosemary's cooking had improved with all the years of Flo's influence.

"Will ye join us for supper, Marcel? I know ye'll like it?" Marcel nodded in agreement. There was a bucket of water and a towel for the men to wash before they went inside. The front door was ajar; they cleaned up, removed their boots and entered the house. Rosemary was waiting to put their dinner out on the plates. The girls were chattering to Rosemary about where they had been and what they had seen. Indeed, Rosemary wanted to see Kate's material and wanted to see the finished skirt. Rosie was still enthralled by Dublin and all she had seen--she could hardly eat for talking. Finally, her hunger got the better of her, and she ate her supper in silence.

Sean told Rosemary about the bull calf that would be for sale in September. The only problem would be taking the young calf away from its mother just as winter was starting.

"Ye might have te bring it inside wit' ye te keep it warm," he warned her.

"Oh, that wouldn't be so bad. The boys would love it--they'd make it feel like their own pet. By springtime, the danger will be over, and the calf will be in his first year and need te be fattened up. The boys can look after him," Rosemary said.

"I told ye Marcel, once this woman gets an idea in her head, that's the end of it, and ye can't change it."

"So, sounds like we'll be going back in September te bid on the bull calf," said Marcel.

"Sounds like it, indeed," said Sean, and Rosemary smiled at the two men.

The stew was good, and Marcel appreciated the hot meal. He said his thanks for supper and made his way out to leave.

"I'll walk home, the horse has earned his keep for the day and needs to rest. I'll enjoy the walk myself."

"If yer sure of that, then fine wit' me." Sean wished Marcel good-night and thanked him again for his help. He stood for a moment outside at the front door. *What a lovely night,* he thought to himself, *nice for a walk home.* The sky was dark but lit up with the light of the full moon. Then he turned back inside. The girls had already cleared up for Rosemary and made their way to bed in the big room. Rosemary was just drying up the last of the dishes when Sean came back into the kitchen.

"It was a good day," Sean told her. "We got good prices for everyt'ing, and Marcel is definitely coming round te his old self. Are ye sure ye want this bull calf, Rosemary?" he asked again. "It's a lot of work over the winter wit' the kids and the house and all. Do ye t'ink ye can cope wit' it? I don't want ye te be taking on too much yerself."

"Of course I can," she replied. "Sure, it's only a baby calf after all, and if it gets too cold we'll bring him inside. The boys'll love him. Don't be worrying about it. I'll manage fine. Now let's get to bed, ye must be exhausted." she said.

Sean banked up the black iron stove for the night to keep the place warm until morning. Rosemary went through to the bedroom to ready herself for bed. First, she walked around inspecting each child sleeping in bed. Then she got down on her knees to say her prayers as she did every night.

Sean finally arrived and undressed, placing his clothes over the chair beside the bed. He sat down on the edge of the bed and said a quick prayer in thanks for the day. He yawned and got into bed and without interrupting Rosemary, he fell fast asleep.

August passed by quickly. Kate busied herself sewing her new skirt; now she had a good reason to get it finished before the month was up. They would be going to the market again in two weeks' time. Neither girl had spoken about their secret. Kate kept the tickets hidden safely out of sight, and never brought them out for fear someone saw them. Finally, it was getting near time for the monthly trip to Dublin. Rosie asked Rosemary if she could go again.

"Of course ye can go." Rosie had a good reason to decide what clothing she could wear. Somehow she had to wear at least two lots of clothes and the only coat she possessed. It was getting cooler in the evenings, and that was a good excuse to carry the coat with her so that she could wear it on the journey home.

Kate finished her skirt. It had full gathering all around, giving her the opportunity to wear another skirt underneath. She also prepared a small parcel, saying it was her old shoes that she wanted resoled, but in fact it was some underwear and "smalls" for both of the girls. Kate knew that Rosie didn't have underwear or socks, or vests or bodices of any kind. She had enough for them both--knew they would need it on their journey. Kate would also wear her cape; it was heavy and warm for the cooler nights. Rosemary was not in the least way suspicious of anything and wished the girls a happy shopping day. She gave Rosie a penny to spend on something nice for herself.

"Kate, will ye look out for a pattern for the children, somet'ing easy for me to sew?"

"Of course I will," Kate replied.

Again the girls had prepared the hamper with food and drinks. Kate made sure they had plenty of boiled eggs and bread for them to take to the ship. She didn't know what food would be available for them on board. She had the tickets safely hidden in her shoe. They set out as before early in the morning, just before five o'clock. They would be in Dublin by eleven o'clock if there was no hold ups and they didn't stop for anything.

Rosie was growing nervous. It was a bad thing to do, and she chastised herself. If her daddy found out, she knew he'd beat the life out of her, and Kate, too, for that matter. She knew Rosemary would be hurt and offended, and she was sorry for that.

Rosemary was kind to her, even when she was an infant. She could remember Rosemary rocking her to sleep in her arms at nights. As the years passed, she and Rosie became good friends and Rosie knew that running away would break her guardian's heart. She could only hope that one day Rosemary would understand that there was nothing for Rosie at the farm and there never would be. This was

Rosie's only chance for a life of her own and she had to take it. She prayed everything would go well, and that one-day, Rosemary and Sean would forgive her. When they arrived at the auction rooms, Sean stopped and let the two girls down from the buggy.

"Be back here at four o'clock and no later," Sean reminded them.

"Of course," said Kate as they walked towards the Main Street. The girls rounded the corner and out of sight.

"What time is it?" asked Rosie.

"Let's go see the big clock and find out," said Kate. They walked down the street to the main crossroads in the centre of the city where the big town clock stood. It was eleven o'clock in the morning.

"We've plenty of time. Do ye want te go now and stand in line te board early? Or do ye want te wait a little and get on last?" she asked Rosie.

"I t'ink we should go early and get on board first."

"Okay, then, let's go now and board immediately. That way we'll be on board, and we can get settled in the cabin before the ship leaves. We'll be well away by the time Sean and yer daddy notice we're missing," Kate said. They made their way towards the harbour. They found the line up for their ship and took their place in line waiting to board. They had no luggage, only the one small package that Kate brought and the bag of food. They could see up ahead that the ticket master was checking tickets and boarding people from the line up. It would be no time before it was their turn. They waited anxiously in line for their turn to board the ship. It would be a new start in a new country far from Ireland and the farm they knew as home.

Back at the auction hall, Sean went to see if Tom Devlin had shown up with his cows and the bull calf that he was selling. "He's already gone," the auctioneer told him.

"What?" asked Sean. "He's been and gone already?"

"Yes," replied the auctioneer. "He was here already, but he went down te the harbour te help board some of the cows he sold on.

They're off te America. The ship leaves in about an hour. He said he'd be back later. I t'ink he took the bull calf wit' him as well. I don't know if he sold that as well or not?" he told Sean.

Sean turned to Marcel. "I t'ink we should go down there in case he sold the bull calf already," Sean said annoyed. "Otherwise, we might wait here for him all day. I wonder if he sold it already? We can pick up our supplies when we get back, but we should find out about the calf first. What d'ye t'ink?" Sean asked Marcel.

"Yes, indeed, I agree with you. We could be here all day waiting for him, right enough," replied Marcel.

The two men stabled the horse and buggy and made their way down towards the harbour. They went to the office to find out which ship was sailing to America. The clerk handed Sean the list. On the top page was the list of sailings including the name of the vessel, destination, and departure time. They found the ship departing at twelve o'clock noon to America carrying livestock.

"This is the one," said Sean. On the next page was the passenger list. They were looking for livestock sold by Tom Devlin. They didn't know the name of the person who had bought the cows and who would be shipping them to America. Sean and Marcel both read through the lists at the same time. When Sean saw the names Kate McGinty and Rosie Murphy, "Orphan," he immediately thought he had read it wrong. However, Marcel read it out loud as he saw the names and a shudder of disbelief rushed through him.

"Kate McGinty and Rosie Murphy, Orphan," Marcel said out loud. Sean saw the stunned expression on Marcel's face--he was angry. He knew that if Marcel got to Rosie first, he would thrash her in broad daylight.

"We'll go together, Marcel," Sean said. "Now stay calm, no need for public display, not today. We'll just fetch Rosie te come back home wit' us. Kate can go--in fact, I'll make sure she does. I'll be rid of her by her own wishes this time. For sure it was Kate who put Rosie up te this," Sean said firmly.

Marcel, silently enraged, stood rigid, only his mouth agreed with Sean.

"Well, let's find out," he said infuriated.

When they reached the line-up for boarding the ship, Sean saw the two girls immediately. They were near the top of the line but still standing on the quayside. They were waiting for their turn to embark the gangway to board the ship. Both men walked up the outside of the line-up. When they reached the girls, Marcel grabbed hold of Rosie's coat collar and dragged her under the rope to the other side where he was standing with Sean. Her legs went limp when she saw her daddy, and she found she couldn't stand. It wasn't difficult to drag her under the ropes--she was so light and small.

"No!" Kate cried out when she saw Marcel and Sean. "She's coming wit' me te Auntie Kitty in New York, I've enough money for us both," she said defiantly.

"Oh, no she's not. She's coming home with us," said Marcel. "You can go to your Auntie Kitty, but she's staying here with me, I'm her daddy." In that same moment, the ticket master reached forward towards Kate and snatched the tickets from her hand.

"No, no, wait," she pleaded with the ticket master. He stopped purposely--took a long look at the situation.

"Well now, what have we here?" he said. "This young lass has a ticket to travel wit' this young lady, and it says that she is an orphan and that this young lady is taking her charge for the journey. What have you to say about that?" he directed his question to Marcel.

"I'm her father, and she's no orphan. I knew nothing of this plot. I do not give my permission for her to go to America with this young lady, as you call her," pointing to Kate. "She's not going to America, she's coming home with me, and that's final," he yelled back at the ticket master. Marcel went to walk in the opposite direction away from the ship with Rosie clenched in his hand when Sean shouted out.

"Stop, Marcel. Wait here a minute," Sean said. "I want te make sure Kate gets on board that ship te America, and that finally we'll be well rid of her." He motioned to the ticket master to board Kate and not let her back on the pier. The ticket master pushed Kate forward and up the gangway as he ushered the next in line for their tickets. Kate had no option she was already on the gangway holding up the people behind her. She had to go forward to let them on and found herself boarded and unable to get back on the pier.

"No, no, wait, let me off," she cried, but the people behind had lost interest and were pushing her forward as they wanted to get on board.

Rosie stood sobbing quietly on the pier, as her daddy held her tight with his fist closed hard on her collar, as his other hand clenched her arm. She couldn't get loose and was afraid to pull against him. In those few seconds, she saw her bright future vanish. Her chance for freedom was gone. Disheartened and afraid of what was to become of her now, she knew she was in big trouble. More importantly, she felt ashamed of herself for being so deceitful, and a direct insult to Sean and Rosemary, who trusted her. She knew that when she got home she was in for a good thrashing, probably with his belt. That was what he always threatened, but until now he had never used it on her.

Rosie didn't realise until now how much she wanted to go to America and leave the farm. It would have been a whole new and exciting life for her. Kate told her that she would find a job perhaps in a tea shop like the one they visited. Rosie would love that, serving and talking to people all day. There were few visitors to the farm and even when the odd person came calling, it was never for her. It was usually for some farm business or other, and not to talk to Rosie. Standing there with Marcel she felt humiliated, caught doing something despicable against the very two people she cared for, and who cared for her.

She knew Rosemary would be hurt and disappointed. She probably could not help her out of this trouble. Rosie felt really alone for the first time since her mammy died. She had no one to turn to. She knew that any affection from Rosemary and Sean was now ended. She was at her daddy's mercy, and she had always been afraid of him. Now, she had given him the perfect excuse to beat her and she knew he would.

Sean, Marcel, and Rosie stood on the pier waiting for the ship to leave. It began to rain. The cold raindrops settled on Rosie's face and ran down her cheeks to join her silent tears. She tried hard not to cry, but she was full of fear and trembled visibly. They could see Kate standing on the deck crying and fearful of traveling alone. Sean felt relieved that she was leaving and that he and Rosemary would finally have their home to themselves.

Her Auntie Kitty would be delighted to take her in. She was elderly now but very well settled in New York with a nice home and money in the bank. Sean had often thought of going himself, like two of his brothers before him had done. However, his daddy wouldn't hear of it. He needed Sean on the farm to keep things going for future generations of McGintys. That was old Mr. McGinty's wish, and he would not be questioned on it.

The three of them waited patiently for the ship to pull away from the harbour. Other people waved in excitement, happy for their departing loved ones. Sean, and now Marcel, were both glad to see the back of Kate and felt relieved that they had managed to get there in time to stop Rosie from leaving with her. Sean worried that Marcel would be too harsh on the girl. He would try to talk with him on the subject before they got home. He felt sorry for Rosie, understanding why she would run away with Kate to America. He knew there was little promise of a life for her on the farm.

Sean also knew that if Rosie asked her daddy for his permission, he would have said no. Rosie was the only reason that Marcel was still alive. He might have ended his own life before now if not for her.

He promised Flo he would care for their daughter, and to him that meant paying for her keep. This was the only way he knew how to care for her in her mammy's absence. Marcel was a man of his word and meant to keep his promise to Flo, even if Rosie didn't want it.

Finally, the ship pulled away from the pier and slowly slipped into the Irish Sea--onwards to the vastness of the Atlantic Ocean. Sean knew Kate was stuck on board, and it was a long way to America. The ship would take three months to get there. Kate had her ticket money for two years now. Her Auntie Kitty had sent it to her, and Kate saved every penny towards her new life. She just wasn't brave enough to travel alone. Now, after all the planning and conspiring, she was traveling alone. They turned and made their way back to the auction rooms where they still had business to complete. Marcel kept a tight grip on Rosie's arm. When they arrived, he made her sit up on the buggy where he could keep an eye on her while he was loading the supplies.

"Sit there and don't move or else."

"Yes, Daddy," she replied quietly. Rosie sat still with her head down. She was silently mortified, and wondered if Rosemary and Sean would ever forgive her. She knew her daddy was not the forgiving kind, and he would never let her forget what a despicable thing she had done.

The men were busy loading the buggy with their animal supplies when Tom Devlin appeared looking for Sean.

"Ah, there ye are, I was here earlier looking for ye, but I had te go help someone load the cattle I sold him onto the ship for America. Ye know, paperwork an' all," said Tom. "I just wanted te tell ye, that the bull calf's not ready te leave the mother yet. I want te keep him for another month. Just te make sure he's well and healthy before I sell him on, but he's yours when he's ready if ye still want him," he told Sean.

Sean knew that if Tom took the bull calf away from the mother too early, that she would pine and often the cow would die from the sorrow of losing her calf. That was the real reason Devlin wanted to keep the calf, to make sure he didn't lose his cow, as well.

"Are ye sure yer selling him?" Sean asked.

"Oh, yes, but next month, so I'll see ye back here then. We can shake on it if it makes ye feel better, but as I said he's yours if ye still want him." Sean held out his hand to Tom, and they shook firmly on the deal for next month.

"We'll see ye then," Sean said.

"Right ye are," replied Tom as he walked away.

Sean turned to Marcel. "I just want te buy some produce for Rosemary, ye know fruit and sugar and flour, and then we'll be off home."

"We're early enough, but it would be good te eat first before we leave. I'm starving," said Marcel.

"Of course, we missed lunch, didn't we? Rosie, get the hamper out and let's see what there is for eating." Rosie reached behind her for the hamper and placed it on the seat in front of her. There was cheese, bread, butter and jam, and some boiled eggs. Rosemary had made scones to go with the jam. There was a large bottle of milk and another that contained the hot tea, which would be warm at best by now. Rosie handed down the milk, bread, and cheese first. She tried to have some bread but her stomach was churning. She was so afraid of what was to come. Sean left to pick up the produce that Rosemary had asked for. When he came back, he sat alongside Marcel, and Rosie handed him some milk, bread, and cheese.

"The tea is just lukewarm if ye want it?"

"No thanks, I'll stick with the milk." The men continued to eat and chat among themselves.

"Quite the day," Sean said.

"Certainly is," agreed Marcel.

"Ye know, Marcel, I wouldn't be too hard on her," Sean said. "Kate probably painted a very rosy picture. Rosie's never been anywhere but Dublin just once before now. She was probably so excited about the thought of going on a big ship, that she didn't realise how hard it would be on ye, or us either, for that matter. She doesn't understand how far away America is, or even that she did somet'ing wrong."

"Oh, she knew alright," Marcel said nodding his head. "She knew she was doing something very wrong indeed. Otherwise, she would have told me, or Rosemary, or you, or at least one of us. She knew enough to keep it a secret--she knew alright. Sneaking around for a whole month knowing what they were planning. Does she really think I'm a fool?" Marcel asked quietly. "Well, I'm not, and she'll find that out the hard way not to make a fool out of me again," he told Sean. "She'll get a good thrashing for this when we get home, and don't try to talk me out of it. She's my daughter, and I'll deal out the punishment for this my way. Do you understand Sean?" Marcel said, in control.

He could see Marcel was angry and nodded in agreement, realising that he had lost his argument for Rosie's sake. She was about to feel the wrath of her father's anger and Sean told to mind his own business. It was a five-hour ride home. The journey was mournful and silent for most of the way. Rosie tried to calm herself sitting quietly on the rear bench. At times, she let her eyes close while holding the bench with her hands but she didn't sleep, just dozed a little. It rained a bit then stopped again. Then it began to get dark, and Rosie knew they didn't have much further to go. Her stomach was empty. She hadn't eaten anything since breakfast, and then only bread and tea. She knew if she ate anything it would make her sick. Her stomach was so turbulent with fear that she was in pain. Finally, they rounded the dirt track into the driveway and up to the farmhouse. Rosie's fear rose to her throat now, and she found it hard to swallow. Sean stopped at the front door to the house where Rosemary stood waiting. She heard them come up the driveway.

"Where's Kate?" she asked.

"On the ship te America," replied Sean. "It's a long story and I'll tell all later. Let's get this buggy unloaded first and then we can have supper." Rosemary's mouth fell wide open as she nodded her head in agreement and turned to go inside again. When Sean finally returned to the house, Rosemary was ready to serve supper to everyone but saw that Marcel and Rosie weren't with him.

"What's going on?" she asked Sean.

"Rosie was going te run away wit' Kate te America. She listed herself as an orphan te travel in Kate's charge. I believe Kate saved enough money for the two of them. They were going to Kitty's place in New York. We saw them both standing on the pier waiting te board the ship," Sean told her.

"My word," she replied shocked.

Sean continued, "Marcel is furious wit' her and I'm fearful that he'll beat the life out of her. I've spoken te him, I asked him not te be too hard on her. It was more Kate's fault than Rosie's," said Sean. "However, he made it clear that he wants no interference from us on this. He says he'll deal wit' the punishment himself." Sean hung his head and then looked up at Rosemary in dismay.

"Oh, dear," said Rosemary worried.

"I feel so sorry for her. Our Kate led her into this for sure," Sean said. "Marcel t'inks she was trying te make a fool of him and he's about te make her pay for it. He'll lose his temper wit' her. I know he will, but it's not our business, Rosemary, d'ye hear me?"

"Yes," she replied.

"We've been warned off, and we might lose her custody if we interfere. She is his daughter," Sean said defeated.

16

Rosie, Rosa, Just Like Mama, 1908-09

The buggy was sitting stationery in the barn. Rosie sat on the rear bench with her head lowered. The men had unloaded all the supplies and stored them. Marcel finally approached the buggy and called up to Rosie.

"Get down here."

His voice was low, but his words were hissing mad and sometimes he spoke in Italian that she couldn't understand him. She heard the odd swear word. Those she did understand and it scared her even more. "*Sciocca*, little fool, just like Mama. *Sciocca Rosie, sciocca Mama*," he spat the words from his mouth. "*Piccola cagna*, little bitch," he called her, "*faccia di merda, sciocca*, little fool, just like Mama."

Marcel grabbed hold of her arm and pulled her towards the back of the barn where the hay was stacked high to the roof. There was a clearing at the rear where the stacks made a half-wall to the front of the barn. It became like an enclosed room made from hay. He threw Rosie down on the floor.

"Take your coat off." She unbuttoned her coat and placed it on the stack beside her.

"Now," he whispered. "Get on your knees and lift your skirt up to your waist, *piccola cagna*, little bitch." Like most young girls at that time, Rosie didn't possess underwear and Marcel knew that. They wore their skirts long instead--underwear was a luxury. Rosie's heart dropped like lead, and she felt totally humiliated as she did what he ordered.

"Think you make a fool of me and get away with it?" he shrieked angrily. "Never!" he roared. Marcel undid the belt on his trousers and wrapped the belt around the palm of his hand. He swung the buckle end towards her bare bottom with a swish, and the metal ripped into her soft flesh as Rosie screamed out in pain. In seconds, the belt was on her again tearing, burning, ripping, and wounding the skin so deeply that it wept blood. He revelled in the power over her and lashed her again and again in quick short strokes, all the while screeching out in Italian and working himself into a seething uncontrollable rage.

"*Piccola cagna...* little bitch." "*Piccola cagna...* try to make a fool of me... *piccola cagna...*"

He continued to beat her in a blind rage and unable to stop when he lost all sense and was suddenly on her, penetrating her body like a wild animal. Rosie screamed out in pain but Marcel pushed her head down into the hay to muffle her sound. She tried to turn her head sideways to breathe, but the pain was unbearable and she fell unconscious. In his rage, he hadn't noticed that she was out cold, and continued to pound on her body, relieving his long-standing, pent-up frustration. This was the first time Marcel raped his daughter. She was thirteen years of age.

When he was done, he threw her to one side like a lifeless rag doll. He stood back and viewed his victim with disdain and contempt. "Just like Rosa," he said. "No respect. Now you know my strength and you will respect me, understand?" He fixed his clothing and replaced his belt without remorse or concern for her. He reached down to Rosie and pulled her over by the arm.

"Stand " he commanded without shame or guilt.

Rosie regained consciousness and slowly opened her eyes. She stood as he ordered. She was shaking all over and unable to control her trembling.

"Let this be your punishment--indeed your purpose from now on. You're old enough to learn how to please your papa. Now clean yourself," he ordered as he walked to the other side of the barn and sat down to watch her.

"Not so smart now," he said in a cold voice. "Just like Mama, a little mouse," he continued. Marcel's rage had unleashed a sleeping monster that lay dormant all these years. He had no feeling for Rosie's pain. In fact, he thought she deserved her punishment for causing him embarrassment in public.

Rosie could barely see through her tears. She had fainted from the pain, but she knew what did to her. She had seen the bull being led to the cow one year, and Kate had instructed her on what was going to happen. At the time, she remembered the girls giggled in embarrassment, and Rosie covered her eyes with her hands as she tried not to watch the event.

Her pain reached all the way up inside her body. She struggled to stand--her legs wobbled, and she thought they would break in two if she put her full weight on them. There was a lot of blood, and she wasn't sure where it came from, but she tried to rub it off with the dry hay. Her stomach rolled over with fear, and she felt like throwing up several times. Aware that he was watching her, she nervously continued to clean herself while trying hard not to cry. When she looked reasonable enough, and the blood cleaned away, Marcel spoke again.

"Don't ever disrespect me, or make a fool of me again. I am your papa, who pays for your life every day. Your punishment is between us--you will say nothing to Sean or Rosemary. If either of them mentions anything to me about this, you'll get more. Do you understand?" he said in a low but controlled voice.

"Yes," she whispered. He walked over to her and picked up her coat.

"Put this on." She did as he told her, and together they walked out of the barn towards the house.

He held her tight by the collar as before. Her legs were weak, and she felt that she might fall, but he was holding her up. When they got to the front door, Rosie pushed it open. Sean and Rosemary sat waiting by the fireside. Rosie walked into the room and without saying a word, turned immediately into the bedroom.

"She's had a taste of my anger for such deceitful conspiracy against me and your good selves. We are the people who care for her and feed her every day. She won't forget tonight quickly, and now she knows what to expect if she ever insults me again," Marcel told them. "I'm going to walk home. I think the walk will do me some good. After all this drama, I need the fresh air about me, and it's not raining. Goodnight now."

"Goodnight, Marcel," replied Sean sombrely.

It was nine o'clock at night. Sean went into the kitchen and spoke quietly to Rosemary.

"We should leave her alone te cry for a while; she'll fall asleep shortly, poor wee lass." Sean shook his head in disbelief that this night had happened at all. It was all Kate's fault he knew for sure, and he hoped they would never set eyes on her again.

Rosie removed her coat and climbed straight into bed. She muffled her face into her pillow to soften the noise of her crying. She cried with pain, and she cried with disbelief at what her daddy did to her. She cried with humiliation, and she cried with fear that this would not be the last time. Rosie couldn't understand what she did that made him hate her so much. How could any daddy hurt his own daughter like this?

She thought over the events of her lifetime since her mammy died. There was nothing she could think of that she had done to offend him, until today.

She made the comparison with Sean McGinty, who would chastise his boys verbally, often threatening things he would do if they didn't behave. However, he never lifted his hand to any of them. Nor would he, for it was obvious to Rosie that Sean loved his children, and wouldn't hurt any of them. Not like her daddy did to her tonight. She didn't understand the years of stifled frustration that she had unleashed with his anger.

The pain in her body made her twitch at times, and the humiliation made her feel unimportant, and empty inside. She was worthless, to anyone, even her own father. Rosie wished that she could die, for now she was nothing--how could anyone love her if her own daddy couldn't? Finally, she cried herself into a light sleep, her little body still twitching from the trauma.

Sean and Rosemary waited for her to fall asleep before entering the room. Finally, after some time, they stopped by Rosie's bed. Neither of them spoke but stood looking down at the little girl. She looked tiny in the bed. So small like a little bird all curled up as if she was giving herself a hug. Rosemary's heart saddened to see the young girl in such a state, and a single tear spilled over and rolled down her cheek. Sean leaned forward and picked up the quilt that was covering her. He lifted her skirt to expose her bloody bottom. Rosemary gasped in shock when she saw Rosie's wounds. Her bottom was severely scarred with deep bloody gouges from the buckle.

"Oh, my God. That's it. I'll be having words wit' him tomorrow 'bout this. He went too far wit' her, and this is too much for any beating. I can't believe he'd do this." Sean said shocked. At that Rosie opened her eyes and rolled on her back.

"Please don't talk te Daddy about this, Sean. He said if anyone spoke te him about it, then he would do it again." Rosie burst into tears. Rosemary sat down on the side of the bed beside Rosie and consoled her as best she could.

"My daddy hurt me bad, Rosemary. He hurt me really bad," she cried.

"I have some lanolin cream. It's good for sealing wounds like this, and it'll help te take the sting away." Rosemary went to fetch the cream and Sean sat down beside Rosie.

"Don't worry, Rosie, I won't say a word te him. Yer Daddy's been brewing his anger for a long time, since yer mammy died for sure. I have te tell ye though, this beatin' he gave ye has changed my opinion for the worst. I didn't know he could be this cruel," Sean told her.

Rosemary stood in the kitchen with her hands over her face to muffle the sounds of crying, shocked that Marcel, the girl's daddy, could do such a thing. She pulled herself together for the youngster's sake and returned with the cream and some warm water to clean the wounds. She asked Rosie to roll over on her stomach and began to clean the wounds with the warm water and a soft cotton cloth. It stung a little each time, but Rosie was silent and lay as still as she could. Then Rosemary saw the bruises on the young girl's thighs, she looked closer and wondered how they would get there. *How odd--poor child,* she thought. Rosemary gently coated the lanolin cream on the open wounds and placed gauze over each one.

"If ye lie still, they'll stay in place and help the wounds te seal over. We're going te bed now. I don't want ye te get up tomorrow, just stay in bed and keep te the house for the next while. I'll look at yer wounds again tomorrow mornin' and see how they've sealed. Stay on yer tummy for the night if ye can," Rosemary said. "Goodnight Rosie." She leaned down and kissed the girl on her forehead.

"Goodnight Rosemary, and thank ye. I'm sorry if I disappointed ye and Sean. I didn't mean te hurt anyone."

She lay quietly on her stomach, still fully clothed as Rosemary covered her with the quilt. Rosemary quickly changed into her long nightgown and got in beside Sean, who lay staring at the ceiling.

"How could he? How could he beat her like this? She's just a child," he said. Rosemary, too, shocked at Marcel's behaviour, had always suspected a violent side to him. Her intuition was right.

"I don't know. I've always known he had a dark side te him, but I would never have guessed he'd do such a t'ing te his own daughter," said Rosemary. "We need te protect her from him, Sean," she said. "Now that he's shown his anger towards her. He might have blamed her all these years for losing Flo? Ye never know what's in his mind," she said.

"I know," said Sean. "All these years of rage let loose on a wee girl. Yes, he might do it again given any reason. We need te keep her away from him from now on. I'll do what I can," Sean said. "If I'd known this would happen, I'd have let her go wit' our Kate. I wish they'd told us about their plan."

"I know," agreed Rosemary. "There's not'ing here for either of them. Rosie's chance of going te America's over now that Kate's gone."

"I wish I'd been able te let her go, but Marcel saw the names on the passenger list at the same time I did. We were reading over the list together," Sean told her. "Ye know, Rosemary, Marcel turned almost green when he saw the names. He was raging mad, so angry. He's been a different man since Flo died alright, like two separate people altogether."

"Hmm," agreed Rosemary.

"Poor child," Sean said again. "Yes, we need te keep them apart from now on. Keep her in the house wit' ye as much as ye can. Goodnight now, Rosemary." Sean rolled over to sleep but couldn't help thinking about the changes in Marcel. He wondered what had come over him and what would happen to young Rosie. What kind of life would she have now?

"Goodnight, Sean." Rosemary said her usual night prayers. She asked God to help young Rosie and keep her safe from her daddy so that he never hurt her again.

Marcel walked home in the dark and silence of the cool night air. A great relief came over him as if a load had lifted. He felt no remorse for what he did to his daughter. Indeed, he had every right being angry with her and felt entitled. He paid for her life, and she's female with no other purpose. If he relieved his frustrations on her from time to time, so what? Finally, he reached his lodgings and went inside to find his meal waiting for him, still hot on the black iron. He picked up the plate and took it into his room. He gave himself a quick wash, hands and face only. The fire was burning brightly, and he sat down in the soft chair by the fireside to enjoy his meal.

The next day, Sean saw Marcel in the far field working alone. He made no attempt to go over there to talk, fearful that he might say the wrong thing. Sean felt that he was better to keep a distance between them--at least until things settled down. Rosemary didn't waken Rosie. She let her sleep on while she dressed her children and made breakfast. She cooked hot oats for the children and made enough to put aside for Rosie when she awoke. Rosie had eaten almost nothing the day before and would be hungry when she woke up.

Rosemary was expecting her sixth child. She sat by the fireside peeling potatoes and vegetables for the stew she was making. Young Rosie entered the room. She didn't stand upright but was slightly bent forward. She couldn't sit down but asked Rosemary if she could take a look and see how it was healing. They went back into the bedroom where Rosie lay face down on the bed. Rosemary lifted her skirt up.

"I t'ink we'll put some more lanolin on these wounds again. They look good but need just a wee bit more te help them seal up. How are ye feeling today?"

"I'm okay," Rosie said softly.

"I want ye to stay in the house today. I know ye can't sit down but if ye want ye can stay in bed for the day and read yer books that ye love so much. I've got some oats still hot on the stove for ye. Are ye hungry?"

"Yes, thank ye, Rosemary. I'm really hungry."

"Ye'll have te stand te eat, I'm afraid, then ye can take yerself back te bed and lay on yer tummy again. That's the best position for ye. Now let's see." She spread the lanolin cream on each wound and placed fresh gauze on top to help seal them closed.

"Now then, let's get te the kitchen," she said, helping Rosie up from the bed.

Rosemary poured the oats into a deep bowl, covered them with a small pinch of cinnamon powder and cream from the milk, and handed the bowl to Rosie. She stood in front of the warm fire eating. The oats would help to bind her stomach.

"Is there more," Rosie asked? Rosemary knew that once the girl started to eat, she would regain her appetite. "Of course there is," she replied. She poured the second bowl and again handed it to Rosie, who finished it quickly.

"Thank ye for taking care of me, Rosemary."

"Back te bed now, lie on yer tummy. Tomorrow ye can get a wash-up and change yer clothes. By then yer sores should be closed over, but we should keep up wit' the lanolin for a bit longer."

"Yes," nodded Rosie as she returned to the bedroom and lay face down on the bed.

Rosie kept inside the farmhouse with Rosemary. As the days passed, she slowly recovered from her wounds. However, she was more reserved than before, and Rosemary noticed the difference in the young girl--she had lost her sparkle. She was more outgoing and cheerful before. Now she seemed always on edge. If her daddy came close to the house, she would disappear and hide until he was gone. Her wounds healed, but her broken heart would take longer, Rosemary thought.

She didn't ask any questions or refer to that terrible night again. Everyone wanted to forget the whole episode. Rosie, most of all, wanted to forget. However, when she was lying in bed at night, she couldn't stop her thoughts drifting back to that terrible night, and she would remember. She tried to get it out of her head, but the shock, the fear, the beating, the pain, the buckle tearing her skin open was still too vivid.

Then there was the other thing, the thing she wanted to forget most of all. The more she tried not to think about it, the more it came back into her mind. She felt the pain of his sudden penetration into her body. At first she didn't know what it was--then she realised what he was doing. What could she do? Tell Rosemary? No. She had to pray, like Rosemary did when she had trouble. Rosie knelt down on the cold floor beside her bed and clasped her hands in prayer.

"Dear Father in Heaven,

Please hear me. I don't know what te do. My Daddy did a bad t'ing te me. He raped me, and I don't understand why. Did I do somet'ing te make him punish me like that? Please tell me what it was so that I don't do it again. I feel dirty, ashamed, and guilty. Was it my fault? Help me Father--I'm scared he'll do it again. I can't tell anyone and I hate hiding it from Rosemary and Sean. They've been good te me, but I'm no good te anyone now. I'm soiled, and no good Catholic boy or man would have me. I have no future here--please take me te be wit' me mammy. I know she loved me. I remember how she used te hold me and brush me hair. It was a lovely feeling, and I was safe then. Please, Father, hear me. Let me die and be wit' me mammy. Amen."

Rosie prayed to God every night after that, always pleading to let her be with her mammy. Kate was never mentioned again. It seemed cruel to bring up that subject as Rosie had missed that opportunity. Rosemary felt so sorry for her young charge and tried hard to enrich her life and give her hope for her future.

"The boys are going te be starting school in the village soon. Would ye like te go wit' them, Rosie? We could all walk together next week te see how long it takes te get there?"

Her wounds healed, and she was sitting without too much pain these days. The idea of going back to school excited her. She learned her letters and some numbers and loved to read. She was very happy about the idea and would work hard at all the lessons. The following week Rosie and Rosemary walked into the village with the boys and the youngest baby in the push-pram. It was only a four-mile walk, but with five young children it took much longer than normal. Rosemary thought to put her first four to school. The oldest boy, Damian was almost eight and the youngest being Miriam was just four years old, but old enough to start school with her siblings.

The children were excited and looked forward to their lessons. Rosie was excited, too. Rosemary spoke to her about her taking charge of the others going to and from the schoolhouse. She timed their first walk together. It gave her a time frame for them to arrive at the schoolhouse, and a time frame for her to expect them home again. Rosemary still feared Marcel. She made sure she knew where Rosie was at all times. She gave her some of Kate's chores; those would keep her busy on her days away from school. They went to the stream together and Rosemary showed her how to do the washing. The stream was about a mile in the opposite direction of the working fields.

"How'd ye like to learn to cook, Rosie? Yer mammy loved te cook, she really did, and she taught me everyt'ing I know."

"Oh, I'd love te cook. Will ye really show me, Rosemary?"

"Of course I will. We'll have fun learning together." Rosemary was trying to make the girl's life a little more interesting and give her some purpose. She continued to come up with ideas to keep Rosie busy and away from her daddy. She didn't want him to see his daughter out playing in the fields, or, in the barn with the other children. He would take advantage of any opportunity to get her alone--no knowing what he might do to her. Rosemary had an uncanny feeling about Marcel--she always knew there was a darker side that not even Flo knew about. Marcel was just too good to be true in her eyes. Unknown to her at that time, her fears were real enough. Her instincts told her to keep Rosie away from her daddy for the girl's own protection.

Rosie was a bright little girl. She delighted in the cooking lessons, and they had fun together baking her first cake. It was for her fourteenth birthday. The whole family enjoyed the fun and Sean reluctantly invited Marcel to the house for the celebration. Rosie felt a cold shudder run through her at the thought of seeing him.

"Don't be afraid," Rosemary told her. "We'll all be together, and I won't leave ye alone wit' him for a second. I'll be watching."

Marcel came to the house as invited. "Hello Rosie, Happy Birthday. I've a small gift for you, but you might want to open it privately." Marcel handed the parcel to Rosie.

"Oh, yer fine te open it here in front of everyone," Rosemary said aloud. "We're all family here, no secrets, eh? Go ahead. Open it," she said. She was afraid it was something that might frighten Rosie and didn't want the girl upset. Rosie tore into the package excitedly. It was her very first gift-wrapped present. She couldn't understand why her daddy had bought her a gift. Perhaps it was his way of saying sorry?

To her great surprise it was a pair of bloomers. They came right down to her knees with big frills all around the leg bottoms. These would certainly keep her warm in the winter months. Rosie's face turned red with embarrassment as she laughed and held up the bloomers for all to see. The boys roared with laughter, though they were young enough not to understand what they were laughing at. Rosie was a little embarrassed and shy, but secretly, delighted that she received a gift.

Everyone sang the "Happy Birthday" song and she blew out a candle and made a wish with her eyes closed. She felt as if everything in the world was good again. Nothing untoward happened that day between Rosie and Marcel. It was a happy birthday, one that she would remember fondly.

She had not faced her daddy since that terrible day, and, still scared of him, she was glad everyone was there up at the party when he arrived. She said nothing to anyone about that night. She told herself that she might be mistaken--it may have been the belt. However, deep down, she knew she was not mistaken. She was quiet towards him, almost shy. He did nothing to give rise to any bad feeling towards her.

"Thank ye, Daddy, for the gift. It's grand " she said, laughing.

Both Sean and Rosemary thought the event had seen its day. The episode over, Rosie punished, and, they could enjoy family life again, without having to know where Marcel was every minute. Rosemary, now relieved felt she could relax her feelings towards him, a little. She continued to teach Rosie housework duties: cooking, washing the clothes, and other chores that she thought Rosie was old enough to cope with. She needed the extra help, too, now that the family was growing in numbers, and she was expecting another baby.

Rosie was a great help to her, better than Kate had ever been. The two enjoyed their time together, Rosemary teaching and Rosie learning. They worked well as a team and shared much fun and laughter. Rosemary was a natural-born teacher who loved to teach her children. She was one to point out the beauty of simple things like a tree or a flower.

"God's creation," she would say. She always followed with a question and then finally would come a story with the answer. The children loved their mammy's stories. She encouraged them to question things to make them think and learn. She wanted her children to grow up knowing happiness from the simple pleasures of life.

She played games with the clouds, the trees, the flowers, and the birds as they walked home from school. They were not a poor family in comparison, but everything they owned came through hard labour, a lot of hard labour, and some luck. Most families in the area were on much the same measure--farming could be profitable, or not, depending on the weather and the seasonal luck. There were few luxuries. Money spent on necessities only, such as food supplies for themselves and their animals. They would only buy items that they could not grow themselves--sugar, flour, or fruit.

Occasionally they would spend on clothing, considered a luxury item. Even shoes were not considered a necessity, and most of the children didn't have any unless they belonged to a sibling before and passed down the line. Clothing, too, was passed down, and nothing wasted.

Often on their walk home from the village school, Rosemary would ask them: "Listen, what d'ye hear?"

"Not'ing, Mammy." They were wrong, and Rosemary would make them listen again.

"What about that bird, can ye hear it? Where d'ye think it is?" The children would take notice and look for the bird until one of them found it and shouted out.

"Look, there it is, up there in that tree."

"D'ye hear any more?" The children would be quiet as mice as they continued walking, looking, and listening, for another bird until one of them shouted out.

"Look, there's one up there."

"Ah, a robin redbreast. Does anyone know why it's called a robin redbreast?" she asked.

"No," they agreed, and Rosemary told them the story of Jesus on the cross when he was dying. A little robin flew down beside him and sat on His shoulder. The blood from Jesus' crown of thorns dripped on the robin's breast, and, the bird forever stained with His blood reminds us of that event.

The children would look up at their mammy in wonder and amazement--she told such wonderful stories. Rosie loved her stories, too. She loved to learn from Rosemary and was always asking questions. They complimented each other well, and the other children learned from their example.

Life on the farm became more interesting for Rosie, and she began to develop a sense of her place in the family. She may not have been a real daughter to Rosemary and Sean, but she was very close to the two of them and appreciated their protectiveness towards her. Rosie had worried that she might have lost their affection for what she'd done. In fact, both Rosemary and Sean now realised that it would have been best if Rosie had gone to America.

17

A Willing Helper, 1909-10

As the months passed and Rosemary became awkwardly more pregnant, Rosie took on more of the household duties. Little by little the girl was almost doing a full day's housework. She dressed the younger children, made their breakfast, and walked them to school, giving Rosemary time by herself with the youngest baby. Sean was always early out of bed, made a pot of tea, and ate some bread before heading out to the fields to work. Mid-morning he would come back to the farmhouse for something more substantial, and at this time Rosemary cooked him a hot meal.

Rosemary prayed first thing out of bed and last thing at night before sleep. She always prayed for the lost soul of little Fin, now long dead but still much alive in his mammy's heart.

"Ye know, Rosie, I sometimes feel Fin is still here wit' us in the house. It just feels that he's around, especially when I pray and I love te feel him close te me, like he's givin' me a hug, ye know?"

Rosie could remember little Fin vividly. They were good friends before he got sick and died that day, now long ago.

"I know what ye mean, Rosemary, I feel it too when I pray wit' ye. It's a good feelin', like he's here prayin' wit' us."

Rosie could read and write, she learned to count and knew her numbers. She was a good student, always willing to soak up new information. She loved it. She went to school three days a week, and on the other days she helped Rosemary. She knew her efforts were very much appreciated, which made her want to help more.

"Yer a grand help te me, Rosie. I don't know what I'd do wit'out ye," Rosemary told her.

"Sure, ye know I like te help out wit' things. It makes me feel like real family."

"Of course yer real family. I'm yer Godmother and yer named after me. Yer like a daughter te me, ye must know that for sure."

"I do, of course I do," the young girl replied.

Rosie would collect the clothes for washing and happily carry them down to the stream, about a mile downhill. She would spend hours washing the soiled clothes in cold water and ringing them through. She carried the damp clothes back to the farmhouse and hung them to dry in front of the black iron stove. If the weather was good she would hang them out to dry in the sunshine. She never complained.

"I just love the countryside, Rosemary," she said, "and all the beautiful t'ings that God gave te us te enjoy." She saw the beauty in things that Rosemary pointed out to her. She would marvel at the water rippling downstream on its journey to the open sea. She imagined herself on the same tour, floating on the water--the wonderful things she could see as she voyaged towards the vast ocean and final destination. She asked Rosemary about things she thought about. She especially liked the way the sun shone on the water, making it twinkle like little diamonds. How pretty it was with all the different colours sparkling through it. She would sing as she washed the clothes and was happy alone with her thoughts. This was the old Rosie, optimistic, innocent, and content. The way she was before that terrible day had happened.

One month when Sean and her daddy went to Dublin, Sean brought back a book that Rosie could read to the children and teach them to read, too. She was overjoyed. She helped the boys read the story first and looked forward to her own private time with the book. At last alone in her bed, she had it all to herself and read by candlelight late into the night. When she finished the book, she read it again to the children, over and over, each one taking a turn at the reading until finally they knew the book by heart. She loved to imagine living in the stories and would daydream the events time and again.

Rosie learned to make bread, scones, and biscuits in the oven, and soup on the top of the black iron in the big pot, all at the same time. She learned to make stews and puddings that her mammy had taught Rosemary. She learned how to cook the meat with whole vegetables and potatoes in one pot. Then to plate it up for Sean's evening meal, leaving the broth for soup.

She pumped water from the well every day and carried the buckets into the house for Rosemary. She always pumped extra buckets because they were always needed as the day wore on. Rosemary taught her how to separate the whey and the curds from the milk to make different types of cheese and butter. She showed young Rosie how to knit and crochet with wool. Rosie loved to crochet and was presently making squares for a warm winter blanket with all the 'bits and pieces' of leftover wool. Rosemary found a way to use everything and instructed Rosie well in all she knew.

"Waste-not, want-not," she told the girl.

"What does it mean Rosemary? Waste-not, want-not."

"Well, it means te find a use for everyt'ing and waste not'ing. Then ye'll never be stuck wanting somet'ing ye don't have because ye wasted it and threw it away."

"Oh, that's really a clever way te remember it--waste-not-want-not," she repeated.

Rosie went to the stream two or three times a week with washing. She found it easier to do small washes more often rather than one big wash every week, and it was easier to carry. It was a beautiful summer's day, and Rosemary had recently given birth to another baby girl named Hanna. She was in the house when Rosemary asked her. "Will ye go down te the stream te rinse out a couple of t'ings for Hanna? She's a little short on t'ings te wear."

"Of course I will, give me them here. I'll go now." It was quiet, and she would have some time to daydream. She sang out loud as she walked down the field towards the stream, carrying the few items that Rosemary wanted rinsed out. She washed out the clothes and thought she would hang them out to dry in the sunshine. She spread the clothing out over the bushes to let the air get through and make them smell fresh as summer. Rosie was down on her knees scrubbing when she became aware of a shadow closing in from behind her. She felt uneasy and turned to see her daddy standing there watching her scrub the clothes in the water.

"Hello, Rosie," he said in a soft low voice. She motioned to stand up, but he insisted, "Stay, do your washing, carry on with your work. I'll just sit back here and watch." He sat down on the grass with his back against the tree for support. Rosie became increasingly afraid as she continued to scrub and rinse in the rushing water of the stream. He said nothing, but she could feel his eyes on her.

"I've been watching you, you know," he said toying with her. "This isn't your usual day for washing. Rosemary busy with her new baby and the rest of her brood" he asked? "It isn't a school day either, so the other children will be at home, playing in the yard. You never do, though, Rosie. I never see you play in the yard with the rest of them. They keep you inside," he continued. Rosie said nothing and kept washing and rinsing as he talked. "They say you're a great little helper. Sean says so," he said teasing. He stood up and walked casually back and forth kicking up some stones into the water.

"They keep you away from me, don't they? Have you said anything to them that you shouldn't have said?" he questioned, leaning back against a tree with his hands in his pockets.

"No, no, I've said not'ing," she replied quickly, shaking her head from side to side. She reminded him of his childhood and the boys at school in Italy, who deserved punishment for being such cowards. That old feeling of power returned to him, and he enjoyed making her suffer and squirm. He knew she was afraid and carried on tormenting her.

"Why else would Rosemary keep you inside the house all the time? I think she's trying to keep you away from me," he said mockingly.

"No, no, she knows not'ing." Rosie's voice trembled with fear. "There's just so much work te do. Rosemary keeps me busy helping her wit' t'ings inside," she explained, hoping he would believe her.

"How are those nice bloomers I bought for your birthday? Still wearing them," he asked, lifting up her skirt with a long piece of broken branch? Rosie's breathing became faster and harder as she tried not to show her fear. She kept her head down while she continued scrubbing. In the flash of a second, Marcel had undone his breeches and was on top of her, like a dog. She gasped and let out a muffled whimper.

"Oh, no, Daddy, no. Please Daddy, don't hurt me, please," she pleaded, as tears blurred her eyes and she held on tightly to the rocks. He didn't hear her and continued to release his frustration on her little body. When he finished, he pushed her forward into the water, as though she disgusted him. Rosie stretched out her arms in front to stop herself from falling completely into the water.

"Wash," he ordered. "Make sure you're clean before you go back to the house, you understand?" She nodded her head and cried at the same time.

"Yes, Daddy," she replied, crying.

Marcel fixed his clothing and made his way back to the field where he was working. Rosie waited for him to go. Then she rolled onto the grass and cried, and cried, and cried. Finally, she realised she was taking too long and had to get back to the house with the clean wash. She cleaned and dressed herself properly, but she couldn't see that her eyes were red with crying. Like a brave little soldier she stood tall, picked up her washing in the basket, and started to make her way back to the house. By the time she arrived, Rosemary was beginning to wonder what was taking her so long.

When Rosie entered the room, she placed the basket where it belonged and hung some of the damp clothes around the black iron for drying. Then she went straight into her bedroom and to her cot with her curtain closed. Rosemary knew something was wrong and followed her. When the two came face to face, Rosemary could see that she had been crying.

"What happened?" she asked anxiously. "Ye've been crying. Why, what for?" she demanded. Rosemary wanted an answer and kept probing the girl for a reason. Rosie finally pulled herself together.

"Don't laugh at me, Rosemary, but I fell into the water up te me waist. I got carried downstream a bit, for I couldn't find me feet te stand up. I got such a fright, ye know, and there was no one around te help me." Rosemary was so relieved that she burst out laughing and then hugged young Rosie.

"Ye frightened me for a minute, and I thought yer daddy had got te ye and hurt ye again." Rosemary rocked the girl in her arms for a few minutes.

"Come get yerself some hot tea and a fresh-baked scone wit' jam. Ye worked hard today wit' that washing, ye deserve a treat. Come now, as soon as yer ready, and ye can have one before the rest get them at supper." Rosie nodded in agreement but just wanted to be alone.

"I'll be through as soon as I change into somet'ing dry." Alone for a few minutes, Rosie tried to deal with the pain in her limbs, and her insides, and quietly stifled a groan as she moved around the room. She changed her clothes and pinched her cheeks a little to hide her red eyes. She just lied to Rosemary for her daddy. How she hated him for making her do that. She hated what he did to her, and she hated lying to Rosemary. It made her feel bad. But she knew that if she told anyone, he would certainly kill her.

Rosie now realised that Marcel was watching her. He knew where she was and when. He knew when she was alone and when she was with others. He even knew that Rosemary kept her close to the house to keep her away from him. Most of all, she understood that it was only a matter of time before he would find her alone and hurt her again that same way. Her daddy and their filthy secret confused her, and she felt her situation was futile. She was lost in a void where nobody saw her, her life annulled and her presence simply a nuisance to everyone. Oh, how the wee girl wanted to be safe with her mammy--being held and cuddled and loved, feeling the warmth that she dearly missed. Often, when she was alone, she would talk to her mammy like an imaginary friend. She always finished with the same wish.

"Oh, Mammy, I know ye can hear me, and I'm longing for the day when ye can put yer arms around me and make me safe and love me like I remember. I wish it were now, Mammy. I want te be wit' ye now."

Rosie was reaching fifteen years of age and still had not started to menstruate as most other girls her age. It was a blessing in some ways, but Rosie began to wonder why, and finally asked Rosemary about it one day.

"Not'ing te worry about at yer age. There's plenty of time for that te happen, and when it does ye'll wish it hadn't for sure. It's a messy business te deal wit' and there isn't much privacy here for such t'ings."

Rosemary instructed the girl on what to expect and how to cope when it did happen. She showed her the cord that went round her waist and how to attach the cotton napkin to it. When the cotton napkin was soiled, she could take it down to the stream and soak it in the cold water to clean it thoroughly for the next time. Rosemary was particularly strict about the napkins being properly cleaned. "Otherwise, disease can set in," she instructed her young charge.

"Now, what about babies and how they're made? What d'ye need te know about that?"

"Not'ing Rosemary," she replied. "Kate already told me all about that business a long time ago when the cows were going te the bull for insertion." Rosie knew this part alright, and relieved to learn that she couldn't have a baby until after she had started to menstruate. She knew that her daddy would know this too, and perhaps this was the reason he felt safe with her. Rosie hoped that one day soon her body would change and "it" would come. She could tell her daddy that it wasn't safe for him anymore as she was now a woman and could have babies. She held that thought in her head as her private weapon for when "it" finally happened. She knew that when Rosemary was pregnant, Sean didn't expect his rights exercised and let Rosemary rest throughout the entire pregnancy. Somehow Rosie was getting the two situations mixed up and thought that when "it" came, that her daddy would also leave her alone, just like Sean did Rosemary.

Rosie stayed close to the house and made sure she was with people as much as she possibly could. She knew Marcel was watching her every move, waiting to catch her alone somewhere quiet, where he could use her again. Rosemary wondered why the young girl was so afraid of being alone with her own daddy. Apart from the time he beat the flesh out of her, a long time ago now. She knew that Rosie was afraid of Marcel. She saw how the girl ran inside the house if she saw him coming near. Rosemary knew there was something more, something hidden. However, she was afraid to question what--for fear of finding the truth. She did have suspicions and once, a thought of them together flashed through her mind. She immediately chastised herself for having such a filthy idea about a man and his daughter. Rosemary prayed for forgiveness. Often Rosie prayed with her, but for something completely different. Rosie prayed for protection. She prayed to all the angels, as many as would come to her rescue.

At such times, when the girls were alone, Rosemary would talk about little Fin and together they would say a prayer for him. She sometimes cried because she still missed her little boy so much. Even after all these years, she still felt guilty for leaving him that day. The young girl understood Rosemary's sorrow and consoled her.

"It would've happened if ye'd been home or not, Rosemary. It was just one of those terrible t'ings that happen. Yer not te blame."

"I know that now, Rosie, but it still feels like yesterday when I t'ink about it, and I wish I hadn't gone te me mammy's for the celebration that day."

Rosie remembered the day clearly as if it was yesterday, as Rosemary did. She too missed little Fin, even though he was younger than she was. They had been very close. Rosemary said she felt Fin close, especially when the two girls prayed together. She could feel his presence, although it was hard for her to see his little face, which dimmed more with each passing year.

The months passed, and it was winter again, and, would soon be Rosie's fifteenth birthday. Would they have a house party this year, she wondered? With all the work to do these days and all these children to feed, there wasn't a lot of spare time--not like the old days when they could bake a special cake together. Rosie always remembered that year when Rosemary showed her how to bake that special birthday cake. They had such a wonderful time, and she smiled to herself as she remembered. Her birthday came and went without notice this time. It was a busy life on the farm, and Rosemary now had five children to care for. Rosie continued to walk the younger children back and forth to school and take the lessons herself as she loved to.

It was springtime when Rosemary announced that she was expecting again and needed Rosie's help in the house even more than normal. Rosemary seemed tired a lot and was losing some of her happier, fun side. Rosie was glad to help and took on more chores. She knew that her daddy always knew where she was, even though she was careful to stay close to the house or with other people. Somehow he always knew when she would go down to the stream to do washing for Rosemary, and often he would just appear without warning. She never saw him approach, even though she was always on the watch for him.

He caught her alone more than a couple of times during her fifteenth year. Each time he had forced himself on her, discarding her like an old rag when he was satisfied.

"Our secret, remember, and keep your mouth shut, or else." It was always painful for her, physically and emotionally. Her body was still small, and she had not yet menstruated as she hoped.

"One day soon," she would tell herself, as Rosemary told her many times.

Rosie often wondered why her daddy didn't let her go to America with Kate. He would have been rid of her and not had to pay Rosemary for her keep. She imagined a nice life there, waiting on tables and talking to people every day, perhaps even meeting a young man.

She began to take some of the children with her to the stream when she went with the washing. It was a good idea and gave her some added protection from Marcel. She was able to make it sound appealing to Rosemary who was more and more in need of rest these days. Rosie would volunteer those who were old enough to help and carry, leaving the younger ones with Rosemary in the house. Outwardly, she appeared less afraid of her daddy. In reality, she was just more resigned to her situation, knowing that somehow he would have his way with her, and when he finished he would leave her alone for a while. Sometimes she cried about it, but only when she was on her own. She wished her daddy was as loving as Sean was to his children. He could see no wrong in any of them and wouldn't hurt a hair on their heads.

She prayed to God for forgiveness, that perhaps if she prayed enough he would forgive her and make Marcel stop. However, that didn't happen. It seemed to her that no matter how often she prayed, Marcel still found her. There was no escape for her, and at times she became withdrawn and silent in her unhappiness with her sordid secret. Rosemary noticed these sullen times and thought it was her age and the young girl's maturing body. She hoped that soon her monthly period would finally arrive, and put an end to Rosie's torment and her mood swings.

18

A Shopping Trip, 1911

*I*t was the springtime of 1911. The fields were coming alive, and new life was all around. Rosie turned fifteen years old that December past. Rosemary's baby was born and to everyone's delight it was yet another little girl. They named her Cora.

That same year a census was being held all over Ireland. *How exciting that a stranger would come to the farmhouse,* Rosie thought. The Government wanted a headcount of every living person--including Rosie, even though she wasn't family, she would be named in the census and that made her feel good. She finally started to menstruate. She practiced a million times over in her head exactly how she would tell her daddy that he had to stop. However, when the time came she just wasn't brave enough to do it and never told him.

They were into March when Marcel surprised everyone by suggesting he take Rosie to Dublin for a weekend of fun and shopping.

"I want to take her on a proper trip to Dublin for a few days. We'll stay at a decent hotel, and I can show her the city and the shops. It's time for her to see the world outside of this farm," he said. "I can take her to a movie at the cinema and buy her a book suitable for a young lady. Now that's she's growing up, it's time she had some nice things of her own to wear and not only hand-me-downs. I've never spent much on her since she's been living here with you and Sean," Marcel said. "What do you think, Rosemary?" he asked.

"It's a grand idea and very timely since she's outgrown everyt'ing she has," Rosemary replied. "And yer right, it's time she had some real clothes of her own. She'll love it."

He was feeling very generous having recently discovered that he was quite wealthy and had substantial savings. Marcel hadn't spent money in years, not even at Christmas, and suddenly felt that he wanted to splurge and spoil everyone in the family. He would lavish gifts on his daughter and the family who raised her for him. It was his way of showing his appreciation when Flo was alive. He loved to see the excitement and love in her face when she opened a gift from him. It made him feel good about himself, and he thought that Rosie might be the same. He would make the effort for her, and anyway, she desperately needed clothes and shoes--everything she wore was obviously too small for her.

Rosemary had her own secret thoughts on the matter but knew she had to keep them to herself. They were, after all, just her thoughts, and there was no evidence that her suspicions were real. She put them out of her mind and let it be. Rosie was going on a trip to Dublin to buy new clothes. She thought the girl would be overjoyed at the idea.

Marcel still had the pouch money that his mother Rosa had given him. If he borrowed from it, he always replaced it immediately. He was not a spendthrift, and when he needed something he always had the cash available. He paid his debts weekly and seldom spent money on himself or anyone else, including Rosie. So, most of his earnings went to savings and when the pouch became too bulky, he would make a trip to the bank in Dublin and exchange his money for large notes. That way the pouch was lighter and less bulky. No one had ever known about his pouch. Even in Flo's lifetime, she never questioned what it was that he kept hidden in his boot.

His plan was to book into the same little Dublin hotel that he used with his mama and again with Flo. Dublin was beautiful in the springtime as he remembered. He would take his daughter shopping for clothes and shoes and more underwear. Rosie was becoming a young lady, and Marcel felt it only fitting that she should look like a young lady. Her overcoat was much too small for her, and it would best be cleaned and pressed and put away for someone else. He could show her the city, and the fine places that he had once shown her mammy.

"It's a grand idea, Marcel, but perhaps take one of the girls wit' ye te keep Rosie company and give her some help choosing t'ings?" Sean suggested.

"No, Sean, I want to spend the time with Rosie myself--our special trip together, daddy and daughter." Sean couldn't argue with that, and so he let it slide. Rosemary just prayed that everything would work out fine.

Rosie's stomach turned when Rosemary told her about the trip. Shocked and horrified at the idea, she kept quiet, afraid to say anything against her daddy. She kept her silence and tried hard to look excited about the outing, all the while her stomach turning with fear.

"A trip te Dublin with Daddy, just the two of us, really?" she said, smiling.

"Ye'll get new clothes, a coat, boots, and shoes, and maybe even slippers," Rosemary said. "He says he'll take ye te the cinema te watch one of these movies. Ye know--the talking pictures. And, he'll take ye te the bookshop, the big one in the centre of the city. Ye'll love that," Rosemary told her. Rosie nodded in agreement but didn't share her enthusiasm. Rosemary was more excited than the girl was. "Ye'll have a wonderful time wit' yer daddy. He's going te take ye te see places and t'ings that yer mammy once visited. It'll be good for ye te see the city properly. Ye'll enjoy it," she said. Marcel saw Rosie's first reaction of shock and quickly drew the attention back to him.

"They've got some really good talking movies out now with all the new film stars. They sell chocolate and ice cream and popcorn, things you've never tasted. You'll love it," he told his daughter.

She had heard about the motion pictures but never thought she would see one in her lifetime. The other children "oohed" and "aahed" at all they heard as they listened in awe--eyes and mouths wide open.

"We'll go, we'll go, if she doesn't want te," Damien said.

"Yer turn'll come in time when yer older," Sean said. "This is Rosie's turn."

She decided to keep her fears to herself and go quietly without objection. Marcel would make her pay for upsetting his plans if she showed any unwillingness to go with him. She would enjoy the shopping part of the trip and the sightseeing, too. The idea of going to a motion picture was tempting--how exciting. The part that frightened her was staying overnight in the hotel. She knew that she would be sharing a room with her daddy and feared what that entailed. He might be buying her lovely things, but he would make sure he had his fun out of the trip too. She put that out of her mind as much as she could and tried hard to focus on the new clothes, the sightseeing, and the motion picture instead.

Rosie always wondered what her mammy looked like. There were no photographs of her and no one ever spoke about her for fear of upsetting Marcel. Perhaps on this trip there might come a time when she could ask her daddy that question. She longed for her real mammy, all of her young life. Rosemary was kind to her, and Sean was, too, but she dreamed of being with her own mammy. To be cuddled by her own mammy, and to feel safe in the warmth of her mammy's loving arms wrapped around her. To feel her brushing her hair and loving her, the way she saw Rosemary with her children. She never felt any of that and longed for the feeling of real love. Perhaps she would get a chance to ask her daddy about her mammy on this trip. She hoped so.

The time came to leave. Marcel arranged to take the pony and trap for the weekend. They would leave early on Thursday morning, stay overnight on Thursday, Friday, and Saturday, and start back home again on Sunday morning after Mass and breakfast, returning to the farm in time for supper.

Rosemary asked Marcel a favour.

"Marcel, I'm all out of fruit and sugar. If there's any time would ye mind picking me up some, any kind, even dried fruit will do, and some sugar?"

Sean's monthly trip to Dublin was almost a full two weeks away, and she had no reserves. Rosemary was hoping to make more jam to keep them going, and so any fruit would be welcome. It was spring and fruit was in short supply at that time of year--so not a lot of choice.

"I'd be happy to and if you'd like anything else just let me know." He felt he was in the good books for arranging the trip with Rosie, and buying her new clothes and boots. Secretly he laughed to himself, as it seemed he couldn't do any wrong at the moment. Neither did Rosemary or Sean know that Marcel had taken the shoe sizes for all the children. He intended bringing back boots for the older ones and shoes for the little ones. It was the one thing they really needed on the farm, and he knew it would be appreciated. He also wanted to get wool for Rosemary as she was always knitting.

Rosie dressed in her best outfit, but everything she wore was either too tight or too short, obviously old and well-worn. Her only boots were falling apart with holes in the soles, and the uppers polished through to the other side in places. Still, she was getting new clothes on this trip, so it didn't matter. She would never complain about such things.

They arrived in the early afternoon. Rosie's head was turning fast to take in all the sights as they headed towards the hotel. "We'll book in first and then eat out. Are you hungry?" he asked. Rosie was looking forward to that part. It was the second time she would eat in a restaurant, and although she loved Rosemary's food, she knew there were more delicious dishes available in the city.

"After lunch we will go shopping for your new clothes, Rosie, that'll cheer you up? Yes?" he questioned.

"Of course, yes. I'm excited, I can't wait te see the shops," she replied.

"Perhaps a coat first, or shoes, or boots or whatever--where would you like to go first?" Marcel knew his way around the shops. He was known to barter for everything, and seldom if ever paid the ticket price for anything. The more she thought about it, the less frightened she became. She had put that bad part out of her mind, telling herself that it was only the evening that would be unpleasant. She would try to enjoy the journey and the experience during the daytime. It is the best way, she told herself.

Marcel wrote a letter to the hotel ahead of time and made a booking for himself and his daughter sharing a twin room and bathroom. He specifically requested a large tub as a luxury for them both to enjoy. They arrived at the hotel and went inside. In her innocence, she was unaware of her obvious country appearance.

"Is there someone to take care of the horse and buggy?" Marcel asked the receptionist.

"Of course, sir, I'll get someone te attend te that immediately," he said signalling a porter. Marcel paid for his room booking and the stable services on arrival.

"When are the meal times?" he asked.

"Here you are, sir, for your convenience, a list of the restaurant hours and meal times." The clerk handed him the schedule.

"Thank you, this will be very useful to us. We'll be back in time for the late supper." It was the same hotel he stayed in with his mama all those years ago. The owners were new, but the hotel still had that same welcoming atmosphere that he remembered. It was central for shopping and sightseeing, being on the edge of the city within a short walking distance to the centre. That memory seemed a lifetime away now as Marcel thought back. He was not the same person now, so much had happened to change him.

"Come, Rosie, we'll eat first, and I know the perfect little cafe where they serve hot meals so mouth-watering, I promise you've never tasted food like it."

He was right. She had the lamb chops and potato fries with beans in a tomato sauce on the side. She had never had lamb in her life until now, and it was delicious. She had never tasted beans in a tomato sauce either, and they were grand with potato fries, which she had also never tasted. It was unusual for them to have a pudding after such a large dinner, but Marcel insisted they indulge. Rosie had no idea what to pick from the menu and so he helped her choose.

"We'll have two treacle puddings with custard," he ordered from the waitress. Again, Rosie said nothing. She tasted the pudding. It was sweet, sticky, and chewy with warm creamy custard over the top. Simply delicious, and he was right--she had never tasted food like it.

"Hmm, this is delicious, Daddy, and I'm so full I t'ink I might burst."

"We'll finish with tea and a sweet biscuit--you'll feel better once we start walking." When they left the café, they went straight to a shoe shop. Marcel knew the owner. He always purchased his working boots, and soft shoes for himself and Flo here, in years gone by. He used the same shoe shop since he first arrived in Dublin and had built a friendly relationship with the owner.

"Ah, Marcel, it's been a while," the owner greeted him shaking his hand.

"Good to see you, too, Tony. This is my daughter, Rosie. She needs shoes, boots, and slippers. She's turning into a young lady with needs. I also have a list; perhaps you could have the order made up for me and we can discuss the price later?"

Anthony laughed and nodded in agreement as he glanced over the list. He knew the ways of this long-term customer, and that he was about to make a good profit, even with a discount. He snapped his fingers and an assistant came forward and took the list. He snapped his fingers a second time, and another assistant appeared to help out with Rosie's choices with another assistant on hand to do the running for the one in charge.

People were buzzing about the shop, jumping to Marcel's every wish. Marcel bought the best of leather--he knew it lasted longer than the rough, hard, cheaper leather. Rosie loved the boots--black or brown, plain at the front, and laced up above her ankles. She knew they would last a long time, and they were so shiny. "I like the black ones," she said. Marcel motioned to the assistant to wrap them to go. Rosie loved the shoes even more because they had a strap that came across the front of the foot and round the ankle with a modern shiny buckle. They had a short square block heel that made her feel tall and elegant. They also came in black or brown and were very modern. "May I have the black, shiny ones, Daddy?" she asked.

"Of course, Rosie," and again he motioned the assistant to wrap them to go.

When Anthony brought out the slippers, with their warm, white furry lining inside and soft red corduroy on the outside, her eyes grew big and wide in delight. Marcel watched her--the transformation was amazing. It was clear to him that Rosie loved the red corduroy and the white fur--indeed she liked showy things just as Flo had. Her expression gave him so much self-gratification, a feeling he remembered when Flo was happy. He never saw his daughter like this, so excited and cheerful. She didn't get nice things very often and certainly they had never been shopping for something new for her.

Marcel felt it was her time to shine. He would buy her a new coat, a new dress, one, possibly two new skirts and tops to go with them, stockings, and new underwear. He wanted that feeling again, for himself. Now he knew he could have it, and he was willing to spoil her and treat her the way he did Flo. She was Flo's daughter after all, and like her mammy, Rosie loved beautiful things.

"Oh, Daddy, so many nice t'ings te see. I t'ink I'll burst, I'm so happy."

"I'm happy to please you today. You've waited a long time to be spoiled like this, so let's just enjoy it."

Her daddy was more than generous and treated her to the nicest gifts she could ever imagine. He had never been this pleasant before. She chose a beautiful crimson coat with black shiny buttons down the front. It had a big hood lined with white fur and edged with black velvet, and a drawstring that went around the hood to the chin. When the hood was down it lay under the collar of the coat and looked like black lapels on the shoulders, or she could undo the buttons and take the hood off completely. The coat had a back pleat with two tiny buttons, one on each side of the pleat. The slit pockets were overlaid in black velvet, as was the edge of the small lapel at the neck. The side seams on the arms had the same two little buttons. The panelled coat shaped and fitted her beautifully. Rosie loved it as she spun around in the shop catching glimpses of her reflection in the mirror as she twirled. Her daddy laughed out loud at her excitement.

"I think this is the one," Marcel said, "and please wrap the old coat, we'll take it home for someone else to wear."

"Of course, sir," replied the assistant.

Rosie wore the new coat and handed her old one to the assistant. Next on the list was a dress, and then a skirt and top. Again, she went for the red pinafore dress with the big patch pockets on the front. It had a black belt with a shiny buckle that she loved, and a full skirt that swirled out when she twirled around. It had long sleeves with a neat cuff and a sparkly black button. A simple but lovely white lace collar rounded at the edges, and little buttons all the way down the back from the neck down passed the waist. She loved it, and what fun she was having looking at the other dresses available.

"Look at this one, Daddy, and this one, too, and oh, there's more over here." Then she saw the pinafore skirt with the front bib and the side pockets tucked into the seams. The waist was slightly higher than normal, but that was the new style. The pinafore was a lovely shade of royal blue with a red and black stripe around the bottom of the hem and around the edge of the bib.

"I love this one, Daddy, and here's the perfect sweater top te go wit' it." They had the tops in all colours. "You can choose two sweater tops to go with the skirt," he told her. "Also pick out a couple of blouses that you can wear under the sweater, for winter, you know?" he said approvingly.

"Thank ye, Daddy," she said excitedly and wasted no time finding two lovely white cotton blouses. She could wear them in the summer alone, or in the winter under a sweater. Rosie was having the time of her life looking through the variety of skirts and dresses.

"Daddy, look at this dress, too, isn't it beautiful?" Again it was the modern look but this time it was straight and without sleeves, and the slit pockets were hidden in the seams like the other skirt. The assistant advised on the new fashions and ways of wearing them.

"This dress can be worn in two ways: wit' a blouse under the dress, or no blouse showing bare arms and wearing a cardigan," she advised Rosie. It was a lovely piece, and her daddy couldn't help himself.

"Try it on and see how it looks on you." Now she had three dresses and a variety of blouses and sweaters, more clothes than she had ever had in her life.

"Now," Marcel said to the assistant, "we need some underwear for a young lady this age. Can you help my daughter on that? I'll busy myself in the men's department until you're finished. She needs tops and bottoms, and stockings and socks, too. She also needs two nightgowns. I'll come back when I'm finished, and we can total everything up."

The assistant looked at Rosie and smiled. "My yer a lucky girl. Yer daddy's so generous, is it yer birthday?" she asked.

"Yes, just passed--I'm lucky te be getting all these new clothes now," said Rosie quietly, wondering about the trade-off later.

Marcel left and went into the men's department where he purchased a few small items for himself and had them wrapped. He then returned to the ladies department and went to the cash desk to barter with the shop owner for a final price.

"Now, what kind of discount can you offer me for such a big purchase?" The owner scowled at him and began to tally up the order. Marcel was right, it was a substantial total, and the owner knew he had to offer him a decent discount. He wrote down the total and showed it to Marcel, who gasped aloud. Then the owner wrote down his price with the discount, and that made Marcel smile.

"I think you'll agree it's a fair discount for such a sale?"

Again Marcel smiled and began to count out the cash into the man's hand. The two shook hands. Marcel and Rosie picked up their parcels and left the shop.

"Daddy, Daddy, thank ye, thank ye," she said in excitement. "I've never had so many beautiful t'ings in me life," she gasped. "Thank ye, thank ye so much."

"I'm glad it makes you so happy, Rosie," he told her. When they arrived at the hotel, Marcel walked Rosie upstairs to their room.

"Now, I'm going out for a while. I want you to have a hot bath in there. You'll find everything you need, soap, shampoo for your hair, and when I come back I expect you dressed in something new of your own choosing. Then we'll go for dinner and on to the cinema." Rosie jumped up in the air clapping her hands in excitement.

"D'ye mean it, are we really going te the cinema?"

"Of course, now you get ready. I'll be a couple of hours or so." Marcel left to do his errands, leaving her alone in the room with all her new purchases. She was so excited--didn't know where to start. She opened all the parcels and hung everything properly on hangers and placed them in the wardrobe. It was as if she was doing it for someone else, making sure the new clothes wouldn't spoil.

Rosie never had a big bath before, not from a proper bathtub with taps, only ever in the little metal bath at home or in the cold water of the stream in the summer. She was so excited about everything that happened that day and thought herself so lucky.

"Perhaps this is God's way of telling me he heard me prayers all those times I asked him for help. Thank ye, God," she said out loud. "Thank ye so much. I'm so grateful and happy, and I love everyt'ing me daddy bought for me today. Thank ye, thank ye, thank ye."

Rosie put the plug in the hole and turned the tap on to run a bath. The water was hot, as if by magic she thought. She undressed and got into the water and sat down in the tub. *Oh, what a lovely feeling,* she thought. She sank into the warm water--a new experience for her, and real soap to wash herself. She just lay there enjoying the splendour, and then she lay down with her head under the water. Everything was so elegant and luxurious. *This is like being in Heaven,* she thought, and for the first time she was genuinely glad that she had decided to come.

Rosie washed her hair with the scented shampoo and rinsed it out with cold water. She ran her hands through her hair, feeling how soft and smooth it was. She lay in the bath for a long time daydreaming about how life could be so beautiful, exotic, and luxurious. Suddenly she realised she was dreaming longer than she should, and thought she'd better get out and get dressed for her daddy who would be back soon.

She decided to wear the red dress with the long sleeves and the white lace collar, black stockings, and her new shoes with the ankle strap. She wore her new underwear and the new-fashioned brazier. The shop assistant insisted she have the braziers instead of those heavy bodices with the rubber buttons, considered old-fashioned for young ladies. She tied her hair up at the sides and pleated it from the centre of her head, leaving it to hang down her back. She looked lovely and felt wonderful, like a young woman should. Rosie sat down at the little table to wait for her daddy. All the while the only thing she could think of was that she was going to the cinema to see a motion picture.

Marcel was busy shopping for the things that Rosemary requested. He arranged for the order of slippers and shoes for the McGinty family be delivered to the hotel. It wasn't Christmas, but he felt generous and he wanted Rosemary and Sean's approval. This was the old Marcel, and he remembered how good it felt. His memory flashed back, and he seemed dazed for a moment as he remembered the fun times long ago. Now, he realised how much he had changed since Flo's death. He was actually enjoying himself today.

He arranged with the concierge to have all his purchases packed and strapped to his buggy for his return journey. Then he made his way upstairs to his hotel room for a bath and change of clothing before taking his daughter to the cinema.

"Look at you, how beautiful you are, and how grown-up you look. Are you happy now?" he asked her.

"Oh, yes, Daddy, and I had the most wonderful bath ever. I feel like a real lady in these new t'ings." Rosie was glowing but remained timid as she gave him a little twirl.

"You look totally different, older and more mature in your new clothes." He smiled at her in a way that she never saw him smile before, lovingly and somehow proud of her appearance. Marcel wanted her to be like Flo so much, but Rosie just wasn't as pretty as her mammy. Nor was he in love with her as he was with Flo. He felt a slight disappointment, but he was kind to her anyway. He was in a good mood, and they were having a lovely time together.

It was early evening when they went downstairs for a light supper before going out.

"We don't want to eat too much now, or we won't be able to eat in the cinema. I want you to try the ice cream and the popcorn."

"Yes, Daddy, whatever you say."

Marcel gave their order to the waitress. "We'll have the cheese quiche followed by tea and a sweet biscuit. No pudding, thank you, we're going out and will probably eat more then."

"Yes, sir, I understand," said the waitress taking their order.

Rosie relished the food and finished everything. Then, off they set to catch the tram to the cinema in the city centre. What a marvellous journey on the tram, and so exciting for Rosie. She saw the lamplighter light the street lamps, and crowds of people going about their business.

"I've never seen so many folks in one place before--it's t'rilling just to watch," she said. The hustle and bustle of movement all around made her feel alive and energised. Marcel watched her, and noticed for the first time that his daughter sparkled. He smiled to himself and was content in a smug way that he was able to give her this new experience. How different from being on the farm.

It was a famous movie star from America who was playing in the cinema. She recognised his name, as she had heard the people at the hotel talking about him. Rosie was so excited she could hardly stand still. Marcel paid for them both and in they went. She was immediately awestruck at the luxurious furniture inside.

"It's like being in a castle in Heaven," she said.

The loungers were beautifully made in crimson velvet, cushioned with big buttons. They had luxurious painted golden arms and curvy legs that were very grand looking. The entire floor, covered in red carpet, was so soft and silent to walk on. The walls had beautiful designs and heavily gilded mirrors hanging on them. Rosie had never seen anything like it in her life.

They removed their coats, and handed them in at the cloakroom and received a ticket in return. Then they entered through the big double doors into the cinema hall. The overhead lights dimmed, and an usherette came forward to meet them and lit the way with her shining torch to their seats.

Marcel pointed out the line-up of usherettes in the shadows at the side aisles, waiting to sell ice cream, drinks of lemonade, and giant bags of popcorn.

"We should let supper settle first, and buy some ice cream and popcorn during the interval. We don't want to be sick now, do we?" he said.

"Yes, Daddy, yer right, that would spoil everyt'ing," she replied.

The huge velvet curtain across the stage opened slowly as if by magic to expose the giant screen where they would watch the movie. There was writing at the bottom of the screen for everyone to read. The voices were quite funny, she thought. Luckily she could read and was able to follow the story. She sat there engrossed, watching and reading everything as it came up. She was in heaven and thought this is what America was like. She found herself wondering if Kate was enjoying her new life in that world?

Quickly she focused again on the story and the movie. She didn't want to spoil things with thoughts of Kate and what might have been. Amazed at everything, Rosie soaked up the luxurious clothes and the fashions, the fur coats and beautiful shoes and the make-up that people wore. The unusual hairstyles of the young girls, who wore red lipstick and had red-painted fingernails, was all breathtaking to her.

She thought it all very modern and exhilarating, how different the world was in America. What a wonderful country to live in, with such abundance of everything. She couldn't imagine anyone in that country being hungry or running out of sugar or oats.

Rosie loved the cinema, and it opened her eyes to the other side of the world--a place that until now, she hadn't given much thought. Until now she wasn't aware of a different way of life. Now she understood why Kate wanted to go so much, and why she had been afraid to go alone. Life seemed so very busy, so many people in one place. How thrilling it was. Intermission came, and the curtains closed.

"How is your tummy now? Are you ready to try something?" he asked her.

"Yes, Daddy, I feel fine. I'd like te try the ice cream, it sounds grand, and maybe a little lemonade, too?"

"That's good," he said, "I'll get some popcorn, and we can share that between us, if you have room that is."

"This is the best. Thank ye, Daddy for bringing me, I love it all," Rosie said after tasting everything.

The movie ended, and it was time to leave and make their way back to the hotel. Rosie talked the entire way back, leaving nothing out. She talked about the clothes, the make-up, the ice cream, the lemonade, and the popcorn. She couldn't wait until she got home to tell the others about it. They wouldn't believe her. When they arrived back at the hotel, Marcel ordered tea at the reception. It would be brought up to the room shortly. They made their way upstairs, Rosie still talking excitedly about everything.

It was ten o'clock in the evening. The chambermaid brought the hot tea, cups, and saucers up to the room on a beautiful silver tray. Marcel and Rosie sat down at the table overlooking the street. He asked her to pour the tea and then he sat back in his chair with a deep sigh.

"So, have you enjoyed your night out at the cinema? You've had a grand day altogether, new clothes, shoes, coat. You've been spoiled like Kate was by her daddy. Now it's your turn to be nice to me," he told her.

"Yes, Daddy," she replied quietly. Rosie knew what her daddy meant, and she expected as much. She knew that there would be a price for all the gifts he bought her, and the cinema--a big event in her life. She knew she would have to pay him back for everything, his way.

Rosie had put that thought at the back of her mind. She wanted to enjoy the moment, buying the new clothes, the shoes, trying on the dresses. Now it seemed that time had come. She would not fight him. She knew better--she would lose anyway. This time she resigned herself to her situation, and would let him have his way with her.

Each time it happened, another piece inside her withered and died. She felt the knot in the pit of her stomach tighten even more, every time. She wanted to scream out loud to let the world know what he was doing to her, but she knew better and suffered silently.

Marcel was strong as an ox and he would hurt her even more if she did anything against him, and so she endured the pain quietly. She knew this was a special night for him--he wanted some new pleasure badly enough to pay for this extravagant weekend to get his way. She knew she'd better play along with him, and so she did without showing any obvious objection. To do so would ignite his inner demon, a fearful mania she experienced once before and never wanted to repeat. So she obeyed his every order without fuss.

Marcel had his way, alright. He believed that she was now his plaything and that he could do whatever he desired, and he did. When he was spent, he threw her aside like a soiled rag and told her to go clean herself in the bathroom.

When she returned to the bedroom, he was already asleep in his own bed. She crawled into her bed and pulled the quilt up over her head. She buried her face in the pillow so that he couldn't hear her quietly weeping and moaning in pain. She knew that it would happen again the next evening.

This was his plan from the beginning. He would take her away so that he could have a weekend of indulgence. Rosemary and Sean would believe that he was being a proper daddy, treating his daughter to gifts, clothing, and evenings out as he had missed during the earlier years. How wrong they were.

The following morning Marcel got into bed beside her. He told her it was the best way to start the day, and it made him feel good. When he finished with her, he took a bath and dressed. Then he ordered Rosie to do the same. "Have a hot bath and get dressed quickly, we'll have breakfast and go sightseeing today," he said cheerfully.

"I want to take you to places that your mama and I visited." He wanted to show her the town, the way he had shown his beautiful young wife. Rosie was almost the age Flo was when she and Marcel married. Although Rosie was not as beautiful as her mammy, he wanted to pretend that she was his Flo, just for the day. He would enjoy that game and get plenty of self-satisfaction from it.

Marcel gave Rosie the most spectacular tour of the city, taking her on the tramcar and even going upstairs to the top seats where you could see the entire city. She had a wonderful time. He took her to the docks to watch the big ships arriving back from America.

"Do you still think about going to America--don't lie to me, I want to know?" he asked her.

"Yes. I would still love te go te America, especially now since I saw the movie. America looks so exciting," she replied.

"I've thought about going myself. Perhaps one day we'll go together. We could start a new life out there. What do you think of that idea?"

"I would be very excited, and yes, I would love te go wit' ye Daddy."

"Well now, let that be our secret. Not a word to anyone, understand?"

"Yes, Daddy," she replied. Now she had two secrets from Rosemary and Sean that made her feel bad.

They had lunch in a lovely little restaurant, and the food was delicious.

"Your mama and I came here a long time ago on our honeymoon--we had a wonderful time together," he said.

There would never be a more perfect opportunity for Rosie to ask him about her mammy. He seemed in a good mood, talkative and happy, and so she did.

"Daddy," she said quietly. "What was Mammy like? I'd like ye te tell me about her," she said timidly, unsure of his reaction.

Marcel's face changed instantly as he remembered Flo. He smiled softly, and the corners of his mouth twitched upwards. His eyes softened, dark and loving, as he reminisced and began to speak gently about his Flo.

"She was unlike anyone I've ever known in my life," he said smiling. Rosie remained silent. She wanted him to talk and tell her as much as possible.

"She had a girly giggle," he continued, "a laugh that I loved to hear. It was like music to my ears when she laughed," he said with a grin. "She lit up the whole room as if she had a light all around her. She glowed from the inside out. Everyone could see it, and everywhere she went, people loved her." He smiled as he spoke about Flo in a soft and gentle voice.

"Her face was beautiful and always smiling for me. She was small but tough, and I could sweep her up high with one arm and she would laugh and giggle," he said now with a broad grin on his face. Then his face changed, and he began talking in a low whisper. His face became whimsical and sad as he remembered. Rosie noticed the change in him and was curious but silently nervous that she made him angry. She said nothing and let him continue.

"She was hard-working and a wonderful cook--I just loved her cooking. She would try to make me Italian meals, and she loved it when I told her it was perfect. She always wanted to please me and made me feel like her champion."

"She looked after me like I was a king. Everything had to be just right for me," he said as he drifted back through his memories. "We were so happy together, so much in love. I miss her terribly. Each day without her, I become less alive, but one day closer to being with her again." He stopped talking abruptly and looked down as he lowered his head. For a moment, Rosie thought that he was going to cry. Then suddenly he snapped back to the present.

"She died and left me," he said in a cold, matter-of-fact way. There was no love in his voice with his last comment.

Rosie sat quietly--afraid to say anything that might break the spell he was under. She was glad to see a different side of her daddy.

It seemed to her that he was still deeply in love with Flo. His words about her were warm and tender, and he even smiled when he was talking about her.

Why can't he love me too? Am I so ugly? she wondered. The agony of her question was so dark and deep--it hurt her physically and profoundly, just to think about it. She had never felt a love that way from anyone. *What a beautiful t'ing and so powerful--te be in love with someone, and te feel love for another person,* she thought. She had such a longing and loneliness that was hard to carry for a young girl. Rosie decided not to think about it any longer. It was too depressing for her. She was going to enjoy her day out in the city and take what was coming later in the evening.

Marcel suddenly spoke. "We have all afternoon now, where shall we go? What about a tram ride around the city?"

"Yes, I'd love that, Daddy." They had a delightful afternoon. It was a beautiful spring day and the sun was out, which made everything look bright after the winter months. They sat up top on the tram in the open air and Marcel pointed out some interesting places educating her on the many historical points of Dublin's fair city. They passed the biggest bookshop in the city.

"Oh, Daddy, can we go in?"

"Of course we can. Let's get off here," he said.

Rosie loved to read, and he knew that. She was a very good pupil when she went to school and learned to read well because she was so eager. He wanted to buy her a book that she could read and keep for her own entertainment for a long, long time. Finally, he found the book he was looking for and showed it to her.

"This is by Elizabeth Stuart Phelps, a young American writer. It was a best seller for young ladies your age. It's been very popular for a long time. It's my gift to you, a reminder of our trip here."

"Thank ye, Daddy, I'll love it forever."

Rosie was so excited and couldn't wait to start reading it. They took it to the counter clerk to wrap carefully in brown paper. It was an expensive book with a hard cover and gold lettering. It even looked expensive. She would take great care of it and enjoy reading it over, and over again.

The afternoon was growing dark and shops were beginning to close. They had journeyed to the opposite side of the city. It was a pleasant day for Rosie, and she truly enjoyed her time with her daddy. Marcel too had enjoyed the afternoon and getting to know his daughter. He began to feel more at ease with her, and found that they could actually hold a conversation together.

"We should start back to the hotel. It's getting late and near time for supper. We need to get a good sleep tonight, it's an early start tomorrow morning," he told her. "You'll have plenty of time to read it on the way home," he laughed. *Grand*, Rosie thought, *maybe he won't want me tonight, maybe we'll just go to sleep*, and she hoped she was right.

They arrived back in plenty of time for supper, as it was just being served. They went upstairs for a wash and quick freshen-up before going down for supper. Rosie couldn't bring herself to leave her cherished book behind--she wanted so much just to sit down and read it all there and then.

Supper was more than satisfying. They were both hungry and finished everything.

"We'll both have the fish and chips with coleslaw and peas, thank you," he ordered. He knew she had never tasted fried fish before, and that she would enjoy it. She did. Then came the pudding, nothing like the ordinary rice pudding that they had on the farm. They both had the trifle, filled with fruit of every kind that she had never seen before. It had whipped fresh cream, custard, and sponge cake, little red cherries and fruit from some far away exotic country that she knew not. Rosie never tasted anything so delicious in her life. They finished with tea and sweet biscuits. She was full to bursting, and so was her daddy.

It was a lovely spring evening, crisp but not cold, and still "in the gloaming," the time before darkness sets in for the night. Time seems to pass more slowly during the gloaming, allowing a space to reflect on the events of the day before it gets dark.

"I'm full, Daddy, what a grand supper. Are we going for a walk te help it all go down faster?" she asked him.

"Yes, let's take a walk along the embankment." They made their way across the road and headed in that direction.

"The first time I came here was with my mama when we first arrived from Italy, many years ago now. I was just a year younger than you are now," he said remembering. "So much has happened since then," he said peacefully. "Here I am today, walking the same pathway with my own daughter, coming sixteen years of age. Where did the time go?" he asked. "What happened to my life? Time just seems to have disappeared, and I've done nothing with it--planting someone else's crops and not my own," he reflected.

Rosie could see that her daddy was in his memories and listened patiently. It struck Marcel that he had been in hiding for many years, keeping to himself. His mama told him to keep a low profile and make a simple life for himself and that one day he would be able to return to Italy to see her and the rest of his family. Marcel knew that was not going to happen. His mama threw herself into the sea, drowned and was dead. He would never see her again. Those days in Italy and time spent with his extended family were gone, never to return. It all seemed so very long ago, almost like a dream to him. Now he felt it was time to come out into the open again and reclaim his life, or what was left of it. His mama brought him to this small country to hide him away from the Italian army. That time was long over. His life with Flo was over.

"America," he said aloud. "I wonder if there is anything there for us. What do you think Rosie?" he said out loud.

"If ye were going, I'd surely come wit' ye. I'd like that, Daddy," she replied.

"Hmm, perhaps, perhaps, one day soon, we'll see," he said.

They walked on, and she could see that he was deep in his thoughts again. He had plenty of money to afford a cabin on the big ship and make a new start when they got there. He would give the idea more time in his head before deciding on anything. Rosie remained silent, somehow knowing not to disturb him.

She took in the beautiful scenery all around her, the tall trees with their new buds ready to burst into life. She watched the way the water flowed downstream quickly and silently, throwing out sparkling lights that danced before her eyes, as the evening sun slowly set in the sky. This was the gloaming--the time between day and night.

She felt peaceful walking with her daddy, even though they were in the middle of a big city and there were noises all around them. There was a feeling of excitement and being alive, people in motion and action around every corner. She watched groups of people talking in the street, some laughing out loud as they walked. She watched as a young man fell out from the doorway of the public house, having obviously over indulged and loudly expressing his happiness to the world. She noticed how the windows were lit up with light as evening set in and people lit their oil lamps. Everywhere seemed alive and she loved the feeling. Marcel broke her thoughts.

"We should start back to the hotel, it's getting darker now and soon it'll be night. Have you enjoyed your day, Rosie?" he asked quietly in his soft voice.

"I've had a perfect day, Daddy, wonderful in every way." She smiled up at her daddy feeling his satisfaction too, and they turned together to walk back to the hotel. It was nine o'clock when they got back, just in time to order tea and biscuits up in their room before going to bed for the night. They talked about their day on the tram, and relived the excitement of the big bookshop and its many wonderful books.

"If I were rich I'd buy up the bookshop and read every book there." Marcel laughed light-heartedly.

It was time for bed. Rosie went into the bathroom first to wash and change into her new flannel nightgown. When she returned to the room, Marcel was already in her bed waiting. Her stomach churned. She knew immediately what was about to take place. She had hoped that because they were getting along so well, that he might not bother her that night.

"You can take that off," he said mockingly. She removed her nightgown as ordered, and got into the bed beside her daddy. It seemed he would have his way for their last evening together.

It was early in the morning when Marcel woke Rosie from sleep. He rolled her over on her back and took her once again. She closed her eyes and told herself that this would be the last time for a while as they were going home today. When he finished, he removed himself abruptly from her small body, went into the bathroom to bathe, and ready for their journey home. It was the last chance for them both to enjoy the luxury of a large hot tub. He felt refreshed, clean, and dressed in his new but casual clothes suitable for travel. Most of all, she thought, he seemed happy, and she felt curiously glad for him. *He's been miserable for such a long time*, she thought.

"Rosie, go and take a hot bath and wash your hair. It's your last chance before we go, so don't take too long but do enjoy. I'll go downstairs and read the newspaper until it's time to order a hot breakfast for both of us," he said.

Rosie got out of bed and ran the bath with hot water to soak her aching body. The bath would help relieve some of the pain she felt in her limbs--she knew this from experience. She immersed herself in the hot, soothing water. She did not want to relive any of the events of the night before or that morning and lay soaking and enjoying the moment. However, her thoughts drifted back to the pain and how bad it made her feel, every time it happened. She tried hard to forget about it knowing he wouldn't come near her for a while now. He'd had his fill of her, morning and night, and she knew that would satisfy him for a while.

Was it worth it, she asked herself? She considered the gifts, the book, the cinema, all the lovely food and things. *He treated me kindly enough and certainly spoiled me,* she thought. The answer came back instantly in her head. "*NO.*" Nothing in life was worth what he had taken from her. Her very soul was lost to him. He had devoured her life, killed her insides, and what she might have been. He took her body, her hope and her dreams--she had nothing to live for now.

Rosie slipped deeper into the water and fleetingly had a thought that she could end it all there and then. She just had to stay under the water. Suddenly, she sat upright in the tub and began to wash herself furiously with the soap. *No more of that t'inking,* she told herself. *He would win if I did somet'ing like that, and God would certainly send me te Hell when I die.* She had to rid herself quickly of such bad thoughts. *Concentrate on here and now,* she told herself. *Last night is over. He won't come te me again, not for a while.*

19

Christmas at Springtime, 1911

The journey home was quicker than expected. The weather was lovely, and it was the perfect day for a buggy trip through the country roads.

"That was a grand breakfast, Daddy, I'm full te burstin'. The food was grand wasn't it?" she said.

"Yes, it was," he replied. "Just as well you're full, we won't be stopping until we get home, and Rosemary will be expecting us for supper." Rosie knew that the children would be waiting excitedly to hear her stories. What they didn't know was that her daddy was bearing gifts for everyone. It would be like Christmas, only better.

It was a quick trip with no hold-ups, and they made good time. In just five hours they approached the pathway leading up to the farmhouse. It was suppertime as expected. Everyone was waiting for them to arrive, and there was great excitement all 'round.

"We've been waiting for ye te start supper," Sean said. Marcel dropped Rosie off at the front door and lifted the boxes down from the buggy.

"My goodness, what's all this?" Rosemary asked.

"Oh, a little something for everyone. Let me go and see to the horse first, and then we can open the boxes," he said. Rosie carried some of the parcels into the house and straight into the bedroom and placed her things on her bed. All the while Rosemary's eyes were scanning Rosie's new clothes: her coat, her shoes, and her white cotton socks. She looked older than usual, and Rosemary felt a slight sense of envy, but then chastised herself quickly. She knew that Rosie deserved the new clothes and the trip to Dublin.

"Ye look lovely, Rosie, all grown-up in yer new stylish coat and shoes." Rosie could feel some slight indifference and decided not to overdo things that might cause jealousy of her new wardrobe.

"I had a wonderful time, Rosemary--Daddy took me all 'round Dublin te the same places he took Mammy. We went te the cinema, and the shops were just huge. I can't wait te tell ye about it all," she said in excitement.

"Look boys, me daddy bought this great big story book for all of us. I can teach ye how te read it. Ye'll love it."

Rosemary finally found her voice. "How was the hotel?"

"It was grand, very posh, hot running water and a huge tub te bathe in, any time ye wanted," Rosie quickly responded. "The food was grand too. They had t'ings I never heard of before, so good it'd make ye fat in no time." Rosie was careful not to make too much of it. She could feel some resentment from Rosemary and knew there was a slight envy for all the nice clothes she was wearing.

"Oh Rosie, ye lucky t'ing, look at her new clothes," the boys were saying.

"One day, when yer older, yer daddy'll take ye. It'll be yer turn te see the city, just wait and see." They helped to carry the boxes inside and finally Marcel returned from the stable where he had settled the horse for the night.

"I put your supplies in the usual place in the barn, just inside the doors where you like them," he said to Rosemary.

"Thank ye, Marcel, Sean'll settle up wit' ye on that."

"I have a few small things I wanted you all to share in," he announced happily. "It only seemed fair that since Rosie was being so spoiled that I could afford to spoil everyone, so let's see what we have here," Marcel said to everyone.

They went inside, and Rosemary sat in her chair by the fireside, quietly surprised but somewhat curious why he would do such a thing. Then she remembered how much he liked to spoil Flo, and it took her back to those early years in the pub. She remembered how he became taller and more commanding when Flo excited by his gifts, giggled and laughed--it made her relax a little as she recalled and understood.

Marcel began to open the boxes one at a time. He picked out a pair of stripped slippers with a fur insole.

"Size two, for a boy, I wonder who?" he called out.

Anthony, Damian, and Sonny, stood in front of him with their eyes gaping wide open. They had no idea what size they were and didn't dare to speak. Rosemary reached out to Marcel for the slippers.

"My, these are lovely, and yer feet will be 'snug as a bug' in them, Sonny." She handed them over to him to try. Sonny, thrilled to pieces, put the slippers on his feet. They were soft and cosy, and he felt grand.

"Thank ye, Marcel, they're so warm and fluffy," the five-year-old boy said, shyly smiling at him. Next was Anthony and then Damian and then the girls, Miriam and Cora. The children had never had such lovely soft warm slippers before.

"These are for wearing inside the house only, not for outside. We have other shoes for that," Marcel instructed. The children jumped up and down in great delight; everyone was getting new shoes. Sean and Rosemary looked at each other in astonishment and silently wondered, where did Marcel get all this money from and why was he spending it now on their children?

"Ye always did like te buy gifts, didn't ye, Marcel?" Sean asked approving. Marcel nodded in agreement as he loved to see the gratitude of everyone. Then finally, he handed a box over to Rosemary.

"This one's for you, I hope they fit you." She opened the box to see a lovely pair of red and white fur-lined slippers.

"Oh, Marcel, they're beautiful. I love them, thank ye very much." Her expression showed delight and surprise, gratifying Marcel. He seemed to grow physically in height, right in front of her eyes. Suddenly she knew why he did it. It was for his pleasure. It made him feel good. Now she understood him, at long last. Rosemary indulged him with her display of gratitude, even though she thought him a self-serving, little man. She hugged him, and put her arms around his neck and gave him a kiss on his cheek. Marcel responded by handing boxes to the others, but his demeanour took on another appearance and self-confidence as if he could do no wrong. The children joined in the excitement. It was better than Christmas for them all. They had never had such beautiful new shoes or slippers in their young lives.

When Rosie brought out the book, the children jumped up and down with joy, clapping their little hands together in excitement.

"A new story!" they shouted.

"A new story for us all te read," Rosie said. "I'll just put me t'ings in the room for now." She laid them out neatly on her bed for Rosemary to see.

"Rosemary, will ye come in here for a minute?" Rosemary followed her through to the bedroom.

"Yer a lucky girl, Rosie," Rosemary told her.

"I know. I am that, a very lucky girl," she replied.

Rosie relieved that her daddy thought to surprise everyone else in the family, watched on as the gits were given out. For Sean, a new pair of boots was a very special occasion. However, to throw in a pair of men's leather slippers--soft warm wool lining was a luxury he never experienced. Sheepishly, and slightly embarrassed at the occasion, he sat down to take off his boots. The children stood around watching quietly, anticipating something they knew not. Sean removed his old boots and tried on the new ones. They were of very good quality that he would never have bought for himself, and they were very comfortable. The room was silent until finally Sean spoke.

"Very nice, Marcel, very nice indeed, and thank ye. I'll make them last until I die." They all laughed. Sean then turned to the slippers. He had never possessed slippers in his entire life. It was a completely new experience for him as he removed his woollen sock and slipped his large foot inside the soft fur lining. He sat there for a few minutes, quietly looking down at his new footwear and shaking his head. Finally, he spoke. "They're grand just as grand as can be, thank ye." That was his final comment, but he wore his slippers every night from then on.

"Are we ready to eat supper now?" Rosemary asked. The family arranged themselves around the table in their usual places. Sean said grace out loud for them all to join in at the end:

> "... *and thank ye, Father, for these gifts and the friends who share this meal wit' us tonight.*"

> *"Amen,"* they all said in unison.

Rosie helped lift the soup plates over to the table as normal. She always helped Rosemary at suppertime and realised that she was happy being home with her family.

Later on, after supper, Marcel left for his digs.

"Goodnight, everyone, see you all in the morning."

"Goodnight, Daddy," Rosie said cheerfully.

Rosie went into the room and carefully folded her new clothes on the bed.

"Here, hang yer new coat on this and put it in the wardrobe te keep it good." Rosemary handed her a proper wooden hanger, one of the few they had. Her other new clothes she folded carefully and placed them in her box under her bed. She put a sheet of brown paper over the top to keep them clean and dust free.

That night in bed, Rosie relived her visit to Dublin with her daddy. She remembered the trip to the cinema, and all the exciting food and flavours she had tasted for the first time. She didn't want to talk about that with the others, as she knew that would raise some feelings of resentment, and she could understand their point of view. So she kept her memories to herself and recalled all the exciting parts that she wanted to remember. The other parts that she wanted to forget, she buried in the back of her mind. She eventually fell asleep in her own bed and was grateful to be alone. She felt safe again, home with Rosemary and Sean.

It was April and then May, and the nights stayed bright longer. At ten o'clock in the evening, it seemed still as bright as daytime.

"You children can play out later since it's still bright, but don't go out of the yard," Rosemary told them.

Rosie found that she had put on some weight. Her new clothes were fitting snugly around her waist. It must have been all that grand food in Dublin that finally caught up with her, she thought. She liked the new extra pounds though; it seemed to give her some shape, and her breasts were finally starting to grow. She was becoming a young lady with a few new curves that pleased her. It was early one morning in June when she felt nauseous.

"I don't know what's wrong wit' me, Rosemary?"

"Ye must have a bug or eaten somet'ing bad. It'll go away soon. Here, drink this, it's boiled water so sip it slowly," Rosemary told her.

As the days went by, Rosie became more and more aware of the changes in her body. She noticed the red mark around her nipples and wondered what that was, but did not dare speak to Rosemary about it. Her breasts were tender to touch and much more swollen than they had ever been before. She began to suspect that she was pregnant.

"It can't be, please, God, make this go away, please," she begged.

She pleaded out loud to God repeatedly. She was so afraid of the idea. She tried to put it to the back of her mind and not think about it. However, her body was a constant reminder, and she could feel the changes daily and became more and more anxious about what she should do. She couldn't ask Rosemary for help. She didn't have anyone that she could talk to about it. *I have te talk te Daddy—he's the only one who can help me now. Yes, he'll know what te do about it,* she thought.

She kept an eye out for his comings and goings, so that if the chance came she would know where he was and could talk to him without anyone knowing. In the meantime, she kept her fears to herself, and ensured her body was well covered to disguise her rounded breasts and recently developed pot-belly. Finally, an opportunity arrived when she saw him going into the barn and not coming back out. She waited and watched for him. Rosemary was out the back of the house hanging up some washing to dry in the night air. The children were with her, helping. This was her chance.

She ran towards the barn, making sure she was not seen by anyone. She stopped at the entrance and walked inside slowly looking around for him.

"Daddy, where are ye, I need te talk te ye. I have something I need te tell ye, are ye in here?" she called out.

It was a long barn with a high timber roof. Marcel was up at the furthest back of the barn where the hay was stacked high. He was stacking blocks with a pitchfork. He was behind the hay where she couldn't see him, so he stepped out into the open and shouted to her.

"I'm up here at the top of the barn." She ran up towards him shouting out all the way.

"Daddy, we need te talk, I've somet'ing te tell ye." As she came closer to him, she called again.

"Daddy, I t'ink I'm pregnant."

Marcel heard what she said and immediately stopped working as his stomach turned in shock. He stabbed the fork into the hay, as Rosie came into his view.

"Did anyone see you come in here?" he asked angrily.

"No, Rosemary's out back hanging washing and all the children are wit' her." He spun around on his heels towards her. The back of his hand whipped her face so hard that she flew across the barn and landed on her knees at the stack beside the fork. Marcel was furious and couldn't contain his rage. He leaned down, grabbing her by the shoulders, and shook her wildly while shouting at her in some garbled Italian she didn't understand.

"What are you talking about, you stupid girl?" Suddenly he was on his knees behind her and started to unbuckle his belt. Rosie gave out a shout.

"No, Daddy, no, ye don't understand " she gasped, as he lifted her skirt and pushed her face down into the haystack. He pulled at her bloomers and in a flash had penetrated her body, pumping her hard and violently. Rosie tried to speak, but he was too enraged and furious to hear her words.

He pushed her head down into the hay and held her in place with his hand around her neck while he continued to ravage her. Again, she tried to speak and twisted her head to gasp some air, but he tightened his grip and continued to pound her harder. He seemed unable to hear her, oblivious at her attempts to catch a breath.

She tried one more time to move her head and break away from his hold, but she weakened, and her world darkened as her body fell lifeless. Instantly, Rosie found herself floating up high in the rafters of the barn looking down on her daddy savagely raping her little body. Now she felt weightless, and the pain was gone. She wondered how this could be, as she watched until he finished with her.

She saw herself lying on the hay, as still as could be, her head bent to one side, and her eyes closed. She looked as if she was sleeping. She could see his one fist clenched tight on her thigh, and his other hand closed around her small neck choking her. That was her last sensation. She had difficulty breathing. Then she became unconscious and confused how she could be up in the rafters.

He proceeded to make himself respectable again as he turned back towards her where she lay. She watched him pulling her by the arm to get her up, but her body lay still, and her eyes did not open. Marcel, shocked when he realised what he had done, had gone too far with her this time. He pulled at her arm and leaned down to shake her by the shoulders, but she didn't respond. Rosie lay dead on the hay. She could see him panick, not knowing what to do as she watched from above.

He strutted up and down rubbing his forehead. He turned back to the body and covered it lightly with hay then he started to feel the wall behind him, as if he was looking for something. He was feeling for the loose plank of wood that he had found all those years ago--the one that comes out, and, goes back in again, the one with the mark on it, now, black with age. Finally, he found the right one and removed it.

She watched as he got down on his knees and started to dig in the ground with his hands. He was feeling for something in the soil on the other side of the wall outside the barn. She saw him lift what looked like a large cover. Then he came back into the barn to Rosie. He lifted her up and carried her over to the hole in the ground and dropped her body into it. He threw some hay over the top of her body and replaced the lid. Then he threw loose soil and hay around and over the top of the hole. He stood back looking at his handiwork showing no remorse or emotion at all. It was as if he had just cleaned up a little mess on the barn floor.

"Yes, this will do, no one will ever find her," he mumbled to himself.

Marcel had stumbled on the secret cellar many years back when he first came to the farm and slept in the barn. He had lost his balance, hit his head on the loose plank, and fell into the sunken earth on the other side. He knew that no one was aware of the hole in the ground. It was never spoken of, and he had hinted at it over many years. Sean apparently didn't know about any secret hiding pit in the ground, and it was never mentioned again. Rosemary was new to the family and wouldn't know about it, either. He felt confident that Rosie's body would never be found, not by anyone.

Rosie watched as her daddy buried her small body in that dark hole in the ground and then hid the opening. She watched shocked, as he dusted himself down and walked across the yard heading home as normal at that time of night. His callousness, so cold and cruel, showed no guilt, no remorse, or emotion of any kind. *How can he be so heartless, I'm his only child,* she thought. She followed behind him, shouting and trying to make him see her. He didn't react. She couldn't understand. Was she dreaming? What was happening to her? She tried to awaken from her state. She rubbed her eyes, but nothing changed. Marcel walked on towards the pathway that passed the house and led to the road that took him home. Rosemary came out of the farmhouse front door and shouted over to him.

"Have ye seen Rosie?" she called out.

"No, I haven't," he replied. "She might be down the lower field. I don't know Rosemary--I haven't seen her in a while. Goodnight now, see ye in the morning."

Marcel continued walking, and Rosemary turned and went inside. As Rosie approached the farmhouse following her daddy, she became aware of a bright light behind her. It seemed to call her, beckoning her to "come." She didn't know what this light was and felt a little anxious. She started to run towards the front door of the house when she saw Rosemary go inside and close the door. She tried to get away from the light, but it seemed to follow her as fast as she ran.

As she reached the door, to her great surprise, she saw little Fin standing there, calling her over.

"Quick, Rosie, in here quickly," he called out to her.

"How did YOU get here?" she asked him confused. "Where did ye come from and how can I see ye?" she said desperately and began to cry.

"Did ye see me Daddy?" she asked. "Did ye see what he did te me, and did ye see him walk away?" she asked frantically. "I can't get him te hear me--he won't stop, he just keeps walking away from me--I don't understand Fin, how are ye here?" she sobbed.

"Quick, in here, Rosie," said Fin. He ushered her in through the front door and into the bedroom, closing the front door firmly behind them.

"Get in here away from the light before it gets ye," he said. Rosie ran straight into the bedroom and sat down on her bed crying.

Rosemary was working at the black iron stove making supper for everyone. She was still wondering where Rosie was when she heard the door bang and thought it was her. She stopped what she was doing and went to look but Rosie wasn't there--the bedroom was empty. Confused, she returned to the black iron and continued with her cooking.

Rosie sat on her bed, crying, puzzled, and agitated.

"I don't understand, why can't Rosemary see me Fin, what's happening?"

Fin sat on the bed beside her. He placed his tiny hand on hers and spoke softly.

"Rosie," he said, "ye must try te understand--yer dead, yer daddy strangled ye te death in the barn. I was there watching. I saw him hurt ye again, and then choked ye wit' his hands around yer neck. Don't cry, Rosie. He can't hurt ye anymore, and now we're together again," he tried to console her. "It took me a long time te understand why Mammy couldn't see me. It was only as the time passed, and I heard people talking about me being dead, that I realised," he said. "Now we're here together--friends again, we can keep each other company. Ye don't have te be alone like I was for so long," Fin told her.

Rosie stopped sobbing and lost her fear--she always loved Fin and missed him after he died.

"I know," she said, "I saw him hurt me. I was up high in the rafters and I could see him and what he was doing te me," she said. "I remember feeling that I was choking. I couldn't breathe, and then I must have fainted and that's when I went up te the rafters," she sighed. "Fin, am I really dead?" she asked him. "I saw him hide me body down a big hole in the ground at the back of the barn. No one will ever find me there," she sighed. "What de we do now?" she asked her little friend.

"I don't know," Fin replied. "I've been waiting for me mammy te come and get me, but she can't see me. We just have te wait," he told her. "I t'ink we're in Limbo?" he suggested. "Ye know, that place where child souls go before they go te Heaven," he said.

"I wonder why we have te wait here and what for?" she asked him. "Why don't we go te Heaven now?" she questioned again. "Ye know, Fin, I prayed every day te be wit' me mammy. I told God that I was ready te die. I did that," she confessed to him. "I told God te let me die and go te me mammy, but now I'm here in Limbo wit' you instead. Why?" she asked, still confused and anxious. "There must be more. Somet'ing else has te happen te release us from this place, but I don't know what it is," she said, wondering.

"Can ye t'ink of anyt'ing that we haven't done, or maybe somet'ing bad that we've done that needs te be forgiven?" she asked him.

"I don't know," the little boy replied. "But we're here, and we should stay away from that light, it scares me, ye know," he said. "Old Papa came out of the light one time and tried te get me te go wit' him in it. He saw me and smiled at me--told me te 'come' wit' him, but then he went in the light, and I never saw him again," Fin said.

"It only comes when yer outside. It doesn't seem te be able te come inside the front door. So, if ye ever get chased by it, run into the bedroom, like I do," he warned her.

"Ye know, Rosie, ye won't feel pain ever again, not like when yer alive," he told her. "Ye won't feel hungry or sick or any of that.

The only t'ing ye can feel will be in yer memories. If ye remember a happy or sad event, ye can relive that feeling again," he explained. "But, ye can also feel the pain ye caused other people as well," he continued. "That's how I felt me mammy's grief when I died. It was so sad for her. I tried te let her know that I was fine, but she couldn't hear me," he said gloomily.

"Oh," said Rosie, interested. "Ye mean I can feel how me daddy felt when me mammy died, if I t'ink about it?" she asked him.

"I t'ink so, because when I'm t'inking about a t'ing that happened, the feeling comes back," he told her. "If yer just watching the others then it's like this, and ye feel not'ing at all," he said. Fin continued to instruct Rosie on being dead, and she listened closely to his every word.

"D'ye mean, Fin, that every time yer mammy said she could feel yer presence when she was saying her prayers, that ye were actually still here in this room?" Rosie asked.

"Yes," he replied. "I never left the place. I've been here all the time since I died. I've watched Mammy saying her prayers morning and night, birthing the other children, now, me brothers and sisters, and everyt'ing that has happened since then," he told her. "When I saw them put me body into that nice white box, I realised I was dead." Fin smiled at Rosie and continued. "I've watched ye growing up and playing wit' me brothers and sisters and oh, how I wanted te join in, especially the reading. The stories ye told them were grand Rosie. I loved them all," he said.

"So, me life is over then," said Rosie. "I don't get te go te America. I so wanted te go there and visit wit' Kate. I used te t'ink that one day a young man would come and take me away from here. We'd go te America together and get married. We'd have lots of children, and we'd live a happy life together," she said smiling. "None of that will happen now, will it, Fin?" she said disappointed.

"No, it won't," Fin told her. Rosie hung her head, silently dismayed. "How unfair that he should get away wit' it all," she said.

"He should be hanged by the neck in a public place where everyone could see him die a slow death," she said crossly and continued. "I'd love te watch him wriggle and squirm in pain, like he did te me." "Not able te cry out and have te keep quiet like I did," she told Fin resentfully. "Why should he get off and be allowed te live his rotten life? After what he did te me," she said again. Fin stroked her shoulder to comfort her as Rosie started crying again. "He stole me life from me, that's what he did. He stole me life, Fin," she cried.

"I know he did," Fin replied. "It's so unfair." Fin sat quietly beside her on the bed. He said nothing but he understood how she felt and she knew that.

"People should know," she said tiring. "They should know what he did." Fin took Rosie's hand again, but still he said nothing. "I want people te know what he did te me. It's not fair," Rosie cried leaning her head on little Fin's shoulder.

The children sat on the bed together. They talked about the time they were friends before Fin died. They talked for a long time. Then they lay down together on the bed holding hands, and they fell into a light sleep. Fin was still four years old, as he was when he died. Rosie was just fifteen and her life was over. She felt cheated.

In time, there would be no sign that she had lived at all and nothing to account for her life. No children to continue her lifeline, her seed lost to the cycle of life and evolution. She would never marry, never have children, never be a grandmother or know a family line such as Sean and Rosemary had. Rosie wanted validity--she wanted justice, and she wanted revenge. She wanted her daddy exposed as a rapist and murderer. She wanted people to know that she had a life and he took it away.

She determined that her life would not be over until people knew her story, and her truth exposed. Only then, would she be set free and able to begin again. Otherwise her life had no meaning at all. Fin, meanwhile, simply wanted his mammy.

"That's it, Fin," Rosie said, an idea forming in her mind. "I t'ink I understand why we're stuck here and not passed into Heaven." Fin listened, eager to hear what she was thinking. "I t'ink there's somet'ing we have to do, like a test, or a final challenge, somet'ing we've missed," she said, thinking out loud. "Then we'll be able to pass through. We just need te find out what it is. Then we get the reward: you wit' yer mammy and me wit' my mammy," she said. "That's the reward for both of us. But what can the test be?"

"I don't know, Rosie," he said, "that's why I'm waiting for Mammy te come. She knows what it is, and, she'll know what te do."

Marcel walked quickly, almost sprinting, in the warm night air on his way home. It was still very light and would not be dark for some hours yet. His thoughts were clear as he worked out in his mind what he was going to do. No one had seen Rosie come into the barn where he was working. No one knew that he was working in the barn at all. He would simply turn up for work the next day as normal. Sean and Rosemary would want to go looking for her and he would go along with that, knowing that she would never be found. He would suggest that she had run away in the night, probably went for the ship to America. He would suggest that she was a bad apple and they shouldn't spend any time worrying about her. She was gone, and this time he wasn't going to stop her.

It was getting later and later back at the farm, and young Rosie hadn't shown up. Rosemary was very concerned. Both she and Sean searched everywhere for the girl. Sean decided that Rosie must have run away sometime during the day, but Rosemary wouldn't believe that for a single minute.

"All the girl's nice new clothes are still in the box under her bed. Her good coat is in the wardrobe along wit' her good shoes," Rosemary said. "No, Sean," Rosemary said, "she would never leave all her new clothes. She would need them if she planned te leave. Somet'ing's happened te her, I feel it," she pleaded. Finally, they returned home late in the night and went to bed. They had waited up as long as they could, hoping that she would return. Rosemary prayed hard for young Rosie that night, but all the time she had a dreadful feeling that something very bad had happened to her.

The next morning Marcel arrived for work as usual when Sean and Rosemary called him over.

"Marcel, d'ye have a minute?" he called out. "Rosie's gone missing. We looked everywhere for her last night and found not'ing. No sign of her anywhere."

"Well she can't just disappear," he replied, "she's probably hurt herself and is lying somewhere waiting for us to find her," he suggested. "We should go look again."

"We went down te the stream last night but there was no sign of her there," Sean said. "We've been out over quite an area and found not'ing. Finally, it got too dark, and we had te go home te the children," he explained to Marcel.

"She might have run away, you know, like before?" said Marcel.

"I t'ink if she was going to American she'd need her new clothes. I don't believe she'd go wit'out them. It doesn't make any sense," said Rosemary.

"Well, I'll have another look for her but you can go about your business since you've done so much already. I am her daddy, I'll look for her now," Marcel said.

Rosemary went inside the house as Sean walked with Marcel some of the way pointing out the places they had already searched.

"We should tell the local police that she's missing, as well. They'll want te know, and probably do a search themselves. Will ye do that, Marcel, or would ye prefer me te go into the village and make the report?" Sean asked.

"No, I'll do it, Sean, but thanks for the offer. I think it should come from me as her father, but I will tell them that you and Rosemary have already made a search for her, as well as me," he replied.

"Good enough, Marcel, I'll leave it in yer hands," Sean agreed.

The days passed. Rosie didn't return. In time, the family got used to her not being part of their daily life. Often Rosemary wondered about her missing Goddaughter, and always with a heavy heart. She included her in her daily prayers, somehow knowing that something bad had happened to the young girl. Sean told her to let it go.

"The girl's gone now, Rosemary. No one knows where, or who wit', but she's gone, so let it go," he told her.

"But what if it was him that did somet'ing te her?" Rosemary replied.

"We don't know that and can't prove anyt'ing. There's no body, no proof, not'ing. She might have run away. Taken the ship te America. We'll never know now, so let it be, Rosemary," he told her again.

Marcel tried to show concern for his missing daughter and continued to work alone in the fields, staying away from people as much as he could. He had the support of people in the village. That gave him some relief knowing that the finger of blame was not being pointed in his direction. People believed that Rosie had run away to America. Rosemary's intuition told her differently and warned her that Marcel had something to do with his daughter's disappearance. She told her children to stay close to the house and never to go anywhere alone with Marcel. She didn't want to scare them, but she did want to impress on them that he could not be trusted. She continued to pray for the lost girl, and every morning after prayers, her broken heart hoped that maybe, this would be the day that Rosie would come home.

20

100 Years in Limbo, 1905-2005

Rosie and Fin stayed together on the farm. They played with each other as they had in their lifetime before and watched the daily events of the family unfold with great interest. A long time passed, although they didn't know time as live people measure it. They continued to stay away from the bright light, and every time it appeared, they would run inside the house and hide. Fin, especially, was very afraid of being captured. He told Rosie many times that his old papa got sucked into the light and disappeared, never to return. Nothing could tempt him into the light, not ever, and he continued to warn her that it was dangerous for them both.

They took great pleasure in trying to make Rosemary hear them. They stayed close to her when she was praying, both morning and night. It was easier to feel near her when they all prayed together. They knew that she ached for them. The children waited patiently, not knowing what for, but intuitively that they were waiting for something.

Rosie remembered a lesson during a Mass service, that when children died, they went to a place called Limbo--a place half-way between worlds, where they stayed for purification until released into Heaven. The lesson taught that the soul, even that of a child, pure and innocent, must be unblemished and in a state of perfection, to cross over. Each morning they prayed with Rosemary hoping for a message through their prayers.

"Heavenly Father, Thank ye for this day, for protecting me children and keeping us safe and healthy, for giving me a good husband and children te love. Thank ye for providing us wit' food te eat and for keeping us strong and happy. Thank ye for a nice warm house te shelter us from the cold. Please help us te stay safe in this beautiful world ye've given us te enjoy. And thank ye for this farm te provide Sean wit' the work and income te keep us. Guide us every day and protect us from all evil, and Father please help us te forgive those who hurt us. Say hello te little Fin. Ask him te forgive me for not being home when he passed over. Tell him I'm proud of him being so brave when he died alone, he must have been very scared--and now Rosie if she's wit' ye. Sean says, we just don't know if she is or not, but if she is, give her a hug from me and tell her I'll never forget her and I'll always love her just like I love Fin. I miss them both, Father, very much. I wish t'ings had been different, better somehow, but I don't know how. We're a lucky family, I know, so much love, and yet I feel I should have done more for Rosie. I hope we find her but if we don't please take care of her and ask her te forgive me for not being able te help her more when she was wit' me. She's a good girl, Father. Thank ye.

Amen."

"Rosie," Fin said, "try te push her, prod her or somet'ing, see if she feels ye."

"I've already tried pushing her, Fin, and she doesn't feel anyt'ing at all, but I t'ink she knows we're here wit' her. I can feel a kind of closeness when we pray. Don't you?" Rosie asked him.

"Well, yes. I've felt that before, but she always just ignores it and carries on wit' her prayers and asking for forgiveness."

"Forgiveness," said Rosie. "Hmm, yes she always asks God te forgive those who hurt us, doesn't she?"

"Yes she does, every day, in her morning and evening prayers. I don't t'ink there's much we can do te make her know we're here wit' her. She can't see us, but I do t'ink she can feel us sometimes," Rosie told Fin.

The children tried every day to alert Rosemary's attention in some way. However, Rosemary never saw a connection that it was the very children she was praying for.

Fin and Rosie tried all sorts of pranks and were the cause of some strange things happening in the house. But their brothers and sisters just ignored the strange events and carried on with their chores. Neither did they know what to think about the odd things that happened--doors closing in front of them when there was no one around, or a bale of hay suddenly toppling over, when there was no one near to push it. It gave Fin and Rosie free range to play all kinds of tricks with the family. They would move small items around in the farmhouse just for the fun of it. Then, they laughed at the bewilderment on the children's faces when an object moved, or some other strange thing happened.

They delighted in every birthday event and Christmas celebration, secretly wishing they were alive to take part in the family fun. They saw the good years' harvests as well as the not so good years. They listened to every conversation discussed. Who was getting married and all about the wedding, and especially about their own brothers and sisters marrying. They heard about the funerals and who had died. They listened to the gossip and what was going on in the village, the hearsay of no jobs in Ireland and plenty in America. They watched as Marcel and Sean finally parted ways and listened intently when the first two siblings decided to leave for New York. Then the next two boys and their sister until finally the family were mostly gone. They watched Rosemary and Sean grow old, and their siblings become adults with their own families. Finally, when farming was too much for Sean, and there was no help to do the work he announced to Rosemary that it was time for them to close up and move on to a smaller homestead.

"What are ye t'inking, Sean? I've lived all me married life here in this farmhouse. Birthed all me children here and lost Fin and Rosie here. This is me home and I'll not leave this place or me lost children," she said adamantly.

"Rosemary, don't be silly now. I've an offer for a small cottage just a few miles up the road," Sean told her. "It's been modernised and has electricity and a proper kitchen wit' a sink basin for yer dishes," he tried to convince her. "It has runnin' water, taps an' all, and there's a proper toilet outside in the garden," he said. "We could be comfortable and warm in our old age and much less work te keep the place. All we need for ourselves is a small garden patch for vegetables. Sonny can take over the farm and make it his own, ye know?" he said. But she wouldn't hear of it and continued to rock herself back and forth in her chair while listening to him.

"I won't go, Sean, and that's me last word on the subject. I intend dying here on this farm, all me memories are here. This is me home, our home. Fin and Rosie would never forgive us if we left them here alone. Our boys can have the place when we're gone. I'm staying put, Sean, and that's final," she said digging her heels in.

Fin and Rosie listened eagerly, knowing that life would be easier for Sean and Rosemary at the new cottage. But they also knew that they couldn't go with them. The children remained trapped in the farmhouse and couldn't be freed until they met their final test.

Rosie understood that the soul must be pure and free from all sin to get into Heaven. But what sin?

What happens if a small child dies before reaching the age of under-standing what lesson might they have to enter the Kingdom of Heaven, she wondered? *How could there be a sin of any kind in a young child? Fin was so young when he died. So, what blemish could he possibly have on his young soul?* And then she remembered her Bible: *"The sins of the fathers pass to the children unto three or four generations."* Family karma, she wondered, *is it possible? But what could Fin's challenge be?* She agonised over and over looking for the answer.

These puzzles were constantly on her mind. It was a conundrum--a riddle--but she had to work it out. *What other virtues would be required te pass into Heaven,* she wondered? *"Purity and innocence,"* she thought again. *What act could purify the soul of an innocent child, and dissolve the mysterious chains that held them stuck?* 'Round and 'round her mind went. Her thoughts filtered, slowly becoming clearer as time passed. She had always been a good girl, honest, loving, and giving of herself. She remembered telling Fin that she wanted her daddy exposed. She wanted him to suffer. She wanted revenge--and that was a sin!

She thought about all the feelings she endured because of Marcel--she remembered the pain she felt, and her fear and terror. Then came the hatred and disgust and that made her resentful, and bitter. He changed her and now she was like him: vindictive and angry. She didn't realise until now, how much "sin" he had caused her, and she wondered if Marcel felt these same emotions when Flo died. He held his anger inside and wouldn't let it go. It explained why he was so cold-hearted and cruel. He was full of hatred, because God took his love away when Flo died. Now, Rosie began to understand Marcel's suffering and loneliness.

The same word kept repeating in Rosemary's prayers, day after day. She always asked God to forgive her and to forgive those who hurt us. Was Rosie meant to forgive her daddy for his cruelty? Was she meant to forgive him for stealing her life? She considered this for some time and truly found it difficult to let go of her anger.

She realised that Marcel held the same bitter resentment towards God that she felt towards him. She would pray to God on this and ask for his help. There was no other conclusion. Slowly she began to realise that her challenge was *forgiveness*, and oh...how impossible that seemed to her.

Her head, consumed with thoughts, but still she didn't have the answer for Fin. Surely his lesson wasn't forgiveness--who did he have to forgive? Was it his mammy for not being home the day he died? Somehow Rosie felt that the answer was in Rosemary's prayers. She must listen more carefully when they were praying together.

"Fin, tell me, did ye forgive yer mammy for not being home the day ye died?" she asked him.

"There was not'ing te forgive, Rosie," he replied. "She had te go te her mammy's house for the family reunion and I wasn't well enough te go wit' her. I wasn't really sick, either, just a wee cold, Mammy thought. All the time it was me heart getting weaker and weaker until it stopped beating," he told her. "But there was no pain, Rosie. I just went te sleep. So ye see, there's not'ing te forgive Mammy for, Rosie."

"Yes, Fin, yer right there's not'ing te forgive," Rosie agreed. "I was just wondering if that might be the final test for us both?" she asked.

"Well, it might be for you but I don't t'ink it fits for me, ye know?" Fin said.

"What d'ye t'ink yer test might be then? There must be one t'ing in yer life that ye have te face. Somet'ing hard that ye never did before?" she suggested.

"I've no idea, Rosie, no idea at all. I love me mammy and the whole family. There's not'ing I wouldn't do for any of them. I can't t'ink what it might be. I'll keep t'inking about it though, for you, Rosie."

"Will ye, Fin?" she asked anxiously. "I'd really appreciate yer help--we need te know what it is, then we can go together when the time comes," she said finally.

One day in summer, the children saw a stranger walking up the pathway towards the farmhouse. To their surprise, the stranger could see them both and he looked just as normal as they did.

"Somet'ing's changed, Fin," she said. "This person can see us, maybe this is what we've been waiting for."

The stranger waved to both Fin and Rosie, calling out to them.

"Hello, at long last," he said, "I made it. The message told me te come here," he told them. "Somet'ing special is going te happen here, and I'm involved, so I came," he said. "There are more coming too, lots more," he told them.

Alarmed and surprised, the children didn't know what to make of this person, or his message that more people were coming. However, as the days passed, people started to drift into the farm, a few at first, and then in larger numbers and small groups, like families. They all had the same message--to come here, that a special event would happen that involved them and they should be here for it.

"Where did the message come from and who told ye te come here?" asked Rosie.

"I don't know who it was," the man replied. "The voice led me here and told me where to go. I was curious and thought I should come." Rosie and Fin looked on, listening but they didn't understand any of it.

"We've had a long time wandering these parts, we all have," he said pointing to the crowd. "We're all stuck in this no man's land waiting--for something," he said. "Just like you two, we didn't pass into Heaven, either. We all had to look inside, examine our conscience, and release our sins. We know now that those feelings of anger and hatred had to dissolve te get into Heaven."

"How did ye know that?" Rosie asked him.

"Well," he said, "in time, it came te me that Heaven is a place of perfection, beauty and love. Only excellence exists there. A blemished or soiled soul cannot pass through the veil, until it's made pure and whole again. That's why we're stuck here--between worlds," he explained. "A time and place te see our imperfections and release them," he said.

"Yes," agreed Rosie, "finally I understand--only in perfection can we pass through," she said.

"I believe the time is near," he explained. "We've all been led here, a gathering of souls, for an event, but that's all I know," he finished.

"Somet'ing special," Rosie said aloud.

"It could be our time for release, a second chance for us all, but I've no idea how or when," he told her.

"Ye sound as if ye've given this a lot of thought?" she asked.

"Oh, I have. Many years. Many years t'inking," he confessed.

"I was t'inking the same t'ing meself. It's good te hear that I'm on the right track," Rosie said.

"They're just like us, Fin," she said. "They're dead and stuck, waiting, just like us. But I t'ink he's right, we must have a blemish that needs perfecting before we can cross over."

"Do ye have any idea yet what mine is yet, Rosie? I was just a wee boy when I died." Fin asked her anxiously.

"No, I don't, Fin, but I t'ink I know what mine is. I need te forgive me daddy. It's the only way te make my soul pure again," she told him.

"Oh, Rosie, I saw what he did te ye, and it frightened me just watching," he said.

"I t'ink I'm ready now, Fin. I have tried te let go of the hatred," she told him. "Even before we spoke te that stranger. Hating me daddy makes me feel bad. It depresses me when I t'ink about him, and holding that anger inside makes me feel as bad as he is," she admitted and continued. "I realise now, that I want te feel like the old me, and be happy again, the way I was before. But te do that I have te let go of all bitterness, hatred, and revenge," she explained to Fin.

"Oh, Rosie, I understand and I t'ink yer very brave," he said.

"I feel sorry for him, Fin," she continued. "I've hated him for so long me heart feels heavy when I t'ink about him," she explained. "He made me feel bad about myself, like I wasn't good enough, pretty enough, or clever enough. A daddy should make his daughter feel good and fill her heart wit' love, like me mammy did."

"Oh, Rosie, I wish I could help ye."

"I know ye do, Fin, but I t'ink I'm ready te try," she said. "Daddy's been so alone since Mammy died, isolated in the fields, keeping te himself the way he does. He must be suffering. His black heart filled wit' such rage that he could hurt another living person. Maybe his own pain is so bad that he didn't t'ink of me at all," she questioned.

"It's a hard one alright," Fin agreed.

"Thank ye, Fin," she said and continued. "I t'ink me daddy needs te remember what love feels like.

When I remember Mammy, she makes me smile," she said and grinned softly. "I feel her warmth, and her love. When yer heart is filled wit' love, there's no room for anyt'ing bad," Rosie explained to him. "I want te feel like that again--the way I felt when Mammy was alive, and my world was safe, and perfect, and beautiful, and, full of love."

"Yes, I remember that, too," said little Fin. "Mammy was loving, I felt it from her all the time."

"When me mammy died, it changed Daddy and he never recovered," Rosie explained.

"Well, I know that after I died Mammy changed and became more religious, praying all the time," Fin said.

Rosie didn't know that Marcel had always needed someone else to make him feel good, even as a young boy at school. When Flo was alive, she adored him and that gratified and soothed Marcel. He loved to hear her giggle like a little girl and the way she would swoon over him when he came home. She attended to his every need, fussing over him. She made him feel like a king and he loved it. She was the only friend he ever had and when God took her away,

Marcel became incensed with rage. After Flo's death, he worked out his aggression in the fields, but his bitterness kept him isolated--a curse and a blessing. All the years of frustration were finally laid on Rosie when his anger exploded and released his dark side that was dormant for so long. She didn't understand any of this.

"What d'ye t'ink my challenge is, Rosie?" he asked again.

"I'm not sure, Fin, but I'll help ye find out what it is. I couldn't go wit'out ye. I want te be wit' me mammy, just like you do." she said.

"I do, Rosie, and thank ye for helpin' me. I want te be wit' me mammy, too. Just don't leave me behind," he pleaded.

"I promise I won't do that te ye, Fin," she assured him.

"D'ye, Rosie? Because it would be terrible te be left here alone again--wit' that light," he confessed.

"I promise ye, Fin. I won't leave ye here alone. When the time comes, we'll go together, hand in hand. I promise ye that."

"Thank ye Rosie, I feel better now," he said.

The drifters continued to arrive day by day. The numbers grew and a large crowd began to form. First a few people, twenty or so, then fifty and then a hundred, and hundreds more. They all told the same story--a gathering of like souls at the farmhouse--included them in a special event. No one knew exactly what--and a feeling of expectancy and intrigue developed as they waited together.

21

Doune, Ireland–1940

When Rosemary's heart stopped in 1940 and she crossed over into the light, to her surprise Fin wasn't waiting to greet her, as she expected. She could see him clearly now, though, to her dismay and shock, he was still in the farmhouse with Rosie. She could see them both, waiting but afraid to go into the light. Perplexed and horrified at first, she became frantic with guilt and fear for her children.

All these long years, pining for her son, praying for him and looking forward to when they would be reunited. Devastated to find that he had been in the farmhouse all that time, her feelings, telling her that he was close by, were right. Now, she saw the children trapped in a world she no longer belonged to.

Rosemary was deeply saddened by what had happened to Rosie and felt that somehow, she should have done more to prevent her young ward from being abused and murdered. But, at that time she was afraid of knowing the truth and causing trouble without any proof. Rosie never confided in her and Rosemary's fear held her back from asking.

Now, she knew that her suspicions about Marcel were real, and she wished she had taken the chance, back then, to confront him. Her instinct warned her that he was an evil man, with a dark and sinister side to his character. She always believed he was just too good to be true--too well-mannered, too charming at the right moment, and too generous with his gifts and money. She had to put things right--find a way to persuade Fin and Rosie to go into the light that they were so afraid of. She determined that somehow, no matter how long it took; she would find a way to release them from their ghostly captivity, and bring them to her after-life dimension.

In the years that followed, Rosemary had several encounters with psychics and clairvoyants on this earth. She was searching for the right person, to work with her and create the bridge between their two dimensions. She knew she couldn't do the work herself and was afraid that her children would be stuck forever in their unearthly world. However, as she found out, with the human condition, ego got in the way every time, and she became a topic of amusement and money making schemes. No one would commit to help her, or even hear her story through. That is, until she found Sophie during her meditation one day. Rosemary tried to connect with Sophie several times in her normal working day. Sophie felt the presence and finally spoke to her out loud.

Now, the connection made, and Sophie aware of the events leading to the present day, their work together could begin. Rosemary wanted Sophie to know their past, and feel their helplessness, and isolation. Sophie promised to help, if she could, and bring the children to Rosemary on the other side.

22

Sophie, British Columbia, Canada, 2005

Rosemary's first visit with Sophie happened exactly one hundred years after the death of young Fin. Sophie carried Rosemary's torment as if it were her own, feeling her pain at his death and the love she felt for her little boy. She understood the weight of her shame for doing nothing to help Rosie in her struggle with Marcel. Rosemary's suspicion about Marcel was true, and her guilt and disgrace for doing nothing during her lifetime had grown burdensome and got heavier in death with the passing of time.

Young Rosie had paid with her life. Rosemary's cowardice plagued her constantly, and she waited a long time to find the right person to help her. Now it was time. Finally she made the right connection and could begin the rescue.

Rosemary knew the children were afraid of the light and would never enter it willingly. She was the only one who could shine the light from her side to create the portal and bridge the two dimensions. But she needed someone on the other side, a living person from this world, who was brave enough and willing to accept this unworldly quest. She needed a medium, an empath, sensitive, and intuitive--someone pure of heart, honest, gentle, and loving, to persuade her children into the light. Sophie's compassion and empathy touched Rosemary. Humbled and honoured, Sophie accepted the challenge with all due seriousness--a privilege. She wanted to end the children's eternal waiting, as well as Rosemary's own torment and pain. Although she had never undertaken anything this critical, she vowed to see it through.

She decided to contact her old friends, Marishka and Chloe. They would know how to handle this. Marishka's group were all experienced lightworkers and had helped many lost souls cross into the light--exactly what Sophie was attempting for the first time. They agreed to call their group together and discuss the options. It took time to organise, with information going back and forth for most of the winter months. Sophie's classes continued to meet and pray for a positive outcome for the children.

Rosemary's connection with Sophie became stronger than ever. So strong, that Sophie started feeling Rosemary's deathbed heart palpitations, which could become dangerous for Sophie. She had to ask her spirit friend to distance herself--sometimes the spirit energy connecting is stronger than the medium and can take over the energy of the living person. Rosemary listened to Sophie's request to stand back and disconnect, temporarily. She did, however, continue to visit her from time to time just to prod things along and make sure that the rescue was imminent. The two had become good friends and Sophie always knew when Rosemary came to visit.

Eventually the day came when Marishka and her group arrived at Sophie's house. It was almost ten o'clock in the morning. It was a Saturday and a beautiful autumn day. The sun was full in the sky and it was still warm from the summer months. Sophie had instructed her own friends to tune in at ten o'clock as well as other friends in different parts of the world at their corresponding times.

"We need to 'feel' out the property before starting," Marishka said. "The energy in the house must be positive," she told Sophie. "No negativity at all, and the link must be strong and positively charged. I brought a cleansing kit for burning before we start. It'll cleanse the atmosphere in the room, to ensure a positive energy."

"Okay, that's all fine with me," Sophie said.

Marishka walked downstairs into the room they were going to use in Sophie's basement, followed by Chloe and the rest of her group.

Sophie's friends from her classes were becoming concerned, and Helen told her what they were saying. "Sophie, you're a good friend to me, but we're all very concerned that you're getting involved in some kind of hocus-pocus."

"Helen, I understand your fear, but I'm being guided through this process by a higher power and it will be fine--have faith, please," she asked Helen.

"Sophie, you don't know what could happen or how dangerous this is. We're scared for you and we don't want anything to do with it," Helen pleaded.

"It'll be fine," Sophie reassured her.

"You're in over your head, Sophie. I'm afraid you're on your own," Helen said disapproving.

"Don't worry, Helen. Everything is as it should. I can feel it," Sophie told her.

Her friends were afraid of the unknown and didn't want to take part. Sophie understood. "It's okay Helen, you can sit this out in the kitchen upstairs. I need to work with the energy from Marishka's group. I can't do this alone," she explained. She told her other friends that they could tune in from wherever they were if they wanted to take part. It was up to them. She needed everyone's energy to make a powerful connection. She felt compelled to continue for the sake of the children. Sophie trusted her old friend Marishka--with all her strange unworldly ways, she knew what to do on an esoteric level. The group went downstairs into Sophie's basement.

"I've been channelling for years, Sophie," Chloe said. "I'll talk you through what's happening in the circle to make the rescue happen. You'll just have to trust me. Will you do that?" Chloe asked her.

"Of course I will," Sophie replied.

Chloe and Marishka worked together as a team. Chloe would lead the group through this rescue. Hers would be the only voice, while the others from Marishka's group would form the circle with Sophie and Helen. Six chairs sat inside the circle, one at each point of a hexagon shape, drawn on the floor with chalk. Candles were lit and placed around the room and the cleansing kit, lit and set on the floor in the centre of the circle.

Marishka insisted on everyone wearing amethyst beads; their vibration is known to provide spiritual protection. Helen became very spooked with all the regalia and refused to take part. She told Sophie, "This is witchcraft, Sophie, and you don't know what you're into." She left the room and sat in the kitchen upstairs, where she prayed on her rosary for protection. Sophie smiled as she left Helen with her rosary--the others downstairs were using amethysts. What difference, she thought? She asked her own friends from her classes to stop whatever they were doing at the appointed time. "Tune into the farmhouse in Ireland, just as I've described it to you, and stay tuned in until you feel it's time to leave," Sophie told them.

The candles cast a soft glow across the dark room that made for a more relaxed feeling, even though the atmosphere did feel electrically charged. Sophie asked Chloe, "What's causing the atmosphere? The room's so cold and yet feels alive with energy."

"That's normal in a place where you've had supernatural activity. That's why it's important to cleanse the room before we begin," Marishka told her friend.

She started the cleansing ceremony first. Sophie sat in her chair and listened to everything Marishka said.

"Would it be okay to say my prayer before we begin?" Sophie asked her.

"Of course. We can do that," Marishka replied. "Do you have a copy of it? I can read it out, or do you want to recite the prayer yourself?" she asked.

"I have it written down. You can read it out since you're leading the cleansing ceremony," Sophie said.

She quickly ran upstairs for the copy. Helen was in the kitchen sitting quietly at the table with her rosary in her hand.

"Oh, Sophie, I wish you wouldn't do this. It's dangerous and these people are strange, to say the least. You don't know what they're into, witchcraft and all sorts," she said anxiously.

"Helen, I've known Marishka and Chloe for years and I trust what she's doing to help these children," Sophie said. "I know you don't want to take part, but I have to go through with this. I promised Rosemary I would, and I'm going to keep that promise. Marishka and Chloe know what to do, and they'll lead the session. I'm going to follow their lead. I'm sorry, Helen. You can stay here until we're finished or go home if you want, but I'm going back downstairs. They're all waiting for me to get started. Are you coming down?" she asked Helen.

"No, Sophie, I'll wait here until you're finished and pray for everyone," she said, defeated.

Sophie made her way back downstairs with a copy of her prayer. She handed it over to Marishka. The group sat in a circle and joined hands to create a united energy for the prayer.

"Oh, I like this prayer, Sophie. Did you write it?" she asked.

"Some of it," Sophie replied, "with bits added to fit a diverse group of people. I never knew who would be attending the classes and didn't want to alienate or offend anyone," she continued. "I just feel it's appropriate to say something together before we begin the meditation. It bonds our energies--almost like saying hello, you know."

"Yes, it's a nice gesture for people who are meditating together for the first time in a group like this." Marishka started to read out Sophie's prayer:

"Heavenly Father, Spirit of the Universe, Omnipotent Life of All:

We ask that you guide and protect our group today during this meditation. You know who we are and what we wish to accomplish. Help each of us to stay on our pathway so that we can gain our soul's perfection and glorify you. Let us always be aware of your light protecting us, and your consciousness guiding us. Should we fall, as we all do, give us your hand to lead us back onto your path. We want to be good and to do good by others so that we never intentionally hurt another person. We offer ourselves to serve without return or reward for the effort. We ask that your light encompass this world to bring peace and harmony to all people, to heal the sick and to feed the hungry. We ask that your love enter every heart, mind, and soul, that we learn to love one another and forgive one another as you love and forgive us. Guide us today and tomorrow in the work we do to spread your love and understanding to all mankind."

"Amen," the group spoke in unison.

"I'll now ask the initial questions for clarity of some issues, as well as during the cleansing ceremony. Then I'll pass the lead over to Chloe, and I'll work within the circle," Marishka said.

"Is there any other spiritual presence in the house?" she asked.

"Yes," Sophie replied, "but I don't know who these spirits are apart from Rosemary. The house has always had 'other' occupants--even my granddaughters who are four and five years old, can see them from time to time," Sophie told the group. "The girls speak openly about them, as children do with imaginary friends."

Marishka nodded in understanding and replied, "We'll find out who they are and why they're in your home, during the rescue." She continued with the cleansing ceremony, lifting the small burning log and placing it on the mantle above the fireplace to continue its purification work. At this point Marishka passed the lead over to Chloe who stood at the side of the fireplace in front of the circle. Marishka took her seat in the circle with the other ladies.

Altogether there was quite a number involved. Sophie and her friends around the world, and her own people from her classes wherever they were at the time, and Chloe and Marishka's group in the basement. The group hoped their combined energies would be powerful enough to connect with Rosemary, who would open the portal for the lost children to cross over.

The energy in the room was quiet and peaceful, although still electric and encouraging, as Chloe began to lead the group into the meditation. There was no fear, anxiety, or apprehension at all--everyone was completely at ease, and being there seemed natural to everyone involved. It was a beautiful experience. Chloe spoke directly to Sophie.

"Is there any other spirit unknown to you in this room at present?" Sophie's eyes were closed but to her own surprise she replied, "Yes."

"Describe the energy," said Chloe.

Sophie described what she could see clearly in her mind. "There's a tall, very regal-looking, well-dressed Indian chief standing in the corner at the opposite side of the fireplace. He stands proud with his arms folded in front of his chest. He's dressed in a fine-looking ceremonial outfit."

"What's his name?" Chloe asked her.

Sophie gazed towards the impressive looking chief as he took one of the feathers from his hair and handed it to her. Neither of them had spoken out loud, but her subconscious mind heard him and she replied to the group.

"Eagle Feather, his name is Eagle Feather." He smiled down at her and nodded in approval. Chloe spoke again.

"Ask him why he's here?" Sophie looked towards Eagle Feather and his reply came immediately, although again his mouth did not move. She understood his thoughts and spoke out loud for everyone to hear.

"He's here to help with the healing. He says he's my guide and a powerful medicine man. He's come to help."

At that point Eagle Feather came 'round to the empty chair intended for Helen and sat down. He took Sophie's hand to join in the circle, and in her mind she heard him speak to her. *"Now the circle is complete, we can begin,"* he told her.

Chloe asked, "What's he doing now?"

"He came to join in the circle. He's sitting in Helen's chair and he's holding my hand to complete the circle. His hand feels so real to me, it's just as solid as Marishka's hand " Sophie said. Chloe spoke again.

"Now we know why Helen isn't involved--it was to give Eagle Feather her chair. His energy is very powerful and he'll help to create the bridge. But something remains hidden. He would only come forward if his power was needed. Let's see what develops," Chloe said.

The energy in the room changed and became more static and charged with a power unknown to any of them. Eagle Feather's commanding presence gave Sophie confidence that everything would go well. He had a strong formidable aura and she felt sure he was protective towards the children and their rescue. She sat there with her eyes closed amazed at how real it all felt. Chloe continued to talk to Sophie.

"Sophie, I want you to stand in front of the house in Ireland and describe everything out loud for us all to hear. How you feel and what you are looking at--the weather and anything else you might see or feel. Tell us everything as it unfolds, that way you will stay grounded to us here in this room." Sophie began to talk.

"I'm standing on the grass in front of the house. The place is old and abandoned looking. It's a very run-down, single-storey dwelling with whitewashed stone walls from long ago," she said looking around her. "Some of the roof is intact but there are missing slates and obvious holes in some places. The front door is ajar, wafting back and forth with the draught." Sophie continued to describe what she was looking at. "There's a window on both sides of the door and the glass is broken in them. The place looks dirty and very unlived in," she said and continued again.

"The grass is long and overgrown. It's been raining. There's a feeling of dampness in the air and I can feel a cool breeze against my face. It's chilly and I wish I'd brought my coat," she told them. "The countryside smells fresh after the rain and there's a whiff of farm animals, but there doesn't seem to be anyone around. I'm alone, and there's a strange whirling noise, like a wind surge would make. Yet I feel that I'm not alone, as if I'm being watched," she said and carried on.

"It's cloudy and dull--a grey day. There's no sunlight breaking through at all. I feel as if I'm actually here, but I know I'm in my basement in Canada. It's very strange," she told them. "The people must be inside the house. In fact, I know they are, but they're all scared to come out. They're hiding from me," she said, realising. "Should I shout out to them, Chloe? Tell me what to do?"

"Call them outside, Sophie," Chloe told her.

"Oh my, Chloe," Sophie said anxiously. "There's a bright light appearing. A brilliant glow is slowly emerging from an opening in the clouds above me. It's spilling down slowly, like a giant waterfall from the sky. It's so beautiful," she described it.

"It's resting on the grass, between the house and me," she went on. "It appears like a golden-coloured light. It looks alive--there's movement inside of it and it's making that whirling noise like the wind. I think it's an energy portal--a gateway," she said guessing, "It's shaped like an archway leading into what appears like a long stairwell, but it's kind of hazy and indistinct. I feel as if I'm in a dream. Is this real or am I dreaming?" she asked out loud.

"Sophie," Chloe called out, "stay with us. Keep describing what you see and stay grounded with us," she warned. "We are all here holding the energy for you until you finish your task, but you must stay connected with us and keep talking."

"Thanks, Chloe, I'll try to remember that and keep talking," she replied. "The light is beautiful, it feels alive somehow, as if it's speaking to me," she told them. "It's intoxicating, alluring and inviting. I feel that I want to get closer to see more. I feel I should go inside. Yes, it's inviting me in. It feels so loving and friendly. Should I go, Chloe? What should I do?" she asked anxiously again.

"No, stop, Sophie," Chloe called out. "Don't go inside the light. It's not meant for you, it's for them--the children in the house, not for you, Sophie," she warned her again. "Stay outside of the light and tell us what else you can see. Promise me you won't go in, Sophie, it's dangerous for you. There's no way back if you enter."

"Okay, Chloe, I promise I won't go inside," Sophie said and continued. "It looks solid enough and glows as if the sun were shining through it from behind. There's a welcome coming from it, a feeling of warmth, and an overwhelming sense of bliss. Somehow I feel it belongs to Rosemary," Sophie suggested. "It feels like her energy, her light, her aura. Something--I don't know what. Perhaps this is the connection being made now. The portal, the bridge we need from this world into the next dimension. What should I do, Chloe?" she asked again.

The combined energy from all the people from both dimensions gave Rosemary enough power to create the portal. It was the gateway for the lost souls hiding inside the house. Somehow Sophie had to encourage them to walk into the light and through the bridge between dimensions into Heaven, but they needed help.

Rosemary spoke intuitively to Sophie.

"Sophie, I know ye can't see me, but ye need te call everybody outside quickly. I don't know how long I can hold this portal open."

Chloe also picked up on this message from Rosemary and told Sophie to call everyone in the house outside. "We don't have much time, Sophie, so do it now," she said. Sophie spoke out loud.

"Everybody inside the house, listen to me. I know you can see me. I know you're there and you've been waiting to cross over into Heaven. You've been lost for a long time wandering, and you must listen to what I'm saying now," she said aloud. There was no movement from the house and Sophie tried calling them again.

"I know you're afraid of the light. But this is your chance, the time you've been waiting for. The light is your salvation, your escape, your way out," she told them. "You must come outside of the house and walk into the light to enter the kingdom of Heaven," she told them. "It's the entrance to the bridge between Heaven and Earth. So please come outside now and walk into the light and eternal freedom," she said anxiously. "Please, we don't have much time. There's no need to be afraid, no harm will come to any of you," she promised them and continued.

"Fin, Rosie, you must listen to me. It's Rosemary's light, your mammy, Fin--she's here for you, and she's come to take you home with her. She's been trying for years to get you to come into the light," Sophie explained. "It's her, Fin--she's inside the light, waiting for you. But she knows you're afraid, and so she sent for me to come and help you," Sophie pleaded. "Fin, Rosie, you must come out and walk into the light. It's the only way to release you both from the farmhouse and set you free forever," she tried to explain to them. "Your mammy's there, in the light, please believe me," she pleaded again. "Don't be scared, I'll help you. Rosemary wants to take you to Heaven with her, and you won't be alone in the farmhouse any longer," she said, getting anxious.

There was still no movement from the house. "Please, we don't have a lot of time before the portal closes. Come now, I beg you. Just trust me."

"What's happening now, Sophie?" Chloe asked.

"At last," Sophie replied, somewhat relieved. "A group of people are coming out through the front door. Rosie is first, her head bent down as if she's afraid to look up at the light," Sophie said. "There are people on either side of her protecting her. They're all 'round her and walking very slowly into the light together. I don't see Fin. Where is he, and who are all these people?" Sophie asked, confused. "The group is walking towards the archway and slowly going up what seems like a slight incline--a stairway," she said. "People inside the entrance are coming forward to greet the newcomers as they enter. There's a great feeling of excitement now. Love and delight exudes all around and the atmosphere is welcoming and filled with joy," Sophie told them.

"I still don't see Fin and I don't see Rosie now either," she said anxiously again. "Where are they? I'm watching the people moving forward into the light and when they're fully immersed under the archway, they just blend into the brightness and disappear," she said. "I can see Rosie now. She's stopped at the entrance, outside of the light. I don't know why she didn't go through with the others. She's just standing there alone and watching as the people nod to her and pass her by," Sophie said. "The light is so bright. I can't look at it. It's calling out, beckoning to come forward," she explained to the group. "There are hundreds and hundreds of people--lost souls--all forming the line-up to walk into the light," she said. "They span four across, and the line-up is solid all the way back to the house. Where did all these people come from?" she asked again puzzled. Sophie stood in front of the house watching in amazement.

She watched in silence as they entered the light and greeted by well-wishers, family and people who obviously knew them. Then immediately, as if on a moving escalator, they went up into the beautiful brightness and were gone.

"I still don't see Fin," she said again. "He hasn't come out yet and Rosie is still standing at the entrance. She's waiting for him to come out," Sophie said. "She knows he's afraid of the light but she won't go without him. I can feel her concern for him. Tell me what to do, Chloe? They need help," Sophie said, concerned.

"Wait... there's a young man coming forward. He's about twenty-one years of age, very thin, but well dressed for the times in a dark three-piece suit. He just stepped out of the line-up and tipped his cap at me. He actually spoke out loud to me," she told them. "He stopped in front of me. 'Thank you,' he said in my face, doffed his cap, smiled at me and nodded his head. Then he stepped back into the line-up and walked past me into the light," she said confused. "I'm amazed, I know this is in my meditation--my minds eye, how can he connect with me like this?" she asked. "I'm in my basement in Canada, he's entering an energy portal into another dimension from Ireland, so how can he see me? Do you know, Chloe?" she asked again.

"Sophie," Chloe said unconcerned, "we can talk about that later. For the moment I want you to continue talking, stay connected with us. It's important for you to do that. Do you understand?" she asked.

"Yes, Chloe, I will. I'm just so amazed at what's happening. It's as if I'm in three places at one time."

"You are," replied Chloe, "but I'll explain that later, as I said."

The line-up continued on and on with people entering the light, but still Sophie didn't see little Fin. Rosie remained waiting at the entrance.

"What should I do? I still don't see Fin."

"Did you go into the house?" Chloe asked her.

"No, I've been outside on the grass all this time," Sophie replied.

"Call Rosie over to you. Ask her to guide you into the house to where he's hiding."

"Will Rosie be able to see me?"

"Of course, just as the young man saw you and doffed his cap," Chloe told her. "Now call Rosie over to you," she said again.

"Okay," Sophie agreed. "Rosie!" she shouted. "Over here," she called and waved her hands in the air to draw Rosie's attention.

"My name is Sophie," she called out. "I'm a friend of Rosemary's. She asked me to come and help you and Fin today. Will you come over here to me?" Rosie walked towards Sophie standing on the grass outside the farmhouse.

"How did ye get here, Sophie? I don't know ye?" the girl asked.

"No, you don't know me, but I am a friend and I'm here to help you and Fin," Sophie replied.

"Thank ye for comin', Sophie. I can't get him te come outside, he's too afraid of the light," Rosie said sadly.

"Yes, I know, and that's his challenge. He has to overcome his fear and replace it with the love he has for his mammy. That's his test," Sophie explained. "Perhaps once we tell him that and he understands, then he'll have the courage to come outside and go into the light with you?" Sophie suggested.

"Oh, I don't know Sophie. He's really scared of the light, but I'll try anyway. I promised him I wouldn't go wit'out him and I mean te keep me promise," Rosie said.

"Good girl, Rosie," Sophie said. "Tell him that the light is his mammy, it's her energy. She's the one who's been chasing both of you all these years--trying to get you to come into her light and go with her to Heaven."

"I'll try, Sophie. Will ye come wit' me inside the house?" Rosie asked.

"Of course I will. We'll go together now."

Sophie reported back to the group in the room. "Rosie and I are going inside the house now, Chloe--we're going in together."

"Good," said Chloe, "keep talking to us. Don't lose contact." Sophie took Rosie's small hand in hers. The girl was shaking with fear but bravely walked with Sophie towards the farmhouse to look for Fin. They went inside and Sophie looked behind the front door. There he was, crouched down, squatting on his hunkers, hiding his face in his hands and visibly shaking with fear.

"Fin, Fin," Rosie said gently as she crouched down beside him, "I'm here, we've come back te help ye, like I promised. I won't go wit'out ye. This is Sophie, yer mammy's friend. She sent her te help us," Rosie told him.

Fin couldn't open his eyes--he was so afraid, and still trembling in his terrified state. Sophie spoke to him softly.

"Fin," she whispered with an accent that he could understand.

"Fin, remember ye wanted te know what yer blemish could be?" she said, adjusting her voice. "Well, this is it. This is yer challenge. Yer love for yer mammy must be stronger than yer fear of the light," Sophie told him. "Now, I'm asking ye te be brave one last time and walk into the light te yer mammy. D'ye t'ink ye can do it?" she asked him. The little boy didn't move, still frozen in fright.

"Don't be afraid, Fin," Sophie continued. "The light is yer mammy, but ye can't see her until ye go inside. Then ye'll see her," she explained. "She sent it for ye te go te her. She's waiting for ye in the light. She's been waiting for years for this day te come. But ye must go te her quickly, now, before it's too late. Don't be afraid," she pleaded with the little boy. Sophie spoke to Chloe and the group again.

"Chloe, I don't know if I can do this. He's terrified and frozen to the spot. I can't get him to speak or move or even stand up. What should I do, Chloe?" Sophie asked anxiously, and very concerned that they were running out of time.

"Fin," Rosie suddenly pleaded. "Please listen te Sophie, she's a friend. Remember we've been tryin' te find yer test. Well, she's right, Fin. Please stand up and come wit' me into the light," Rosie cried anxiously. Fin didn't move and Rosie began to cry, dreading that they would miss the crossing.

Suddenly, Sophie sensed another presence behind her in the room. Rosemary had come as close to Fin as she could. She too was anxious that Fin would miss the opening and be left behind. Sophie couldn't look at her because the light was so intense--it hurt her eyes. At that moment a large hand appeared through the light. The hand was strong, manly and beautiful, beaming as if the sun was shining through it from the inside out. There was a blue glow around the hand. Sophie looked up to see Eagle Feather standing beside her. He smiled softly at her and nodded. Then he moved his gaze to Fin and slowly stretched his arms down to the little boy.

"Thank goodness you've come," Sophie said. "He's terrified and I don't know what else to do." She wiped a fearful tear from her cheek. It was obvious to Eagle Feather that she was comforted to see him and immediately the air was filled with a sense of relief--help had arrived.

Sophie and Rosie stood silently, watching as Eagle Feather spoke intuitively to Fin. The little boy slowly looked up towards this commanding Indian chief. No words were spoken between them, but there was a feeling of safety all around. Fin knew that Eagle Feather was taking him to his mammy. His strong arms lifted the trembling boy and cradled him like a baby. Eagle Feather carried him out of the house and walked towards the light carrying the little boy in his arms, reassuring him all the way.

"You're a brave little boy," Eagle Feather told him. "Your mammy will be proud of you. We're going to walk into the light now; she's standing inside waiting for you, but you can't see her until we go inside, so hold on and be brave just a little longer," he said.

Fin turned his face in towards Eagle Feathers's chest to hide from the light. He had been running from the light for years, hiding inside the farmhouse when it appeared. Now he was going inside under the archway, right into the middle of the light. He remembered this was where he saw his old papa disappear. He held on tight to Eagle Feather, still hiding his face away from the light, as they walked inside. Then Eagle Feather stopped and spoke again to Fin.

"We're here, Fin, and your mammy is here, too, as I promised. Just be brave one more time and take a look. She's longing to hold you and give you a hug," he encouraged the boy. "Now open your eyes and look, turn your face around and see, she's standing right in front of us waiting for you," he said. "I won't let you go until you see her. Rosie is here too, standing right beside your mammy. They're both waiting for you, Fin. Be brave this last time, Fin, and open your eyes."

Eagle Feather gently rested Fin on the ground beside his mammy and Rosie. Still trembling, Fin opened his eyes and saw Rosie first, then instantly recognised his mammy, just as he remembered her.

"Mammy, Mammy," he cried out, reaching his short arms to his mammy. Tears of relief spilled over and rolled down his cheeks. Rosemary's arms enveloped her little boy. She hugged him tenderly for the first time in a hundred years. She kissed his little face all over and wept tears of joy and happiness. "I'll never leave ye alone again, Fin," she assured him.

"Oh, Mammy, I've missed ye so much," he said, clinging to her.

Rosemary's task was almost ended. She proved her love was stronger than her fear. She put right a dreadful wrong done to Rosie. The power of her love reached from beyond the grave, exactly one hundred years after Fin had died, to connect with Sophie and make the rescue happen. Now she took her son's tiny hand in hers, and Rosie held the other. There they stood, all three of them together at last. Her heart was bursting with happiness as they prepared to walk into the mystery of the Divine Light and its wonderful miracles.

The scene was breathtaking. The light, radiating a strong sense of love, was emitting beautiful waves of euphoria that touched everyone, inviting them all to come inside and live in harmony for eternity.

Rosemary turned to thank Sophie and Eagle Feather for their help.

"I can never thank ye enough for what ye've done," she said as tears welled in her eyes. "I'm in yer debt forever for yer courage and compassion."

Eagle Feather bowed his head respectfully in acknowledgement. He knew Rosemary understood his power and why he had come. He was Sophie's spirit guide and although Sophie did not know it, her deep compassion for the children and Rosemary impressed him. He knew she wasn't experienced enough for the task, but he was.

Sophie was so grateful that Eagle Feather had come to help her fulfil her promise. She felt humbled by Rosemary's gratitude and exhilarated at the outcome. Finally the children were safe and free to cross over.

Rosie spoke softly. "Rosemary, will me mammy be there?" Rosemary looked down at the young girl and smiled as she replied.

"Yes, darlin', she's waiting for ye up there," and she gestured towards the light.

"I t'ink I'm ready now, Rosemary," Rosie said. Rosemary glanced towards Sophie and smiled again for the last time. There was an air of peace surrounding the three, and holding hands together they slowly walked into the light.

"Oh my, a surprise for ye, Rosie," Rosemary exclaimed. "Look up there darlin', who d'ye t'ink that is?" Further ahead, Rosemary saw the outline of a small, slender woman step out from the crowds formed at the side of the stairwell. She couldn't see her in detail--the woman was just a silhouette against the bright light behind her. She was standing with her hands gripping the sides of her apron. Rosemary instantly recognized Flo, her long ago friend and little Rosie's mammy.

"It's yer mammy darlin', right up there in the light. D'ye see her runnin' towards us?"

"Oh yes, but are ye sure it's her?" Rosie asked anxiously.

"Yes darlin', I'm sure it's her. She was me only friend in all me life, and *yer* mammy. I was lost wit'out her for a long time. I'd recognise her anywhere," Rosemary said warmly.

Rosie looked ahead into the light and saw the outline of a young woman. Her heart skipped a beat and excitedly she couldn't wait any longer as she let go of Rosemary's hand and ran into the open arms of her mammy. Sophie's eyes filled with tears as she clasped her hands under her chin and watched them embrace.

"I'm going te brush yer hair lovingly forever more, and we'll never be parted again," Flo said to her daughter. Rosie was so happy--her dream had come true. She was with her mammy and threw her arms around her in absolute rapture. Sharing a giggle and clinging to each other, the two little female figures slowly disappeared into the light. Sophie heard them chatter and chuckle as they gradually vanished out of sight.

Contentedly, and eager to catch up with her old friend, Rosemary and Fin walked into the light behind Rosie and Flo. All the while Rosemary spoke softly to Fin. "Just be brave a little longer for me," she asked him.

"But Mammy, I'm not scared now. I have you," he said as she lifted him and they cuddled each other.

Sophie watched on tenderly, grateful that their suffering was over. Slowly they too were engulfed by the light and were gone. She breathed a deep sigh of satisfaction and looked over to where Eagle Feather was standing, his arms folded in front of his chest. He seemed pleased, and they smiled at each other in acknowledgment that the rescue was successful.

"I realise now why you came to help me," Sophie said, "and I thank you so very much. I know now I wouldn't have been able to complete the task I promised to do. I'm so glad you stepped in and took over. Thank you, Eagle Feather. I'll never forget you, or what happened here," she said modestly. Eagle Feather smiled at Sophie and in her mind she heard him say, *"You're welcome, Sophie. I was glad to help. You are a rare example of human kindness and compassion."* Overwhelmed by his words and somewhat stunned she thanked him again and went to take a last look inside the farmhouse. Sophie walked through the two little rooms to make sure that there was no one left behind. She marvelled at all the people who had crossed over into the light, still confused as to the number involved. She didn't understand why there were so many people, but the house was empty and she went back outside into the garden. When she came out Eagle Feather was gone. She hoped he understood her gratefulness towards him.

Chloe spoke to her again. "What do you see now?"

"The house is renewed," Sophie replied. "It's all painted new and clean. The grass is bright and fresh, and wild flowers are growing in the garden. It looks and feels happy again and the sun is shining down on everything."

Chloe spoke again. "It's time to leave the farmhouse now, Sophie. I want you to come back into this room, here with the group where we started. Take a deep breath and exhale a couple of times, blowing out sharply, as if blowing out a candle. Wriggle your toes and your fingers, and when you're ready, and in your own time, open your eyes back here in this room."

Sophie did as she was told and slowly she opened her eyes. She was in her basement with her group of ladies. Eagle Feather was gone and the chair beside her was empty.

"Awe, what a shame," she sighed. "Eagle Feather's gone and I'm sad to lose him. He's such a strong guide and that was an amazing experience, some meditation!" she exclaimed.

"You'll never lose Eagle Feather now that you've met him. He's your spirit guide and will always be bonded with you," said Marishka. "It's very seldom we get to meet our own spirit guide in person. You're very lucky, you know," she told Sophie.

"That was an excellent rescue--a very powerful connection with everyone and the strongest I've ever felt in a group. Did everyone feel it and see what was happening?" Chloe asked.

"Yes we were all there, every step of the way, sharing the same vision," said Marishka. "It was a powerful link. Our bond the strongest I've ever experienced, too, and I believe our work here is finished. Job well done, everyone."

"How are you feeling, Sophie?" asked Chloe.

"I feel amazing, full of energy and just buzzing and exuberant at what's taken place here with you all. Thank you so much for coming to help, everybody. I could never have done this without you. Eagle Feather knew we needed his energy, too. Such a powerful event we made happen together. Thank you all for being involved," Sophie said. "Now anyone ready for a cup of tea?" Sophie announced as they left the basement for the upstairs kitchen.

Helen was waiting in the kitchen, eager to hear what had happened, but a little embarrassed about not taking her part in the event.

"How did it go?" Helen asked.

"It was great, so amazing, Helen. The energy was incredible," Sophie replied.

"Sorry I wasn't there, Sophie, I just couldn't do it."

"Don't worry about it," Sophie told her. "Everything turned out as it should have. I'll tell you all about it later. All you need to know just now is that it worked and the children crossed over safely. We're going to have some tea now. Will you join us for that?" Sophie asked her friend.

"No, I'll go and let you all get on with your business. Give me a call later tonight and we can talk then."

Sophie showed her friend out the front door to her car.

"I'll call you tonight, and thank you Helen. Even though you don't think you did anything, actually you did a lot, so thank you."

Sophie closed the car door and went back to the house to join everyone in the kitchen.

The group discussed the event in great detail. "Rosemary, determined to make this work," said Marishka. "Her energy was amazing."

"And Eagle Feather too," said Chloe, "what a connection," she exclaimed in awe. It was the strongest any of them had worked with.

Marishka explained more about Eagle Feather to Sophie. "Now that you have identified your spirit guide and met him in person, his energy will become part of you. You will work together in the future. You only need ask him for his help and he will be there for you," she told Sophie.

Sophie felt privileged. She didn't even know she had a spirit guide and felt honoured they had met. "He had such a regal air about him and appeared proud without being arrogant," she told the group. "I'm so grateful for his help during the rescue. I couldn't have completed it without him," she admitted.

The ladies finished up and made to leave Sophie's house. Marishka invited her to join them again any time for a group meditation and Sophie promised she would.

After the group had left, Sophie started to phone around the world to tell the others involved how it had all worked out. One of the girls in Scotland had actually been drawn into the group vision and described the events that she saw happening. She described Fin hiding behind the front door of the house and detailed exactly what he was wearing to Sophie. That just proved to Sophie that everyone's energy had bonded and the entire group were operating as one unit to help the children. The other ladies involved were happy to hear that the children were now safe on the other side and no longer trapped in the farmhouse in Ireland.

The following week when Sophie went back to work, a co-worker came up to her with something closed in her fist. She extended her hand towards Sophie and asked her to hold out her hand. Sophie did, and her friend opened her palm to release a small metal figurine of a very proud-looking Indian chief dressed in his finest regalia.

"Oh my goodness, where did you find this?" Sophie asked. It was Eagle Feather. The detail on the figurine was amazing, right down to the two eagle feathers in his hair. Sophie was astonished.

"I was on vacation on a cruise ship and came across this figurine at the gift shop. I knew I had to have it. Not for myself though. At the time I didn't know who its intended owner was," she told Sophie. "When I got back to work and heard the story of the spirit rescue, I knew the figurine was for you so I brought it in today," her friend told her. "Here he is," she said, as she placed the figurine into Sophie's hand.

It was Eagle Feather manifest into a solid form, a sacred symbol known as a totem. This was Sophie's gift from him for her courage and her compassion. It was a keepsake from her spirit guide to remind her of their bond. She was dumbfounded at how the universe works its mysterious magic.

The meditation classes continued. As time passed, people's situations changed and the classes began to get smaller until finally Sophie and her husband sold their house and moved to a new location further away.

The following years were to prove difficult for Sophie. Her sensitivity and beliefs were challenged through personal events within her family and at work. It was a time of significant change in her life and many times she called on Eagle Feather and his great strength to sustain her.

The death of her younger sister left her devastated and confused. Her sister was just forty-five years old when she developed pancreatic cancer. The doctors tried a new laser treatment on her. Six patients, all terminally ill, were chosen for the experiment. The laser would burn the tumour out. It had never been used for this type of cancer before and it worked. They got her tumour, all of it. Some months later she was given the all-clear and returned to work, a job she loved. Within the next six months the other five patients died one by one, but Sophie's sister did not. She survived. Sophie sent healing energy and love to her sister every day in her prayers and felt sure it was helping. Finally, a few years later, the cancer returned in her spine and spread all through her body. Sophie's sister died three months later at forty-eight years of age. It was a shocking blow to the entire family who had thought the cancer was gone. Sophie was stunned. Her siblings mocked her healing efforts and scorned her for her strange beliefs.

Sophie was heartbroken. She absorbed the negative energy directed at her like a breath of air into her lungs. Ultimately she fell into a state of despair and disillusion, which resulted in her own illness. Sophie knew that she was being tested. She loved her family dearly but finally realised that she had to forgive them and let them go in order to begin healing herself.

During that time Rosemary continued to visit with Sophie, as if pushing her forward for more. She didn't understand for a long time what Rosemary wanted and thought she was just keeping in touch as the two ladies had developed a strange but solid friendship.

Some years passed, and Sophie was home recovering from surgery when some friends came to visit her. They brought a parcel full of gifts together with a card signed by many of her friends from the old classes. The card read:

> As your friends, we are trying to inspire and motivate you to write the book that is inside of you, waiting to find its way onto paper. It is our intention, by way of these gifts and tools, to suggest you use this healing time as an opportunity to start your next chapter.

Sophie realised that this was the answer she was looking for. The reason for Rosemary's continued visits and prompting. Rosie always wanted people to know what had happened to her--that she didn't just disappear. She wanted a book written about her life. It was the best way to tell how her young life was cut short by a tragic end. She was no longer seeking revenge for her father's deed towards her. She learned that only love matters in the end. It was through her love for her mother she was finally able to forgive her father. Love replaced hatred. However, she did want her short existence to have some meaning, and not just end silently in her secret grave. A storybook would sooth her soul, and each time someone read it, they would be validating of her life on Earth.

Rosemary's connection with Sophie remained strong. She supported the idea of a book and did what she could to encourage Sophie to write. Within the story, Rosemary could finally expose her own regretful guilt, and reveal young Rosie's dark secret to the world. The courage of her heart replaced her shame and proved that the power of love was the strongest virtue of all. *"The truth will set you free."* These words haunted her over and over. She would find a way to enlighten Sophie to write the book. Finally during meditation a message filtered through:

> *When something special happens in your life, you have*
> *a choice to keep it to yourself and remain quiet, or share*
> *it with the world.*

It is Sophie's choice to share this story, in the hope that it will help some to heal, some to forgive, and some to believe in the power of love.

Author's Note

"Love and compassion are necessities not luxuries,
without them humanity cannot survive."
The Dalai Lama

*A*s it transpired, and as channelled by Rosemary, the hundreds
of people who went into the light from the farmhouse starved
during the famine years 1845-1880. In time they all realised they were
dead and spent their years wandering and looking for release. They
too avoided the light and were left grounded on this Earth as ghosts.
For whatever reason, these souls did not cross over and remained
stuck in this dimension. During the famine years in Ireland over one
million people died from starvation.

Rosemary initiated the rescue. She guided the lost souls to the
farmhouse. Her love had no boundaries. She demonstrated the power
of excellence--perfection and love triumphed from beyond the grave.
Finding her truth not only set her free, it filled her heart with love
forevermore. She would never be afraid again.

If only one person learns something from reading this story, be it
courage, forgiveness, love, or compassion, then Rosie's short life had
meaning. This book is her testament to humanity and the validation
of her dreams come true. She wanted exposure but not revenge and
now every time someone reads this book, they know her story.

Fin found his courage and his way back to his mammy. Sophie's
loving compassion compelled her to help. She couldn't leave them
suffering.

There is no explanation for any of the events reported in this story and no way to prove it happened. Only you, the reader can decide what you believe.

I believe in another existence after this life, form unknown. I believe that love is all-powerful. It is the energy that holds our world together. Love never dies--even in death, love can heal all, and reach from beyond the grave, its power infinite and supreme. I believe that lack of love, its opposite--hatred, is the enemy, causing division, loneliness, sickness, fear and even death.

All life is energy and energy does not die. It converts to a higher vibration during the death process. Some people have been lucky enough to see the light from the soul separate as it departs the body.

We are slowly becoming conscious of our ability to control our life and our universe. As a nation we are beginning to understand that we attract what we emit, just like a magnet. Every thought, word, and action creates energy every second of our life.

Be conscious of your moods and feelings because this is what you are transmitting through the power of your thoughts and beliefs, and this is what we attract back to us and into our world. Our life is a result of our feelings. Be open to change and new ways for as the world evolves, so must we.

Do what you want to do in life because you love to do it, and do it with love. Ensure that it's not at the expense of someone else, for then it becomes a selfish act, and self-gratification is not love. Send love out to everyone, everywhere. Wish the world love and the same feeling will return to you. We are all on the same journey in this life, evolving in our own time at different stages of development and understanding. Our duty is to love humanity--we are here to help each other, and teach one another freely. We each hold the power to make this world a truly perfect and heavenly paradise. Only positive loving energy will perpetuate this beautiful universe. Negative energy causes life to wither and die. It's your energy, your world, and your choice. Be careful what you think, feel, do, or say. It will return to you as your own creation.

"and the truth shall set you free." John 8.32

Drawing by Keely Macleod – age twelve

Author Biography

Jo Macleod was born in Glasgow, Scotland in March 1951. Her father, Frank Devlin, was an Irish Catholic. Her mother, Jessie Summers, was a Scottish Protestant from Stirling. Jo was the second oldest of eight children. The family was quite wealthy for the times. She was just nineteen years old when her father died and her life changed. She was raised to be responsible for her younger siblings and to help her mother. Jo's sensitivity and intuitive instincts became a protective tool for her. She was fourteen years old when she grew interested in astrology and her books became her escape from family life. It was through her reading she realized that she had a special ability and a definite interest in associated subjects began to develop. Jo lived in the Isle of Man for twelve years with her own young family. There she joined the Spiritualist Church to learn meditation and energy healing. Later, she immigrated to Canada with her husband Peter, and two children, Simon and Ruth. Today she loves being a granny to Keely, Harmony, Callum, and Hamish. She lives in Langley, BC, with her husband Peter and their very lovable Airedale called Toby.

Photo of Eagle Feather

CPSIA information can be obtained
at www.ICGtesting.com
Printed in the USA
BVOW09s1155310118
506848BV00001B/88/P